KILTMAN® III

Once Upon a Time in Rome

Dermid Strain

ISBN: 978-1-916820-48-7

PublishNation
www.publishnation.co.uk

*Kiltman® 3: Once Upon a Time in Rome is
dedicated to Steve Schnall and
Vladimir (Volli) Sapožnin*

*Two phenomenally talented and caring men -
whose friendship I was privileged to have been
blessed with.*

And always on my mind and in my heart...

Georgie, Max, Bruce, Anne, Angie and John

*Mum, George and Margaret
We miss you every day*

"Remember me to one who lives there."

Prologue

The desperate, anguished scream competed with the noise of artillery fire and grenades exploding around the building.

"Push! Push!" she shouted, trying to resist succumbing to the panic seeping through the walls of the small apartment. She had only come to help her neighbour escape the shelling. Now she was surrounded by the isolation - and desperation - of this woman's abandonment.

"You can do it! Come on!" Her voice sounded more like a bark than a recognisable language. She had to help her find the strength. The newborn would be lucky to survive the birth, but the mother would become another anonymous casualty of war, her wounds trickling blood onto the stone, cold floor.

The next scream was higher pitched and croaky - the baby's first cry, a reach out to the world beyond.

The neighbour snipped the umbilical cord just as the door burst open. A gust of wind blew into the small space - a blizzard of dust and debris. A soldier in an American uniform halted at the scene of life and death.

It may have been the despair of the moment that made her react in the way she did. She had not planned for it. Or it may have been his face, kinder that it should be for a war as brutal as this one.

"Please! Take the baby!" She thrust the bundle of crumpled flesh, streaked with mucus, at the young soldier. Then, in a more hushed tone, she whispered, "The mother is dying, there is no hope." She lifted a warm bottle of milk from the saucepan and stuffed it into his pocket.

The soldier could have refused. He could have walked away. In a normal scenario, he would have. However, with the same instinct he had relied on in making split-second decisions over the last few years on battlefronts across Northern Africa, and now Italy, he grabbed the baby and ran from the small room, creaking under three floors of broken masonry.

If one positive outcome could emerge from this war, he was determined that it would be this most delicate of lives, nestled inside his thick army coat.

Sunday, April 10
2005

Sacco

The soft, spring breeze billowed through watchful trees on the banks of the misty River Thames. Small boats jostled against the strain of their anchors and buoys - dancing to the light rhythms of Puccini's Madam Butterfly drifting past from a nearby restaurant.

The pleasant temperature for this time of year had encouraged him to leave the comfort of his spacious room in the Petersham Hotel in Richmond, and enjoy a late evening stroll. Lately he had become conscious of the increase in his weight. Although it did not concern him. At his age - and considering his lifestyle - an accumulation of girth was to be expected. An expensive Armani belt punished his protruding stomach while his shirt buttons fought for survival.

The lump of bread roll in his pocket, sequestered from the restaurant table, bumped against his hip with each step. He had set his *passegiata* goal at the river's slipway - where geese and swans mingled with ducks and cranes. On each of his business trips, he had made a point of feeding the birds. In one of the world's busiest metropolises, with a variety of entertainment options, this was the highlight of his evening.

Paolo Capello reflected on his professional achievements. His beginnings had been humble. Growing up in a small family apartment in the gritty streets of Rome's Trastevere - before its metamorphosis into a chic, bohemian haunt - his parents had treated him like a special gift. A child who had arrived in their later years, after they had stopped hoping. They would do whatever they could for him, as humble and challenged as they were financially. They found the money to put him through the best schools in Rome, and ultimately the prestigious Bocconi University in Milan. He had played his part - rising to the challenges demanded of him in the competitive world of finance, achieving levels of success unknown to someone from his neighbourhood.

Throughout his life he had made - and lost - numerous friends. Very few became close, while most were just necessary to help him achieve. Now he could not tell the difference.

His nickname from an early age had been Sacco. His full head of black hair as a child combined with his last name meant he was recognised as '*Sacco di Capello*' (full head of hair). He had been proud of his thick, wavy tresses, until his early twenties saw them wave good-bye. The hair was gone, but the nickname had stuck.

Over the years, Sacco had found a way through the competitive world of banking in Milan to a role worthy of his training and dedication. As President of Banco d'Aiuto - Bank of Help - he was renowned for his efforts in unlocking funding to help the less well-off finance their dreams and aspirations. He had not done this alone; he had developed a structure of banking partnerships across Europe. With their support - while enjoying recognition of their altruism - they had helped Banco d'Aiuto flourish over the years. In the process, he had grown to enjoy the acclaim, even earning himself the unofficial title of '*Banchiere del Popolo*' - the People's Banker.

As he relaxed into his late walk, he let his thoughts drift to the meeting arranged for the morning with the Bank of England. Some issues had arisen making this a complicated - potentially, confrontational - event. While it was not going to be an easy conversation, he was confident in his ability to answer their questions.

The sharp sound of a twig cracking barely registered. It came from a two-metre-high wall beside a local café. During the day Tide Tables Café thrived with walkers, bikers and shoppers taking a well-earned break. At this time of the evening, it was empty except for plastic chairs and metallic tables under sprawling trees.

The two men in black clothing and dark balaclavas landed on top of Sacco, with the grace of gymnasts scoring a perfect ten. Despite Sacco's feeble attempts to struggle, Luigi, the smaller of the two, applied the chloroform-saturated rag to his mouth with ease - while his accomplice, Luca, held their victim in a vice-like embrace. They would agree later that he had hardly put up a credible fight. Not unusual, when the prey had a sense of expectation - a fatalistic acceptance that this day was coming.

Sacco crumpled into a heap of flesh. With clinical efficiency, the men slipped a thick rope's noose around his neck - before tightening it to restrict the supply of oxygen to his brain. They manoeuvred him to the bridge's nearest arch, making sure not to drag him along the dusty pathway. The taller assailant tossed the rope up over an iron bar protruding from the underside of the bridge. As Luca pulled the rope to haul their victim up from the riverbank, Luigi placed a black brick in each of the jacket side-pockets.

Luca's heavy breathing told Luigi that Sacco was even heavier than expected. He wrapped his hands around the rope and leaned back pulling hard, helping his accomplice hoist Sacco to where his feet dangled just above the bank. Once Sacco was in place, Luca bent down to tie the rope to a metal railing underneath the arch. He tugged it twice to make sure it was not going to loosen. Luigi placed a chair under the arch. He made sure it was close enough to the swaying body that observers would reach the expected conclusion.

Stepping back, they surveyed their work. They waited until Sacco took his last, halting breath. He had not awakened since the application of chloroform. They had not wanted to torture their victim; their job was to deliver death – simply and with dignity.

In the same manner of an artist stepping back to appreciate a painting, they paused and nodded at one another. Before turning to run back into the dead of night.

Teenagers

"Roddy!" Kenny shouted from the kitchen. Despite half the grated cheese falling onto the floor, he was determined to complete the sandwiches. Numerous slices of buttered bread, open packs of ham and rocket salad littered the worktop - interspersed with chopped tomatoes and cucumber slices.

Their 6-month-old puppy hovered underneath the worktop, catching errant slices of cheese and bread. A bearded border collie poodle mix, Maisie could sense the tension and drama building this evening; the humans would need some corralling.

"Yes?" Roddy replied from his first-floor bedroom. The rucksack was nearly packed, just a couple more items to be added.

"Roddy!" Kenny called again.

"Yes?" The reply louder than before.

A moment passed - Maisie enjoyed a brief but welcome silence.

"Roddy?" Again, the shout from the kitchen.

The teen yanked open his door, and yelled, "What is it?"

"Don't you dare talk to me in that tone of voice. Come here to the kitchen." Kenny did not try to hide the rising irritation in his voice.

Thump! Thump! Thump!

"What is it?" Roddy stood at the kitchen door, folded arms and splayed legs underscoring his teenage defiance. Maisie slinked behind a stool, dropping down into a crouch, ears flat.

"Were you deliberately ignoring me?"

"Of course, I wasn't! I answered you."

"Yes, but you answered me in a disrespectful tone of voice." He had not looked up from his sandwich-making, a process that seemed to be much more complicated than it was supposed to be. Roddy was not going to mention that.

"That's how I speak. Especially when I have to *raise my voice* to shout down to the kitchen. Anyway, 'deliberately ignoring' doesn't make sense. It's one of those expressions where an extra word is added, but it makes no difference. In English grammar, it's what you would call an 'expletive'. Not a swear word expletive. It's a different type of expletive.

"My point is - you could just ask 'was I ignoring you'. The answer would still be the same, although at least you would have saved a word. For some reason, *certain people* add an expletive to sentences to create an accusatory layer of emotion."

The emphasis on *certain people* was not lost on Kenny. He could not stop the smile. He wanted to ask if *certain people* was an expletive too. Instead, he leant his head down towards the cheese, pretending to smell to make sure it was not off. Roddy could always make him grin. At fifteen, his son had become a baffling lad. He could infuriate his father to the point of exhaustion, and then with one simple comment, he would remember why he loved his son. Why he loved this independent, strong-minded boy, with his bright auburn hair, downy facial fluff and haphazard acne.

Before Kenny could think of a response, the back door opened a few centimetres. A white handkerchief fluttered just above the handle. Maisie had already started barking, relieved that some sanity was about to descend on the house.

"Is it safe to come in?"

Maggie stepped into the kitchen, her thick brown hair tied tight above her head, accentuating the hazel in her eyes. She bent to stroke Maisie, watching her lower half wag along with the tail, threshing the air with happiness. Maggie had heard the tension when she put the key in the door. She was tired after her shift; a three hour stake out at a renowned cat burglar's home. Until they found out he was on holiday in Spain. They had called it a day around 10 pm. She agreed to a quick glass of wine - which became two - with her colleagues on the way home, not in the mood to hurry back to Uisge Beatha. Friction had been running high in the Morgan family opera of late. She expected the performance to come to a crescendo this evening under the stress of the trips planned for the following morning.

Roddy was excited to leave home for a week to participate in a football tournament. He played for the school under sixteen team, Chesters F.C. The name baffled most spectators since it was different to their school's name, until they were informed that by choosing the name of a local senior seminary for trainee priests, they could use a pristine, full-size grass-covered pitch in Bearsden, a plush, leafy suburb west of Glasgow.

Chesters had secured an invitation to Cincinnati to participate in a tournament against other schools from the Midwest US. It was what the Americans called a Co-Ed event – teams comprised of boys and girls. This week would be the longest period he had been away from home without his mother or father. While some parents had been invited and had agreed to chaperone the team, neither Fiona nor Kenny could make it. They had been divorced now for nearly as many years as they had been together. Roddy could barely remember them married; although he now enjoyed watching their post-marital friendship develop into a strong bond built on a shared love for him and respect for each other.

His mother had accepted an invitation to attend a 'once in a lifetime' conference in Paris on climate change and the role households and communities could play in changing mindsets and behaviours towards protecting the planet. Roddy had laughed when she said. "It's hard to ignore a conference called *Armageddon Nervous About the Future: Why Aren't You?*"

He knew his mother's decision not to go on the US trip was her way of encouraging him to be independent. It was his chance to bond and make some solid friendships - without interfering parents to worry about. His adopted sister, Angie, would also be going. After her adoption - and after what she had to endure as the child of a psychopath - Fiona was pleased Angie was maturing into a strong, self-sufficient young lady. While there was still a wall that would rise when Angie was upset, they were making progress in helping her settle into her new, quirky family.

Fiona was sure the trip would help her bond with Roddy.

Mask Wants to Talk

Kenny had wanted to go with the team. He had made it clear that he was concerned about safety in the USA, with its liberal gun laws. It was therefore a source of vexation for him not to be on the flight with Roddy in the morning. Maggie knew the Smörgåsbord of sandwich fillings - remnants on the worktop, chunks on the floor, and the majority in Maisie's tummy - was his way of distracting himself from this dilemma, while showing Roddy how much he loved him.

Kenny had his own trip to think about. He thought he had heard the end of his most recent nemesis, Mask. Every day they counted their blessings that Mask's daughter, Angie, was safe now under Fiona's watchful eye and Roddy's brotherly love. Her father remained under lock and key, three years after Kiltman and Maggie outwitted him at the United Nations, when he came close to killing nearly 200 UN representatives.

Recognising the prisoner's public profile and capacity for evil, the US Department of Justice had decided to move him to a high security penitentiary outside the USA. The Americans had built a prison for the most dangerous of prisoners, in a remote clearing in the Amazon jungle. A special agreement with the Brazilian authorities ensured this facility was used on an 'as needs' basis, when 'crazies' - as referred to by the US President - needed to be locked away and forgotten about, far from the shores of 'our great nation'. Brazil had been happy to accept this proposal - as well as the zero interest borrowing rates on a substantial aid package.

Mask had been a model prisoner. His repentance - he explained in a four-page letter to the General Secretary of the United Nations - was a direct result of his time to reflect. He felt he had made progress in addressing his psychopathic urges, working with therapists to iron out the 'startlingly gargantuan zeniths of imbalance' he had displayed in his former actions. He believed he was now a changed man and wanted to make a positive impact on the world. As the letter progressed, he was at pains to communicate that he was not looking for freedom. He was guilty of the crime, and acceptant of doing the time. However, the letter went on to explain that in the spirit of working towards a higher goal, he did want to bring to the United Nations' attention certain worrying facts he had been told by one of the other 'crazies'.

In his letter, he wrote: "The information I have is vital to the safety of millions of people, I would only feel comfortable sharing it with one man. One special person. I would even call him a 'super-man'. The individual I want to impart this knowledge to is Kiltman."

In the morning, Kenny would fly, as Kiltman, from Glasgow to London, and then onto Brazil, to land at São Paulo, known as 'the land of drizzle'. Despite his misgivings about the trip, he had acknowledged to Maggie that he was curious to see a place owning a title that Scotland deserved.

In an effort to turn a negative into a positive, he had booked a five-day spa for 'just the two of them' after his visit to Mask. She was coming out to South America in two days' time to meet him at Iguaçu, on the border where Brazil meets Argentina. From there they had booked a helicopter to take them to a location well off the beaten track, close to Iguaçu's famed majestic waterfalls.

Kenny and Maggie were looking forward to bathing in spring waters and taking long walks in the forest. The hotel was so remote there was limited Wi-Fi access. She rarely took a break, but she knew this trip was necessary. She had agreed with the Scottish Constabulary that if an emergency arose, they would arrange transport to get her home.

They had spent evenings after dinner convincing themselves they were going to enjoy the luxury of 'quality time' - a concept they thought they understood, because they heard other couples talking about it. The void growing between them meant they had some rebuilding to do. When they had discussed this, Kenny had said it was more of a decoration than a renovation. While she was thinking their relationship needed a complete extension, a new floor and a landscaped garden. However, she was saving her comments for when they were in the remote nether regions of Brazil.

"Hey!" Kenny called out before Roddy said something like, "Yes, it's safe to come in. Be prepared for a grumpy dad, who makes a meal out of making sandwiches."

Maggie walked to Roddy and enveloped him in a tight hug. He had not quite reached her height, waiting for that growth spurt everyone said was just about to happen. The look on his face had told her all she needed to know about his mood. He fell into her arms, settling into the first stress free moment he had felt all day.

Kenny had enjoyed watching their bond and mutual love develop over the years. He walked over to join the group hug - and enveloped Roddy and Maggie in his arms, inadvertently rubbing a blob of butter onto the shoulder of her new jacket. Maisie had joined in, finding a way to wrap her front paws around Roddy's legs, tail slashing the air. Kenny absorbed the warmth of their embrace, unaware of how much their relationships would be tested in the days ahead.

Packing Troubles

Roddy threw a sweater into the rucksack just in case the evenings were cooler than expected. He had researched the climate for springtime in the Midwest and realised it could be even more unpredictable than a summer in Scotland.

He had been enjoying the group hug downstairs, until Maggie's phone buzzed. She had pointed at it while mouthing 'Gemmill' - her prickly Chief Inspector - before wandering off to a quiet corner of the spacious kitchen. Roddy had decided to extricate himself from his father's man hug and continue packing in his room.

He had just packed his toiletries, when he was startled by the loud knock on his door.

"Hey, Mr. Traveller!" Kenny said as he entered the room.

Roddy turned, "Hi, Dad."

"Are we good now?"

"Yes, we are," he said with the slightest hint of tetchiness. Sometimes it just appeared in his voice, even when he was feeling fine. This teenage puberty had been a long-drawn-out form of torment. If the spy world ever ran out of torture techniques, Roddy felt they should create a drug for their prisoners that replicated teenage angst and paranoia. Secrets would be revealed faster than acne after a bar of chocolate.

He rubbed his son's head, as if in recognition of the emotional turmoil rumbling underneath.

"Aw, look at you," Kenny said. He reached down into the rucksack to extract a plastic bottle of Irn-Bru. "You're bringing a wee bit of Scotland with you on your trip."

"Eh, that's right." Roddy prised the bottle from his father's fingers, wrapping his hand around as much of the container as he could. The contents were a tad more golden than the traditional amber colour. In the shaded light of the room, Kenny had not noticed. He placed it back inside the football boot, where he had tried to conceal it, unsuccessfully.

"I'm saving it for the final - if we get there," he said, pulling the zip around the outside of the rucksack.

"Aw, you will, I'm sure!" Kenny said. "Have you remembered to pack TCP?"

This was his father's question on any trip Roddy or Maggie planned. He was not interested in whether the suitcase included an antiseptic medicine for sore throats. It was a reference to whether they had packed Tickets, Cash/Cards and Passport.

"Yes, Dad. It's all under control." He felt a wave of love for his father and his quirky, repetitive ways. His father had learned over the years that being a parent required an infinite number of corny one-liners, and the ability to repeat them whenever the situation arose. Which was always more often than anyone else wanted.

Maggie walked into the room, with a look on her face that Roddy had last seen when she had washed his father's Celtic top alongside her pink sweater.

"Everything okay?" Kenny asked, noticing the same look. Also remembering the washing incident.

"No, not really." She paused, coughed, then said, "It looks like I won't be able to make the Brazil trip."

He did not speak. He had sensed this coming when he saw Gemmill's call.

"There has been an incident in London, and they've asked me to go down and help them investigate." She knew what was coming next - but waited all the same.

"Hmm. The last time I looked I think there were over thirty thousand police officers in London." He had decided not to stem his annoyance. This trip was important for them, he was not going to stand down easily. They had been living a double life since Mask's capture. She now knew that he was Kiltman. While that should have made things easier between them - and in some ways, it did - it also meant a higher level of subterfuge.

In any situation that would be difficult. Where they were working together nearly every week, were lovers, and lived as a family with Kenny's son, this made their lives complicated and confusing. They had considered telling Roddy his father was Kiltman, but the burden would be too much. She had to work hard to keep it secret - Roddy would have no chance.

This football trip had become the perfect opportunity for them to take a break without feeling guilty. It was the chance to reconnect and talk about their relationship. The fact they had found a place in Brazil, when Kenny was going there anyway, had sounded too good to be true.

"So, it really was too good to be true," he said aloud.

"There has been an apparent suicide. It's an Italian banker, who has been on radar recently for alleged financial crimes. They have reached out to me because they believe my recent training will help them on the investigation."

She kept her eyes on him, sensing Roddy's awkwardness, but did not dare look away. She had recently completed a two-year diploma at Glasgow University on international financial crimes - mainly money laundering and terrorism financing. In the aftermath of 9/11, the police force needed officers with such expertise. She should have been pleased they had recognised her potential to help, but Kenny's evident hurt was all she could see at that moment.

"Well, that's it, then, isn't it?" he said. "It's a done deal." His slumped shoulders conveyed his acceptance. He had to realise he was in love with a Detective Inspector, who was good at her job and in demand.

"I do need a break though," he continued, with a hint of defiance Roddy would have been proud of.

"I know," Maggie said. "I was going to suggest you go ahead anyway - chances are I'll be in London for at least a week." Although she wondered how much of a break he needed. Unless he was trying to escape afternoon TV adverts on releasing equity from your home, buying gold, and subscribing to a cremation service - presented by actors smiling while opening bottles of champagne.

Kenny nodded his agreement. He would go for a 5-day spa in the Amazonian rainforest. Alone. He would pack one less item than he had originally planned.

Monday, April 11

Flight of Fancy

Their checked luggage bumped and rolled along the carousel before it dropped out of sight. Next time they would see those bags was in Cincinnati. The team huddled around a row of connected chairs, perfectly designed to allow a seat for a few minutes, but absent the back support needed for a prolonged sleep.

A week was going to be the longest most of the team had spent away from home. The excitement had been building over the last term, growing in momentum until it was the single topic of conversation at school break time. Now at the airport, most could not contain their excitement, bantering with their closest friends; while, for others, the weight of pending distance was beginning to sink in. Parents were on hand to hug and kiss their children, with reassurances they would have a great time. Roddy felt a tinge of melancholy, despite his anticipation for the trip. He just wanted to get on the plane and have some alone time.

"Hey, Roddy. You all set for the tournament?" Mr. MacDonald approached him and placed a hand on his shoulder.

"Yes, I am, thanks," Roddy answered. Mr. MacDonald was father to Reilly, the team's best player and top goal scorer. He had spoken to him on several occasions after games and in the evenings after training. There were two types of parents, he had decided, when it came to children's sporting activities. The committed ones, like those at the airport, and the *kiss and fly* parents, like his; they always seemed to have somewhere else to go. His mother was off to Paris to save the planet and his father was going on a spa trip to Brazil.

"Don't worry, you'll have a great time." When Reilly's father spoke, his words carried a gravitas, a combination of his deep voice and unconventional look. His long hair was tied back in a ponytail, and his beard - the only father who dared to have one - was a shaggy bush of speckled grey. Every so often he would tie a few coloured beads onto the strands, calling it his *whiskerewellery*. Older than the other dads, he encouraged a degree of respect mainly because of how he carried himself. He remembered his father describing him as having a *presidential* aura; before Maggie responded. "Depends which president you're talking about." One of those comments that make grownups laugh and teens shrug in bemusement.

"I know." Roddy nodded. "I just want to get there and play."

Mr. MacDonald laughed. "Typical teenager. Don't wish your life away. Make the most of today: you'll regret it if you don't."

Roddy nodded at another phrase adults make expecting children to understand. He pointed in Reilly's direction. "Is Reilly all set?" His team-mate was sitting in the middle of a cluster of boys. They were throwing a plastic bottle in the air, trying to get it to land on its base. Without much success but generating a lot of *ooohs* and *aaahs*.

"What do you think?" Mr. MacDonald said.

Roddy smiled. "Just as well we're not going to a tournament in bottle tossing."

"Funny. Truth is, Reilly needs to get his act together. He has too much nonsense in his head. Hopefully you can help him be sensible. Like you." Mr. MacDonald reached out and gave Roddy a fist bump at a comment that was meant to be a compliment although felt wrong on several levels.

"Okay, everyone," Mrs MacLeod shrieked. She was the mum who organised everything and made the other mothers feel guilty. Not out of intent, just because she had been gifted with a huge amount of energy, efficiency and, most important of all, time. Her daughter Jo-Jo, the team's maverick player, always seemed to take a deep breath when her mother stood up. She bristled when her mum made the clumsiest comments with the best of intentions. Jo-Jo had confided in him that she was pleased to get away from her for a few days. They had joked that her mum was the *VO* that separated proactive and provocative. Roddy had said it stood for *Verging On* breakdown. Jo-Jo shook her head, saying it had gone beyond that; she was just *Very Old*.

"Come now, Chesters!" Mrs MacLeod clapped her hands as if they had not heard her high-pitched shout. Roddy looked at Jo-Jo. They smiled at their shared insight of a woman who created chaos in the midst of calm.

Healing on a Jet Plane

"Howdy, ladies and gentlemen. As you can see, we have started our descent to the airport," the pilot announced into the microphone.

"You know," he continued in a tone he probably saw as uplifting, "I have to say I find it ironic that even though Cincinnati is in Ohio, the airport is on the other side of the river in Kentucky. It might not seem strange to you folks from Europe, but that river was part of the Mason-Dixon line in the 19th century - the border separating North from South during the Civil War. Back then they would never have contemplated putting an airport for the North over in the South."

The pilot paused for a moment.

"My co-pilot has just informed me that such a contemplation would have been a massive anachronism since the first plane was not invented till 1903." He paused again.

"Well, apart from learning some history and aviation, you folks will have also realised that my co-pilot is a bit of a smarty-pants."

"Anyway, in a couple of minutes, if you look on the right side of the plane, you will see downtown Cincinnati and its famous sports stadium." The pilot sighed. "Let's hope the Reds can do better next baseball season. Please, don't get me started on the Bengals football squad. It has been tough watching these teams over the years. They just seem to struggle to gain momentum at the start, and then it becomes downhill from…" The stream of consciousness stopped.

"Oh, right. Some people are just no fun at all. That was my very helpful co-pilot telling me to concentrate on landing the plane. Okay, I guess, here we go. Hold your nose!"

Roddy felt the plane dip and swerve, lining up its landing approach.

He had been enjoying the pilot's brief rant. It had provided a welcome respite from the thoughts running through his head for most of the flight.

A week earlier he had stumbled across a Cancer Research shop in Glasgow, where they were selling second hand self-help tapes. On the plane he had taken the time to listen to the smooth, calming voice of an actor between roles. Roddy's main takeaway from the tape was that we need to break our issues down into 'bite-sized' chunks, and approach them one at a time, finding solutions for each.

The first was easy. Angie. He could see her five rows ahead on the right, sitting beside Reilly. Her adoption by his mum was the easiest case Social Services had probably ever heard – liberated from a psychotic father intent on unleashing death and mayhem. Roddy was proud of his mother. She had signed the papers without hesitation, knowing - and loving - Angie from the many playdates she had shared with Roddy over the years.

Angie adapted well to their busy world, joining in social events and going on holiday as a family. Their relationship had grown into a unique version of brother-sister. Their mutual respect and love for each other as friends had developed into a strong sibling bond - absent the rivalry.

The issue he was struggling with had started halfway through last term. She was sitting beside 'the issue' on the plane. Reilly, their centre forward - a naturally gifted player. Not forgetting his athletic physique, straight A's in all subjects, and what he had heard the girls calling a 'devilishly charming smile'. Roddy had expected - and wanted - him to be a nasty, selfish bully. Annoyingly, Reilly MacDonald was a kind, gentle, caring kid who went out of his way to support and befriend the other team members. He was the glue that held the team together. How unfair could life be, Roddy thought?

If that was not bad enough, Angie played upfront on the right wing, while Roddy was a substitute. She not only spent her social time with Reilly, she was the first to hug him whenever he - or she - scored a goal. Roddy would have to watch from the bench while he quartered oranges for half-time.

The self-tape had encouraged him not to 'invest in wound-licking' but to decide on - and work towards - a goal. Okay. Fine. He had worked hard during the flight to find the key to unlock this issue. He decided he could not stop Angie hanging out with Reilly, nor did he want that, really. He liked seeing her happy. It was just that he missed her. He wanted to be part of it all, included in the hugging and bonding inspired by goal-scoring and winning. He made his mind up. He was going to get off the bench and into the team proper. If that meant getting up early every morning to practice, then so be it.

Then there was his father. Or rather his father and Maggie. The tension in the house was thicker than the marmalade his dad layered on top of his breakfast toast. On one level he understood why the friction had evolved. His dad was Kiltman. He realised it as soon as he had discovered the source of his powers in his sporran after they had captured Mask. All the secrecy and trips away from home suddenly made sense to him.

His first reaction was to feel an immense pride. He had never thought about it before that moment. His dad was his dad. He always knew he had a benevolent, caring side and would 'do a good turn rather than a bad turn' - he had expressed it to Roddy in that way on many an occasion. His father had used his special potion to help others - no matter the self-sacrifice involved.

He also knew - through the numerous superhero movies he had binge-watched - that living with such a secret could take its toll on loved ones. Especially when the hero was co-habiting with his crime-solving partner on the Scottish police force.

Initially he had not been sure if Maggie knew about his dad's secret identity. Over time, after having walked into enough kitchen conversations created for his benefit, he accepted that she was aware too.

He had not been invited into the secret, which was fine by him. Pretending not to know could be fun, watching his father make up stories to disguise his activities. It made it easier not to deal with the reality that his father faced danger on a regular basis, putting his safety on the line for others.

That is what made it difficult for Roddy to comprehend why the same man would stomp around the house complaining about socks, books and plates 'making the house look like a bombsite'. His father had even told him off for coming in late after football practice a couple of times. How could he become independent with his dad breathing down his neck? Kiltman or not, his father was out of sync with how teenagers should be treated.

Just when he felt he could explode at this constant nagging, his father would - without any prompting - tell a complete stranger how proud he was of 'his son'.

Ten out of ten in trying to confuse your child, Dad.

Hair o' the Dog ala Roddy

Roddy shook his head. He had to focus on the tape's request to identify a goal for each problem. Okay, he decided he would work harder to be patient with him and not be critical of his grumpiness. He would remember that his father's secret was the source of his behavioural problems, and he would be empathetic - he decided to help his father work through his own issues. He would help him become a better person, a better role model.

It would be easy to tell him that he knew he was Kiltman. Clear the air. Although everything would change - bringing a new set of problems - particularly for Roddy.

How could he tell his father that he had found out about his superhero secret when he was rifling through his sporran - and found the source of his powers; his Hair o' the Dog 'whisky'. It tasted quite adult and soothing.

And alcohol-free.

This became clear after his first generous glug – when he had expected to start singing Irish ballads and dancing. To his surprise nothing happened. Well, not exactly nothing.

It took a few minutes - he started to see things. In the air all around him. Letters, words, numbers, names, dates. The air had filled with a thick alphabet broth. It frightened him at first. But then he started to see the soup for what it was. Communication. Each combination of data was a line, a sentence. They were texts. Emails. Even faxes. Information transmitted by phones or downloaded from the internet. Telephone conversations appeared as transcripts. It became clear. He could see the airwaves; the invisible data being transmitted all around him.

In the beginning, he felt afraid of the claustrophobia fuelled by this viscous soup swirling around his head and body. He had rushed to open the window and gulp the fresh night air. It had helped at first, but the sight of more, bigger clouds of moving data and information stretching as far as the night sky panicked him even more.

After a couple of hours, it had eased off. When he woke the next morning, he was determined to get to the bottom of this phenomenon. He snuck into the basement and found his father's secret stash. There were crates of bottles lined up along the wall, full of amber liquid. Each container had a label stuck on with Sellotape, describing how long the whisky had been kept in a barrel and when it had been bottled. On the table, a notebook showed the inventory ins and outs. That is when he saw the name, *Hair o' the Dog*. A strange title, he had thought. Some googling told him that Hair o' the Dog was a colloquial expression for a drink that helped you recover from one too many. All a bit pointless and paradoxical, he had thought, but not a surprise.

With a couple of tweaks to the notebook he was able to free up a few bottles and maintain a balanced inventory ledger. He had pilfered enough to explore this power-inducing enigma over the weeks that followed. He kept his own stash in the shed at the bottom of the garden, underneath a shelf stuffed with mowers and rakes. His father would never find it there.

Learning about its capability had been fascinating. He tuned into people on the bus texting their friends that they were on their way; customers in cafes messaging their boss they were not feeling well; men and women texting their love for each other; men and women texting messages far from loving to each other. Over time he had cultivated a skill that allowed him to identify the data with the sender, linking the floating stream of words back to the source phone or computer.

It had gone well for the first few weeks. Then it started. The enemy of teenagers, the scourge of the young. Puberty. Not just puberty. It was the manifestation of the arrival of adolescence. Acne. Little mountain ranges of red peaks revealing the seismic shift of hormonal tectonic plates in his body. He feared the moment of looking in the mirror in the morning, afraid of what would look back at him.

It became evident after a couple of sips of Hair o' the Dog that acne thrived on non-alcoholic, superpower-imbuing whisky. His face would flair up into an angry speckled range of volcanic craters, threatening eruption. A liberal splashing of cold water would add some calm to the simmering lava, but he would not be able to stop the most determined from breaking through.

Superpower-imbuing or not, he had no choice; he had to protect his skin - and self-esteem. He had not touched Hair o' the Dog in nearly two years.

That was why he now had an issue.

He was quite sure the ex-actor on the tape did not have a solution to this one. Roddy knew he had access to a power others could only dream of. Until now he had been under-utilising its incredible strength, wasting his opportunity. This trip, far from home, was his chance to up the ante - and probably the acne - and use these powers to full effect.

As the wheels touched down with a deliberate bump on the runway, he was determined to use every drop of the bottle to help him become the teenager he was meant to be.

Sacco meets SOCO

DI Wilson enjoyed the pleasant morning air settling around the river. The trees swayed in the breeze, while the small boats and dinghies sat motionless in the calm water. It would have been pleasant to walk further along the bank to the clearing ahead, however the large, yellow tent - her destination - spanned the length of the riverside walkway.

"Excuse me, Miss, you will have to walk up over the other path. This area is restricted." The young policeman's outstretched hand reinforced his message.

"That's okay, Officer." She flashed her police ID. "I'm here to join the investigation."

"Sorry, Ma'am." The officer inspected the ID before lifting the plastic tape surrounding the crime scene. She had preferred 'Miss'. She flashed him a courteous smile, as she ducked under the tape and entered the tent.

"Hey, Maggie!" A policeman approached her. He looked familiar. As she tried to recall where she knew him from, he reached out and took her into a tight hug.

"Hi, Cameron. I didn't expect to see you here." She should have realised there were not too many Urquharts around. Last time she had seen Cameron Urquhart, he had been on mini-sub duty when they were in the closing stages of capturing Cullen Skink a few years earlier. A shiver coursed through her veins at how she had avoided what he had in store for her.

"I've been in London now for the last couple of years. I applied for a move after we caught Skink. This is my latest case." Urquhart pointed a thumb over his shoulder to where a body lay outstretched on a table. It was being poked and prodded by three SOCOs - scenes of crime officers - dressed in typical yellow suits with goggles and mask.

"Well," he continued before Wilson responded, "it was me who mentioned you to the Chief of Police. When he realised who the deceased was, he asked for recommendations on expertise in investigating financial crimes. I hope you don't mind."

She allowed herself a rueful smile. She did not mind, although she knew someone who did.

"Thanks, Cameron, I appreciate that."

She paused for a moment. "What have you found so far?" She nodded over his shoulder.

"His name is Paolo Capello. He is…"

"President of Banco d'Aiuto," she finished for him. "Answers - or answered - to the handle of Sacco. What happened?"

Urquhart led her by the arm outside the tent and pointed to the arch under the bridge. She had read about Richmond Bridge on the plane. Built a quarter of a millennium earlier, it spanned the Thames, connecting the counties of Middlesex and Surrey. It was truly a beautiful construct, she thought. Pity it had been put to its most recent use.

"Capello was found late last night hanging from that bar. He had a couple of bricks in his pockets, for weight I assume, and an upturned chair on the path."

"Suicide?" she asked.

"Yes… if he had found a way to procure a rope after leaving the hotel. Yes… if he had not really wanted to feed the ducks with the bread roll in his jacket pocket. Yes… if you assume he was not intending to use the ticket we found on his bedside cabinet for La Boheme in La Scala next weekend." Urquhart stopped for a moment.

"So, it's *No* then," Wilson replied.

"Yes, it's *No*." He smiled at the awkwardness of the statement. "Once we have the DNA analysis, I'm sure we won't find any of his on the rope or the bricks, and probably not even the chair."

They turned to duck back into the tent. "Any thoughts on who the perps might be then?" she asked.

They approached the table and stopped a metre away from the body, allowing the SOCOs to continue their picking and bagging.

"Well, with a situation like this," he shrugged, "we can't rule out the Italian Mafia. There's suspicion Capello has been working with them over the years, potentially laundering some of their black money. Hence why you are here. The Chief is hoping you can work with us in finding a motive. That should help us towards identifying those responsible."

Wilson inspected the body between the SOCOs methodical movements. Her attention was drawn first to Sacco's small, delicate hands. He could have been a piano player. They seemed so out of place against the rest of him. The corpse's girth bulged out over his designer, black belt. He had been living the good life - *la bella vita*. His expensive navy blue, silk suit contrasted with a face contorted by the strains of someone choked to death. Urquhart was right. The evidence pointed to murder. Even the method of death told her it was not suicide. She knew enough about Sacco to know he would not want to be found dangling from a bridge, even if he had a mind to kill himself. A man known for his style and panache, he would have found a more noble - and painless - way to go.

"Probably better at this stage not to jump to conclusions," Wilson said. "You're right, I don't think we are going to find much in the way of evidence to know who did this. We'll have to work backwards, starting with a potential motive. Yes, it could be Mafia, since they do the whole bricks in the pocket thing. Or could be someone wanting us to think it's Mafia. Or could be some other group of ne'er-do-wells intent on punishing him."

She waited for Urquhart to respond, but it was clear he had settled into focusing on Wilson. He seemed a little too focused, she thought. She kept going, determined not to let the silence become uncomfortable.

"Anyway, traditionally people make a connection with Mafia in these cases. Especially when the victim is Italian. However, more and more since 9/11, we are identifying banks used to move money around for international terrorists. If that's the case here, then we are potentially looking at a broad spectrum of suspects, from Al Qaeda to Russia's Caucasus; and more besides."

She could see Urquhart's eyes twinkle. She decided to assume he was excited about the chance to investigate global financial crime.

"Right then," she said. "Where next?"

"Central London, somewhere we will both feel at home." Urquhart replied, barely able to restrain the broad smile and chuckle. "New Scotland Yard."

Business Class Superhero

Kiltman pushed the button to recline his chair to a comfortable position, before draining his glass of orange juice. He was in the process of placing the container back on the table, when the steward appeared at his side.

"Good morning, Kiltman! Would you like a refill?" To say the steward was well-coiffed would have been an understatement salons across the country would have balked at. His black hair was slicked back with a parting that could cut glass. Eyebrows had been plucked to within a centimetre of Bram Stoker's original Count Dracula. Eyes glinted with a turquoise blue - even without his earlier Hair o' the Dog swig, Kiltman could have seen the edges of the contact lenses.

"Oh, hi! Good morning to you too!" Kiltman handed the cup over for a refill.

"I am Darius, and I will be serving you on this trip to São Paulo." He winked. It was the slightest of twitches, but it was a wink.

"Thanks, Darius." He was annoyed at himself for feeling vulnerable in his reclining position. Dressed in his full Kiltman regalia, he sometimes forgot how odd others might find a man in a kilt, cape and mask, decorated with a white cross against a blue background: the St. Andrew's cross.

"Anything you need on this flight, just let me know," Darius smiled before applying a slight tap - or was it a rub - to his shoulder. Before he walked away with poise, filling glasses and smiling at passengers.

Kiltman pushed the button to recline his seat to a more horizontal position, in the comfort of knowing Darius would be keeping an eye on him. He was tempted to go fully flat, then realised a kilt was not the best accoutrement in the circumstances so settled around a gentle gradient.

Until recently he had never been in a business or first-class seat. Now when he approached the check-in desk, the airlines would usually find him an upgrade. It had all started after the high-profile capture of Mask after his attempt to annihilate United Nations General Assembly members in New York. In the early days, he had considered refusing politely - a quiet rebellion against class distinction. Until he sampled the luxurious seating, and delicious meals.

He closed his eyes and let his mind wander. His thoughts spanned a range of topics, all vying for priority. First, he wanted to think about Roddy. Ah, that wee boy! Kenny adored the ground he walked on. When he observed his son connecting with his friends, and even with strangers, he could see a massive dose of kindness and compassion. It was when Kenny approached that Roddy's hackles would spike. It was as if he changed from the inside out in a millisecond. One moment, he was exploding with banter and repartee. One father later - the mood changed. He knew what the cause was, he just had to figure out how to address this cavity that existed between them.

It had started when his son had turned fourteen, a fully-fledged teenager - the early days of facial hair and spots. Until then, Kenny felt he had handled the situation well. He had adapted to the late arrivals at breakfast - which became known as lunch at the weekend; the grumpy one-word answers; the long silences when on his phone - Roddy's responses to questions a somnambulistic, startle reflex to keep his father at bay.

There had been a time when he thought humour might bridge the gap; until he realised his one-liners achieved two things; self-satisfaction and annoyed teenagers. Of late, he had decided to stop bombarding him with puns and quips; they both felt the vacuum.

When Roddy turned fifteen, he adopted the mindset that covering every piece of furniture and floor with his plates, books, clothes - especially smelly socks - was normal, because someone - yes, muggins - would pick them up. He had made a decision a few months earlier that enough was enough. The gloves were off.

He sighed aloud attracting a quizzical glance from a seasoned, mask on the forehead, earplugs in hand, passenger across the aisle. This was his greatest regret. He should never have taken the gloves off. In fact, boxing metaphors should never have entered his vocabulary. This was his son, his precious wee boy. Roddy had not said the words, 'I didn't ask to be born', but if he did, Kenny would not argue. His job as a father was to guide his son through the fog of life. These teenage years were as much a learning ground for Kenny to cut his teeth as a father, as they were for Roddy to find himself.

Why did it take a reclining seat on a twelve-hour flight and an affable steward for him to reach this conclusion? When they were both back home, he was determined to make sure they re-booted their relationship. At the weekend on the radio, the breakfast show DJ had stopped him in his tracks. Usually, the DJ's spouting was out one ear soon after it entered the other, however this last Sunday one comment stuck. Kenny had half a slice of toast in his mouth, when he stopped mid-bite, the radio turned up loud to drown out Maisie barking at a plane coming to land in Glasgow airport.

The DJ made a point of explaining that, by the time a child leaves home at 18 to pursue studies or a career, they will have spent 94% of all the time they will ever spend with their parents. He shivered whenever he thought about that statistic; he had work to do.

Next was Maggie. She had been a rock, making Uisge Beatha a home and not just a perfunctory house where father and son came and went. Kenny had told her once that she 'put the 'well' in dwelling together.'

She had smiled back. "Thanks, but let's try to remember not to put the 'hospital' in hospitality."

He knew it was a dig at how he had been reacting to Roddy and his friends messing up the house. When he thought about it, he had not noticed any friends around Uisge Beatha of late. Maybe he had made one comment too many, one admonishment beyond the limit acceptable to teenagers with an abundance of places to go.

If that was the main issue with Maggie, he knew they could deal with it. The bigger - and more pressing - matter was his Kiltman identity and their professional relationship. At work she feigned she had no idea who Kiltman was. He pretended not to know she was faking. When they were together on a job, even when alone, she would call him Kiltman. She would not let her guard down for a moment. Once during a quiet moment when they were walking across the hills at the back of their home, she had mentioned that life sometimes needed the equivalent of *control/enter* on a keyboard - a way to start a new page, make a clean break with the past. She made this comment around the time he felt the distance build between them.

They had both brought baggage to the relationship. Hers was a neat, well-packed, carry-on bag with a couple of marginal sized bottles of liquid. While his was a checked in suitcase and a colonial style trunk decorated with stickers from all over the world. He wondered in his quiet moments what would happen when their *metaphorical flight* landed. Would she wait for him? What worried him more was whether he would say 'go on ahead and I'll meet you outside after bag collection'. Would he ever be able to bring himself to exit the terminal?

He realised he was not doing well with either Maggie or Roddy. A 'game plan' was needed. In a couple of days, he would be alone in a remote part of Brazil, with time to think things through. The plan would have to be more than trimming the edges of overgrowth in their relationship garden. He was prepared to plough through his personal allotment, turn it over and replant seeds of growth. That meant nothing was sacred - not even his Kiltman persona - or annoying mixed metaphors.

Hint of Menace

Darius placed a mega-sized portion of chocolate and vanilla ice cream on the table.

"Crikey," Kiltman exclaimed. "I don't think I'll manage that."

"Okay," Darius lifted the plate. "I can go back and prepare a smaller portion."

"Wait." Kiltman placed his hand on Darius' arm. "Let's not be hasty. What kind of superhero am I, if I can't face down a challenge like this."

Darius twinkled a smile at him. "That's the spirit! First there was Cullen Skink. Then Mask. Now… *Gelato!*"

Kiltman nodded his appreciation of the steward's knowledge of his nemeses. He picked up the spoon just as Darius walked down the aisle, touching him again on the shoulder. This time it was definitely a rub. Kiltman found it quite soothing.

He lifted the bottom of his mask to create space for the spoon. Most of the ice cream made it to his mouth with some splodges landing on the inside of the mask. One day, he would need to create a detachable mouthpiece that allowed him some dignity when eating in public.

As he enjoyed the soothing, chocolatey mixture, he realised something had been niggling him since he boarded the plane, lurking at the back of his mind. An ever so slight hint of menace. There was no denying it. He had first sensed it in the Heathrow departures lounge. It felt like a wave of hot air touching the pores of his skin - not the first time he had experienced something like this. Hair o' the Dog had become adept at boosting his five senses to extraordinary levels of sensitivity. Of late, it had also given him something he could only define as a sixth sense. That was the beauty of the whisky he had created in his basement several years ago, using local hillside water. When he discovered that the power-imbuing, alcohol-eliminating ingredient was a meteorite nestled in a pond above his house, it made sense. He had stumbled upon a treasure that allowed him to turn his life around and give something back to the world.

Before boarding he had wandered into WH Smith, although he had no intention of buying anything. It was more to stay away from the main thoroughfare - avoiding photos, autographs and well-wishers. There were times when he would invest in encouraging the interaction - he felt that showing a human side would make people want to support not just him but, more importantly, the law and order he was trying to protect.

Then there were days like today, where he felt out of sorts. Partially because of the issues at home, but also because he could feel this strange hint of danger. From his vantage point in the bookshop, he had surveyed the spacious terminal. His eyes and ears had focused in on each of the several hundred travellers and staff. He could hear what they were saying, see what they were reading - yet found nothing of note.

Now on the plane, he failed to shake off the sensation. He decided to visit the facilities to clean the inside of his mask; but also, to observe his fellow passengers. On his way to the toilet at the rear of the plane, he noticed nothing out of the ordinary. Other than a woman on a hen party trying to use a mirror to see if he was a 'true Scotsman'. The journey back to his seat felt like the 'walk of dames' - an orchestra of whistles and screams. The plane had departed at 10 am, yet this group of ladies looked like they had been 'flying' since well before take-off.

He managed to retain his pride by giving the bride-to-be a latex kiss on the cheek. When one of her friends put her hand up the back of his kilt, he whirled around, and said, "Hey, you've got ten minutes to stop that, young lady!" In the midst of the laughs and cheers, he was able to walk away – his head held high and his hand on the back of the kilt.

When he sat back in his seat, he considered the Hollywood version of Superheroes; they spent an inordinate amount of effort protecting their identity. Yet he seemed to spend the majority of his time protecting his dignity.

A few hours and a brief nap later, he was walking through São Paulo airport to the helipad, accompanied by a Brazilian named Jose. Jose had met Kiltman at arrivals, holding a sign reading *Celtman*. It was close enough. Back in London, he had been given a picture of Jose, to make sure he could identify him on arrival. There had been a spate of kidnappings at South American airports recently. Jose would have been a handsome man, were it not for the four-inch scar on his right cheek, the boneless, squidgy nose, and the brown, crooked teeth.

"If he was the good guy," Kiltman had said when he showed the picture to Maggie, "he did not want to meet the bad guys."

A twenty-minute walk later, they arrived at the helipad, where they approached a red four-seater helicopter. The pilot stepped down from inside. Kiltman was not sure if he should feel reassured by the resemblance to pilots in war comics he had read as a child. The goggles and headgear had more scratches than any peace-time outfit should warrant.

"Hallo, Kiltman!" the pilot extended his hand. "I am Martim."

Kiltman shook his hand, "Nice to meet you, Martim. How long will this take?"

"Weather good. Skies clear." Martim nodded. "Two hours max. Let's go."

Kiltman turned to thank Jose, but he had already wandered off to the smoking area beside the helicopter pad, lit up a strong-smelling cigarette and was busy tapping his phone.

Within fifteen minutes, the rotor blades were slicing the air noisily. As the chopper floated up above the terminal buildings, Kiltman glanced towards Jose. He was stamping a foot down on what looked like the remnants of his phone - an array of plastic and battery splattered around the ground. Whatever words had been communicated had now become victims of 'verbal abuse'. Strange, Jose did not seem to show a hint of anger or passion on his pugilist features. In fact, he was smiling in Kiltman's direction, waving in a halting, slow-motion gesture.

The chopper soared high above the streets of São Paulo, the doors on either side open - the wind and noise eliminating any chance of chit-chat. He could focus on the task at hand. Meeting Mask, finding out whatever information he wanted to share, deciding whether he believed it, then a relaxing well-earned break in Iguaçu.

Then he felt it again. That hint of menace, even more sinister than before.

Icarus

"*Icarus* is now high in the sky." He hit *send*.

Beep.

"*OK*." The receipt message read.

He waited a few moments unsure whether the conversation was finished.

Beep.

"*Destroy the phone. Goodbye.*"

"*Ok, will do now.*"

Assuming that was the end of the conversation, he removed a knife from his inside pocket. Using the tiny point at the weapon's tip - while ignoring the sharp, serrated edge used for much more fulfilling exploits - he removed the sim card. He enjoyed the satisfying snap of it breaking in two between his gnarled fingers. The phone dropped to the ground in a clatter, shattering on impact. The heel of his boot sealed its fate.

The splinters and fragments scattered across the tarmac in a disarray of shards. He smiled realising the mess underfoot was a precursor for the destiny ordained for the *Icarus* package climbing high into the sky above him.

He waved at the weirdly costumed man who should have known better at his age; not to dress like a Halloween muppet - and not to trust strangers.

Game On

"Ok, team, huddle round!" Coach Stone liked to use Americanisms - even back in Scotland - when talking about football. 'Coach' had played for several teams over the years, in both Scotland and England. The toll of physical stress over the years manifested itself in a snapped knee ligament. Two years of operations and stuttered recovery saw him drop down the leagues until he made the decision to pass his skills onto school kids. Despite the look he presented with his five-day stubble, baseball cap round the wrong way, maturing belly and dry sense of humour, he got the best out of the players.

When Coach explained strategy, Roddy tuned out - he was rarely on the pitch to participate. It did not help that Coach was dressed in his usual gold and white tracksuit. Roddy had heard a couple of the players talking on the plane about how Coach's garb made him look more like a Russian oligarch than a football manager; making it even harder for Roddy to engage with his instructions.

The team sat in a semi-circle focused on an A3 sheet of paper spread flat on the ground. Coach was kneeling on the grass pointing a stick at various crosses and lines on the page.

"Okay, listen," he said. "This evening, we have our first game against the Galatians. They are a physical team, and, on average, are a head and shoulders taller than us." He paused to let that sink in.

"There's no point in us trying to beat them in the air, so we are going to keep our passing below head height. This also applies to set pieces."

"Roddy," he continued, "you will be on from the start. I want you to take the free kicks. Thanks to that strong right leg of yours, you're very comfortable at passing at a height lower than this." Coach stood and positioned his hand level with Roddy's head.

Roddy was surprised, this was the last thing he had expected. He knew he could hit the ball hard - probably harder than anyone else in the team, including Reilly - however, his sense of direction was as accurate as a blindfolded four-year-old trying to pin the tail on a donkey.

He felt Angie beside him, squeezing his arm - he was glad she was pleased for him. Although he was not sure if Coach had factored the accuracy issue into his thinking, until he went on. "No offence, Roddy, but once you let rip, the ball might go anywhere. However at least it will go anywhere at a low height. The rest of you upfront should be on your toes to pick it up and move fast."

The players looked at each other. Nobody was under the illusion this was a great play. In fact - they realised in unison - this 'set piece' tactic was the best they could hope for considering the height disadvantage. Roddy was in effect being brought in to make the best of a bad situation.

"Okay, let's practice the 'Pin Ball Wizard' play." Coach smiled at his ingenuity and clapped his hands, eager to get started.

The rest of the training went better than usual for Roddy. He hit the ball under his head height - and as planned, it rarely went twice in the same direction. His team-mates' reaction time improved the more he kicked the ball.

Considering they had arrived a few hours earlier that day, they showed no signs of flagging - spurred on by the excitement of being in the USA, and about to play in an 'international' football tournament. This was their last chance to train prior to their first game that evening, so they kept it light, just enough to warm them up.

The Galatians were based in Cleveland, Northern Ohio, the other end of the state from Cincinnati. A faction within the Catholic Church, they were a recent media sensation, challenging the church's teachings and seeking reforms. Roddy did not know much about them other than they were quite influential in evangelising Catholics and members of other religions to join them. He was not expecting a party atmosphere at the game.

At the end of training, as they prepared to drop their bags back at the accommodation area, Coach announced the bunking arrangements. There were to be two per room - boys in the West wing and girls in the East. Roddy and Reilly had been picked to share a room overlooking the football pitch. Reilly slapped his roommate on the back. "Cool, pal! I really wanted to share with you."

Roddy did not buy that for a second. Either Reilly was faking or wanted to impress Angie. Whatever the reason, Roddy struggled to conceal his disquiet.

"Yeah, great, Reilly. Me too!" was all he could muster.

As he said the words, he realised that even though he had not meant to be sarcastic, his facial expression had not kept up with his words - he had probably presented an archetypical display of the lowest form of wit. Reilly's flicker of an eyebrow was enough for Roddy to know how it had been received.

Once in their room, they set about unpacking their bags. They had three drawers each - two drawers more than either of them needed. They exchanged wry smiles when they realised they had been equally parsimonious in their packing.

Roddy felt bad about his earlier sarcasm and knew it warranted an explanation. "Reilly…"

Reilly's phone sounded. It then rang another five or six times. Roddy noticed the ring was not the normal mono-beep sound. It had been customised to a deep low tone, akin to the sound at the start of a funeral march.

"Hey, Reilly, are you not going to answer it?"

"I'll get it later," he answered, before rearranging his t-shirts and shorts for the third time.

"It could be important."

"No, it's just my dad. He can be a real pain sometimes. I find it better to ignore him when he goes off on one." He turned to his roommate and spread his hands wide. "Dads. Can't live with them; definitely can live without them."

New Scotland Yard

Maggie stifled a groan as she exited the police car onto the pavement.

"Good morning, DI Wilson!" Grant MacTavish already had his microphone in hand and trusted cameraman at his side. Darn, she thought, he seemed to get younger looking every time he accosted her. His boyish good looks landed somewhere between Brad Pitt and Robert Redford in The Spy Game. Intensely cunning, annoyingly handsome and not to be trusted for a moment.

"Hi, Grant!" She smiled despite herself. She could not dislike this bizarre reporter who had studied at university with Kenny. He had an uncanny ability to show up whenever she worked on a high-profile case. "What's up?"

"Hah!" he said. "I see what you did there." He paused for a moment, before thrusting the microphone under her chin. "Do you want to shed any light on the breaking news - the Italian financier, known as the People's Banker, Paolo Capello's apparent suicide in Richmond?"

"Well, Grant. As you know," and as I told you several times on other cases, she thought, "I can't comment on a case that is being investigated. We will make an announcement later today at the appropriate time when we have information to communicate."

"Thanks, DI Wilson. Is it true there was a brick in each pocket, indicating there may be a Mafia involvement?"

"Grant!"

Her voice had sufficient admonishment embedded in its tone to prompt him to concede.

"Okay, thank you!" He turned to the camera making sure he did not block her walking away in the background. She proceeded up the stairs into the UK's most famous police station, with his final words drifting towards her. "Well, we can await DI Wilson's report later. It does seem like Richmond has witnessed a scene normally at home in back alleys of Sicily or Brooklyn.

Capello - colloquially known as Sacco - has garnered a reputation for himself as a modern-day Robin Hood of the banking world. Well, if we are looking for a Sheriff of Nottingham, there is nobody better than DI Wilson to lead the investigation. We can rest assured Kiltman will not be far away."

"MacTavish!" His earplugs buzzed with the rasping shout. Grant's cavalier spirit irked his producer, Dominic Gallagher, getting worse over the years they had worked together. There were several broadcasts where Grant had crossed the line; today looked like it was going to be no different. "Listen carefully, the BBC does not harass interviewees, especially those we need to stay close to. Keep it calm and friendly while still insightful. Clear?"

"Yes, Boss." MacTavish hated being restrained; he would wait for his moment. The sound in his headset stopped. He looked at the cameraman "Okay, let's get ourselves a curry. Boss's paying."

Wilson entered the station with a shake of her head. Overworked clichés were Grant's bread and butter, although she could not remember one as puerile as his most recent Prince of Thieves analogy.

"Hello, DI Wilson!" a tall policeman wearing a neat, pressed uniform extended his hand. Her engaging smile switched to a grimace when Chief of Police Armstrong's handshake crumpled her fingers. She wondered if anyone had mentioned to him how well his grasp fitted his name. From Northern Ireland, Armstrong was known for his ability to confront danger head on. As a policeman on the streets of Belfast, he had no shortage of training. She sensed that while he was broad shouldered and physically imposing, his booming voice with its broad vowels and rolling consonants would have made most criminals think twice.

"It's a pleasure to meet you, sir," she managed to say through clenched teeth.

"Welcome to London. I'm pleased you can join the team on this case." He had already turned on his heel and was striding along the corridor. She hustled beside him, trying to match his long stride, with the odd half skip to keep up. "Let me take you to the control room we have set up for this case."

He pushed open a door halfway down the corridor and she followed him in. Two long walls were being used as extended whiteboards, already half-covered in photos, sheets of papers and scribbles with lines and bubbles drawn around and between them.

"Goodness," she said. "You guys have been busy already."

Closing the door, Armstrong nodded. "Yes, we have. However, most of this was done before Capello died last night." He looked at her, encouraging her to speak.

"I see," she said. Sacco had already been under some sort of investigation before his death. She walked towards one of the walls to study a series of mugshots, names handwritten underneath: Roberto 'Mucky' Marciano, Gianni 'Pirla' Sconi, Mauro 'Zio' Papetti, Carlo 'San' Babila.

She had heard of each of these individuals before, the leaders - *capos* - of various Sicilian families. She could see a circle drawn around each photo and a line in red ink leading to Paolo 'Sacco' Capello's picture above them.

She turned to Armstrong. "Looks like you've already made some connections here."

Armstrong had folded his arms, with a hand stroking his chin. "Yes, we have. Sacco was not what he made himself out to be. We have plenty of evidence to connect him to these Mafia bosses. At a minimum he was laundering money for them through Banca d'Aiuto. While we believe there is more to it than that, we have hit the proverbial brick wall, I'm afraid."

He rested for a moment to let this settle in. Wilson studied the data as he continued. "We would have arrested him already based on what we have found. However, there is a bigger prize here - we don't know what it is yet, but we do know that based on the sums of money involved, there is more to this than washing some Mafia ill-gotten gains. Our People's Banker was into something bigger and more clandestine than that."

She nodded. She decided not to say that laundering money for the Mafia - four different families - was already a major crime compared to the issues she dealt with daily in Glasgow. "I appreciate the invite to help on this, Chief. Who will I be working with?"

Armstrong beckoned to three officers seated at computers at the back of the room. A man and two women stepped forward as if they carried a ton weight on their shoulders.

"Here are officers Crawford John, Alison Modine and Mary Best. They are experts on extracting and mining data. Where we need help from you is in making sense of the reasons for, and connections between, the information we have collated. A fresh pair of eyes, if you like."

She reached across and shook hands with each of the officers. Crawford was taller than Alison and Mary. "I'm looking forward to working with you," she said. They each nodded their welcome to her, only Crawford attempted a smile.

"Hello, Ma'am," Crawford said. "We've met before."

Wilson recognised him. Handsome - although not in a conventional way - he sported a half-smile when he spoke. She clicked her fingers. "New York! A few years back. You and your friends in the pub were accountants."

"Yes, I'm pleased you remember me, eh, us. Since then, I have taken up investigative work helping the Met. They seem to appreciate my approach to scrutinising finances." Wilson smiled, remembering how Crawford was badgered for spending too much time *scrutinising* and not enough time buying his round.

"Okay, small world," Armstrong said with a hint of impatience. Although much less than Gemmill would have expressed in the same situation. "I'll leave you four to get to know each other. I don't need to mention that Sacco's death has upped the ante here. We were already behind the clock. Now we may be forced to show our hand on the Mafia connections and approach those mobsters sooner rather than later. I'm going to make an announcement to the media this evening. If you don't find anything soon, then I will be forced to contact our Italian colleagues and get them moving. Not ideal, I admit. However, we have to be seen to be doing something here."

She detested politics strong-arming policing. The irony of the Chief's name - something Kiltman would have enjoyed - was small comfort.

Amazon Delivery

Kiltman had never been happier to see a top-security prison in the middle of the Amazon rainforest. The four-seater had proven to be a bumpy two-hour ride over an endless span of treetops. He had tried to converse with Martim to explain how the compact forest resembled a panorama of oversized broccoli. He gave up after the third attempt - the noise of the blades had reverberated on the inside of the chopper, shaking him to his core. He would keep the broccoli metaphor for a future moment deserving of his whimsical observations.

As they approached the high-walled prison surrounded by turrets, search lights and guards, he understood just why such a facility was considered a secure home for some of the world's most violent criminals. While the outside walls and protective surroundings were impregnable, the inside was a large box-shaped block with a myriad of tiny, fortified windows; all prisoners kept in solitary confinement.

They slowed down for their landing on the helipad close to the main building, but outside the prison walls. Kiltman could see a row of tombstones one hundred metres or so further away towards the trees, the final resting place for prisoners who would never make it home. There was some activity at the top end of the small cemetery, where it looked like a convict was being added to the rainforest's human fertiliser program. He felt a twinge of sadness before he conceded that some people did not deserve sympathy.

"Governor Fernandes, welcome." A tall, striking man in a pressed uniform introduced himself as Kiltman stepped down from the chopper.

"Pleased to meet you, Governor." Kiltman bowed awkwardly.

"Come. Let's enter. The prisoner known as Mask has been informed you are arriving. You can meet in my office." No small talk suited Kiltman just fine. He wanted this over and done with.

"Sounds good," he answered, following Fernandes as he was buzzed through a series of gates and barriers, until they reached a large spacious office on the ground floor. The smell of fresh coffee greeted them. Fernandes poured two large cups and pointed towards a sugar bowl and milk jug. The disdain with which he indicated the crockery deterred Kiltman from taking his usual two sugars and splash of milk. Obviously, tough middle of the Amazon rainforest types drank their coffee bitter and black.

The Governor pressed a button on his phone. Without waiting for a response, he spoke in an even tone. "Ask the guards to bring prisoner 2101 here. He should be ready."

"Yes, sir," a male voice responded.

Kiltman was amused that they were speaking in English - it somehow made him feel less like an unwanted guest.

The Governor walked towards the main table in the room and pointed at a strong, wooden, cushioned chair. "Make yourself at home. Although I expect you would like to be out of here as soon as possible."

"Maybe on another occasion, I can make a weekend of it," he responded. Trying to sound as wry as the Governor - while realising Scottish accents do not lend themselves to cynical overtones.

The Governor tapped the table impatiently. "I personally believe this is a piece of nonsense. This Mask thug is, how do you say, jerking the UN's chain? I would not have entertained this ridiculous request, if it had not..."

The desk phone beeped loudly. Two seconds before the prison alarm sounded. Fernandes rushed to his desk to press the phone's speaker, sirens shrieking in the background.

"What the..." he started.

"Mask is gone, sir. He is not in his room."

"What do you mean, not in his room?"

"He was there an hour ago, when we last did our rounds. So, he can't be far away. We have started a full facility-wide search."

"Okay, officer, you know the drill. He can't have gone very far. Keep me informed."

He turned to Kiltman. "Looks like your Mask friend has taken cold feet. We need to get you off the premises immediately. This meeting is no longer going to happen." He walked towards the door.

Kiltman did not need an instruction to follow - he stepped into line behind Fernandes as he strode back along the corridor, they had walked along a few minutes earlier. The alarm shrieked in his ears with guards running past, stopping to ensure doors were shut tight, peering in through slots no bigger than a postcard.

Within five minutes, Kiltman was outside the gates, after a brief farewell from the Governor. Martim was sitting on the chopper's landing skids sucking hard on a strong-smelling roll up. "That was quick. What's all the fuss about?"

"It's been a wasted journey. Let's get going." Kiltman did not want to explain something he still had to digest himself. He climbed into the cabin, squeezing past Martim.

"Okay, you're the boss," Martim took a long drag, before he threw the half-smoked cigarette onto the ground.

Kiltman had just enough time to click his seatbelt before the chopper lurched into the air, to begin a graceful glide away from the prison. He felt like a fool - he had come all the way to the Amazon to be stood up. Mask had not lost whatever sense of cynical humour he had nurtured in his years in isolation. It would be interesting to understand how a prison punishes inmates who are on a life sentence with 100% solitary confinement. Take away their TV time, he wondered?

He bunched his cape up behind his head, closed his eyes and leaned back against an iron bar behind his seat. He hoped the shuddering of the chopper would induce the sleep that had avoided him on the incoming journey. He was drifting towards slumber, when he heard the click. In a chopper as deafening as this, there were lots of sounds and noises alien to his hearing. It was the cough that made him sit up and look - a high-pitched two-tone throat clearance a teacher would make to interrupt a naughty child.

He hardly registered the Glock 26 pointed at his face. It was the sight of the bearded man wrapped in a dirty cloth shroud that drew his attention. In another situation, he would have commented on the biblical overtones.

"I hope you don't mind me hitching a lift back with you, Kiltman." Mask's smile - a sardonic sliver of scorn - switched his mood from tiredness to trepidation in as brief a moment as it takes to load a bullet in a gun's chamber.

Jungle Jackanory

"Surprised at my ingenuity?" Mask tilted his head to the side. "Before I dispose of you, it would be fair to fill you in on a few details."

"You are a piece of work, Mask... or should I say, Omar... or why not Alois?" Kiltman shook his head. "You really are a confused individual, eh?"

The butt of the Glock felt as hard as it looked. He felt warm blood trickle down his forehead.

"You're not in a position to be funny, you freak." Mask's fury flashed, before he relaxed back into his story. "I'm going to continue despite your uncooperative attitude. Which I find strange since you came all the way here to meet me. Oh, and to help me escape!" Mask tossed his head back and laughed.

"I am sure you saw the burial taking place as you landed. Timing was perfect." He turned to pat Martim on the back, "Thanks to my loyal Brazilian mate." Martim raised his thumb in acknowledgement without looking back. Not able to hear the conversation over the rotor blades, he still enjoyed his boss's show of affection.

Mask scratched his beard. "This thing is quite irritating. Although it did serve a purpose. It may go down as one of my greatest impersonations - a dead Islamic fundamentalist."

Kiltman leaned forward, "So, you killed Khalil Qatari." Other than Mask, Qatari was the prison's most high-profile prisoner. He had been responsible for terrorist attacks across Europe and the USA over the years since 9/11. In the airport, Kiltman had watched a CNN breaking news story announcing Qatari's suicide. He had not realised Qatari had died in the prison he was visiting. It came on the back of another report related to Pope John Paul II's death earlier that month after a long fight with Parkinson's disease. The Angel working the Pearly Gates had an easy shift that month - he would know where to send them without looking at his notes - one up, one down.

Mask continued to enjoy the moment. "Don't be surprised! It gave me pleasure to add some homegrown poison to that crazy terrorist's morning coffee."

Kiltman decided not to draw attention to the irony.

"It went like clockwork. I had sized him up a few months ago. Same height. Although a bit thinner, so I had to go on a diet. Not difficult when you are eating jungle food all day. During this morning's guard rotation, I was able to remove his body from the coffin, crawl into that tight space and close the lid. That was the worst part. I hate small spaces.

"Then when they realised I was missing, the guards ran back inside leaving the coffin in the clammy heat. Fortunately, Martim was there to let me out." He slapped the pilot on the back again.

"Thanks to you providing a reason and an exact timing for a helicopter, I am free. When they find Qatari's body, they'll not recognise him. Let's just say that he had an acid attack." Again, the head throwback and guffaw. Kiltman dared not mention how well Mask fulfilled the role of an archetypical villain in a Victorian theatre. His temple was still throbbing from the Glock thump.

"Qatari's ruined remains, wearing my favourite underpants and socks will be all they need to believe one of the other prisoners attacked and destroyed me out of madness. No shortage of lunatics in there to blame.

"Meanwhile, they are in the process of burying what they think is Qatari. Although it's a coffin full of carefully weighted rocks and bricks." He jerked his thumb towards Martim. "Yes. He is much more than a helicopter pilot, you know."

Kiltman could see that the chopper was flying a hundred metres above the treetops. Martim was taking a prudent precaution to stay below radar. Even though he had nothing to worry about since the Governor would have considered them out of sight, out of mind; two dead people accounting for two prisoners less.

Kiltman began to realise they were not travelling in the direction of São Paulo - or even Iguaçu. His accentuated navigational intuition told him they were flying west to the densest - most forbidding - region of the rainforest; south of

Manaus, Brazil's *Paris of the Tropics* due to the vast wealth created from the sale of rubber in the 19th century.

"You must be wondering why I am talking so much."

Kiltman nodded. "Well, you can imagine I don't want anyone stumbling across a dead, kilted superhero lying in the middle of the forest. A superhero, I may add, who should be on his way to a '*spa week*' in Iguaçu." He laughed as he looked out the window to the drop below the chopper. "Oh my, how *posh and girl's blouse* has Kiltman become?" he said in a high-pitched effeminate tone, with a flap of his hand. In this context - Kiltman realised - it was hard to argue.

"Before we close this discussion down, I want you to know that there are many things I hate you for. I don't need to list them. Although there is one action you catalysed that I do have to admit being somewhat grateful for."

He paused and Kiltman saw a tear in the corner of his eye. He was showing more mood swings than Kiltman liked for someone holding a gun close to his face. Mask wiped his cheek with the scruffy edge of the off-white shroud draped across his back.

"My daughter, Angie, is living a normal life with her adoptive mother and brother. By going to prison I left her parentless. My greatest crime was not to wreak havoc in the UN Assembly. Rather, it was to leave that girl half-finished, ill-prepared for what the world will throw at her. If she had gone to an orphanage, even my hard heart would have broken."

Kiltman's antenna had peaked. He did not like where this conversation was going.

"I look forward to hugging her once again. I will make sure to, eh, how can I say, *compensate*, lovely Fiona and weird Roddy for their well-intentioned meddling in my family. Angie might not like our reunion at first, but I will make sure she realises her destiny is with me."

Kiltman was sweating, trying to keep his head clear. He had to believe Mask did not know his true identity was Kenny Morgan. As soon as he realised that things would get ugly.

"Okay, Boss. Anywhere around here works," Martim shouted over his shoulder.

Mask nodded slowly. "Well, there is one thing left to do, my Scottish friend. Before we see if that cape of yours can help you fly." He moved the gun closer to Kiltman's head. Reaching across with his free hand, he tried to peel back the mask. It refused to budge. He jerked and pulled at its underside. Kiltman made the task difficult by shaking his head, thankful the combination of sweat and blood had created a welcome adhesion inside the latex.

Mask cursed under his breath. He moved the barrel of the gun a tad, just enough to allow a thumb under the edge of Kiltman's face covering, working both hands to prise it away from the sticky skin.

He knew this was his moment. This had to be all instinct and luck. And whatever help Hair o' the Dog could provide in the circumstances.

He drew back his arms as far as he could in the confines of the tight space and chopped both sides of Mask's midriff. While there was not enough power to hurt, it did wind him. He crumpled into a stoop. Kiltman followed up with four or five rapid punches to his stomach. Despite the blows, Mask rolled to the side and lifted the gun towards Kiltman.

Placing his weight on his right leg, Kiltman sprang from his seat and kicked out at Mask's hand. Mask stumbled to get to his feet, firing the gun at Kiltman. The bullet passed over his head, missing the pilot by an inch, smacking off the inside of the chopper.

Martim - who had been oblivious to the scuffle until that moment - heard the bang and turned around, to see Kiltman direct his leg to kick Mask in the head. He yanked the controls to force the chopper into a turn, throwing Kiltman off balance. The manoeuvre achieved its aim of tossing him backwards. Kiltman reached out to take hold of the seat, but Mask smacked the gun on top of his fingers and kicked him in the stomach. Kiltman did not have time to react to the pain, the momentum carrying him out the door. He watched the chopper soar away from him as he fell towards the trees, thrashing around in the wake of the rotor blades' noisy whooshing.

In the midst of the clamour, slipstream and fear, his first instinct was to get his bearings and figure out if he had a chance to break his fall. That was not going to happen - his cape had wrapped around his face like cellophane on leftovers from Christmas lunch. As he hurtled towards the ground, he hoped some of those rubber trees had survived deforestation.

Skyline Chili

"This is amazing!" Roddy proclaimed through a mouthful of Three-Way Skyline Chili – (a trio of chili, spaghetti and cheddar cheese). Before the waiter brought the food to the table, he had explained that Skyline Chili was a speciality of Cincinnati, created at the end of the Second World War by a Greek immigrant, Nicholas Lambrinides.

Judging by the noise of the thirty young footballers in the busy restaurant, Nick had created something truly wonderful. Some, like Reilly and Roddy, had exercised a degree of restraint in opting for the Three-Way, while the majority of the team went for full immersion in the Five-Way - a Three-Way plus diced onions and beans. After 90 minutes of non-stop running and chasing, they would have had a Ten-Way if Nick had invented a double figure version.

Chesters and Galatians players were intermingled throughout the restaurant amidst a frenzy of forks, napkins, slurps and belches. Roddy, Reilly and Angie shared a table with three Galatians' players: Chuck, Brad and Brit. What struck Roddy even more than the monosyllabic names he could have bet on being included in their team somewhere, was how they appeared. Not just the three at their table, but all the Galatians - they looked identical.

When their opponents emerged from the changing room after the game, they walked stiff-backed towards the car park. To a person, the boys had their hair combed in a side-parting, hair greased back flat. The girls' tresses had been pulled back into tight ponytails.

The boys wore black suits, white shirts and black ties - a Midwest teen version of Reservoir Dogs. The girls had dressed in white blouses buttoned to the neck, with long black skirts - akin to any fifties Rock 'n' Roll movie.

This could not have been more different to Chesters apparel. None of them shared an item of clothing - George of Asda and TK Maxx had outdone themselves.

Apart from their strange garb, the Galatians wore a medal - the size of a 2p coin - around their necks, secured by what looked like a rolled gold chain. Roddy could see a large letter **G** inscribed in the centre of the medal, in bold Gothic typeset.

A couple of hours earlier, the teams had been pushing and tripping each other – not a feast of football beauty by anyone's standards. As hard fought and physical as any game Chesters had played - save for the match against the renowned Drumchapel 'Demagogues' F.C. back home, living up to their motto 'if you can't get the player, get the ball''.

Galatians scored two goals early in the first half, putting Chesters under pressure from the start. Both strikes were celebrated by touching each other's medal with their own; rather than the traditional high five hand smack. If this was a tactic to distract the opposition, it worked until the last minute of the first half when Chesters managed to salvage a goal. Towards the end of the second half with full time approaching, Chesters were down 2-1. It looked like the Galatians were heading for a win. They had stopped attacking and had settled into defending their lead for the remainder of the game. They used their physical advantage to push the Scots off the ball whenever they felt threatened. Two free kicks outside the penalty box allowed Chesters to employ the Pin Ball Wizard play twice. Roddy's talent for kicking haphazardly proved to be the secret factor gifting Reilly two scoring opportunities, which he took full advantage of. The score ended 3-2 to the Scots.

Now they were all in the diner together, Roddy watched them fiddle with their medals. It seemed they touched them more often than their cutlery, sometimes absent-mindedly but mostly when they were speaking. In the same way an Italian would gesticulate with their hands and shoulders, the Galatians team would point the medal to stress words or phrases.

He placed another heaped forkful of chili in his mouth, wondering if his teammates had noticed this focus on their medals. Angie had been quiet throughout the meal. Her mood had changed soon after training when she approached Coach Stone. Roddy observed her walk towards him - she had lost the carefree, joyful air of earlier that day.

"Coach," she had whispered, head bowed lest the others could hear.

"Hey, Angie!" Coach Stone bellowed in a congenial voice that made everyone feel like the most important person in the world.

"I'm feeling a bit under the weather," she continued. "Is it okay if I sit it out for this game?"

"Aw, that's a shame." Coach stepped forward. His face flinched as he moved; the ACL injury seemed to hurt whenever he had been standing for a while. He called it his unwanted best friend, reminding him it was there whenever he stood up or started to walk. He leaned forward to Angie and touched her forehead. Whenever a player complained about an ailment, he checked their temperature. "Hmm, seems normal. Okay, probably better for you to take it easy. Are you feeling tired?"

"Yes, I am," she said. "Maybe it's jet lag."

Jetlag, my backside, Roddy had thought. This was not like Angie - she had been pumped for this trip since its announcement months earlier. No amount of jetlag - whatever that was - would have prevented her from playing.

"You really not well, Angie?" Roddy had been standing behind Coach.

"What, do you think I'm making this up?" She had turned on him in a manner that took him by surprise. He could see the anger in her eyes.

"Sorry, I didn't mean that I don't believe you. Just…" he paused, "I'm just worried about you, that's all."

She did something then with her head - a sort of half nod, half shake. Whatever it was, he knew she was not going to respond. She had turned on her heel and strode across the park. Angie was hiding something - but he had blown any chance of being the empathetic brother he wanted to be. They would not have been at the same table at dinner, had Reilly not put his arms around their shoulders and led them into the restaurant.

"So, what do you guys do for fun, other than play football… I mean, soccer?" Reilly's attempt to introduce conversation into the feeding frenzy was an attempt to move the Galatians players onto a topic that did not include football. The Galatians should have won the game. They were taller, stronger and - contrary to a misconception about US ball control - were skilful on all areas of the pitch. They would be hurting at the loss; despite the brave face they were presenting above their Skyline Chili. The Galatians had one more game to play. If they could win, then there was a good chance they would achieve a place in the quarter finals. Chesters were already just one game away from the quarters - they just needed to win their next match against Delhi Druids, a local team from Cincinnati.

"To be honest," Brit said, "we spend a lot of time in the church, while also helping on local community projects." The fact she answered on behalf of Brad and Chuck was not missed by the trio of Scots at the table.

Brad spoke up, "*Let us not become weary in doing good, for at the proper time we will reap a harvest if we do not give up.*"

"Nice one, Brad," Chuck said, touching his medal against Brad's. "Six nine. Way to go!"

"Six nine?" Reilly repeated.

"Galatians chapter six, verse nine," answered Brit. "We like to introduce quotes from St. Paul's letter to the Galatians, when we converse. Whatever the discussion, or problem, this influential letter penned by St. Paul in the first century has a line that addresses it."

"Amen," said Brad. "*Cursed is everyone who does not continue to do everything written in the Book of the Law.*"

"Three ten, buddy." Chuck reached out with his medal, for Brad to bump it with his own. They nodded towards Brit, who conceded a wink and a shrug.

Roddy looked sideways towards Angie. On a normal day, this would have been a moment for them to exchange a glance. An ever so slight connection the others would not have noticed - enough for them to acknowledge the weirdness of this conversation.

She did not look up from her food, which she had barely tasted. Her focus seemed to be on how best to use her fork to cover cheddar cheese with chili. Even that exercise appeared half-hearted.

"Come on, Angie," Reilly pushed his shoulder against hers gently. "You know your bible! How should we answer these guys?"

Angie did not look up from the plate but spoke in a subdued timbre. "*If you keep on biting and devouring each other, watch out or you will be destroyed by each other.*"

"Five fifteen," Brit answered - her tone lacking the conviviality of earlier. Brad and Chuck shifted in their seats. Reilly savoured the moment. Roddy sensed trouble on the horizon.

When Will Those Clouds All Disappear

Roddy rapped his knuckles on the door with all the resolve he could muster, considering the reception he anticipated. He waited for a response. Then knocked again.

The door opened just wide enough for him to see Angie's pretty face peeking through. "Look, this is not a good time."

He felt the door push against his hand - he had expected her resistance.

"Look, sis," he used the nomenclature they had created to help redefine their friendship after her adoption. He was 'bro'. Although - he realised - she had not called him that in a long time. "What's going on? Is there anything I can help with?"

"Please leave me alone." She looked down towards her feet for a moment, then lifted her head with a hint of resolve. "Roddy, I know you're trying to help. I'm sorry for being distant. I just need some space."

They looked at each other in silence until he dropped his hand. She considered him for a moment, unshed tears misting her eyes, as if she might say something, but then closed the door. He turned and walked to the end of the corridor, a couple of rooms down from Angie. He had not wanted to use it for this type of a situation, but he had no choice. He extracted the Irn-Bru bottle from his inside pocket. Placing the bottle to his lips he took a hefty slug of his father's concoction. One day, he thought, he would be man enough to ask him how he had been able to create something so satisfying.

The grainy liquid invigorated his taste buds and warmed his throat like no other liquid he had consumed. He felt it drop down into his stomach and mix - sacrilegiously, his dad might have said - with the remains of the hefty Three-Way. It took just a few moments before he started to see a mass of words - speckled with the occasional number - drifting across the corridor. As per usual, they appeared less a data highway and more a spaghetti junction - jumbled and criss-crossed in every which way. This had been the difficult aspect in the beginning: trying to make sense of the information avalanche. He had learned to take a deep breath and focus on the streams of data, and within a minute each communication took on a different colour, or different font. He did not understand any of this – how his brain was able to cluster connected information through formatting typical to a standard Word document.

"hey mum hope youre all well we won today then had this massive dinner gotta go sofie xx"

Roddy smiled. Sofie was their left-back. Tall, strong and ate twice as much as the rest of the players. She was considered the funniest person on the team, able to find a joke in any dire result.

"Whassup amigo? Hangin here in the Cinci hood... getting doon with local rap jingo : -) Havin a blast hombre! Jo-Jo x"

He grinned at Joanne *Jo-Jo* Johnstone's message. Team right back, she was the quiet, pensive one in the locker room. Her boots did the talking. Full of running and a great passer, she could change games with a burst of speed and a strong tackle. He enjoyed knowing that she had a sassy side too. Considering how much of a whirlwind her mother was, Jo-Jo needed it.

He was invading the privacy of his teammates - the female side of the Chesters team, relaxing in the East wing. This made him uncomfortable. Although considering the texts they were sending, he was not worried he would stumble across any deep, meaningful messages. Until…

"Please don't do anything crazy. I will do what you want. Let me know. A"

His heart skipped a beat. He recognised the number, which showed up as an underlined portion of floating text. Although he did not need that on this occasion. Perfect grammar. Signed 'A'. His pulse raced.

The thread continued to weave its way across the corridor. After a few moments of searching and reading, he could see the number she was sending to - it started with +55. He memorised the remainder of the number as best he could absent pen and paper. Although this was more difficult than it should have been. His number literacy and memory were fine - except when interrupted by a wave of despair for someone he loved dearly.

Eye of a Needle

"As you can see, we have run a thorough computer-assisted audit of all Banco d'Aiuto's cash movements over the last 12 months. It's clear which ones relate to Mafia deposits."

Alison stopped talking and folded her arms, looking at Wilson. Wilson noted that the police officer's bright blue eyes and hair pulled back tight gave her the air of a frozen tiger. Hypnotically still while seething with innate rage.

"How can you be sure?" Wilson had found the three-hour presentation tiring. She was exhausted by the nonstop barrage of numbers and banking codes. Alison was convinced of their findings, Wilson less so.

"We know these accounts belong to Mafia renegades." Alison looked towards Crawford and Mary, pointing at a list of numbers on the screen.

"Yes," Mary stood. She was taller than she should have been for a desk job, Wilson thought. How on earth could she maintain that perfect posture huddled over a computer all day?

"We have 15 specific bank accounts in the names of known Mafia members. Look." She pressed a couple of keys on the laptop, to display a series of photos. Wilson surveyed each of them, concluding that Italy most probably had the best-looking hoodlums in the world. She could have been studying a casting agent's notes for Beverly Hills, 90210. The names of the four family leaders they had already identified were among them: Roberto 'Mucky' Marciano, Gianni 'Pirla' Sconi, Mauro 'Zio' Papetti, Carlo 'San' Babila.

"Okay," Wilson nodded. "How much money are they depositing?"

Crawford was younger than the others, a schoolboy air about him - fresh-faced and eager. Despite that, he was old school. He had an A4 pad, which he flipped over a couple of pages. Wilson knew she would get on with him. He ran his fingers down the sheet until he stopped and looked up. "In total they paid in around €10 million in the last year, spread evenly across each account."

She clasped her hands, holding them under her chin. She stood and walked towards the back wall of the small room. "Then what happened?" A phrase her mother used to ask her when she told a story. As a child she found it infuriating as her mother's constant questioning took the story way beyond the intended punchline, encouraging her to think on the spot. As an adult, she found it a perfect technique to squeeze every last ounce out of a discussion. Whether with a perp or a fellow officer.

Alison tapped the keyboard, and a list of transfers showed money leaving the accounts. Each transaction went to accounts in one other bank. "Banco Discepolo is affiliated to the Vatican…"

"Banking network," finished Wilson. "Created a few years back to collect monies earmarked for charitable works. Named *Discepolo* after Jesus washed his disciples' feet on Holy Thursday - recognising the true work of the Church must be generosity and humility in helping those in need."

Alison nodded. If she was impressed, she was a good poker player. "That is where we have got to so far."

Wilson gave a slight nod of her head. "I know. It's easier to get a camel through the eye of a needle than gain access to protected banking records."

Crawford laughed. Alison remained expressionless, while Mary admonished him with a tilt of the head.

Wilson continued. "The difference now is that we have a dead body on our hands. If we are not able to use Sacco to get us the access we need, then we are caught between the Devil and the Deep Blue *Holy See*."

Crawford laughed again. Alison was deadpan. Mary could not hide her frustration. She knew that with a name like *Mary*, she should have been getting these jokes faster than Crawford.

Bad News Travels Fast

"Turn on the TV!" Armstrong burst through the door. "Quick!"

Alison had been in mid-flow explaining the process of how they had collated and synthesised the Banco d'Aiuto evidence into worthwhile clusters of data. She did not need Armstrong to ask twice. She picked up the remote and pressed the green button. The screen popped up with a reporter standing outside the United Nations building in New York, talking to the camera.

"… and this is what we can call a bittersweet day. Evil to the core, many people wanted this criminal to serve out his time for the rest of his life under lock and key. However, nobody will mourn his passing."

Wilson looked at Armstrong. He turned and said, "Wait for it!"

The reporter continued. "His remains were found in a concrete tub in the basement. Some of the other prisoners must have figured he deserved an end fitting for the monster he was. He had been dropped into a bath of acid. Well, this is one evil mastermind who can hang up his mask." On the left side of the screen a picture of Mask appeared. It was the photo taken when he was led away from court after sentencing, Kiltman and Wilson in the background.

She stood and leaned on the table; the blood drained from her face.

"Well, well," Armstrong boomed, "looks like your prisoner has had his last bath."

She could not force a smile, not even an attempt to take satisfaction from the event. "Yes, looks like he's gone once and for all."

"I wonder if Kiltman is celebrating somewhere," Mary said. "Hey, DI Wilson, what's his favourite tipple? Does he have a drink now and then?"

"Eh, I don't know." Her face had gone from drained to blushed. "Probably likes Super Lager."

"Ha!" Crawford laughed. "I get it."

Mary shot him a look of scorn. "So, is he a party animal, then?"

"Seriously?" Wilson answered. "Is that all you can think about when you see breaking news like this?"

"Hey," Armstrong said. "Take it easy, Wilson. Mary's just joshing."

Her head was filling with questions she could not ask. Did Kiltman see him before he died? Why had he not contacted her?

"I know, sorry," she answered. "Look, I need to call into the station back home. I think we have covered enough here today. We can give you a briefing first thing tomorrow morning, Chief."

"Okay," Armstrong said. "That's fine. See you in the morning. Don't celebrate too much tonight."

Bzzzz. Bzzz.

She looked at her phone. Gemmill.

This was one occasion when she wanted to talk to him. She picked up the phone, waved to the Met officers and left the room.

"Chief?"

"Wilson, have you heard the news?"

"Yes, I have." She wanted to ask if Kiltman was okay; but it was Kenny who told her about the trip to the prison to meet Mask. Not Kiltman. She was not sure if she was meant to know.

"Good enough for him, if you ask me," Gemmill grumbled. "Anyway, you might be interested to know that your partner in crime went out there to talk to him."

She heard him slurp his tea.

"Kiltman, really? And did they meet?"

"No. Kiltman had to turn around when they realised Mask was missing from his cell."

"Oh..." she was not sure how to respond.

"The best part is... wait till you hear this. He contacted me last week to say that he was going to take a break for a few days after his Mask meet. What a cheek!"

"Oh, I see, but..."

"The rest of us have to keep the country safe, while Kiltman can waltz off for a - what do you call it - comfort break?"

"I guess that might be the name for it, although..."

"Well, they saw him leave prison in the chopper. Then found Mask's remains shortly after. I wanted to let you know; I expect this will be meaningful for you."

"Thanks, sir. Yes, it is kind of eh, bittersweet." She could only mimic the news reporter - thankful Kiltman had left without harm.

"Tomorrow, I'd like a briefing on this Sacco gig you're working on down there. You do know we have crime in Scotland too, don't you?"

She did not respond.

"Listen, go out and have a glass of wine tonight. You deserve it. Make sure you charge it to the Met. I'm not picking up their tab. They've taken our oil - I'm not giving you to them for free too."

She heard the line go silent.

Kiltman had left the prison. He was seen leaving in the chopper. At that point he would have known Mask had gone missing. He would now know that Mask had been found dead. Why not send a text to say what was going on? Whether as Kiltman or Kenny, she did not care. The least he could have done is make sure she heard the news from him, rather than over the BBC.

She admonished herself for feeling like the *woman indoors* when her hubby does not come back from the pub in time for dinner. Technically he had not done anything wrong. She knew he was going to Iguaçu. It had hurt to know he had still gone even when she was not able. Or maybe this was his way of sending her a message.

Okay, she was not going to spend time worrying about his teenage mind games. She could give as good as she got. She hit speed dial on the phone. The smooth, polished voice answered immediately. "Hey, this is a surprise!"

"Fancy dinner?" She had the phone trapped between her ear and shoulder as she pulled on her jacket.

"Sure, where?"

"Gaucho, Richmond. In an hour."

"Perfect, see you then," Grant answered.

Galatians

"Are you people mad? Has someone put a spell on you, in spite of the plain explanation you have had of the crucifixion of Jesus Christ?" The preacher held the edges of the lectern till the white of his knuckles became the most visible object on the stage.

"Let me ask you one question: was it because you practised the Law that you received the Spirit, or because you believed what was preached to you? Are you foolish enough to end in outward observances what you began in the Spirit? Have all the favours you received been wasted? And if this were so, they would most certainly have been wasted. Does God give you the Spirit so freely and work miracles among you because you practise Law, or because you believed what was preached to you?"

The priest paused, letting the sound of his voice settle across the atrium. Roddy was halfway down the hall on the far right. He reckoned there must be around a couple of thousand people listening to the preacher.

On either side he could see his teammates drawn into the hypnotically powerful voice. They had been invited to the evening event by the Galatians team. Coach Stone had agreed in the spirit of *'connecting with our fellow footballers and their cultural nuances'*. At a minimum it was a distraction from their game next day against the Delhi Druids. Their team briefing after the Galatians' match had made it clear it was going to be a tough match. The Druids were the Ohio State champions, considered to be the fittest team in the competition. They were from a Western Hills suburb, Delhi, pronounced with a hard 'H'. A quiet leafy area outside the city, renowned for its family life and high ethical and social standards.

"Those words I spoke to you are not my words," the preacher continued. "They come from St. Paul's letter to the Galatians. Word for word." He pointed at Brit, who was sitting in the front row.

"Three, one to five, Your Eminence," she beamed towards him.

"Yes, thank you, Brit! Chapter three, verses one to five. Those words are as valid today as they were two thousand years ago."

A murmur rolled through the audience, heads nodding, hands clapping. Many of the listeners held their medals in the air. In the light of the hall, they sparkled a bronzy gleam he had not noticed at dinner.

"St. Paul's letter to the Galatians was a plea to ask this group of followers to leave behind their old, outdated laws and practices. He wanted them to move forward into the future and embrace the true message of Christ; he wanted substance, not form."

The preacher took a minute to survey the room. He was dressed in an off-white tunic, tied around the waist with a rope. Underneath the lectern, Roddy could see his toes protruding through leather sandals. However, it was his face that captured his attention. Clean-shaven, with trimmed hair and a freshness of complexion that conveyed a man approaching sixty, he carried a youthful, energetic air. There was a poise about him that affected Roddy. Some would call it charisma, but it was more subtle.

"We need change in the church. In the communities we live, across the world. We have gone too far and are at risk of falling off the precipice. Do you really believe Jesus wanted us to build infrastructures that allowed us to worship ourselves?"

Louder murmuring and bench slapping.

"Where can you find the sermon on the mount in a mountain of idolatry? That is our mission as members of the Christian community. We need *to bring back that loving feeling*." He sang the last few words in a decent rendition of the Righteous Brothers - a twinkle in his brooding eyes. "Let us spread the word. Dear brothers and sisters, we don't need to create a new message."

He held up the book he was reading from, to show a cluster of post it notes and tabs dangling from the pages.

"All we need to do is go back to the Gospels and St. Paul's letter to the Galatians. Those words are as relevant today - more relevant today - as then."

He lifted the book high above his head.

"Grace and peace to you from God our Father and the Lord Jesus Christ."

Brit shouted, "One Three!"

Then another voice from the middle of the audience called, "One Three!"

More voices yelled louder, "One Three!" Until there was a resounding ONE THREE booming across the pews. A melodic, tuneful sound floated over their heads from a group in the back row, singing, "One Three will set us free. One Three will set us free. One Three will set us free…"

Before long the hall was echoing the chant, a mantra in its most adolescent form. People stumbled to their feet, hands raised, medals extended skywards. They swayed from side to side, chanting.

Roddy looked to the side to see some of his fellow Chesters team on their feet singing and swaying. Angie was seated at the edge of the row, her head in her hands. He wanted to take her in his arms and comfort her - help her out of this place she was inhabiting alone.

He prayed that he could somehow set her free from whatever trouble she had gotten herself into.

Cardinal Damascus

"So, these are the Scots who beat you, three two?" The Cardinal focused on each of the players one by one.

"Yes, Your Eminence," Brit said. She appeared somehow enchanted, or maybe it was anxious. Roddy found it hard to tell.

"I would like to learn just one thing from you. Did you receive the Spirit by the works of the law, or by believing what you heard?" The Cardinal was looking Brit in the eye.

There was an awkward silence. Even Coach Stone looked uneasy. Roddy wanted to take a step back and make sure he was not next in the Cardinal's line of vision.

Brit's face lit up with a broad smile. "Ha! Yes! Three Two, you are right, Cardinal."

"You see," he continued. "There is a message in every experience. You just have to be open to finding it. Chapter three verse two. Listen and the Word will find you."

The Cardinal reached across to Brit's medal, bowed and kissed it. He lifted his head and studied the group of young players - Galatians and Chesters - before turning towards Coach Stone.

"Please let me introduce myself. I am Saul Damascus. The Church has conveyed on me the title of Cardinal. However, feel free to call me Saul." He turned to Brit and smiled. "Some people find it hard to be informal."

"Yes, Your Eminence," she said, with a half curtsey and a full-on red blush.

He took Coach Stone's hand and held it between his own in a strong clasp. "I thank you for arranging this trip to join our Midwest Spring Cup. I hope you and your players are enjoying Ohio. I am pleased you could attend our Galatians gathering this evening."

"Thanks, Cardinal," Coach said, looking into the Cardinal's eyes. "It has been an interesting day all in all." Roddy tried not to smile. He had never seen Coach so captivated; waiting for each word to spill from the Cardinal's mouth.

The Cardinal reached across and laid his hand on Coach's shoulder. "Don't worry, my friend. *The righteous will live by faith.*"

Brit whispered to Roddy, "Three Eleven."

He tried not to roll his eyes. *Enough already* - he thought in his best American accent. He watched Coach nod his head, his eyes not leaving the Cardinal's face.

"I am the shepherd guiding this Galatians flock. I hope our paths will cross again before you and your team of Bravehearts go home to Scotland."

Coach nodded. *At a loss for words* was not a phrase often associated with him. Something had happened in the minutes they had stood in the company of the Cardinal. Something more than unusual - extraordinary.

"Goodbye, enjoy the rest of the tournament. May the best - and most humble - win." The Cardinal bowed and walked away from the group. Brit and several of the other Galatians fell into step behind as he walked out the door and into the distance.

"Hey, Coach," Reilly tapped him on the shoulder. "Coach?"

Their manager shook his head and ran his hand across the bald pate where he usually wore a flat cap. "Sorry, guys. Drifted off then. Right," he slapped his hands together, "who fancies some more of that Headline Chili?"

The group of players laughed together, some openly, others quietly.

"Boss, it's Skyline Chili," Reilly said, smiling.

"Well, whatever it is, I'm famished. We have another big game in the morning, so we need to stockpile the carbs. Let's go." Coach walked towards the atrium exit, where their coach was parked. He really was hungry, Roddy reflected, although not sure why the Coach had to load any more *carbs* than usual. That would be two dinners in one day.

Coach usually took time to move from one scenario to another - it gave him a sense of deliberation. The team had become used to waiting for him. Now, he was moving towards the exit ahead of the players. Something was missing, Roddy thought. Then he realised as soon as he saw Coach walk onto the bus.

His limp had gone.

Malbec y Lomo

"How's the steak, Grant?" Wilson sipped her medium-sized Malbec.

"It'sh rooolly tashty," Grant replied.

"That's good, glad to see you're enjoying it." She took another drink. She knew she had Grant where she wanted him, calling him out of the blue - reporters loved to be contacted instead of having to chase news sources. Her choice of Gaucho, an upmarket Argentinian restaurant on the banks of the Thames in Richmond, was metres away from Sacco's death. The table on the terrace overlooking the calm, mesmerising waters may have led him to believe this was more than a courtesy dinner between sources.

She was not responsible for Grant's oversized imagination.

He ordered the 400g lomo. The waiter smarted when he requested it *well-done*. Kenny had once commented to her that a well-done steak was the culinary equivalent of an ex-hire kilt, a quintessential marvel that had seen too much heat.

Grant was surprised to see she was not eating, and at first did not appear concerned. As the meal progressed, she made a point of asking a question whenever he put the fork in his mouth.

"Did you see the news about Mask?"

"Yesh. Unbooloovabill." Perfect timing, she acknowledged silently.

He had not mentioned Kiltman's visit. If he had been aware that Scotland's superhero had been requested to visit Mask in the Amazon jungle, it would have been the first topic he asked about. This made her task this evening more difficult.

She waited a moment.

"I'm surprised you weren't able to convince the news channel to let you travel to Brazil and lead on this story. Are you not the expert on Mask?"

He nodded, took a long drink of his Quilmes beer, wiped his mouth with a large napkin and put his fork on the side of the plate. There was about 200g of steak remaining - despite twenty minutes of industrious eating. "I would have liked to be there, but the boss wanted me to follow up on what happened here. Sacco's death is potentially an explosive report. You know, one of those stories that might not be a story unless the right reporter asks the right questions - and knows the right people." He winked at her when he spoke the last few words.

She worked hard not to cringe.

"I see. Your boss is a smart guy, Grant. As snouts go, your proboscis is as probing as they get." She could see he liked to be complimented. Although she should have mentioned the brown speck of pepper sauce dangling on the edge of his nose.

He picked up the fork and crushed mashed potatoes and spinach onto a chunk of well-done lomo.

She added. "I'm sure someone as resourceful as you can stay close to any story no matter where it is."

"Ha! You goat me, Maachy!" He wiped the napkin across his mouth, managing to clear the sauce from his nose. Pity, she thought. He took a few moments to chew, swallow and take another swig of beer. "I do have my contacts out there. I have a mate called Rafael - he studied at Glasgow Uni around the same time Kenny and I did. He was also centre forward in the football team. That's where I got to know him, he appreciated my ball control and passing technique." He lingered a moment for that to sink in. "I spoke to him this afternoon. To be honest, they're treating it as a non-story really. Until they find who killed Mask, there isn't much to report."

"I know what you mean, Grant." She twiddled the glass between her fingers for a few seconds, looking across the rim at him. "You know, I have a detective's curiosity, probably not too dissimilar to that of a hound-dog reporter."

"Two peas in a pod, Maggie - that's what we are!" Grant's embodiment of a child in adult form was sometimes a wonder to behold. Now was the moment to make her move.

"Symbiotic, Grant!" She laughed and put her hand across the table for a high five. Grant responded eagerly, snagging the edge of her wine glass. Her reactions proved fast enough to catch the glass but not before a splodge landed in the middle of the white tablecloth.

"Oops," Grant man-giggled, with a shoulder shrug.

It was becoming harder to suppress the cringes.

"Anyway, can you give me the name and number of your contact out there? I'd like to have it in case something pops up in the future." She waited while Grant considered the request. "I promise, if I get anything useful, I'll make sure to pass it to you. You'll have access to the best of both worlds - Sacco in London and Mask in Brazil." She placed a hand on his arm and smiled.

Grant already had his phone in hand scrolling down his list of contacts. Here it is - he showed her the screen. Wilson nimbly punched the number into her phone, under the name Rafael.

"Thanks, Grant. I appreciate it." She raised her glass.

"Here's to friendship and collaboration, Maggie," Grant lifted his beer and hit her Malbec with a solid clunk.

Yes, she thought, it was important to keep friends close and reporters closer.

Tuesday, April 12

Armstronging

"Good morning, sir. I'll dive into the detail if you don't mind." Wilson had not expected such a large audience. There were around twenty officers in the room, including Crawford, Alison and Mary. Chief Armstrong was seated in the middle of the front row. Everyone knew the meeting was about bringing him up to speed. Whatever follow up work was needed would impact the rest of them.

"Go for it. I'm all ears," Armstrong boomed in his Northern Ireland brogue.

Dinner with Grant had been a pleasant experience, she reluctantly acknowledged. He had a quirkiness that became endearing once she got beyond the self-praise and flirting. When she returned to her hotel in the peaceful, village neighbourhood of Marylebone in West London, she realised sleep was not even a remote possibility.

She had so many ideas running through her mind. Why was Mask killed? Who by? Was Kiltman ignoring her? Had he arrived at the spa resort? His phone was going straight to messages, consistent with the limited Wi-Fi they had yearned for when they planned the trip. She had toyed with the idea of contacting the resort to enquire if he had arrived. However, if he was annoyed at her, then that would add fuel to the fire. In the end she called Rafael, leaving a message.

Then there was Sacco. Most of the night was spent on her laptop, analysing bank transfers and online correspondence. The presentation had been prepared in haste, with Crawford's support, in the morning, an hour before the meeting. The one practical suggestion Crawford offered with a twinkle in his eyes, was to avoid *TLAs*, since Armstrong detested them. When she asked the baited question, he had answered 'Three Letter Acronyms'. Evidence, if needed, that accountants should get out more.

"Right, sir. Let's talk first about the death itself. This is not my main focus, since I am here to help with the financial aspects.

However, based on forensics and - to be quite honest - common sense, this was not a suicide. The Met team reached this conclusion when they saw the body. The bricks in the pocket… a roll for the ducks… improbable access to a rope… and so on.”

Armstrong nodded. His team would have already let him know all this.

“So now, to help us find the killer - probably killers - we are investigating his bank’s transactions.” She paused and nodded towards the team who were helping her. “Crawford, Mary and Alison have already done a lot of good work. We know that Banco d’Aiuto received more than €10 million in Mafia deposits this year alone. The funds were then transferred out to another bank. The receiving bank was Banco Discepolo. Interestingly, Banco Discepolo is affiliated to the Vatican. I should stress it is not a Vatican bank, it handles funds for various charities supported by the Church.”

She stopped and took a long sip of her coffee. It was already cold.

“I did some further analysis on the transfers from Banco d’Aiuto. We had been focusing on the Mafia deposits, determined to find a link there to another lead. But what is even more interesting is that over the twelve months of data in the analysis, around fifty percent of the bank’s total transfers have been made to Banco Discepolo.” She waited for this to sink in.

Armstrong exhaled a long, slow breathy whistle. “How much would that be?”

“Well, that’s my next point, sir. Over the last year, Banco d’Aiuto has transferred around one billion euros to Banco Discepolo.” She saw a few heads nodding around the room. “Of course, that could just be a series of valid business transactions. However, in my experience, it’s highly unusual to find one bank transferring fifty percent of its deposits to another bank.”

“I agree.” Armstrong was rubbing a clump of stubble on his chin with the tips of his fingers. She imagined he was annoyed to have missed it on his morning shave. “So, what are the next steps?”

“We are limited in what we can do here. I think we’ve come to the end of the road in terms of what’s achievable from New Scotland Yard.”

Armstrong's folded arms told her how enthusiastic he was about what he expected to hear next.

"We need to go to Rome to meet with Sacco's colleagues in Banco d'Aiuto and potentially Banco Discepolo HQ to get their perspective on our findings." She looked towards the Met threesome to see Alison and Mary smiling at each other.

"Ideally, I would ask for the whole team to go, but considering budget constraints, let's keep it to myself and Crawford for the moment."

"Okay," Armstrong said after a few moments thought. "I will contact the Italian force in Rome and ask for their support on this. You and Crawford should pack your bags and make sure you get there at some point today. Time is of the essence here."

Armstrong stood up and strode out the door. If Wilson were a betting woman, she would have placed a tenner on him going to his office, closing the door, extracting his battery-operated razor from a drawer and buzzing the rogue stubble off his chin. The rest of the participants left after him, some nodding their appreciation while others yanked cigarettes from their pocket en route to the outside smoking area.

She walked over to the team to find Mary and Alison huddled over their documents. They did not look up - their hands hunting around the inside of their bags.

She coughed before she spoke. "Look, I hope you don't mind the choice I made. There'll be plenty of officers in Rome to help - I couldn't see the Chief allowing us all to go. Crawford is a forensic finance expert, and that's what we need to focus on here."

If Wilson ever had to describe passive petulance, she would have taken a photo of the two pairs of hunched shoulders and fastidious handbag rearranging.

Crawford was already packing up his laptop and notes. He sensed that silence was the best option. If he knew what lay ahead, he may have volunteered to step back and allow the others to go.

Homesick

Morning Maggie. Hows things?

She smiled when she read the text. She always liked to hear from Roddy.

All fine pal. Early there for you no?

She calculated it was 5 am Cincinnati time.

Couldnt sleep any news from dad?

None. I didn't expect to hear. He's spa-ing!

I know but would be good to talk with him

She felt her antenna activate. *You alright Rod? You know you can talk to me.*

Thanks Maggie I know nothing urgent gotta go

Okay bye. Good luck with the football.

:-) LOL

Oh, dear, she thought. When it came to text acronyms she was in trouble. Was he loving or laughing? She settled for it being a term of endearment whatever it meant, and texted back :-)

She considered telling Roddy that Mask had been killed but chose to hold off for the time being. Later that day, when she had more time, she would call him. She was seated in the back of a taxi with Crawford heading to Heathrow - for a lunch time flight to Rome. She was already living out of a suitcase: packing had been easy. Crawford was travelling light - just a briefcase with their case notes. He seemed to be happy to purchase his toiletries at Heathrow Boots. Considering airport prices for clothes, she wondered where he intended to buy underwear... then remembered he was a man.

She dialled Fiona's number.

"Hi, sweetie!" She could hear Fiona shout above a backdrop of drums and music.

"Hello, Fiona. Where are you?"

"In Paris. Armageddon outa here, for sure. It's super loud," Fiona laughed. "Hold on, I'm going outside."

After half a minute of banging and crackling, Fiona came back on the line, absent the noise. "Sorry. Yes, I'm in Paris. It's going well. Only got here yesterday, and I'm already an expert on polar ice caps and ozone layers. I wish I had studied Geography and Science at school instead of Latin and Greek."

"Never too late to learn," Maggie said. "Anyway, just wanted to check if you'd been in touch with Roddy and Angie."

"Oh, yes, they both messaged when they landed. Although not heard anything since. I'm trying not to harass them. It's their time away from claustrophobic parenting." Fiona giggled in an endearing, childlike manner. At these moments, she knew why Kenny had fallen in love with her all those years ago. Truth was Kenny and Fiona were the last parents to be accused of micromanaging their children.

"Is there something I should be worried about?" Wilson caught the edge of angst in her voice.

"Oh, no," Wilson said. "Just thought I'd check, that's all. You know what we police officers are like."

"Ah, don't worry. Coach Stone will keep a watchful eye on them."

"That's good!" Wilson took a moment to pick her words. "What about Kenny? Any news from him?"

"Maggie! My goodness," Fiona laughed. "I do believe you are getting homesick. You've only been away a day and you're missing us already!"

Wilson smiled. "Yes, I admit it. You are my new adopted family: how could I not be missing you all?"

"Well, you know that he's off to darkest Brazil, getting his legs waxed and toenails manicured. He called before he left to say that he would be off radar until Saturday. He has gone to his mancave in the jungle!" Wilson heard Fiona's hearty chortle. "Between you and me, I'm not sure why he needs all that space. Or why he had to go all the way to Brazil for a spa. It's not as if he has a stressful, full-time job. He's already a man of leisure. What does he have to *get away* from? Anyway, it's not for me to ask. Exes are not supposed to enquire."

Wilson chose not to explore where the conversation was going. "You're right, Fi. I have to admit. I am missing him. I guess it's true, *absinthe makes the heart tick faster.*"

"That's the *spirit*," Fiona laughed. "Look, I need to go, they're calling us back in. Next speaker is going to talk about the impact of car fumes - called The Planet is *Exhausted*. Keep in touch."

"Wait, Fiona!" Maggie was not looking forward to the next part of the conversation.

"What is it?"

"There is something you need to know, it's already on the news over here."

"Oh, should I be worried?" Maggie could hear the tension in her voice.

"It's Mask. He was killed in prison. Looks like it was the other inmates who did it."

"Oh my!" Fiona waited a moment, exhaling a long, measured sigh. "Can't say I am upset. I don't know how Angie will take it. Do you know if she knows?"

"I don't think so. I just texted Roddy and he didn't mention it. They will probably hear soon enough when they all wake up and watch the news. I thought it might be better coming from you to Angie directly."

"You're right. I'll contact her now and tell her. Thank goodness Roddy is with her over there."

"Okay, Fi." The taxi was pulling into the drop-off area. "I need to go."

"Thanks. I'll let you know how I get on with Angie, poor thing."

Wilson closed her phone and placed it in her bag. She smiled at Crawford - who had been sitting patiently on the bumpy ride along London's notorious, congested M4. He returned her smile with a nod; he could sense her tension.

The car pulled up outside the busy Heathrow terminal. She unbuckled her seatbelt, and turned to him as she exited the cab. "Crawford, are you beginning to notice that everybody seems to be using puns nowadays to emphasize their messages?"

"I know what you mean," he answered as he looked through the rain-spattered window at a row of black cabs dropping passengers outside the terminal. "I find the increase in this type of humour quite punishing." He grinned with pride in the same way she imagined Alexander Fleming did when he discovered penicillin.

Missing

Roddy enjoyed his interactions with Maggie. She seemed to get him, much more than his mother and father. While he knew his parents loved him, it was annoying that their unconditional love seemed to be full of conditions - homework, tidying, chores. Maggie allowed him to be himself and feel free. He knew she did this because she saw how his parents misunderstood him. She would never admit to that, but he could sense her empathy and understanding for what he had to endure.

The knock on his door took him by surprise. It was 8 am, he was about to wander down to the canteen for breakfast. He loved breakfast in America. He could put syrup on whatever he wanted with nobody to stop him. Glazed donuts were a wonder to behold. The jam inside was clearly not sweet enough, so a layer of icing sugar was spread liberally across the outside. Considering how much football they were playing, the sugar would not remain in their systems for longer than a few hours.

The knock sounded again. This time much louder than before.

"Hey, Coach," he said, yanking the door open.

Coach walked into the room. He pointed towards the bathroom. The sound of the shower blasting drifted into the room. "Is Angie in there?"

"Angie? No, that's Reilly having a shower. Angie will be in the other wing." Roddy was struggling with this interaction. Coach should have known the room set up.

Coach scratched his chin. "Well, she's not in her room."

"Maybe she's already at break…"

"Nope," Coach said. "Her roommate said Angie had left when she woke up this morning. I checked her room. Her backpack has gone too."

Roddy felt his stomach lurch. He grabbed his phone from the table and checked for messages. Nothing. He looked up to see Coach holding an envelope.

"This was on her desk in the room." He handed it to Roddy. In small capital letters he could see his name on the front - R O D D Y.

He snatched it from the outstretched hand - noticing a hint of a tremble. Ripping the envelope, he found a half page letter. Angie's writing was rushed. She prided herself on her flowing calligraphy, but this was not her best effort. He read aloud.

"Dear Roddy,

I know this will be a surprise, but I am okay. Don't worry. Please tell Coach I am sorry not to be able to play in the tournament. You can take my place :-)

There is something I need to do, and I can't ignore it. I know it sounds cryptic. Please trust me. I am fine. This was my decision; I have not been kidnapped.

I will let you know where I am once I get there. I will text Mum too when I arrive. Tell her not to worry. I love you both and will explain all to you when I see you.

Lots of love,

Angie xx"

Roddy looked up at Coach, who was rubbing his cheeks with the flat of his hands. "Is that it?"

He turned the page over and back again. "Yes, that's it." His instinct was to make an excuse for Angie, to explain away this behaviour - find a reason to make sense of her disappearance.

"Okay, we need to report this to the police," Coach said. "I'll have to call your parents. Before I do that…" He looked at Roddy scrutinising every feature of his face. "You have to level with me, pal. Do you have any idea of where she might be?"

"Seriously, Coach? I had no clue about this until you gave me the letter a couple of minutes ago." He sat down on the bed. "I'll be honest, I did find her behaviour yesterday a bit weird, and I tried to talk to her about it. Something was upsetting her, although she wouldn't say. I really wish I had pushed her more to find out." Roddy dropped his head into his hands.

Coach sat down on the bed and put his hand on Roddy's shoulder. "Don't beat yourself up. This was Angie's decision. At least she seems to be in control of what she's doing. We just need to figure out what that might be."

Roddy knew he had to mention the texts. He could not figure out how to tell Coach Stone without creating a separate issue, but he had to try.

"There was something," he said. Coach waited. "I saw a text she sent. She was asking someone not to do something crazy."

"What? Who?" Coach was struggling to retain his composure.

"I don't know. There was no name, but it had a country code of 55."

"55?" Coach asked. "Are you sure?"

"Yes, why? Do you know it?"

Coach nodded. "It's Brazil. I used to have a Brazilian friend many years ago. Who on earth would she know there?" It was a half-question, not expecting an answer. Roddy's head was racing. He knew his father would have arrived in Brazil for his spa week. Although he could not imagine she would text his father like that - and not without first discussing the issue with Roddy.

The bathroom door opened, and Reilly walked into the room in his towel, combing his wet hair back from his forehead. "Hey, Coach, what's up?"

"Reilly," Coach stood up. "Angie has gone. We don't know where she is. Did she say anything to you?"

"Seriously? She has gone, gone?" Reilly's concern was palpable. Roddy and Coach nodded at the same time. "I've got no idea. She has been a bit weird since we got here. I was going to ask her today if everything was okay." Reilly sat on the bed, his concern evident in his pale features and half-combed hair flopping across his eyes.

The door sounded. A strong knuckle rap. Coach opened it to find Jo-Jo standing there. "Oh, hi, Coach. I didn't expect to find you here." Her petite, friendly features could not hide her surprise.

"What is it Jo-Jo? What's that you've got there?" She was holding a USA Today newspaper.

"I picked this up at breakfast this morning. I was flicking through it and came across this." She turned to page three - and pointed. "I thought Angie should know but she's not around, so I came to show Roddy."

A picture of Mask stared back at them, underneath the headline - *Mask Murdered in Prison*. Coach flattened the paper on the bed - they huddled around to read the article. Without a suggestion of remorse or sympathy the article explained how the terrorist *'had received the end he deserved at the hands of inmates who had a greater sense of justice than the judges who sentenced him'*

They all knew that Mask was Angie's father. It was one of the reasons she was so loved and befriended within the team. They had an unspoken mutual respect and admiration for this girl who had endured so much.

Coach pointed at the article and looked at Roddy. It referenced the high security prison in Brazil. Roddy's mind was racing.

She was in danger, he felt it with every sinew of his body.

Arnalda

"My sweet, lovely Angie." His tender words did not match the stern look on a face she barely recognised - the ginger beard and red hair perfectly coiffed to an auburn shade Vidal Sassoon would have been proud of. He lifted the pint of Guinness to his mouth. He had waited until the white head contrasted with the darkness of the stout.

"You know, Arnold's was the first pub in Cincinnati to offer draught Guinness. Forty years ago! When Guinness was rarely available outside Ireland and the UK. Its growth had been restricted - limited to the point it could not reach its full potential." He took a long, slow drink from the glass, before placing it back on the table. "Look at how the white head has remained intact, even though half the contents have gone." He rubbed his stomach to the sound of a satisfying belch, while licking a sliver of errant foam from his prickly moustache.

She had said little since their meeting earlier in Fountain Square, Cincinnati's symbolic town centre - famous for its 43-foot fountain of a lady pouring life-giving water down onto people and animals. He had barely acknowledged her presence as he explained how this grandiose water feature - The Genius of Water - represented his rebirth into freedom. She was in no doubt the Guinness metaphor was another attempt to send her a subliminal message about his tough life and fight for release. They had walked - and he had talked - along the Ohio River, crossing bridges back and forth into Kentucky and back again. She was exhausted listening to him. He used whatever detail in their line of sight to reinforce his message to her. He was free - and she was now back under his control.

It had been difficult leaving the football camp that morning; she knew how much confusion and upset this would be causing. She had no alternative. His messages had made it clear that Fiona and Roddy were in mortal danger if she did not comply with his commands. Part of her hoped they would come searching, but that was the emotional part of her brain. The pragmatic side told her she had to stay as far away as possible. Whatever her father intended to do, she was powerless to stop him.

"My daughter, please do not be afraid. I have waited for this day for so long, I want to cherish these first, precious hours of our reunion. Tell me, how are you?"

Angie shifted in her seat, never losing eye contact with him. This was a loaded a question which she had to navigate carefully. If she said, "Fine", or any words that conveyed a sign of contentment, he would challenge her on how she could have survived so well with a new family knowing her father was in prison. This would then lead to questions - accusations - why she had not written to him, not even a card.

If she said, "not so fine" or "terrified", he would become angry at her lack of appreciation for this seminal meeting - this reunification of a family divided by laws and continents. She knew him well enough to know that, for every answer, he had a position and a strong message.

"Of course, I am happy to see you are healthy and well, Father," she said. "Although I am confused and concerned as to what we are going to do now - where we are going to go."

"Hah, my little *shnooky* bear! I ask about how you are, and you answer by talking about me." He took another drink, smiled and said, "Indeed, I have taught you well."

He leaned over the table towards her. "No matter, we will have time to catch up and talk through these last years and our distance apart. Please understand one thing." He took each of her hands in his, looking into her eyes. "Fiona and Roddy's safety and future rely upon your cooperation. As a father, I know I should not issue such threats to my child. However, I am quite sure you have been brainwashed into believing the things that have been said about me. You will have begun to feel comfortable in this world they live in – maybe even thinking that this would be your future."

He lifted his hand and wagged his finger from side to side slowly.

"My dear, your future is with me. Your adoptive family are now part of history. Maybe one day you will see them again, although not when I am here to protect you."

Angie fought hard to quell the rising panic and sense of loss. When she was younger, she had lived in fear of her father every day. She had learned to cope, to manage her life and emotions around him. Fiona and Roddy were too precious, too important for her to risk their lives on the altar of her father's demonic dreams.

"I understand, Father. I am pleased you recognise what I have been through. Don't worry, you can rely on me to be at your side." She did not shift her eyes from his stare. The truth was, she did not know if he believed her - or whether this acceptance of her role would be enough for him.

"That's my girl," he answered. He put his hand in his jacket pocket and withdrew a blue document, placing it in front of her. "Open it, *Arnalda*."

It was a British passport, dog-eared and scratched. She leafed through it until she came to the photo page - to see a picture of a girl, with red hair, glasses and a rather fetching mole on her right cheek. *Arnalda McGuinness* was written in typeset below the picture. She looked at her father, who smiled back at her. "I hope you can appreciate that I wanted your new name to reflect the cementing of our reunion after these years apart."

She realised that her stay in the US would soon be over. "Where are we going?"

"I will tell you once we are at the airport. I like to keep you in suspense."

He took a final gulp of his stout before placing the glass back on the table with a thump. "We have work to do my newly reborn child, Arnalda. Let's go."

Angie, Where Will it Lead Us

The yellow cab bumped and jostled its way along the autostrada at speeds she would not have contemplated driving unless she was chasing a perp. Behind their car, she could see a sleek red Ferrari two metres off their tail. If she had not been in Italy, she would have assumed they were involved in a high-speed car chase. Truth was the driver was probably late for lunch. Their cabby seemed oblivious to the millisecond gap between full health and obliteration.

"I know you! Si! I know you!" He banged the steering wheel with the ball of his hand. You are the Scottish police lady who saved San Siro with your kilty man, no?"

"Eh, yes, I guess I am," Wilson said from the back while gripping the headrest in front. Crawford's discomfort was evident from how he had clasped his arms around his knees. "You know, we are not in that much of a hurry. Why don't you move over a lane and let the red car pass?"

"Ah, not you worry about him. His big car not impress me!"

"For goodness' sake, move over to the other lane!" She had given up being polite.

The driver snatched a look in his mirror. There was enough anger in Wilson's face for him to realise he would need to save the bravado for another customer. He veered to the right and let the car pass - not without a flash of a raised pinkie and index finger.

The rest of the journey into central Rome went without a hitch or a life-threatening manoeuvre, giving her time to reset her phone to Telecom Italia. Barely had it begun to receive a signal, when it let out a barrage of beeps. She looked at Crawford who had also connected his phone - he received one beep: probably Telecom Italia's welcome message. She made a note to self to ask him later about his social life.

She had 4 messages and 5 missed calls, most from Fiona with a couple from Roddy.

Maggie, please call me. It's urgent. F

Where are you? Please call me back? F

Mum is going to call you Maggie. Angie has gone missing. Roddy

Angie is gone. I don't know what to do. I need to speak to you, F

She felt the beads of sweat on her temple before the kick of anxiety in her stomach. Angie gone? What did that even mean? She hit speed dial for Fiona.

"Maggie? Maggie?"

"Hi, Fiona. What's happened?"

"It's Angie. She disappeared from football camp this morning. We found out just an hour ago." It was hard to understand what Fiona was saying, between the high-pitched whine of the cab's radio and her voice cracking with emotion.

"Have you informed the local police?" Wilson asked.

"Yes, they are not taking it seriously. Angie left a note for Roddy to say that she was going somewhere, that there was something she had to do. She made a point of saying she had not been kidnapped. Because of the letter, the local police expect her to show up later. I don't think they are overly worried. Seems to happen all the time over there." Fiona fought back the tears. "Although that's not Angie. Something must have happened to make her take off like that."

"I know," Wilson answered. "She would normally do everything in her power to stop you panicking. This is unlike her. Did you tell her about her father's death?"

"No, I was going to call her today, although didn't get the chance. I was waiting until she had woken up. I don't know if she knows, she didn't mention it in the letter to Roddy." Fiona paused for a moment. Wilson knew she was struggling to control her emotions and focus on the discussion. "Roddy said he saw a message from Angie to someone in Brazil, asking them not to do anything crazy."

"Brazil?" Wilson asked.

"Yes, Brazil, 55 country code. There was no name. Maybe it is something to do with her father's death. Or could it be Kenny? He went to Brazil for that spa trip you cancelled out of, didn't he?"

Wilson's head was racing. Fiona would not know of Kiltman's visit to Mask. "Maybe, but I doubt it."

Fiona continued to speak, her words coming faster with each thought. She had become a stream of consciousness, not waiting for answers. "Could the message have been from his killer? Maybe they are trying to punish Angie for being her father's daughter?"

"Look, Fiona, let's not jump to conclusions. It's easy to join pieces of information together that are unrelated." Wilson already had a few frightening thoughts of her own, but she did not want to share them with Fiona just yet.

"What about Angie's phone? Can they not trace it?"

"That's the thing; I called as soon as I got the news she was gone. Her roommate found the phone ringing underneath Angie's bed. We literally have no way to contact her." Fiona's tears were now unrestrained. Wilson felt her anguish with every sob and splutter.

The rest of the call was taken up with Wilson working hard to comfort Fiona between her tears. It ended with Fiona saying, "Please Maggie, I beg you. Find Angie. Bring her home."

Kiltman in Absentia

"Hello, is that Iguaçu Spa Resort?" Wilson said, unsure if the operator understood English.

"Yes, that's correct. How can I help you?" The answer came back in a clear diction. At least Wilson did not need to engage a local translator. Having just arrived in Rome, she did not want to request Portuguese translation services from the Polizia for a case she was *working on* in Brazil.

"Ah, thank you. I am looking for Kenny Morgan. Can you please put me though to his room?"

"I am sorry. I cannot confirm who our guests may or may not be." It sounded as if she had read it from a card.

"Look, I know he's there. I am a Detective Inspector in the Scottish police force and I need to talk with him. We have an urgent family situation. I am sure he has let you know that he can be disturbed in an emergency." She was finding it difficult to maintain a detached tone.

"I understand what you are saying. However, I am sure you will appreciate that I cannot check who you say you are."

"Okay, okay! Look, let's make a deal. Please tell Kenny Morgan that I called. I am Maggie Wilson. He has to call me back as soon as possible. Tell him, we have an emergency situation." She was pacing in circles around Bernini's fountain in the centre of the *Piazza Navona* - an ancient oblong piazza where Romans competed in athletics two thousand years earlier. At that moment, the magnificence of the Eternal City's *centro storico* was the furthest thing from her mind. She waited in silence until another voice came on the phone, a man with a deep gravelly voice that felt a tad unnerving in the current situation.

"Hello, this is the Manager of the Spa. How can I help?"

Wilson explained again the urgency of the call.

"I see. Well, normally we do not confirm or deny whether guests are in the hotel. However, I feel in this case we should bend that rule."

"Oh, really?" She did not like the tone the conversation was taking.

"Yes. You see, Mr. Morgan sent us a suitcase with his belongings which he asked us to deposit in a coded lockbox in the town bus station."

This made sense to her. The original plan was for her to meet Kiltman at the local airport, and for them to drive to a quiet spot where she could give him his *Kenny Morgan* clothes. Without her on the trip, his plan B made sense.

"We did find it quite unusual, but then again, it's not the most bizarre thing we've had to do. All types of people with many issues come to our resort. This is why our security is so tight."

There was something he was not saying - she was unsure if she wanted to hear it.

"Well, my point is that Mr. Morgan has not turned up. He has not checked in."

Wilson ran her hand through her hair looking up at the bright blue sky over Rome to quell the tears. It was now Tuesday evening, two days since he left home.

"Did he contact you at all?" she asked.

"No, nothing."

"Has he picked up the suitcase?"

"This morning, one of our staff went to the bus station to check. The case was still in the box. Of course, we left it there. Just in case he shows up today or later this week."

A rogue tear rolled down her cheek. She swiped it away with a determination she did not feel.

"Okay. So please tell me. How was he supposed to get to your hotel?"

"He was coming by helicopter. There is a helipad not far from here, which the majority of our guests use. I should say that it's not possible to know which specific helicopter he was supposed to be on. They arrive at various times of the day, every day - and they do not have to register their passengers in advance."

Wilson's mind was racing. The chopper had been arranged by administrative staff from Glasgow Pitt Street police station. She recalled Kenny saying that they had taken care of the trip. All he had to do was show up at the airport. The last time she had heard from him was when he texted just before his flight departed.

When she later heard from Gemmill that he had been to the penitentiary - albeit for a meeting that did not happen - she felt content, knowing he was going to take a few days off. At some point after he left the prison, he had disappeared.

"Okay, thank you. Please call me back if Mr. Morgan checks in or contacts you. I appreciate your help." Wilson gave them her mobile number. Minutes later, she was running through the back streets of *centro storico*. This was not a conscious decision - her legs seemed to take a life of their own, as if they sensed the growing tension in the rest of her body and had to find a release. In quarter of an hour, she had reached the Polizia Commissariato. She flashed her ID at the desk officer and sprinted up a flight of stairs to the room where she had left Crawford settling into their new place of work. She could not shake off the anger and self-recrimination for not checking in on Kenny, for letting her pride get in the way of common sense.

She exploded into the room as Crawford placed a handful of flaky pastry in his mouth.

"Is everything okay?" he mumbled, before taking a large slurp of what looked like a café macchiato.

"Eh, yes," she answered, inhaling deep breaths. She opened her briefcase and removed a slim laptop. "Another case has popped up that I need to deal with just now. Can you crack on with the Sacco stuff in the meantime?"

"Sure," Crawford responded, spraying a splatter of flakes onto the notes on the table. She raised an eyebrow. "Sorry! I'll clean it up, Boss."

She searched her inbox for the emails Kenny had sent her with the details of their spa trip. Embedded halfway down one of the messages, she found his travel schedule with day and time of pick up at São Paulo airport. The helicopter was operated by a company called *Helicópteros Voando Alto*. Underneath there was an address in São Paulo and a telephone number.

She typed the number into her phone and said, "Hey, Crawford. Would you mind doing me a favour? I'd love a pastry and a macchiato. I'm famished."

"Sure," Crawford said, grabbing his jacket from behind his chair. "See you soon." He was relieved to leave the room;

Wilson's edginess was palpable. He closed the door gently as he left.

"Oh, hi, do you speak English?" The call had rung for a minute before it was picked up. Her nerves were on edge - she could not cope with delays.

"Yes, I do. How can I help you?"

"Ah, thanks. One of our colleagues was flying with you on Monday. We just need to know where you dropped him off. He was from Scotland and known as..."

"Kiltman! The Scottish man." the voice on the other end laughed. "Yes, we waited for him, however he did not arrive."

"What do you mean?" she asked.

"Just what I said. We were excited to see him, but he did not show up at our helipad. Then we realised that it must have been a joke. Hah, Kiltman! Very funny. The British have a funny sense of humour."

"It was not a joke," Wilson said, impatience breaching her polite tone. "You were supposed to take him to a high security prison."

"Look, lady! We waited for him. He didn't show. It's not our fault. I don't like your attitude. We have done nothing wrong."

She closed her eyes and focused on regaining her composure.

"I'm sorry," she said. "Are there other helipads near you?"

"Yes, of course there are, we are at an airport." The apology had not worked.

"Okay, thanks," Wilson answered as she heard the line going dead.

This did not make sense. She pushed her chair back from the desk and put her head in her hands letting her thick, brown hair cascade down until it touched her knees. This was a mess. She had started off trying to find Kenny to tell him that Angie had disappeared. Now she was dealing with his disappearance. She rose from the chair and walked back and forth across the room, taking deep breaths. It was important to call upon her years of training and objectivity; there was no point in succumbing to panic.

Crawford walked into the room, "Hey, Boss. Got you some cannoli. Bit sweet, but think you'll like it." In his hurry to close the door with his heel while balancing the food and drinks, he had not noticed Wilson's fast pacing. She stopped and reached across to take the food and coffee.

He rubbed his stomach as he handed her two large creamy cannoli. "You know, Italians are the best at combining things other countries don't consider. Tomatoes and cheese. Ham and melon. Then cannoli - ricotta cheese and pastry. Yummy!"

As she took a bite of the soft - yet bristly- tubular shape, she closed her eyes and enjoyed the ricotta and pastry mix. The combination of contrasting tastes and textures made her realise that sometimes two events occurring together was not always a coincidence, not even a mistake. Rather it could be a result of genius - and in some cases, maniacal genius.

Back in Cincinnati

"Well done, team. You made me proud this morning." Coach Stone stood at the front of the bus, arms resting on the seat headrest. His face belied his words. His rugged features seemed more harrowed today. They had heard nothing from Angie. Some of the team were concerned about her disappearance, while others felt - with a hint of envy - that she had decided to have a jolly across the hinterlands of the USA.

"I know this is not exactly how you wanted to celebrate beating the Delhi Druids, but I think it will do us all some good." There was a spontaneous nod around the players on the bus. They were parked outside a church nestled in the Western Hills area of the city.

It had been Reilly's idea to come and say some prayers for Angie, in the absence of anything else that could be done. Coach accepted the suggestion. He then took it one stage further inviting Cardinal Damascus to come and say a few words. Roddy had found Coach's reaction to the Cardinal surprising. Something had happened between them - of that, he was in no doubt. Something spiritual - or at least reverential. He and Reilly had talked about the absence of limp, it left them feeling uneasy.

Coach turned to leave the bus, the Chesters team following behind onto the sidewalk. As they entered the church, they could see Cardinal Damascus on the altar, hands resting on the pulpit. There were around two to three hundred people in the church already, men, women and children of all ages. Roddy recognised Galatians players spread throughout the congregation - medals hanging around their necks, the **G** glittering under the overhead lights. Both adults and children were dressed in the same formal black and white clothes they had seen the previous day after the game.

"Here come our brothers and sisters from Scotland now," the Cardinal said. It seemed to him that the Galatians had been there for a while already, judging by how settled they seemed in their pews.

"Please, my friends, come and join us. We have kept seats for you here at the front." He pointed towards the first three rows close to the altar.

Coach led them to the front, where they hustled into the pews. Some of them struggled to hide their unease at being inside a church, not helped by the silence and stares of the elegantly dressed Galatians.

The Cardinal continued. "St. Paul tells us in his letter to Galatians: *'carry each other's burdens, and in this way, you will fulfil the law of Christ'*. This is why we are here today. One of our sisters is burdened. Angie is out there somewhere, dealing with her challenges, trying to find a solution. I ask you all to pray with me that our Scottish sister reaches out and lets us know where she is and how we can help her."

The Cardinal raised his hands above his head and closed his eyes. He moved his head from side to side and began to emit a slow and steady baritone hum. As it rose in crescendo, the Galatians community hummed along. Roddy noticed that some of the Chesters team joined in too, relaxing into the pleasant ambience the sound created through the rafters of the church. He found it soothing – imbuing a sense of peace he had not felt in a long time. The experience lasted no more than a minute; yet it was profoundly calming, layering an air of somnolence across the church.

The Cardinal restarted his sermon. "My children from Scotland. Coach Stone. We are honoured for you to visit us here in Cincinnati. You may not know it, but Scots have been influencing our city since the day it was born. Literally.

"Cincinnati has had several names over the years. Porkopolis, because of the influential role it played in the pork industry in the 19th century, was a contender. Thankfully, this was not given too much credence. It has had the nickname, Queen City, for many years - in recognition of its drive for culture, as well as its strong anti-slavery position at a time that ripped this great country apart.

"This is where the Scots become important in our history. Arthur St. Clair - a soldier and politician from a town called Thurso in one of the most northerly regions in Scotland - back in the 18th century, gave our city the name, Cincinnati. I don't know if our Scottish friends have been to this remote Highland town. I believe it gets chilly there in the winter - and come to think of it - in the summer too." He gave a smile that encouraged the congregation to grin, some to laugh.

"He named our city after a great Roman soldier and politician, who lived over two thousand years before Arthur was born - Lucius Quinctius Cincinnatus. Cincinnatus was known for his leadership, kindness and humility." Damascus stopped and looked around the church. He lifted his gaze to the ceiling and raised his voice to a loud booming echo.

"*The Spirit produces joy, peace, patience, kindness, goodness, faithfulness, humility and self-control.*"

"Amen! Amen!" members of the audience shouted back.

"Five Twenty-Two Twenty-Three," came from the middle of the group. Roddy was sure it was Brit's voice.

"My brothers and sisters we are here tonight to ask the Lord to find our Scottish sister, to lead this lost soul back to her flock. Fill your hearts and souls with prayer and ask for His intercession."

"Amen! Amen!" resonated again through the church.

Roddy closed his eyes and whispered his own prayer. The Cardinal continued to talk and explain the importance of Galatians and St. Paul's influence on the early days of the Church. Roddy was positioned behind Coach Stone. He was going to take full advantage of his girth. Hunched under his shadow, he removed his phone from his pocket carefully. He saw several missed calls from his mother and a bunch of unread messages.

Roddy please call me. It's urgent. Love mum xx

Roddy call your mum. She needs to speak to you. M. xx

My gorgeous wee boy please call me. I need to talk to you. Mum xx

He checked the time of the calls and messages. They had all been made after he had spoken to his mother about Angie earlier that day. His heartbeat quickened. Maybe they had found her already. That really would be an uncanny response to the power of prayer.

He stood up into a half-crouch and sidled along the pew towards the side aisle. When he reached the end he fell into a half jog, rushing out onto the street. He had dialled his mother's number before he reached the outside.

"Roddy? Roddy?" his mother said, her anxiety unabated.

"Yes, Mum, it's me." He hated to think his mother was suffering.

"Thank God!" she responded. "Look. Have you heard from your dad since Sunday?"

He felt the disappointment - Angie had not been found. "No, Mum. Dad's on a spa. Remember? We laughed about him having a leg wax."

"Oh, Roddy," his mother was struggling to speak. "Your dad didn't arrive at the spa. He has gone missing."

"What? How could that have happened, Mum? Did the plane crash?"

"No, son. That's the thing. Everything seems to have gone according to schedule. It was after he got to Brazil, he went off radar. Don't worry, Maggie is looking into it." His mother was asking him not to be concerned, yet he could hear the pain in her voice.

Roddy was fighting the surge of worry. He had to focus. "Mum, what can we do?"

"Maggie is getting people in the area to investigate. All we can do is hope, son. Say a wee prayer."

He wished he could hug his mum and snuggle into her loving arms. Both Angie and his father missing. This did not make sense. He fought back the tears, he had to be strong now.

"Don't worry, Mum. We will find them. Are you going to stay in Paris until the end of the week?"

"I am going back to Scotland. I wanted to come to the US, although they advised me against it. All I can do is wait at the phone and hope Angie contacts me."

Roddy reassured her, said good-bye and turned to walk back into the church. As he knelt on the kneeler in the back row, head bowed, face in his hands, he remembered the words of Jesus. Drummed into him in his catechism classes, *man does not live on bread alone -* words that had stood the test of time. The book of Deuteronomy, written 1,400 years before Jesus, had used the same expression to highlight that humans should not rely solely on the needs of the flesh. Roddy agreed with this spiritual dietary advice - and when he returned to the hotel, he was going to take a hefty swig of his father's liquified grain.

Wednesday, April 13

Cloud Data

"I understand, you should sit this one out." Coach rubbed Roddy's arm, in a manner unusually tender for someone so ungainly and reserved.

"Thanks, Coach. If I can think of anything that might help the police, I'll call them directly." Roddy rose from his chair to indicate he wanted to spend some time alone.

"Sure, pal," Coach spoke quietly.

"Good luck in the game." Roddy felt a pang of regret at not being able to join the team. They were in the quarter finals against another Ohio team, Dayton Dragontails. He wanted to support Coach and his teammates - they had researched the Dragontails and become mildly nervous. With more yellow and red cards than any other team in the tournament, they were going to have a battle on their hands.

He knew that Coach would have cancelled their on-going participation if he could. He seemed to be struggling to find the energy to make this tournament an event the Chesters players would remember for the right reasons. Roddy could see concern in the moistness of his bright blue eyes.

"Thanks. We will give it our best, as usual." Coach turned and exited the room. When he saw the door close, Roddy bent down and reached under the bed. He picked up the Irn-Bru bottle and took a decent swig. He was never disappointed at the comforting feeling infused by Hair o' the Dog. He could feel a tingling across the bridge of his nose. He had stopped looking in mirrors - vanity would have to take a back seat. In the afternoon, he would take a walk in the sun, hoping Vitamin D could reverse Hair o' the Dog's teenage backlash.

Turning to his laptop he typed in IATA - International Air Transport Association. He drilled his search down to the IATA headquarters website. His fingers began to take a life of their own. Like a classical pianist playing a Rachmaninov concerto from memory, He closed his eyes and let his fingers take control. He had not done something like this before - he was not sure what was happening. Somehow his brain and fingers developed a harmonious connection that sidestepped the conscious part of his brain - he had become a spectator in his own body.

Around him the room was filling up with data and threads of information. His fingers were like magnets drawing information out of IATA systems and databases - breaking down security walls and passwords - then splurging it into the Cincinnati hotel room. He could see two search patterns guided by his alter-self. One for his father, the other for Angie.

Reams of names and numbers spilled out of the laptop into the cramped confines of the room, the majority disappearing as quickly as they arrived. He realised most of the numbers were PNRs - 10-digit Personal Number Records - registered when a customer books an airline or flight ticket. Travellers have a unique PNR number for each ticket purchased, recording passenger and itinerary. His fingers moved so fast, they merged into a blur of pink skin - pressing keys, moving the mouse, identifying then excluding data points.

And then they stopped. On screen, Roddy could see the PNR number for his father's trip to Brazil. It took him as far as São Paulo airport - consistent with his expectation. His search moved to the helicopters that left the airport soon after his father's flight landed. Before he realised what he was doing, he had breached air traffic control security screens - not knowing exactly how – and began unlocking information for chopper excursions.

Lists of trips appeared, identifying call codes for scores of choppers and related flight paths. He had not realised so many helicopters could fly in a confined airspace at the same time. After a few minutes of searching and eliminating, with the room an extension of the laptop screen, one flight stood out from the rest.

It was for a four-man helicopter, São Paulo to Manaus. The interesting aspect of this one was it did not leave. The slot had been booked, then cancelled. Roddy went back to the screen showing Kiltman's PNR and saw that he was booked onto that excursion.

He began a search for trips leaving around the time of the cancelled flight. There were several within half an hour of this time. A chopper belonging to *Martim's Manaus Manoeuvres* caught his eye. He opened another screen and googled the company. They offered trips over the Amazon jungle, advertising *breath-taking views of parts of the rainforest where other choppers fear to go*. Whatever that meant, it was enough for him to drill down into the detail of its latest flight. The data came up on screen in a staccato march. It showed an address for a destination helipad right outside the high security prison. Followed by a return trip to São Paulo. He could see the chopper left the prison half an hour after landing. Instead of flying directly back, it took a detour southwest of Manaus. After twenty minutes, it U-turned for its return trip to São Paulo.

This could be the key to unlock his father's disappearance. He had no time to lose. The sense of danger was tingling through every pore of his body. It was as though Hair o' the Dog had set off an internal alarm that was belting out a siren inside him forcing a reaction.

He pressed speed dial on his phone. Maggie answered within seconds.

"Roddy? Are you okay?"

"Yes, fine. How are you getting on looking for Dad?"

"Nothing yet. We're trying to retrace his steps. It's not easy dealing with the Brazilian authorities." What she chose not to disclose was the challenge she had in looking for him. There was no record of a Kenny Morgan travelling to Brazil. Only Kiltman. Maggie was spending most of her time talking to Gemmill and the Brazilians about Kiltman while keeping Fiona up to date on Kenny. At this stage there was nothing to report on either of them. Now Roddy had to be managed. This was becoming too complicated.

"Look, I might have something for you." He was not yet ready to confess what he knew to Maggie about his father's alter ego. He understood the dilemma she was in - he wanted to confess but she would have to cope. "I have, em, a friend here in Cincinnati. He works for the international travel authorities."

"A friend over there? Really?" She was not sure where this was going.

"Yes, look, it's hard to explain. I asked him to search for Dad's flight details and itinerary in Brazil. Funny thing was, he can't find anything. Then, he sees that Kiltman was flying the same day! Also, to Brazil. They might even have been on the same flight. How weird is that?"

She felt her pulse quicken. Roddy was getting too close to the family secret. "That really is weird," she managed to say.

"I know, I thought so too. This guy is going to keep looking for Dad. His data must be there somewhere. There may be a glitch in the system." He waited a moment before delivering his key message. "Guess what? When he looked at Kiltman's data he realised that he didn't take the chopper he was supposed to take."

Wilson rose from her chair, slamming it against the wall. Crawford looked up from his computer screen. She put her hand over the mouthpiece. "Crawford, could you get me another of those delicious cannoli things please? I'm starving."

"Sure, Boss." He smiled as he walked towards the door. If it was possible to get addicted to Italian food, he was happy to be co-dependent with his boss. He left the room whistling a tune he could not get out of his head: *I started looking for excuses*, from Coldplay's song Warning. He may not have Wilson's years of experience, but he recognised a forced decoy when he saw one.

She was struggling to keep up with what Roddy was saying. How could he know that Kiltman did not take the chopper? She had requested the Brazilian police investigate Kiltman's disappearance - they had presented a list of excuses as to how difficult it was to trace travellers who switched from international airlines to local.

He continued. "I know which chopper he took. It belonged to a company called *Martim's Manaus Manoeuvres*. Kiltman was not even booked with them."

"How on earth do you know all this?" Maggie was scribbling down the name of the company. "Who is this friend of yours?" How could Roddy's 'friend' be able to do all this? Grant's mate, Rafael, had not even returned her call.

"Sorry, the phone is crackling. My battery is dying here. I'll keep looking and let you know if I hear anything. Just thought you'd want to know this unusual blip in Kiltman's itinerary. Bye."

"Roddy?" The line had gone dead. Maggie's head was racing. She would try and make sense of all this later - for now she had to follow his second-hand lead.

She hit speed dial on her phone. Gemmill had called just before Roddy to give her the number of the São Paulo Police Chief, Cesar Sampaio. Gemmill met him at the Brazil versus Scotland world cup match in 1998 - when the Brazilian's namesake scored against Scotland. The hopes of a nation evaporated in the five minutes it took for that goal to happen. She knew that Kenny would consider it a debt repaid if the police version of Sampaio could help save his life.

Cesar Sampaio

"Yes, please wait. I will connect to Chefe de Polícia, Senhor Sampaio." The secretary had not needed much convincing. Gemmill had called the police station in São Paulo in advance to advise that Wilson would be in touch.

"Thank you." Wilson was still on her feet, pacing the room. From the first-floor window, she could see the cobbled streets of Rome glimmer with a rare sprinkling of rain.

"Yes, how can I help?" She could tell he was a heavy smoker, with a deep voice that commanded attention despite the discernible weakness it belied.

"Hello, Senhor Sampaio. It's Detective Inspector Wilson here. Thank you for taking my call."

"Ah, DI Wilson. It's my pleasure and honour to speak with you. I have a very clear memory of how you and your hero friend intervened in the United Nations. The world - and in our case, Brazil - truly owes you all the help you need." No matter how many times she heard the warm comments about that day, she could not shake off the anxiety it triggered. The alternative would have been horrendous.

"Thank you, sir. I appreciate your kind comments." She waited a moment to allow a subtle shift of gear. "A friend of ours has been doing some digging. He has advised that Kiltman did not take the pre-booked chopper from São Paulo to the prison. In fact, he found out that another chopper left about the same time, and Kiltman was on board."

"Oh, this is interesting. Can you advise the name of the company or owner?" Sampaio said.

"Yes, it was *Martim's Manaus Manouevres*. Have you heard of them?"

The silence lasted longer than she would have expected.

"Ah, now that is odd," Sampaio replied. "Martim, the owner of this company, was found dead on Monday evening, lying on the floor of the hangar where he kept the helicopter. Apparently, he shot himself. The local police have been looking into it since then. They say he had financial difficulties - his business had been finding things challenging of late."

She had decided many years earlier that while coincidences were subject to the laws of probability, she would never accept their existence in any of her investigations. "Sir, it is more than odd."

Her heart was racing. There were more loose ends than the last time she had her hair done.

"Could someone else have been on the chopper with them?"

"Yes, it's entirely possible. I'm sensing you are ruling out suicide." Sampaio was writing on a pad of paper. "Okay, DI Wilson. We will review the CCTV footage from the helipad area and outside the hangar. We can at least understand who came and went. Then take it from there."

"Thanks, Chief. Yes, that would be great. I'll keep my mobile handy. Just call whenever you have something."

"Okay, will do. Speak soon."

She closed the phone as Crawford walked into the room, armed with a cardboard container overflowing with pastries. "Hi, Boss. The lady who works there gave me extra cannoli. Who can argue with a gorgeous girl called Valentina?" He did not mention that Valentina appeared to have taken a shine to him. She had told him her name the day before when he tried to charm her with his faltering Italian. Today, he had been able to say, *"due cannoli e due caffè macchiato."* Without faltering. This earned him an eye twinkle, a smile - and three extra pastries.

"Thanks, Crawford." Wilson stuffed three quarters of a cannoli into her mouth, letting the flakes drop onto her crimson top. Crawford handed her a paper napkin which she accepted distractedly. As she busied herself cleaning her blouse, Crawford realised it was going to be difficult to stay focused on this job.

Chief Commissioner Pisacane

"Look, DI Wilson. I appreciate your contribution to finding Kiltman, however this is not your case. Am I clear?" It had been a while since Gemmill had shouted at her.

"Yes, sir, I understand." She had just communicated to Gemmill her update from Roddy and conversation with Sampaio. "Rest assured; I am very aware of the importance of this Sacco case. However, I really believe something seriously bad has happened to Kiltman." Hardly her most informed summation of an open case, but it was all she could muster. She was struggling with not being able to disclose Kenny's non-arrival at the spa.

"I agree, the circumstances are a tad odd. However, let's not just turn a logistic hiccup in Kiltman's travel plans into an all-out red alert. He said he was taking a break away from it all. He apparently is taking a break. He would call it well-deserved. I won't use that expression. For the moment, I am not worried."

She wanted to ask what would concern him but held back from antagonising him even more. "Are we done here?"

She heard the door open behind her. A tall, elegant, well-dressed police officer entered. He was peeling off his white gloves by the fingertips. "Yes, sir, someone has just walked in. I will be in touch."

She heard the line go silent before she finished her sentence.

"Signora Wilson. It is my honour to host you here in our station. I am Chief Commissioner Pisacane."

The man - who ticked the drop-dead gorgeous box in her mind - extended his hand. She was not old enough to have grown up watching Clark Gable; although had seen plenty of photos to think that such crushingly handsome hunks had *gone with the wind*. She had to stop herself from curtseying and kissing his ringed fingers. At the last moment she remembered to take a firm grip and squeeze with as much authority as she could manage.

"Thank you, Chief Pisacane. Em, we have been treated very well by your team." She heard a quiet cough from behind her. "Oh, and this is my colleague, Crawford."

Crawford leaned in from behind her and shook the Chief's hand. She could have sworn he bowed slightly. "Pleased to meet you, sir."

"Likewise," Pisacane answered. "So, let's see what you are working on here."

Before she could intercept, he had hit enter on Wilson's laptop. A map of central Brazil flashed onto the screen, with lines identifying flight paths between São Paulo, Manaus and Iguaçu."

"Oh!" Pisacane said. "Have you found a Brazil connection to the Sacco case?"

The silence in the room turned awkward - until Crawford said, "Oh, that was me, sir. I was just planning my holiday for next year. I am booking flights next week."

"I see," Pisacane looked at Crawford carefully. Wilson closed her eyes and groaned inwardly. "I like to see officers mixing business with pleasure. I do love Brazil. I was there for Mar di Gras last year. Truly amazing time to go to Rio."

He turned to Wilson. She was not sure how to read his expression. "So, please advise what you have found on the Sacco case?"

"At this stage, sir, we are still crunching data. We are finding strong links between Mafia deposits and contributions to various charitable organisations."

"Anything else?" His face continued to be inscrutable.

"Well, that Banco d'Aiuto is making very material deposits into Bank Discepolo, which is connected to..."

"The Vatican banking system," he answered for her, in the same way she tended to do when listening to others. He rubbed his chin with a thumb, while shifting his gaze from her to Crawford. He slipped his gloves back over his delicate, smooth fingers. She tucked her hands into her pockets, wondering if she would ever have the courage to ask for his manicurist's number.

"I am sure you are aware - this is an interesting time to be in Rome. Our beloved Pope John Paul the Second died earlier this month. God rest his soul." Pisacane blessed himself. "Soon there will be a meeting of the cardinals, a Papal Conclave, to decide on the next leader of the Catholic Church. This is a great moment in history; and it means I will be focused on supporting the Vatican's security teams and Swiss Guards during this process."

"Yes, we are aware, sir. We fully understand." Wilson was not sure if she should say 'sorry for your troubles'. She knew how respected and loved 'JP II' had been across the world.

Pisacane continued. "Many thanks to both of you. Please keep me informed. My team here are at your disposal. Use them as you see fit." He bowed, turned and left the room.

When the door closed, she turned to Crawford. "You didn't need to do that."

He shrugged and smiled awkwardly. "Don't worry, Boss. It was better than him thinking you were distracted by another case."

"God forbid!" She returned a goofy grin of her own. "Let's focus on Sacco."

She hoped Sampaio would come back soon with news of Kiltman's whereabouts. How hard could it be to find a kilted man in Brazil?

Awake

The soft draught of air felt good on his face.

He had yet to open his eyes. A layer of cloth across his face oozed a cool liquid onto his skin with every wave of air that wafted over him. He had awakened to a sensation of pushing and stroking on various parts of his body. Both arms and legs were being kneaded like lumps of dough. He wanted to lift his head to look but could not find the energy to move.

His throat was parched, his tongue stuck to the top of his mouth. "Water," he croaked in a voice he did not recognise.

The kneading and air flow stopped. He could hear several people breathing slowly. They began to make unrecognisable noises - a cross between the sound of a finger click and a whistle. There was a strange soothing quality to the guttural sounds coming from somewhere - everywhere - in the room. A hand peeled the cloth from his eyes. The brightness of the light startled him. He tried to lift a hand to create some shade, but his arm was pinned to his side.

His eyes began to adjust. A face was up close staring at him; small, round, with a charcoal complexion. The eyes were studying his own. A voice clicked and whistled in a melodic, hypnotic rhythm. Several droplets of liquid were dripped into his open mouth. It was a flavour he could not recognise. Bitter yet soothingly sweet. The tiredness became impossible to ignore. He had no energy to fight it. A deep sleep descended on him like a heavy blanket, the air again drifting across his face, his body absorbing the massage, desperate for its healing power.

Hamilton County

Roddy felt small as he entered the sheriff's office in downtown Cincinnati - flanked by two tall, burly officers. The car ride from the soccer campus had been enlightening for him. Officers Pat and Brian were determined to outdo themselves in explaining how influential Cincinnati had been on the world through commerce and the arts.

The conversation had continued from the car until they were now walking up the steps into the police building.

"Oh, I forgot to mention." Roddy was feeling confident with these two men. They had a sense of peace around them that rubbed off on him. "I just heard recently that a man from Scotland, Arthur St. Clair, christened the city as Cincinnati."

Officer Brian clicked his fingers "Hey, that's cool. I am born and bred here and didn't know that. Pity he didn't call it MacCincinnati." He chortled to himself, only interrupted when Officer Pat punched him on the shoulder.

Officer Brian continued. "Yeah, they could have started a fast-food restaurant chain, serving Skyline Chili on a bun, calling it a MacSkyline."

Officer Pat stopped, looked his colleague in the eye and wagged his finger from side to side. Officer Brian put his hands up. "Okay, I get it. I took the whole thing one stage too far. Got a bit carried away, mixing up your fast-food fetishes." There was a moment of awkward silence, before they both put their hands in the air and whacked a high five that resonated off the building wall. While it seemed a strange ritual, Roddy was sure it was an integral part of their partner modus operandi.

"By the way!" Roddy said, wanting to join in with the banter. He pointed at the sign above the door: *Hamilton County Sheriff Office*. "I have another Scottish factoid for you. You know how Cincinnati is the county capital for the area we are in - Hamilton County? Well, it's named after Alexander Hamilton, one of the USA's founding fathers. Which I am sure you know. Although I bet you didn't know that Hamilton's father was born and bred Scottish."

Both officers nodded their acknowledgement. "Cool," said Officer Brian. "One day I'm going to visit Scotland. I'll find a place called Hamilton and have a beer there." Roddy smiled, imagining this huge American walking into the town of Hamilton's Butterburn Bar and asking a local if he was related to Alexander Hamilton.

They had arrived at a small office towards the back of the ground floor. The room was filled with computer hardware ranging from printers and monitors to mainframes - surrounded by an invisible blanket of melodic, soporific hum of technology in process.

Officer Pat pointed towards a table in the corner. "You can make yourself comfortable here, Roddy. Use this laptop to search the internet." The officers looked at each other and shrugged. At first, they had not wanted to bring him to the station. Then when they considered how upset he was, they saw no harm in allocating a desk and letting him look up whatever he felt would help them. It would at least make him believe he was contributing to the search for Angie.

"Thanks, Officers. You have been super-helpful." Roddy had taken a genuine liking to the two men, who had gone out of their way to make him feel comfortable. The door opened and another officer walked into the room with a tray loaded with donuts and Coke.

"Just in case, you get hungry, Scottie!" His warm smile and decent attempt at the Star Trek engineer's twang made Roddy feel at home.

"Aw, thank you, Officer Brucague." He had learned to look for name plates on their shirts. He looked forward to enjoying the 'stakeout food'.

"No problem, buddy. You carry on and we'll leave you alone. Password to the internet is there on the table. Don't forget, *you're an engine worker, not a miracle worker*." Officer Brucague walked out of the room, smiling, happy to have an excuse to practice some Star Trek speak in public.

Within a minute, the officers were gone. Roddy stuffed half a donut in his mouth and logged onto the internet. Earlier that day he realised he could only get so far with the small, school laptop he had been working on. With the police station's mainframe at his disposal, he could download and generate data at a pace matching his ability to analyse.

Maggie would be following up on his dad with the Brazilian police - she would not rest until she had a tangible lead. In the meantime, Roddy would turn his attention to Angie. The more he considered her disappearance, the more concerned he became. Yes, her note had all the confidence and resolve he would have expected from her. Although it still did not make sense - how her mood had changed so soon after arriving on campus. Then there was the Brazil texting exchange - odd in its own right – even more so when it happened at the same time as his father disappeared on a trip there.

After cleaning his hands with a paper napkin, he typed in the +55 number that had been messaging her. As expected, a torrent of data appeared on the screen telling him nothing other than 55 is a very common combination of digits. He directed his search to *Brasil Telecom*. Before long he had logged on as a senior manager in their diagnostics department, breaking down internal password and security barriers with an ease he did not quite understand himself. His brain seemed to bypass his consciousness again and direct his fingers to the correct keys and combinations of letters and words. Once again, the room morphed into a large screen capturing and spreading the data from wall to wall, moving in constant motion, layer upon layer.

Within ten minutes, he found the number she had texted. A few more drilldowns later, he unlocked a series of text exchanges currently in progress. This time it was not Angie, but a number beginning +39. A quick search showed this was Italy. He would worry about the specific location later. For the moment, he just needed to see the detail. He watched the texts appear on the screen.

+39 - *185323, 69188?*

+55 - *14*

+39 - *5052, 785216, 16197418, '7'61*

+55 - *819*

The exchange had no words, just strings of numbers and some punctuation. It made no sense. At least, not initially. It was some sort of code. He had never been adept at code-breaking games - Maths was not his forte at school. He rubbed his stomach enjoying the sensation of Hair o' the Dog still in his system, willing it to address the mix of jumbled numbers. He copied the texts down onto a sheet of paper and wrote the alphabet alongside hoping that a simple matching of ordering of numbers to letters would work. He was not surprised when it failed. He tried again, reversing the alphabet. Again, nothing. Before he knew it his brain had taken over - or rather Hair o' the Dog had. He began scribbling row after row of letters, sometimes skipping vowels, other times, counting in clumps of 2 then 3 numbers and so on. It proved fruitless - he could not break their code.

He smashed his hand down on the desk, his other hand flat against his face. This was not a game, not a piece of school homework.   This was life and death. He turned to the +39 number. He tracked it into the Italia Telecom system - it was not registered to a specific owner. Maggie would have called it a *burner* phone - a simple mobile phone criminals use for specific jobs. Once the specified series of communications were complete, it would be disposed of, never to be used or seen again.

He shivered and hoped that fate would not befall Angie and his father.

Accountants at Work

"Are you sure they can do this?" Wilson looked across the desk at Crawford. She was uneasy about expanding the investigation any further. Truth was, they had hit the proverbial brick wall and needed help; a higher degree of expertise than they had on their own.

"This is what they do, Boss. They're all still based in New York and spend their days reviewing cases and investigating forensics, either to support businesses or the police. It's their bread and butter, so to speak." Crawford was literally sitting on the edge of his seat. It was his first real contribution to the case - other than providing cannoli on a regular basis. He had already been to the Pasticceria three times that day and it was not yet 6 pm.

"Okay," she said. "How long to set up the call with them?"

"Well, I've got a confession to make." He waited a moment, more out of nervousness than dramatic effect. "They are waiting for us to call them."

"Seriously?" she asked. "When did you arrange this?"

"This morning. A few minutes after Chief Commissioner Pisacane left us."

She nodded. They had both felt the increase in pressure after he left them. His politeness and courtesy were underpinned by a tangible impatience. He would not give them much more time to work this out. The press reported regularly on Sacco's death, raising unanswered questions as to his financial dealings. There was also the small matter of killers out there who had, so far, escaped justice.

Crawford *fired up* the computer screen. *Fired up* was an expression that amused Wilson. He had said it a few times over the past days. She cringed whenever anyone in the world of computing used an expression that was as far from hardware as she could imagine. The fact they did it with an air of excitement fascinated her.

Within a minute, she could see a row of faces crammed into the small screen. A chorus of *HELLOs* and *HIs* came at her from the group she had met once, a few years earlier. She smiled remembering their afternoon in Murphy's Pub in New York City on a bitterly cold winter's day. She and Kiltman had been chasing shadows hoping to find a way to thwart Mask. Their chance meeting with the New York accountants proved to be the turning point in the search for their nemesis.

Aiden, the thoughtful one with the intelligent, cheeky sense of humour, raised his hand in a half wave. Braz, even on a small computer screen, looked gangly. He was already flicking through pages of numbers, pointing his thumb as a salute. Huggy, she noticed, had lost some weight, and was looking fitter than she expected an accountant at his stage of life to look. Early retirement beckoned, she sensed. Shayne was nestled at the edge of the table they had huddled around, enjoying group thinktank mood.

Crawford coughed. "Hi, guys, thanks for being available."

"Wouldn't have missed it," Braz said - in that North Dublin way of making the listener unsure as to whether he meant what he said or was just cracking a joke.

"Thanks, everyone. Good to see you," Wilson said. "I appreciate you helping out here. What have you got?"

Huggy spoke. "I'll take the lead. Okay, we have dug into the Mafia donations to Banco d'Aiuto. In the last year, we know that you already found there had been around €10 million in deposits. You see, we have forensic systems here which ..."

Please don't say it, Wilson thought.

"... are based on *state-of-the-art* software."

She sighed in resignation.

"They have allowed us to go back over the last ten years, analysing ins and outs for all accounts in the bank." Huggy waited for this to sink in.

"What? Since Crawford contacted you this morning?" she asked.

Aiden spoke up. "It's not as difficult as you might think, Maggie." She did not see Shayne nip Aiden's leg at his audacity to jump in. He shifted in his seat and continued. "You see, once we have made the links and defined the universe of the search, we *bang out* a couple of algorithms, and the system does the rest."

She had to admit it sounded easy when articulated like this.

"Thanks, Aiden. I'll take it from here," Shayne said. "You see, Maggie," he looked sideways at his fellow Irishman, "we can now look back to the inception of the bank. Which was…" he leafed through a booklet on his desk.

"1990," Braz interrupted. "January 6, to be precise."

"Thanks, guys," she said. She would have enjoyed the subtlety of their banter if it were not for the fact this case was getting in the way of her search for Kiltman and Angie. "Please don't keep me in suspense."

"Okay, let's cut to the chase," Aiden started again. He really did seem to be the voice of reason in the group. "Over the last decade and a half, there have been numerous deposits made to these accounts, all made on a monthly basis. Like clockwork. The only thing that has changed is the scale. They started at around €1 million a year to the €10 million we see now. In total around €70 million has been deposited."

She pursed her lips and blew out a long slow whistle.

Shayne continued, "If they deposit the same amount every year for the next 10 years, it will be another €100 million." A piece of information that bordered on obvious and irrelevant - he just wanted to see her whistle again. Although this time she disappointed him.

"I see," she said. "Have you been able to identify the account holders?"

"Yes…. Maggie." Braz was doing it too. "Other than the regularity of these deposits and the increasing scale in size, we have seen Banco d'Aiuto increase its payments into Banco Discepolo, practically in the same ratio of year-on-year increase. As you picked up from your own investigative work, Banco Discepolo is the recipient of over half of Banco d'Aiuto's total transfers. That proportion is also growing each year."

"Hold on," she said. "Just a bit slower if you don't mind."

"Sorry," Huggy stepped in. "Let me try. You see, if the deposits in total increased from one year to the next by say 20%, then Banco d'Aiuto's transfers - in total, not just these accounts

- to Banco Discepolo would increase by very close to the same percentage."

"I see," she said. Huggy's one-up-man look of satisfaction did not go unnoticed by any of them. "So, in effect, Banco d'Aiuto's ins and outs are really a product of how much these accounts deposit. Somehow, they determine the bank's overall money flows."

"Yes," Huggy responded. "That's the conclusion I got to. I mean, the team got to." He did not skip a beat.

"Okay. Now that we have this insight, what would you recommend from here?" She sat back in her chair, arms folded.

"Well, Maggie," Braz interjected, "this is where we hand it back to you and *Robin* - I mean Crawford." The group laughed in unison, including Crawford. "You see, we have given you what you need now in terms of money flows. It's up to you to find the people moving the cash and find out why they're doing it."

"Yes, makes sense." She had reached the same conclusion. "In your review, did you manage to find addresses of the main account holders?" She glanced at the faces stuck to the whiteboard wall.

"Yes, we did," Aiden said. "We will email them to Crawford." He lingered for a moment, before he spoke in a voice sounding much too ominous for a charming Irishman. "They all live in Sicily, in or near a town called Corleone."

She understood the implications of this comment. She looked at Crawford, and could see he also realised the potential consequences of a trip to the heart of Mafia-dom. A slight twitch in the corner of his eye gave away the underlying tension.

"Look on the bright side, eh, Robin," she said, placing her hand on his shoulder. "We're going to a place where someone may offer you a cannoli you can't refuse."

Thursday, April 14

Quarter Finals

He pushed back on his elongated leg, stretching his taut calf muscle. Then did the same with the other. Roddy had tried to resist the Coach's request for him to play in the quarter finals against Dayton Dragontails. He used as many excuses as he could invent in a short conversation - searching for Angie, emotionally exhausted, stressed beyond limits. He had not even mentioned his father being missing, for obvious reasons. With every excuse, Coach nodded and said, "That's another reason why you should be out there playing football today".

He had sealed his own fate.

Standing in the morning sun, on freshly cut grass, with a mild breeze in the air, felt invigorating. The smell of the nearby flowers would have added a picnic atmosphere to the moment, if it were not for the team facing them.

The Dragontails looked like adults squeezed into kids' soccer strips. Muscles bulged in places muscles were not supposed to be. As they walked onto the grass, Roddy whispered to Reilly that they looked more like a Mr. Universe pageant. Reilly had shrugged. Opponents did not frighten him - the bigger they were, the easier it was to 'turn them inside out'.

The team had done well to reach the quarters. There had been a few casualties along the way, nothing too serious. A couple of minor sprains and hamstring tweaks. The injury list meant Roddy was in the starting line-up whether he wanted to be or not. They were down to their minimum with only two substitutes on the bench.

Coach had asked him to play up front alongside Reilly, who was stretching close by. "Roddy, how you doing?

"Okay, Reilly, you?"

"I can't stop worrying about Angie, to be honest. You must be the same," he said. "Did you come up with anything when you were at the police station yesterday?"

"No, nothing. At least I got to meet the officers looking for her. They are very committed. I'm sure they'll do everything they can." Roddy recognised his words were meaningless, comfort fodder for Reilly, to make him feel better.

The whistle blew, the Dragontails passed the ball back from centre and everyone ran into spaces and positions. The first half became as scrappy a game of football as any of them had played. Both teams seemed to spend more time stopping the opponents than trying to score. Roddy felt his heart pump as he ran backwards and forwards cutting off passes and intercepting plays. He was not a natural forward, but he did know how to disrupt others when they were trying to be clever.

Halftime approached; he could see the ref checking his watch. One of the Dragontails had proven challenging to control during the first half. The spearhead for most of the Dragontails' attacks on goal, he had won player of the tournament a year earlier. Roddy remembered his name from Coach's pre-match talk, Brandon Scobie. It was common knowledge across the other teams that Brandon Scobie had the skills, talent and mindset to go all the way as a professional footballer. He was also known to be an accomplished rugby player and had even dabbled in the colonial sport of cricket. When Coach had told Roddy before the game to chase this talented opponent whenever he got the ball, Roddy knew he would have his work cut out.

They were minutes away from halftime, Roddy already looking forward to a few orange slices and a jug of iced tea. It happened in a flash; a long pass flew over his head and was taken on the chest by Brandon Scobie. The player turned and sprinted towards Chesters' goal. Roddy had no time to think; he turned and chased the football wizard as he ran with the ball close to his feet.

Over the length of the pitch, Roddy gained a yard for every ten the Dragontail covered. Just as Brandon Scobie reached the inside of the penalty box, Roddy lunged forward to kick the ball from his feet to avoid the impending shot.

His tackle was perfect in every way - except precision. He connected with his opponent's shin, just below the knee, sending him up into the air before landing with a crash on top of Roddy. He heard the ref blow his whistle and shout, "Penalty!"

Within a few minutes, Roddy was yellow carded, Brandon Scobie scored the penalty kick, and the first half was over. He walked back to the changing room a few paces behind the rest of the team. He was gutted. What on earth got into him? To have the gall to think he could chase a player like that and land a perfect tackle had been an absurd overestimation of his ability. As he wallowed in self-pity, he felt an arm around his shoulders. It was Brandon Scobie. "Hard lines, buddy. You did really well to cover the ground to catch me."

"I'm sorry, I hope I didn't hurt you; it was a bit reckless." Roddy felt awkward at having to apologise to an opponent.

Brandon Scobie smiled and ruffled Roddy's hair as if they had known each other for years. "Don't sweat it, man. You did great. You know, it's a pity you're not going to be here for longer than a week, I could get you a spot in my rugby team. We could use someone who tackles like that."

Roddy laughed and said, "Maybe next time."

"But seriously," Brandon Scobie replied, "Don't give up. Remember what the basketball giant Michael Jordan said: *Don't be afraid to fail. Be afraid not to try.*"

The player gave him a thumbs up and walked into the Dragontails' dressing room, leaving Roddy appreciating how much that brief moment's conversation had lifted his spirits.

"Hey, Roddy," Reilly caught up with him at the door. "What was Brandon Scobie saying? Was he giving you a hard time?"

"No," Roddy answered. "The opposite, in fact. He is a cool guy; he just reminded me I need to keep trying."

"That's the spirit we need for the second half," Reilly said.

Roddy nodded, although his thoughts were not on the game; Angie's life depended on him not being afraid to fail.

While he was not failing to be afraid, very afraid.

Galatians II

The dining hall was crammed with people balancing paper plates in one hand and drinks in the other. Brit had invited all the teams in the tournament. She and her fellow Galatians had worked hard to arrange the hall. Tables were pushed back against the wall; chairs had been removed and stacked in the corridor. Roddy noticed one table with five large black boxes - stamped with the letter **G**.

Along the walls, six wide screen televisions were placed an equal distance apart. Roddy assumed the room was used for conferences and business meetings when there were no sports activities on campus.

The atmosphere was abuzz with conversations between the players. They were mingling well, enjoying anecdotes and comments about subjects ranging from soccer to movies.

He was feeling sore after the game. His legs had taken a few knocks more than usual. During the half-time talk, Coach had used Roddy's run - and ensuing bad tackle - to highlight what he expected from the team. He had even used a weird metaphor about a hen and a pig.

"I want pigs in my team, not hens. Do you understand? Do you know what I am getting at?"

When he saw the blank faces - which he expected - he continued. "When you sit down to breakfast and look at your bacon and eggs, who do you think has made the biggest contribution? The hen or the pig?"

He had waited for the point to sink in, then said. "Exactly! I don't want *Hens* in the team, ready to do the minimum then walk away. I want *Pigs* - all in, leaving part of yourself on the pitch!

"Now, get out there and be like Roddy. Be the best *Pigs* you can be!'"

Chesters won 2-1. Two strikes from the goalscoring *pig*, Reilly, had sealed Dragontails' fate. Tomorrow's semi-final would have a Scots' team in it.

Roddy was struggling to enjoy the collegiate mood of the gathering in the dining hall. He was trying to find a way to get back to the sheriff's office and connect to the mainframe. It had been Brandon Scobie's comment about being afraid to try that struck a chord. He had realised *being afraid* could apply to lots of things. It could also be used for being afraid to 'think outside the box', an expression he knew Maggie disliked. He smiled when he remembered how many times his father used it to wind her up.

His *outside the box* thinking had made him realise that Maggie could help him with the +39 number. Considering she was already in Italy she should be able to access the location of the phone. All she had to do was triangulate the number by connecting its signal with the relevant phone towers. It was a simple geometric drawing of lines between masts. Wherever they crossed, that is where the phone would be. He had made up his mind to call her as soon as he got a break. He had not bargained on being escorted into a lunch gathering.

He could see Coach at the other end of the hall, engaged in energetic chatter with the Dragontails' manager, who was working hard to understand what Coach was saying in his strong, Glasgow accent through a mouthful of pizza. As Roddy navigated his way through the group, the television screens switched on. A loud crackle of music burst through the speakers.

Roddy was surprised to see Cardinal Damascus' face peer down at them. "Greetings to the world," he said. "It's my pleasure to speak to you all today. This is a great day for the Church and for our Galatians community."

The screens showed small images of other groups of gatherings. The name of the location was noted in the top corner of each. New York, London, Rome, Beijing, Sydney, Paris, and so on, covering most of the capitals and noteworthy cities across the world. No matter what time of day or night, people across the globe wanted to be part of this moment. What struck Roddy as even more unusual was that in many of the screenshots he could see large boxes like the ones in their hall.

The Cardinal's face came back on the screen. He had his hands in the air.

"Why is this such a great day? Well, we all know that we are between Popes. Our beloved John Paul II died earlier this month. God rest his soul. In a few days, there will be a Papal Conclave, when the cardinals will gather behind closed doors to elect our new leader. It is truly a great time in our Church's history. The first newly elected Pope in this new millennium will soon be announced."

He brought his hands together, bowed and prayed for a moment. The Galatians in the hall lowered their heads and prayed silently with him. Some non-Galatians joined in.

Looking up, the Cardinal continued. "To mark this incredible moment in our history, we have produced a new set of medals to commemorate the passing of Pope John Paul II and the election of our new Pontiff."

"Pope John Paul II led the Church with passion, humility and true empathy for the challenges facing the world. Please pray that our next Pontiff leads with wisdom and a sense of purpose - ready to change the unchangeable, tear down walls of division and hierarchy."

He rested his hands on the lectern and surveyed the group, before looking into the camera lens.

"I will be leaving for Rome in the coming days to join in the pre-conclave activities and spend time with my fellow Cardinals. Our main purpose is to select our next leader. I will then be locked behind the Vatican walls with over a hundred Cardinals. I am sure you appreciate just how much I am looking forward to that. Please remember me in your prayers."

He looked up as the Galatians in the room laughed and nodded knowingly. He smiled back at them. *"Each will have to bear his own load!"*

"Chapter six, verse five," was shouted from the back of the room. Somebody had beaten Brit to it this time.

"In the meantime, let's try and convince as many people as possible to believe in the true meaning of Christ. We want the message we are sending out to be embraced by everyone. With the same passion and faith Paul showed when he spoke to the Galatians."

Roddy saw several members of the group approach the boxes. They took them from the tables and opened the coverings. Soon they were handing out medals with slim bronze chains. After a few minutes they had covered most of the group in the hall. Roddy could see on the screens, the same thing happening in cities across the world.

The camera switched back to the Cardinal - his head lowered in a state of prayer. After ten minutes or so, everyone in the room had a new medal around their necks - the letter **G** glistening. They studied the medal, caressing it, turning it from side to side, enjoying the light shimmering on its surface.

"Ah, it warms my heart to see you all adorned with your new medals. Now, many of you will think that these are just like the ones the Galatians congregation were wearing already. Let me tell you, they are not. They are subtly different. Press the medal with your thumb and forefinger. Feel the tiny bumps underneath your skin. Close your eyes and enjoy the sensation it brings. Let yourself appreciate how the medal connects with you and your feelings. If it helps, keep your eyes shut, and let the moment linger."

Roddy looked around the room to see everyone doing what the Cardinal had asked. He decided to give it a go. Pressing his fingers onto the medal, he could feel tiny pin pricks under his skin. As he applied pressure, it was unmistakable. A pulsating throb rose from the metal, absorbed by his fingers. He let his eyes close and allowed his thoughts to drift to Angie and his father. Where he had felt panic and hopelessness, he began to experience a sensation of calm and optimism. A wave of positivity washed over him. He would have found it unnerving if it were not so uplifting. A growing determination that he would find a solution took over. Nothing was going to hold him back.

He opened his eyes and looked around the room and at the screens. Faces seemed different, somehow more relaxed. He was a few metres from Coach - his face had never seemed so youthful. He still looked ten years older than his age although that was better than the twenty years at the beginning of the quarter final.

He tucked the medal under his shirt, still on its chain. He approached his manager and tapped him on the arm, whispering. "Coach!"

Roddy waited. Coach's eyes were closed, head bowed.

"Coach!" he said more loudly.

He looked up and said, "Hey, how you doing?" as if he had not seen him minutes earlier.

"Fine. Would it be okay if I went to the sheriff's office again? I think I can help them."

"Sure, pal. Just make sure they come and pick you up. You need to be back for dinner at six."

"No problem. See you then."

Roddy manoeuvred his way through the large group, out into the hall. As he pressed Officer Brian's number on his phone, he could still feel the tingling in his fingers.

Triangulating

The call was drawing to a close. Wilson had gleaned what she needed. It was critical to move on now. She had not wanted to be impolite and finish the meeting soon after the information had been communicated - she also had not expected the call to disintegrate into the witty banter Celts engage in when left to their own devices. No nerve-ending was left untouched without being quipped upon or slurred - national football teams; which part of a city/country they came from; whose turn it was to buy dinner next time they met (they all agreed on that one - Crawford).

Her phone buzzed; it was Roddy. She put the mobile to her ear, waved goodbye and walked to the door.

"Hey, pal? How are things? Any news from Angie?"

"Nothing yet, Maggie. Listen, I've got something that might help you find her." He waited for her question.

"Really? I'm all ears - you do know I am in Italy, don't you?"

"Well, that's the thing. The person over here that's helping me dig into all this, well, he, em, he found a number in Italy connected to the Brazil number that was texting Angie. It had a +39 code."

"Now, that is interesting. Keep going."

He read out the number, which she scribbled down onto her notepad.

"My friend tried to locate it – but it's not possible from outside the country. He's wondering if you can do this from where you are."

Wilson waited a moment before responding. Roddy was working with a *stranger* in the US unearthing leads the police may not yet have become aware of. Her first instinct was to advise him to go to the local police and ask them to incorporate this into their investigation. She smiled. Family comes first. In this family, Roddy was showing himself to be a *chip off the old block* - even if he might not be in a hurry to accept it.

"Okay, leave it with me. By the way, what do these messages say?"

"Well, that's the thing. My friend said they were just texting each other a series of numbers. Maybe it's some sort of code. He's still working on it."

"Talented guy, this friend of yours. How do you know him again?"

"Oh, you know, Maggie. On social media you can meet lots of different people. Some you trust, some you don't. This guy is trustworthy, I can vouch for him." His heart had quickened. He did not need her taking this off track. He paused in the hope she had heard enough.

She had not. Although she knew when to stop and wait. "Okay. I'm on it. I'll call you back later. Please do me a favour. Keep the police over there close to this."

"Sure, will do," Roddy said. He had already decided he could only trust Maggie. He would not let anyone else in on this until he had an idea of what was going on.

Wilson knew what she had to do but was unsure how to do it. There was one person who could help her. She hit his number on her phone. It buzzed for a couple of seconds before a reassuring baritone Scottish voice answered. "Hello, DI Wilson?"

"Hi Sergeant McNeil. How are you?"

"All the better for hearing you," he said. She could hear Dvorak's New World Symphony playing in the background of his apartment.

She smiled and replied, "Ah, you're a charmer."

McNeil was her right-hand man back in Glasgow, helping her work through several complicated cases over the years. Since his early days as a *beat bobby*, he had excelled in any challenge the police put in front of him, relishing puzzle-solving nearly as much as finding a solution. One of the most intelligent officers she had worked with, he had a knack for hiding it surprisingly well. She had told him that once, and he took it as a compliment.

"So, how can I help you, Boss?"

"I have a mobile telephone number and I am in Italy. How can I locate it?"

She heard him take a drink. Probably an espresso. Too early for his favourite tipple at the end of a hard day's work, a shot of

Courvoisier. "All you need to do is find a signal tower receiving the strongest signal from the phone you're looking for, which of course has to be turned on. That gives you a radius within which the phone is located. Then you find two more signal towers receiving a signal from the same phone, draw radiuses around them too. And where all three radiuses meet, that's where the phone is. Quite easy if you have the technology which I'm sure the Italian Polizia will be able to help you with." She heard him sigh with the satisfaction he enjoyed when he explained a solution.

"Seriously, McNeil? Where do you think I've been hiding since mobile phones were invented?"

"Okay," he spoke slowly. "But I answered the question you asked."

He had a point, she realised. "I should have said: how do I find it without asking the local police to do it for me?"

"It's impossible. You'll need their help." He waited and then added. "I am sensing that's also not the answer you wanted to hear."

"You're not a police officer for nothing, Sergeant."

"Ouch, Boss. Bit harsh!" He did a good job of feigning hurt. She did not feel bad. He was so naturally smart; she was not worried he would be upset if she teased him.

"Okay, I need to go, McNeil. Thanks for your help."

"My pleasure. Just be careful, Boss."

She closed the call knowing that on top of his IQ, he also scored high on the EQ scales. She was quite sure he would have detected the anguish in her voice.

Sense of Urgency

"*Avanti!*" announced the Chief Commissioner.

Wilson entered the neat office, walls decorated with charcoal drawings of Rome's many attractions. She could smell the Gio aftershave as soon as she crossed the threshold. While she enjoyed a waft of scent like any woman, this was an onslaught on the senses.

"Hello, sir. I was wondering if you could help me with something."

"Sure. As I said, anything I can do." He pushed his chair back from the desk and pointed at the seat across from him.

"Well, we have a telephone number. It may be nothing, but my gut says we should investigate it."

"Really? Where did it come from?"

"During my review of the data, it popped up. I'm not overly confident it leads to anything; I just want to close it down." He did not need to know about Angie's disappearance. White lies were invented for situations like this.

"Can you show it to me?" He leaned across the desk.

She presented the page in her notebook.

"I see. Yes, it's a mobile number. I assume you want to triangulate the location."

"Yes, sir. Would that be okay?"

He was already dialling a number on his desk phone. A man's voice answered, "*Pronto!*"

Pisacane rattled off a request in staccato Italian into the speaker, enunciating the number at a measured pace. They could hear someone on the other end of the line tapping on a keyboard.

Pisacane tapped the mute button. "So, anything else, I should be aware of?"

"Well, yes, sir. We've tracked the holders of the accounts to Corleone in Sicily. Yes, I know." He had raised one eyebrow. She had only confirmed what he suspected.

"I wanted to ask if you could arrange a trip for me and Crawford to go there tomorrow morning."

"Yes, of course," Pisacane said. "You do know that you will be diving into the deep end of a shark infested tank." No shortage of melodrama there, she thought.

"Yes, I know. We have to meet the depositors and challenge them with the data we have collected. It's quite compelling."

"Compelling? Hmm." Pisacane picked up a biro and pointed it at his head. "A bullet can also be compelling, DI Wilson."

There was an edge to his tone she had not noticed before. She did not respond. He continued. "Leave it with me. I will arrange the trip for you. I will also connect you with the local police for support. They will meet you at the airport."

The speaker crackled, sparking off a verbal exchange between Pisacane and the officer.

"Officer Bonizzi will meet you downstairs at the entrance. He is tracking the number you gave us. Interestingly, it is not far from here. It is on the move, close to the Tiber. I suggest you move quickly."

Wilson shouted, "Grazie!" over her shoulder as she pivoted and ran out the door. Pisacane raised another eyebrow; he was pleased to see her enthusiasm, but sceptical as to why she was so eager to track down a clue she was not 'overly confident' about.

Castle of the Angel

The city of Rome is famous for an abundance of outstanding monuments and breathtaking architecture - Vatican, Colosseum, Forum, and the Vittorio Emanuele monument, some of which dated back more than two thousand years. Wilson and Crawford were in the backseat of a comfortable Alfa Romeo, speeding past the city's unique sites as if they were not there. Giovanni Bonizzi seemed to have a sixth sense as he guided the vehicle between cars, vespas and jaywalking pedestrians. He could not have been more than 25 years old - young enough to take pleasure from speeding through Rome's cobbled streets, siren blaring. The sprinkle of rain that afternoon exaggerated the slippage when he hurled the car around right-angled bends.

He was clearly a talented driver - which he had to be, considering he was only partially focused on managing the car. His attention was distracted by the monitor he had placed on the dashboard, as he tracked a yellow light flashing on screen.

"We are five minutes away! It's very close to Vatican City, moving along the banks of the Tiber." Bonizzi shouted over his shoulder. They could see the stunning form of Emperor Hadrian's nearly two millennium old mausoleum - Castel Sant' Angelo - silhouetted against the evening sky. The sun's downward drift signalled evening was approaching. Over the centuries the castle had been used as a tomb, a residence, a fortified castle, a prison and a setting for an opera. In any other city, this would have been the centre of attention. In Rome, the castle had to accept its place as a site visited on the way to the Vatican, if you had time.

The car swerved right to avoid three tourists strolling across the road, huddled over a map. Bonizzi missed them by a couple of metres - then took the opportunity to sound his horn and shout an obscenity through the window. The tourists stopped and waved at him. One of them had a camera in hand - capturing the high-speed police car in action.

"Turisti!" Bonizzi muttered - turning his attention to navigating the car towards *Ponte Sant'Angelo*, a formidable bridge as old as the castle.

"Signora Wilson! The phone is on the other side of the bridge. I will park the car up ahead. Then we need to run. Okay?"

"Sure, Giovanni. Ready when you are." Wilson looked at Crawford as they unbuckled their belts. She wondered what he was thinking. He had not asked about the telephone number clue they were following. He must be questioning what had prompted his boss to take it this far. Whatever he was contemplating, he had not hesitated in joining this unexpected, dramatic pursuit of a random yellow light on a satellite device.

The car screeched to a stop. Bonizzi grabbed the tracker and hurried out onto the sidewalk. He ran towards the castle. Wilson and Crawford were a few metres behind, working hard to keep up. When he reached the end of the bridge he turned left and sprinted down a stone staircase, leading to a walkway on the riverbank. They caught up with him at the bottom. He was kicking the wall of the two-thousand-year-old bridge.

"Va fa!" he shouted angrily.

"What is it?" she asked, trying to control her breathing.

"Look!" He lifted the tracker to show Wilson the light fading from the screen.

"What does it mean?"

"We are here, right where the light was last seen." He stabbed his finger in irritation at the screen. "They turned it off here at the river; or may have even thrown it into the water."

"Hold on. That means whoever had it must be nearby." She scanned the walkway and the stairs leading back to the bridge. She could see nobody of interest, just tourists.

She ran up the steps to the bridge, taking two at a time. She knew it would be useless, but she had to try. Crawford overtook her as they reached the top. He was fitter than he looked, she realised. Without speaking they ran in different directions. He sprinted back towards *centro storico* while she ran along the upper bank in the direction of the Vatican - a few hundred metres behind the castle.

After five minutes of running, she let out a loud screech, before kicking a discarded can of Coca-Cola along the pavement.

Her cry attracted the attention of a group of camera-toting tourists.

What was she even looking for? Was the suspect just going to walk along the upper bank with a t-shirt saying '*Hi, anyone who wants to find out - I know where Angie is*." This was beyond futile. She stopped and focused on controlling her breathing, leaning back against an ornate wall overlooking the river. She could see Giovanni below, sitting on the bottom step, twiddling dials on his scanner. He and Crawford would have reached the same conclusion she had. If they could not find the person holding the phone, then their search was futile.

The buzz in her pocket interrupted her thoughts. Roddy's name appeared on the screen. She felt a pang of guilt.

"Hi, Roddy," she began. "I've got bad n…"

"Maggie, we don't have time to lose. I know where they are."

Physics Can be Useful

Outside the church, Roddy dialled Officer Brian several times without an answer. In the end, the call went to voicemail. He was about to leave a message, when he felt a firm tap on the shoulder. He swivelled to see Coach Stone making a T-sign with his hands, shaking his head.

"Oh, sorry, Officer, will try again later. By the way, this is Roddy here."

He closed the phone. "Hi, Coach, what's up?"

"Roddy, I figured you were calling those police officers. Truth is, I made a decision. I can't let you bunk off. I know it's important to visit the sheriff's office, but I don't think they want you with them when they search for Angie."

"Coach, they need all the help they can get. They have no clues yet as to where she's gone."

"Well, that may be. You have to accept they are doing their best. Look, we can't stand here debating this. Because of everything that has happened here with Angie, you've not been doing your classwork."

Roddy rolled his eyes upwards. The feel-good factor of the Galatians medal had clearly worn off.

"Don't forget, part of the deal in coming here to the US is that the players all have to make sure they do their midterm homework. The rest of the team have been focused, but you haven't done anything yet from what I can tell." Coach had his hands on his hips, his posture showing this was not a debate.

Roddy sighed. Some battles were not worth fighting. "Okay, I get it. I'll go back to my room. But can we make a deal?"

"Sure, I'm listening."

"If we get any news about Angie, I can get involved again in helping the police."

"Fine," Coach answered. "Seems fair." He patted Roddy on the back.

Half an hour later, he was sat at his desk. He had taken care of the pre-homework set up. His books were open at the correct page. He had found a radio station playing non-stop Bruce Springsteen - *Can't Start a Fire* blasting from the speakers. His cup was filled with Irn-Bru - the real version. Coach had managed to convince the Irn-Bru distributor in Glasgow to sweet talk their US counterpart into shipping a week's worth of the soft drink to the campus.

His cup was a gift from his dad, a tongue in cheek present after last term's mock exam results. Roddy had performed well in English, Drama, Religious Studies and History. Less well in the sciences, most of all Physics. The surface of the cup displayed the Periodic Table of Elements, wrapped all the way round. He had enjoyed his father's cheekiness, although was less fond of the reminder of his knowledge gap.

During the midterm break he had to cover Energy and Gravitational Forces, and while the periodic table did little to help with those topics, it reminded him of his dad's encouragement - hence he had packed it in his case, stuffed inside and out with football socks to prevent it breaking.

As soon as he looked at the first formula in his revision book, $W = Fs$, his heart sank. Could someone not find a way to teach Physics by capitalising on the richness of the topics of energy and gravity? He enjoyed learning about these incredible forces. Yet academic institutions felt it better to camouflage it in numerous equations which, of course, required algebra - why not make it even more difficult? Then they would invent a bunch of words that meant something different in physics versus how they were used in everyday language. Why not just use some of those algebraic letters in different ways? *m* represents <u>metres</u> one minute - logically enough - and then <u>mass </u>the next. He still had to figure out why mass was different from weight - and did the 5 kg dumbbell in the gym really weigh 5 kg? Or should we really say that it had a mass of 5 kg. Physics just turned small, innocuous questions into gargantuan, frustrating problems.

He had already started to yawn: an involuntary spasm of his nervous system triggered by Physics in particular, homework in general. He took a large gulp of the Irn-Bru, hoping for a lift in his mood and *energy* levels - too close to the topic at hand to be funny, he mused.

Placing the cup back on the desk, he looked at the periodic table of abbreviated letters, representing the chemical elements. The fact that someone had numbered them in some sort of order made revision that bit more manageable. Each element had its own identity, characterised by an acronym and a number.

Where it came from, he did not know. It was not Hair o' the Dog. He had not touched it since the previous day. Maybe some still lurked in his system, although not enough for the eureka moment he was about to experience.

He stuck his hand into his backpack and searched around pushing aside confectionery wrappers and paper. He tugged his notebook from the inside pocket and leafed to the page where he had written down the exchange of texts. He looked at the surface of the cup, then back at the texts. Nothing extraordinary jumped out at him.

He searched through the periodic table for each of the numbers – finding that sometimes an element was signified by a single number, other times by a pairing of digits. Where he found the numbers, he wrote down the acronym connected to that specific periodic element.

+39 - *185323, 69188? - AR I V , TM ARRA ?*

+55 - *14 - S I*

+39 - *5052, 785216, 16197418, '7'61 - SN TE , PT TE S , S K WAR 7 P M*

+55 - *819 - O K*

He felt a wave of frustration at the futility of the exercise. An attempt to create hope from the jumbled letters and numbers of a periodic table was an indication of how desperate things had become.

Then he read the letters aloud, making sure to articulate each one slowly. The more he repeated them, the less disjointed they sounded. After several iterations, he shouted aloud, "Yes!"

His heart pounding, he turned the letters into meaningful words.

ARRIVE TOMORROW?

SI - he assumed was used for *YES*, since Y was only included on the periodic table once although had a b attached to it, rendering it useless. He imagined the senders used this code often

- they would have established short cuts and workarounds to compensate for the limitations of their chosen coding.

SAINT PETERS SQUARE 7 PM

OK

He was quite sure there were Saint Peter's Squares all over the world. Considering the +39 was an Italian number, he was convinced they would be referring to the most famous Saint Peter's Square in the world. The home of the world's largest church.

A rock's throw from where Wilson was working.

Needle in a Haystack

"Seven pm, Roddy, are you sure?"

"Yes, that's what my friend said."

"Did your friend say what or who I should be looking for?" Wilson had grabbed Crawford by the arm and was pulling him in the direction of Vatican City. It was hard to miss with St. Peter's immense, white dome dominating the skyline.

"Sorry. I have nothing else." Roddy's heart sank. He knew how vast the area was - the square was huge, and the cathedral a large, sprawling cocoon of altars, statues and naves. Adding swarms of pilgrims and tourists in their thousands, he realised how much of a dead-end clue he had given her.

"Okay, I'll let you know." She started running, Crawford alongside making the sprint look easy. They waved farewell to Bonizzi, sitting on the upper bank trying to connect with the phone. She could see that he felt somewhat responsible for not getting to the phone before it stopped signalling.

She felt the buzzing of the mobile in her pocket. Still running, she looked at the caller. Cesar Sampaio.

"Hello, Cesar?" she rasped into the phone.

They had just run onto the bottom end of *Via della Conciliazione*, a broad, majestic avenue, dominated by a row of commanding, flat-roofed buildings leading to the square. At its far end they could see St. Peter's Cathedral dictating the evening's ominous mood.

"Hi, DI Wilson, are you okay?" the heavy accent added a sincerity to the question.

"Yes, I'm running. All fine. Please, go ahead." They were beginning to attract attention the closer they came to the square. Some pilgrims smiled - others shook their heads at the disrespectful noise of their boots on the cobbles.

"Well, we looked at the CCTV footage of the airport and helipad area. It took us a long time to get it - the airport authority was quite obstinate. Anyway, we ran the tapes for Monday of this week, when Kiltman was travelling."

The suspense really was killing her. Her chest pounded with the exertion and rising futility of their pursuit of a random clue.

He continued. "The funny thing is, we did see him get on the helicopter to go to the prison. He was with Martim. When they came back later in the evening, Kiltman wasn't there."

"Oh, really?" She hunched down towards the pavement, her hand over an ear to block out the intensifying shouts and chants in the background.

"Yes. We looked at the route the chopper flew back from the prison. It was hard to track, as it flew just above the trees for some reason. Maybe issues with cabin pressure, who knows. It took a strange detour over the Amazon for a while. Then came straight back to São Paulo, no detours or landings anywhere en route."

"Very strange," she said. Although, it was consistent with Kenny not arriving at the spa resort.

"Yes, it's strange alright. Although that's not all. When the chopper arrived in São Paulo, there was another man with Martim."

She stood up and leant her back against a wall of one of the reddish buildings facing St. Peter's Cathedral. "Another man? Did you get a good look at him?"

"Not great. We could see that he was taller than Martim - who we know was already quite tall. He had a bushy black beard and hat pulled down over his head. Otherwise, there was nothing else of note." The height factor alone ruled out Kiltman.

"Could you see where he went?"

"No, there's no CCTV beyond the helipad exit. That's all we've got."

Her mind was racing - if they had not made any in-flight stops, then the stranger must have boarded at the prison.

"Did you check with the prison if they had someone else on the chopper?"

"Yes, we did already. Governor Fernandes told us that Kiltman left on the plane with the pilot. They had no-one else leaving the prison that day."

"Sure, maybe they hadn't scheduled someone to leave. That doesn't mean nobody boarded the chopper." This was basic policing - she was struggling to hide her growing sense of panic.

"Okay, I'll go back to them," Sampaio conceded.

"Thanks. Please call me as soon as you know." Crawford handed her a bottle of water. He had visited a drinks kiosk, nestled in the corner of the square. Before she put the phone away, she checked the time. 6.50 pm.

She yanked the top off the bottle - and necked the entire contents, some droplets drifting down her chin onto her top. Without thinking Crawford reached across and dabbed a napkin on her chin.

"Seriously?" she asked, shaking her head.

"Oh, sorry, I wasn't thinking." Crawford put the tissue back in his pocket. He liked to keep souvenirs from the cases he worked on.

"Look, there are some perps - maybe two, maybe more - meeting in the square at 7pm," she said. Crawford waited for some additional guidance. "That's it. All I've got."

"Eh, okay. Just a wee bit more would help."

"No. Nothing. Crawford, this is your chance to show me what you can do. Look for the sinister, the unusual, the out of place. Keep your phone handy. I'll work my way through the left side, you go right."

They stood and looked ahead at the square, daunted by the crowd of people carrying crosses and banners, chanting and singing. Wilson noticed many of them carried messages of hope and love. Others referenced the passing of Pope John Paul II with drawings of hearts and crosses. She realised that of all days to try and find a clue in this sprawling square, the days after a Pope has died were not the ones to choose. There was an air of expectancy; similar to a maternity waiting room before a baby is delivered, with thousands of people thrown in. She knew that a Papal Conclave would start in a few days to bring the cardinals together to vote on the new Pope. People had begun to accumulate to prepare for the decision that would result in a new leader.

"Needle in a haystack comes to mind," Crawford said rubbing his head with the palm of his hand.

Wilson paused for a moment, looking at the *haystack* widening out in front of them towards the colonnades on either side. Without warning, she smacked her hand off his back. "You're a genius!"

"Sorry?" he asked. "Am I?"

"Yes. I think so." She smiled. "If you were going to meet someone in a busy square like this, where would you plan to meet them?"

He scanned the square. From the curved rows of columns to the Basilica in front. None of the columns stood out as unique. The front of the cathedral itself was full of people leaving through its large bronze doors. Too frenetic for a meeting spot. His eyes were drawn to the large obelisk planted smack in the middle of the circular square. In the shape of an upturned, pointed needle, it represented another era in humanity, long before Christians were making their presence felt. He recalled reading about the obelisk's history. Stolen by the Romans from Egypt two thousand years earlier, it was estimated to be around four thousand years old.

At 40 metres tall, it was so large it somehow avoided notice. Like electricity pylons on a country landscape. The mind blocked them out - until someone mentioned them.

Pointing towards it, he said, "That's where I would choose to meet."

"Exactly - I agree. You go round the right side, I'll go left. See you at the obelisk."

They both set off on their separate paths, weaving and jostling through the crowds. The chanting and praying increased in intensity the closer to the centre they progressed.

Wilson's mind was bursting – too much to think about. Kiltman had somehow been replaced by this unknown man. She had not fully engaged gear on the Sacco case - yet she was flying to Sicily in the morning. Now she was following up on a clue - a fragment of a clue in reality - that had been given to them by a 'friend' of Roddy's in the US to help find Angie. She was beginning to feel overwhelmed.

She hoped their hunch about the needle would not be pointless.

St. Peter's

The closer she ran towards the obelisk, the thicker the crowd became. People seemed happy to be standing shoulder to shoulder, singing and chanting. Initially the banners and placards were indiscriminate in praising God and thanking Pope John Paul II for his leadership. As she squeezed between the hordes, she noticed more of the signs above their heads were dedicated to specific Cardinals.

There was a slew of names which seemed to cover countries across the globe, held up by people of varying ethnicities. Several appeared more often than the others: Martini, Bergoglio, Ratzinger and Damascus. None of the names meant anything to her, although she could see from the energy in the crowd, they inspired passion in many of the pilgrims.

The congestion exacerbated the futility of the quest. She was recognised as a good cop, renowned for her ability to read faces and get behind the mask of poker-faced criminals. This skill, while useful in a police interrogation room, was less helpful in a wide-open space crammed with thousands of faces, intent on praying for divine intervention.

She reached the obelisk in less than a minute. From a distance it appeared diminutive against the backdrop of St. Peter's Basilica. Now from below, it towered above her, reaching as high as 13 floors in height. Around its base, several large, evenly separated stones defined the base of this grandiose Egyptian plunder. She placed her leg on the nearest and leveraged herself up onto it, allowing her to see above the heads in the square. To avoid slipping from the curved stone she placed her hand on a random pilgrim's shoulder. He was so caught up in the frenzy of the singing, he did not notice.

The basilica bells clanged out the time, seven pm. Even with thousands of noisy pilgrims, the ringing dominated the atmosphere. Dusk was already settling in, making it difficult to discern faces in the distance. Her line of vision was just high enough to allow her to see Crawford on the other side of the obelisk standing on a similar stone. He was waving at her. So much for remaining incognito.

His gesticulations seemed more energetic than a cursory greeting. She realised he was pointing at something or someone in the crowd. His other hand was waving her to come over to his position. Her eyes had adjusted to the light – his face was lit up with excitement.

She jumped down onto the cobbles and weaved her way round the obelisk. It seemed to take forever to wiggle her petite frame through the tiny spaces available among the swaying and dancing crowd.

She had just reached the stone he had been standing on, when she heard the first screams. At first, she had thought they were high-pitched, tuneless chants. The cries and shouts were soon followed by a surge in movement, terror filling the air. People were running to the edges of the square away from the obelisk.

"Crawford! Crawford!" The panic in her voice surprised her, she sensed her partner was in trouble. He did not answer. She kept shouting until she rounded a group of pilgrims hurrying away from the obelisk.

He was lying on the cobblestones, blood-soaked hands clutching his stomach. A couple of pilgrims, a man and woman, wearing blood-stained Cardinal Damascus t-shirts, were on the ground bent over him. The woman looked up as she saw Wilson run towards them. Not much older than twenty, she shook her head from side to side as she pushed her hands down on his wound. The man had a phone at his ear shouting in Italian. It took just a few seconds, before Wilson heard the wailing of a siren.

She dropped down onto her knees and put her hand under his head. His face was white, bottom lip trembling.

"I'm here, Crawford. An ambulance is on its way. Hold on, please hold on!" Wilson did not care about the tears rolling down her cheeks. She could not think in a straight line, so many thoughts competing for priority.

On hearing her voice, Crawford reached across and grabbed her arm. His bloodied hand wrapped around her wrist. Turning to her, pain and panic in his face, he croaked, "Mask! I saw Mask! He has a girl." The strength of his grip weakened with each word. His hand fell back down onto a reddened cobble, and his eyes closed.

Friday, April 15

Glasgow in the Amazon

The bitter scent of acridity filled his nostrils. His consciousness - absent for days - sputtered to life with a series of rasping coughs. He forced his eyes open - smarting against the sharpness of the light. The noises around him were unrecognisable - yet they had become a source of comfort and calm in between long, delirious sleeps. The gentle thump of a cushioned drum beat to a tune hummed by several voices, harmonising imaginative, gentle rhythms.

Words were choked by the dryness in his throat. A hand prised apart his chafed lips and poured water onto his tongue. He heard an energetic wave of clicks and whistles - mesmerisingly tuneful. He knew it was time to open his eyes fully: the darkness of the last few days had become too comfortable.

Hands touched and rubbed his arms and legs, soothing his muscles into life. From his horizontal position he was able to take in a group of five people, men and women. They were naked save for fragments of covering, attached with twine. Their hair and features were dark, their skin a golden brown. As his eyes adjusted to the light, he could see more clearly. Handsome and beautiful, male and female, their faces benign and innocent - wide, dark eyes revealing their mutual concern for their unexpected visitor.

"Where am I?" Kiltman asked.

As hackneyed a phrase as it may have been, the question inspired a high degree of activity and sound around him. A cascade of clicks and whistles met his question. He realised the sounds were coming from their mouths, directed at him.

"Do you speak English?" he tried.

The sounds began to abate. Some of them tried to copy what he said, but they could not get beyond whistles and clicks. He reached out his hand. They helped him into a standing position, although his legs were weak and unsteady. Arms wrapped around his waist as they moved him forward urging him to take steps.

They were inside a tent made of tree bark covered with thick, long leaves. At its entrance a row of long, trailing branches dangled down to the floor. He moved his legs forward, feeling his muscles and ligaments strain with the effort. His right knee - usually the slowest part of his body to awaken - made a loud snap, reverberating off the walls. A cheer erupted from his helpers, with a raucous barrage of laughs and giggles. Followed by excited whistles and clicks. If knee cracking was such fun, he knew a lot of ex-footballers back in Glasgow that could entertain them for hours on end.

Stepping out into the open, the heat and humidity slapped him in the face like a hot, wet flannel. He had never felt such intensity on his skin. Beside him two men, small in height, powerful in stature, carried large, chunky leaves. As they waved them above his head, they produced heavy, cool droplets of water that fell onto his scalp and shoulders. Facing him, over an area no bigger than an acre, a sprinkling of tents like the one he had just left covered an uneven patch of land.

Whatever activity had been going on before he stepped outside had stopped. A group of people were crouched down in front of him, heads bowed, hands placed flat on the earth. A young child, half Roddy's age, walked up to him and took his hand. He led Kiltman to a makeshift wall that had been created from the inside of bark. It had been flattened and rolled, attached to a tree on either side, akin to a large, wooden manuscript. Kiltman enjoyed the softness of the boy's hand – it brought back long-ago memories of when he walked with Roddy along the canal at home, feeding swans and waving at neighbours. A pang of sadness washed over him.

The boy pointed at the wall - pictures had been drawn from left to right. He touched his thumb against his chest with a look any seven-year-old would make, proud of his art. Kiltman rubbed his head, mussing up his hair playfully.

The boy placed his hand on the first picture. It showed a bright, orange sun beating a strong beam down onto the trees below – broccoli trees, just like Kiltman saw them. The next was of a person flying from the sun across the sky, a cape flailing behind him. The kilt and sporran were unmistakeable - the criss-crossing tartan drawn skilfully.

He moved his eyes along the wall to a drawing of a large, round bird. It had sharp, sabre teeth, wild eyes and flaring nostrils. Above its head had been drawn a messy cluster of long lines – a chopper's blades. A similar bunch of swirling, stripy marks were drawn where its tail should have been.

The next picture showed the flying man in the kilt and cape fighting the savage bird, his hands and feet delivering blows to the body and head. The final picture depicted the bird flying off into the distance with the man falling lifeless through the trees.

The group had been silent, waiting for him to digest the picture and its story. He turned to the boy, put his hands together in a flat prayerful shape, and bowed his head. This act spurred a degree of clamour from everyone. They sensed their guest's appreciation of the drawing, shouting and calling. The boy could not contain his excitement, jumping and twirling.

Kiltman pointed at the sun, and said, "How many days am I here?" He rolled his arms over each other and pointed at the sun again. He counted along each finger. "One, two, three." When he said a number and showed an extra digit, he hoped they would stop him. "Four, five."

At the show of five fingers - five appearances of the sun - they delivered a loud response of whistles and clicks. Five days. It was now Friday - Mask had been on the loose since Monday. The feeling of anxiety welling inside him threatened to manifest itself as a scream. He could not let that happen. He had to stay calm - he sensed that the more dignified he appeared, the more respect and support he could rely on.

It took a couple of minutes for calm to return, during which time Kiltman came to realise he was standing completely naked in front of twenty to thirty people.

He looked at his body as if seeing it for the first time. He had hardly registered the embarrassment of his nudity, when he caught his breath. His trunk was a mess of scratches and bruises, strips of flesh torn from his legs and arms. He brought his arm close to his face to look at a deep wound above the elbow. There was a veneer of thick, gooey liquid spread over the top of his wounds. Touching it with a forefinger, it felt sticky, a texture not dissimilar to a liquified version of Play-Doh.

A man slightly taller than the boy approached him and bowed his head. His hair was much longer than the rest, its tresses intertwined with leaves and berries. He whistled and clicked a series of utterances. Reaching across, the man rubbed some of the goo on Kiltman's wounds back into the wound, inserting his finger into an open wound to push the mush down deeper. All the time, he nodded and smiled.

Something was missing.

Kiltman realised that with all these wounds and abrasions - especially the touch of this man - he should be in an enormous amount of pain. In fact, he felt nothing; other than a feel-good sense of energy that was inexplicable. Whatever they had rubbed onto him had a healing power like nothing he had experienced before.

The man handed him a leaf – and placed his fingers in his mouth to demonstrate eating. Kiltman took the leaf and placed it on his tongue. At first it burned like a spicy, peppercorn sauce. Followed by a soothing, sweet taste. A few seconds later, he felt his wounds tingle - not with pain, but with a welcome sense of healing. Whatever they had given him was not yet available at his local pharmacy - of that, he had no doubt.

The boy whistled and clicked at Kiltman, then pointed behind him at a couple of trees. A long piece of twine had been tied between the two thick trunks. It drooped with the weight of the items hanging there. A cape with the saltire barely recognisable - although stitched back into the shape the villagers thought it should have been. After their best efforts they had turned the Scottish flag into a Pisces sign of the zodiac. His top with the KM sign on its chest was in better shape, although that had also been sewn back together - KM now appeared more like XL. Back home he would have said, 'just my age and trouser size'.

The mask - which had triggered the fight with his nemesis of the same name - was intact, dangling beside the kilt. His kilt had survived quite well, its edges in tatters, but largely wearable. There was still enough length to cover his privates, although considering he was living everyone's worst nightmare, this was suddenly less important.

He looked at his sporran dangling from the twine. The chain had snapped, replaced with a thick, twine rope. He walked towards the line, his heart beating faster with each step. Lifting the sporran, he moved to enter the code, 1402, to spring its catch open. It was already unlocked. Its lightness should have told him already - it was empty. The catch had been snapped; its contents lost.

Realising his task to get home had become much more difficult, he snatched the kilt from the line, before wrapping it around his waist. While it did not compensate for the loss of Hair o' the Dog, the empowerment of donning Scotland's national costume transcended his dilemma. Naked, stuck in a remote clearing of the Amazon rainforest, far from his family who were in mortal danger. One kilt later, self-assurance, confidence and sense of purpose were all back on track. More or less.

As he pulled his top on, he felt a tap on his shoulder. An elderly man with a strong physique and a lined, thoughtful face held a shiny object high in the air above his head. Kiltman put his hand over his eyes to shield a flash of sun glinting off its surface. It was his flask. He reached across to take it, enjoying its welcome weightiness. It was still full.

"Thank you! Thank you!" he said. Without thinking it through, he pulled the man into a hug. The eruption of noise and clamour froze him mid-cuddle. The man clicked and whistled with excitement, flapping his arms in the air in a growing sense of panic.

Kiltman stepped back, bowed and said, "Sorry. I am so sorry. I got carried away." The clamour eased and voices returned to silence. The tension was palpable.

Until the boy contorted his mouth into a strange position and blurted out, "So -eh…Aye so - saw -eh. Go ca-heed ha-way!"

A cacophony of laughter followed - everyone trying to copy the words the boy had repeated in as near perfect a rendition of a Glasgow accent to be found west of Rio.

Escaping the Jungle

Back in the tent, he sat down to a feast of vegetables, meats and fish. He did not recognise any of the contents and was not in a hurry to ask. Language barriers were sometimes useful. He tucked into his first meal since Darius' tasty ice cream, realising this may be his last for as long as it took to get to his next destination.

There were four men and a woman there too. They were kneeling, heads bowed, passing him food and water. He placed his thumbs in the air. "This is very good. Yummy!" He rubbed his stomach.

His hosts raised their thumbs and rubbed their tummies, giggling innocently. They turned back to lowering their heads, whispering to each other in clicks and whistles.

He was fighting the growing sense of angst. Mask had escaped. His threats to Fiona, Roddy and Angie had been clear. Kiltman had no way of communicating with anyone outside of the tent. His phone was somewhere in the Amazonian jungle, or in the belly of a fish.

He had taken a drink of Hair o' the Dog – its restorative powers had already kicked in, in addition to whatever drugs and potions he had received from his new friends. He looked like a walking corpse, yet felt strong and energised. His clothing and cape added to the sense of the living dead - stitching akin to Frankenstein's monster.

His internal navigational antenna, thanks to a mouthful of Hair o' the Dog, was now on full power. He had been able to identify where he was: latitude -5.70194 and longitude -68.025. One of the gifts his special whisky gave him was to know exactly where he was at any point in time on the world grid. It struck him that in the current situation, this knowledge was like knowing the size and circumference of a tin of beans. Not very helpful when you want to open the tin and eat the contents. It also struck him that this metaphor - with the advent of ring pulls - had reached its sell-by date.

The tent floor was covered in a grainy sand-like surface. He bent down and used his finger to draw a map of Brazil. He took a berry from the table and placed it on the latitudinal-longitudinal coordinates of where they were. It was in the West, not far from the Peru border - nowhere near anywhere resembling a town or city with the communication or transport he needed.

He pointed at the berry, making a circular sweep of his hand. "We are here."

The faces remained blank.

He was not surprised at their lack of response. He had heard of tribes of Amazonians who had never met anyone from the cities or towns. They lived in the ways of old – traditions and customs intertwined with their desire for survival in a harsh climate. There was nothing around him or on his walk in the village that indicated any exposure to the outside world. Everything they wore, ate or used as tools came from their surroundings. Even the medicine that had saved his life was 'homegrown'.

He put his hand on his chest. "Me must go." He then stood and walked on the spot, striding, moving his arms. He made an inquisitive face, and said, "Hmm. Where can I go?"

One of the men stood and pointed at him. He sounded a few whistles and clicks and flapped his arms, imitating a bird flying at speed.

"Eh, no. Not fly, I." Kiltman shook his head and flattened his arms against his sides. If they did not follow English, then pidginising was not going to make him more understandable.

He bent down to the ground again and drew a picture of various stick people – two tall and two small. "My family!" He wrapped his arms around himself, closed his eyes and said, "Aaah!"

The group became excited. They spoke to each other for a moment, before standing and making a circle around him. He felt he was getting through to them. As one, they stepped forward and wrapped their arms around him, humming, "Aaah!"

Or maybe he was not getting through to them. He decided to wait a few moments before extricating himself – although the group hug had proved to be just what he needed.

Once they were all sitting back on the floor, he drew a line through the map. His powers allowed him to remember infinitesimal details from maps and charts. He drew a snaking, curved line in sand around the town and said, "Is there a river here?" He made sure to depict the curves and bends of the river local to their village. He picked up a cup of water and poured it onto his cupped hand. To make sure they followed, he drew a fish.

Whether it was his artistry or his map drawing, he did not know. They grabbed him by the arm and pulled him out through the entrance. Walking behind the tent, they led him to a cluster of trees that created a natural barrier around the village. The villagers ran through the foliage, ducking underneath dangling branches and leaves. He struggled to keep up with them weaving through the tress. After a minute he heard the pounding of a fast-flowing river, its powerful current pulling shrubbery from the banks. He walked out onto a small clearing to watch it cascade past them. A woman pointed at the sky, then at Kiltman and finally at the river. The water had broken his landing. The torrent of the flow was so strong, he had hit a moving target. Like falling onto a downward elevator, minimising the full force of the impact.

Kiltman blew a kiss at the river. "Thank you!"

As he was growing to expect, the villagers joined in and blew their own kisses. "Da-koo!" Followed by another surge of laughter, whistles and clicks.

One of the men walked towards a clearing further up the river. He beckoned with his hand for them to follow. Rounding another cluster of trees, he pointed into the bushes. Nestled under drooping branches and vines, a small boat sat lopsided on the bank. Kiltman could only assume it must have floated down towards them from somewhere upstream.

It was a 15-footer. Not made of bark or local materials. A real boat, equipped with an engine. The marks where it had been dragged up onto the bank were still visible. Its name had been painted in red flowing letters on its side, Esperança, meaning *Hope*.

He climbed up into the cabin and looked around. It was in reasonable condition. There were no holes to indicate it would not be seaworthy. Under one of the cushioned seats beside the steering wheel, he found the battery. As expected, it was flat. Placing a hand over the connection points, he closed his eyes and summoned Hair o' the Dog's potency. He had started a car battery at home once in the middle of winter in a similar fashion. This task was just the same - absent the snow and biting winds.

It took a few moments and sapped much of his strength, but he kept his hand there until the battery reignited. He could feel the power build inside. All he needed was enough to ignite the engine. It would take care of itself after that. He pushed a couple of buttons on the dashboard and the boat's engine kicked into life. It let out a slow, gentle tremor of energy.

Standing from his crouched position in the boat, he turned to find the villagers looking at him. Several others had come to join them. They were whistling and clicking realising something inexplicable had happened. He had just confirmed his divineness with superhuman abilities reserved for the Gods.

He pointed at the boat and then at himself. "Please may I take the boat?"

They nodded in unison, and said, "Pee -lees mai tek bo."

He smiled and bowed in thanks at their generosity - thinking that imitation is sincerest after fixing a flat battery.

Pasta alla Paura

Mask ran water over the knife for several minutes, confining DNA remnants through the plughole into pipes deep beneath Rome's affluent Northern district of Tomba di Nerone. Escaping the square had proved more difficult than expected. Thousands of people and near hysteria over papal elections had been challenging enough. He had not bargained on the wannabe policeman spotting him. He could see him signalling to Wilson. How they had tracked him made no sense. His disappearance from prison had not been discovered. Something did not add up.

The knife had been a precaution he did not expect to employ. The man had made the mistake of advertising his presence. He was surprised Wilson was working with someone so naïve. Although smiled at the realisation she had no choice - her old partner would have been consumed by piranhas or jaguars.

He turned on the TV when they arrived at their temporary home on the outskirts of Rome. RAI TV reported the incident at the beginning of the news bulletin. The victim had been taken to a local hospital, had lost a lot of blood and was critically ill in a coma. His chances of survival were slim, according to the correspondent. Mask shrugged, annoyed that he had not finished him off. If they did not have such a busy agenda in the coming days, he would have considered paying a visit to the hospital. *A job done well, is a well-done job.* His father - Alois, named after Hitler's father - had shouted that at him with every slap of the leather belt.

He dried the knife on a towel, before slipping it back into the holder beneath his sock.

"Father?" Angie was holding a plate of steaming pasta topped with pesto sauce, sprinkled with cheese. She was working hard to conceal her fear for this man who was proud to be her parent - she had to do whatever he asked. She had witnessed him plunge the knife into the man's stomach, without a hint of remorse or care. Fiona and Roddy could not fall victim to a similar act.

He took it from her and walked to the kitchen table - to join his accomplice. Angie had already given the other man a plate of food.

which he had been toying with his fork. He had barely eaten any of it.

This man, who had introduced himself as *Tantalus*, carried an aura of restrained power she had never seen before. He said little but when he spoke, she saw that her father paid close attention. His long, grey beard and tied back hair added a sense of sixties hippy. From an early age she had loved the Rolling Stones – spending many hours studying the birth of modern rock and the culture it had inspired. Hence the decision to change her name from Agnes to Angie.

"Next time, Arnalda, less salt." Tantalus spoke in a refined, cutglass English accent. He nodded at the plate. "You need to know that you can never remove salt, while you can always add more." He looked at her directly. "Do you know what I am saying?"

"Eh, yes, sir," she answered. She had sat down at the table, placing her hands below her legs to stop them shaking. "You mean that when we do something, we should do it cautiously. We should not overcommit too soon."

Tantalus slapped the table with the flat of his hand and roared with laughter. "No, young girl. I mean, make sure not to put too much salt in pasta when you boil it! Why does everything have to mean something sinister and deep? You are spending too much time with your father." He continued to laugh until he could see Mask readying himself for a conversation.

"Are you sure everything is ready?" Mask asked once Tantalus had calmed down.

"Yes, his flight arrives at 8.30 am tomorrow morning. This is the beginning of the next and final chapter in our adventure." He ate a forkful of pasta before wiping the side of his bowl with a lump of bread. He took a long, slow drink of red wine, then released a loud belch. Angie struggled not to lift a napkin to her nose.

Mask nodded. He raised his glass in the air. Tantalus lifted his and touched it to Mask's. They both looked at Angie. She took a deep breath and lifted her beaker of water, nestling it against theirs.

Here is to the next Pope." Tantalus announced.

"Ad multos annos," Mask responded, smiling at Angie.

"Pope Damascus," the two men said in unison.

Intensive Care

In the two hours spent at his bedside, she had struggled to shift her gaze from the wall above his head, where monitors recorded his vitals. He was alive but only just - the machines were doing all the work for him. Pumping and extracting. His family had been notified - parents on their way from Scotland. She hoped they would arrive on time.

The doctors had been frank - they had never seen so much blood loss without death. The knife had penetrated deep into his stomach, causing significant damage to the intestinal walls. One of the doctors, more senior than the others, had tended to Pope John Paul II's wounds when he was shot in the abdomen in 1981. He held Wilson's hand like a close friend and said, "Our dear Pope also lost a tremendous amount of blood in St. Peter's Square. While we doctors did all we could to save him, we know it was a miracle that he survived. Pure and simple. A miracle."

She knew what he was saying. Crawford needed a miracle.

Her phone buzzed. Pisacane's number appeared on screen.

She rose from the chair and rubbed Crawford's foot gently before ducking around the olive-green curtain protecting them from prying reporters. "Hello, sir."

"Okay, DI Wilson. Let me be clear with you. You have not conducted yourself in a manner I would consider acceptable."

"Sorry? What do you mean?" She was surprised at his tone. He seemed to have ditched the smooth, calm, controlled Chief manner. Maybe he had taken a mini course in Gemmill leadership.

"You run around Rome chasing phone signals, pretending to me and my team you are working on the Sacco case. Then you wander into a volatile situation in St. Peter's Square, unprepared for the outcomes. With no back up: and to be blunt, no plan." She could hear the anger burning down the phone.

"Look... Sir!" Pressure was building in her temples. "I am at the bedside of my colleague. He is within a millimetre of losing his life. Each breath is a bonus. I really don't care what you think at the moment, to be quite honest. I am a police officer. I don't just switch off one investigation because another one starts. It is called good policing. You should try it!"

She had gone too far – she would kick herself later, she knew it.

His intake of break was muffled, but unmistakable.

"I am sorry," he said. She waited, she sensed he had more to say. "I truly am. How is your colleague?"

"Very bad shape, Sir, to be honest. It's touch and go."

"I will pray for him. He seemed to be a good man, someone you relied on."

She fought back the tears, focused on controlling her voice. "Yes, I did." She hated talking in past tense about this young man lying on the bed. She had overstepped the mark in taking him with her in chasing the phone signal. He was not a police officer. He had no training. Just a cordial accountant with a flair for forensics.

"Sir, I wanted to tell you. I am travelling to Sicily tomorrow morning. Obviously, you should cancel Crawford's flight, I am still going." She brought a sleeve up to her cheek and rubbed at a tear escaping the corner of her eye.

"That will not be necessary. We will make alternative plans." His voice had returned to his usual formality.

"I insist. Crawford worked hard on this case. Yes, you are right. I distracted him onto another investigation. I will carry that burden; and deal with it in my own time." Practically and also emotionally. When that was, she had no idea. "I know he would want me to follow through on the Mafia capos and take this lead as far as I can. That is what I intend to do."

"Okay, I will not try and convince you otherwise. I admire your resolve. Above all..." he paused to find the correct words, "your passion and loyalty. You have just put me in my place in this call. Not many people would have dared to do so. You did. Because you care. I cannot ask for more than that. Keep me informed. Good luck."

The line went dead.

Before she could digest the call, the door to the room opened. A pretty young woman with dark brown eyes and long chestnut coloured hair walked in. Her eyes were moist and nose red - tissues stuffed into the sleeves of her blouse.

"Is Crawford here?" she asked.

"Yes," Wilson answered, shielding the curtain surrounding the bed. "Who are you?"

"I am a friend."

"Friend?" Wilson was on guard.

She opened her bag and produced a cardboard box. Lifting it to Wilson's face, she said timidly. "I know you love cannoli. Crawford told me you are a wonderful woman."

Despite herself and all the years of training, Wilson's tears flowed freely. The girl did not need encouragement - she too began to weep uncontrollably.

"Ah, you must be Valentina," Wilson said, taking her into a hug.

News

Wilson sat in front of the hotel TV, barely registering the news. She had switched from the energetic, entertaining Italian RAI channel to the more sedate, highbrow BBC. Grant had somehow shown up in Rome with the backdrop of St. Peter's dome, and a look of severity on his face he reserved for serious reports.

Back in Uisge Beatha, she and Kenny would have fun watching Grant deliver a news piece. They would guess what type of story it was going to be based on how he furrowed his brow or leveraged the dimple on his right cheek. She remembered Kenny saying, 'Grant had a face that launched a thousand stories'.

Grant spent a few minutes covering the 'Vatican Square Stabbing' withholding the name of the *British subject*. It would not be long before he connected Crawford to her. It was just as well she was going to Sicily in the morning. The last thing she needed was for Grant to be on her tail. It was difficult enough responding to questions she had the answers to. Right now, she was more or less clueless – not a great place for a police officer to be when she had three separate crimes on the go. Two of which were already personal, and a third that had just become personal.

Grant felt relaxed today. Dominic Gallagher had a doctor's appointment. He had not been looking forward to reporting from the Vatican. His boss was a pious man who attended mass every Sunday, and during the week whenever possible. Grant knew he would be hypersensitive about any reporting from Rome.

Grant coughed and looked into the camera.

"Rome is really where it's all happening right now." He looked at the camera and paused to let it sink in. "A Papal Conclave has been called to elect a new Pope. As you can see from the people in the square behind me, there is as much campaigning as there is praying today."

The camera scanned the square focusing in on pilgrims and their banners. Despite being late evening, more people appeared to have gathered - Crawford's stabbing had not deterred the crowds.

"A Papal Conclave is a rare event where the College of Cardinals come together to elect a new Pope. Any Cardinals aged 80 or older when Pope John Paul II died are excluded. That still leaves more than 100 who will be voting. The date has been set for the conclave to begin - Monday, April 18, three days' time.

"Over the centuries, these meetings have lasted from a couple of days to months. Although in recent Papal elections, a result has usually been announced in a few days. The Cardinals will lock themselves away in the Vatican, with voting to take place in the incredibly beautiful and famous Sistine Chapel, Michelangelo's Last Judgement painted on the wall above the altar and his Creation of Adam on the ceiling." He paused and let the camera turn back to him. "No pressure, eh?" He laughed despite himself.

"Word on the street here in Vatican City is that there are four real contenders." He touched his ear to acknowledge that he heard the comment - 'this is not a sports bulletin, be respectful'. While Dominic was not there, the assistant producer was not going to let Grant off the leash.

"Sorry, I meant to say, potential candidates for new Pontiff." Not perfect but would have to do, he thought. A picture of an elderly man in Cardinal's robes appeared top right of the screen.

"Cardinal Martini, the Archbishop of Milan. Famous for his liberal views, an advocate for change in the church. Some believe it may be too soon for many of the other Cardinals to vote for him. Although others say he does not go far enough. He divides opinion. While some hope he could create fertile ground for change, others fear radical adjustment could break the church."

He waited a moment before turning the page on his notepad. The photo on the TV changed at the same time to another elderly man, this time in clothing humbler than the prior picture.

"Then there is Cardinal Bergoglio, who comes from Argentina and has lived through some of the most difficult periods in that country's troubled history. Known for his strong desire and initiatives to help the poor, he has chosen a simple, modest lifestyle - rejecting the pomp and ceremony that normally comes with a Cardinal position. Some say he emulates Saint Francis of Assisi, who walked away from family wealth to embrace a life of poverty. He is considered to be a strong candidate, although some say potentially too liberal. Others acknowledge that even if he doesn't make it this time, he could make it the next. The only issue is whether another conclave will happen in his lifetime."

Grant turned another page and on cue, the picture changed to a rather sombre man, who appeared older than Martini and Bergoglio, dressed in eye-catching, red robes.

"Next is Cardinal Ratzinger, widely considered to be the favourite in the competition… I mean, the Papal election. For many years he has been a close friend of the previous Pope, some would say, a confidante. More traditional than Bergoglio and Martini, he is seen as a safe pair of hands, to counterbalance some of the more liberal and forward-thinking advocates for change in the church.

"Which brings me onto our last but not least," Grant was enjoying this way too much, she thought, as she opened a bottle of red wine from the mini bar. One small 33 cl bottle would do no harm. A picture of the next papal candidate appeared on screen. Dressed in simple priest's clothes, a man stood with his hands clasped in front of him. Significantly younger than the other cardinals, he was handsome with a charismatic smile.

"Cardinal Damascus is relatively unknown across the world, although he is a rising figure in the church in the USA. Born at the end of the Second World War - an orphaned, refugee baby - he was smuggled into the US by a soldier. From those humble beginnings, he is now seen to represent the face of change that many in the church desire. He is the head of the Galatians congregation, a sect within the church that asks its followers to see Christ and the church through the eyes of St. Paul when he wrote to the Galatians two thousand years ago. In the words of a source close to the Vatican, he wants to rip up the play book and start again. He has said, and I quote, '*we must renounce tradition and the abundance of formalities surrounding today's church. Let's break down the obstacles we put in our own way and embrace the true message*'.

"Some compare him to Cardinal Martini and his quest for a more liberal church. However, the difference seems to be that Cardinal Damascus is not a liberal intent on keeping up with the world's social evolution. Rather, he wants to go back to the original message of Christ and embrace the true essence of Christianity. He is considered to be a *retro-liberal*, which sounds like a contradiction in terms, but seems to sum up what this Cardinal is all about. He has been known to say he wants to free the Church from the burden of rules and regulations that inhibit it from being what it was meant to be. Rather than be seen as a formidable, powerful Mountain, the Church should be more like the *Mount* where Jesus preached in the Holy Land two thousand years ago."

Grant looked over his shoulder, as the camera panned across the formidable statues and imposing domes of the Vatican and surrounding churches.

"Hard to argue." He touched his ear again, and grimaced. "…if you are a Catholic who feels the same way as Damascus, I mean."

"This revolutionary Cardinal's well-known slogan is, "*You who are trying to be justified by the law have been alienated from Christ; you have fallen away from his grace.*" Someone shouted from behind Grant, "Chapter five, verse four." Grant did not like hecklers - although turned to acknowledge the shout.

"The square is full of Damascus followers. They are identifiable by the medals they wear proudly around their necks." The camera focused in on a group of pilgrims wearing the **G** medals outside their shirts, some holding them aloft.

Grant continued, "Technically, according to the rules governing Papal elections, the Cardinals are not allowed to campaign. In fact, if they are caught doing so, they can be excommunicated. Bit harsh if you ask me, but them's the rules."

Wilson smiled at Grant's cheeky delivery. How does he get away with this?

"There is no shortage of support for Cardinal Damascus in this square. These medals have been widely distributed over the last week. Many people across the globe are wearing them to promote an opportunity for change in the church. Not just Catholics, Christians from other denominations and non-Christians too. For some, a moment of truth, for many, it's as simple as meddling with a medal. We all like to fidget. This is Grant MacTavish, in the Vatican." He grinned, placed his hand inside his shirt and extracted a shiny bronze medal with the gothic letter **G**.

So much for impartiality, Wilson thought, as she drained the last of the wine into her glass.

No Good News

She woke in a daze, the TV playing a BBC Hardcore interview with a senior politician challenging him on why USA and UK had invaded Iraq. She hit the off button on the control – she did not want to listen to 25 different ways of avoiding a question.

Rubbing her eyes, she stood and stretched her back in an arc, letting out a long, slow grunt. The creaks and cracks felt satisfying. Her watch told her she had been asleep for four hours. She had needed it.

Picking up her phone, she feared the worst. Before leaving for the hotel, she had exchanged numbers with Valentina. Wilson had wanted to stay, although when the parents arrived, they were in no mood to spend time with the officer who had led their son into an ambush. Anger was never in short supply in these situations; she knew from bitter experience. Valentina had walked her to the door to allow the exchange of numbers. The first message on her phone was from Valentina to say there was no change and that she was at Crawford's bedside with his mother and father.

Wilson scanned the hotel room, two small bottles of red sat alongside a Gordon's Gin and Bacardi. All empty. No wonder she had fallen asleep. She should have felt worse, were it not for the adrenalin that had already kicked in. Running a finger through her messages, she saw that she had missed some incoming calls. Roddy. Rafaele – she had forgotten about him. Sampaio. Also, Gemmill. It was 3 am, the only person this side of the Atlantic, who would mind receiving a call, was her boss in Glasgow. She could leave him till later.

She tapped speed dial.

"Hey, Roddy. How are things?"

"Aw, okay, Maggie. I just called to see how that Vatican clue worked out." She felt a pang of guilt, she had meant to call him. He continued, "I saw on the news that terrible incident of a British man being stabbed in the square. I hope it was nothing to do with what you were following up on." He waited for a response. Her sigh confirmed his concerns.

"Yes. Crawford was one of ours. I mean, IS one of ours. He is on life support at the moment."

"Oh no, what happened?"

She had thought twice about telling him, but she had no choice. "We don't have anything yet. Local police scanned CCTV footage. Unfortunately, crowds were so dense, there's nothing to see. They got away." She paused for a moment, unsure whether to continue.

"Go on. I can tell there's something else." Roddy had taken a swig before the call; he was not going to miss a hint of hesitancy.

"Well, before he passed out, Crawford said he saw someone. Apparently, it was Mask."

"Mask?" Roddy had been pacing his room. He stopped and looked out at a darkness that matched his mood. "How can that be? He's dead! And was Angie there too?"

"I know, it's a lot to take in. Yes, he thinks he saw a girl with him, although he has never met Angie, so wouldn't have recognised her anyway." Her immediate assumption was that somehow Mask had smuggled Angie into Italy. She knew not to underestimate him; she did not want to impose her half-baked hunches on Roddy.

"If Mask is still alive, then Angie is in real danger. It's too much of a coincidence. I know your colleague thinks he saw him in Rome and Angie disappeared over here. But we have to accept that anything is possible with this nutter."

"I couldn't have put it more eloquently myself," she said, which made him smile despite his concern.

"Could Mask have anything to do with Kiltman's disappearance? Or maybe even dad not contacting us? Maybe Mask is angry that we adopted Angie."

She startled at the bluntness of his tone. "Easy, easy, Roddy. Yes, there are lots of aspects to this we need to consider. But let's remember, I don't have anything yet to confirm whether Crawford did see Mask in the square, so let's not run riot with our assumptions." The connection was all too evident for her, she needed to gather her thoughts and work out what it might mean.

"I'm waiting for a contact in Brazil to come back to me about Kiltman. He is also helping with tracking your dad." This was beyond cringeworthy, thank goodness she could not see her face.

"In fact, I've got a missed call from him so will call back after we're finished."

She had pushed her worries deep down inside. Succumbing to the anxiety would paralyse her. She could not give in to the fear Kenny was gone; she was relying on her innate belief that she would sense if he were dead.

Her eyes stung with the build-up of tears she refused to let flow, when she heard Roddy stifle a sigh, the weight of worry taking its toll. In an effort to end on a positive note, she asked, "Oh, by the way, how's the football going?"

"Quite well, to be honest." His tone picked up a notch. There was no point in cornering her, it would achieve nothing until she had more information on Mask. "We beat the Cleveland Collies in the semi-final today. So, we play in the final tomorrow."

"Oh, that's great. It's refreshing to hear some good news. Who are you up against?"

"Well, that's the thing. We are playing a team we beat in the first game. They managed to win their games from then on and are up against us in the final. They are a strange sort of religious group. Kind of cultish, yet quite warm and friendly. You know how Dad always talks about Marmite separating people's opinions? Well, they're a sort of Catholic Marmite. They are called the Galatians."

"That's funny. I've just been watching the news about them." Two mini-bar bottles of wine, one of gin and one of Bacardi ago. "Their leader is coming to Rome for the conclave - they say he might become the next Pope."

"Yes, I met him. Cardinal Damascus. He's quite strange to be honest. Although his heart seems to be in the right place, I guess. Hard to tell."

"Small world," Wilson said. "Well, good luck in the final. Do your best. Make your mum and dad proud." Her voice cracked at the end. Roddy heard it. "Thanks, Maggie. Bye for now."

She waited a few minutes before she called Sampaio. It was the conversation she did not want to have. She could not avoid it any longer. He picked up before she began to hear the ringtone. His deep, strong voice felt comforting. "Hey, DI Wilson. Did you hear my message?"

"Eh, no, sorry. Just saw you'd called. Any news?"

"I'm afraid I have bad news." She remained silent. Her pulse raced. "They performed a DNA test on the remains in the prison. It was not Mask."

"How could that happen?" she asked through a dry mouth.

"Well, the remains they thought were Mask's belonged to Khalil Qatari. They then dug up Qatari's coffin. It was full of stones. Mask must have used the coffin as his getaway. Martim, the pilot, would have taken him in the chopper. With regards Kiltman…"

He did not need to continue. She finished the sentence for him. "… he was disposed of somewhere over the Amazon jungle."

"Yes, it looks like it," he said. "I am sorry. I know you two worked very closely together." More past tenses.

"Have you activated a search?" She preferred business as usual.

"Yes, we have, but…" he paused before continuing, "the Amazon is a big place. The chances of finding his… him are very slim."

"I know, but it's comforting to know you are searching. Look, I need to go. Please keep me informed."

"I will. Goodbye."

She had held herself together through sheer willpower. Once she hit the *end* button, she collapsed face first onto the bed. Her heart pounded with the onslaught of grief, as she punched the pillow and let her tears cascade onto the sheets. The room seemed so small as her cries and sobs echoed around her, as if she was listening to someone else's heart breaking.

After a few minutes of lying curled up in a ball, arms wrapped around her knees, staring at the wall, she realised she had to shake herself up - and face the reality that had been confronting her for days. He was gone – and was not coming back. Now, Fiona and Roddy needed her to focus on finding Angie. Sacco's killers were also out there, maybe with another victim in their sights.

She could either stay in the hotel room, escaping via numerous small bottles of booze, or get on with her search.

What would Kenny do?

She looked at the empty bottles on the table and sighed.

Saturday, April 16

Sicily Bound

"Yes, I am fine." Wilson was pacing the length of the departures area at Ciampino airport. Her flight was boarding in ten minutes – she did not need any more pep talking from Gemmill.

"I am not one for soft talk, Wilson," he understated. "You can take time off. I mean it. I recommend it. I know you and Kiltman had a thing going on. I mean… I don't mean… well, just that you were a strong partnership. In policing, a partner can become the most important person in your life. I lost a partner many years ago, and it hurt beyond words."

"I'm sorry, Sir, I hadn't realised."

"Oh, no, nothing like that. She went to have a baby. Still, while it may have been a rift I knew was coming, I still struggled with it."

Crikey, she thought, he had to go on some training courses. "Don't worry. I'll be okay. I have to see this case through." An announcement bellowed from the speaker above her head. "They are calling my flight; I need to go."

"Okay, keep me informed. Be careful."

"Will do. Bye." She closed the phone down. At times like this, she saw another side of her boss. His normal approach was to push and cajole his officers until they could take no more. Then, when he sensed a vulnerability, he would become supportive. If he ever had to meet a psychiatrist, it would be interesting to hear how he answered the question about his relationship with his father.

She checked her phone and saw Tommy MacGregor had called when she was talking to Gemmill. She had not spoken to him in months. Kenny's best friend, he had a special place in her heart. Despite his unpredictability and mischievousness, he had proven to be instrumental in capturing both Cullen Skink and Mask.

She wavered whether to make the call. In the end, she hit the Estonian number on her phone.

"*Tere! Kuidas laheb, Maggie?*" Tommy answered.

"*Tere*, Tommy. Fine thanks. How are you?"

"Okay. Can't complain. I just called you there because I've left a few messages for Kenny. He hasn't called back. Is everything okay?"

She leant the back of her head against the wall and closed her eyes. It had been difficult that morning telling Fiona that Kenny was still missing. She could not go into the Kiltman/Mask/Martim events with her in the call. She needed something more substantial before she could explain the full picture. Which meant a body. Kenny's body. Fiona had cried during the conversation - it was as if she realised, he was not coming back. On top of Angie's disappearance, Fiona's world was crumbling. Her son's father had vanished too.

And now Tommy.

"Well, we're a bit worried about Kenny. He went to Brazil on Monday – we've not heard from him since. He was having a spa break but didn't show up at the resort." She was struggling to maintain this double messaging.

"Och, typical Kenny," he said. "He'll be off on some beach enjoying himself. Spas are not his thing."

"Maybe you're right. Anyway, how are you?" Poor Tommy, when was she going to tell him he had lost his best friend?

"Not bad. I have a few days off and was calling him to see if he wanted to hang out. Looks like that's not going to happen this time."

"Looks like it." Wilson's head trapped the phone against her shoulder as she presented her boarding card to the stewardess.

"What are you up to?" he asked.

"I'm about to board a flight to Sicily. I'm working on something."

"Cool," he said. "I've never been to Sicily. Supposed to be nice weather in April."

"Yes, I guess. Look, I need to …"

"Hey, you've given me a great idea."

Oh, please God, no.

"I'll come to Sicily. I'll give you a shout when I get there. Bon, eh, flight."

The line died before she could speak.

Tommy MacGregor roaming around Mafia-controlled Sicily. What could possibly go wrong?

Tantalus

"How are things going with Mask?"

"Not easy," Tantalus whispered into his phone. "He is not to be trusted. Also, with his daughter here, it has become somewhat awkward."

"I will be there soon. We need him for the next couple of days. Once we have the money transferred into the accounts, he will not be needed any more."

"I know. Listen, are you sure you can deliver the package as planned?"

"Do you doubt me, Tantalus? I've played my part perfectly until now. You have your job and I have mine. When I come, I don't want to see anyone. Keep them busy. I know the code to the basement entrance. The package will be deposited, don't worry."

"Okay. From now on let's connect by text, and in code."

"Agreed."

Tantalus placed the phone beside the screen. He rubbed his hand over the mainframe computer in the centre of the room. His eyes were closed - he enjoyed the hum and vibration of the energy underneath the smooth, metal surface. At moments like these, he took a second to appreciate his achievements. He touched the lettering inscribed with his penknife on the top left corner: *Damascocles*.

Tantalus was satisfied with how he had bound two ancient stories together to capture the essence of his life's work. His favourite Roman story was of Damocles – how he thought he had landed on his feet when Dionysus of Sicily allowed him to enjoy the pleasures of a royal lifestyle. Only for Damocles to realise that as he did so, a sword dangled over his head, attached by the thinnest thread. The perfect analogy for the *Sword* Tantalus would dangle over the millions of people living carefree lives without a care for what truly mattered.

And his second favourite tale was of St. Paul's Road to Damascus. The moment of revelation and conversion, when a persecutor of Christians becomes the greatest evangelist the Church has produced.

Damascus and Damocles: two tales so beautifully intertwined. Soon the world would see the power of *Damascocles* and accept a conversion to a new ideology.

The location had been selected years before the upcoming Papal election. A sinister, abandoned villa nestled in a wooded area in Northern Rome, just off the *Via Cassia*, the city's main tributary north towards Florence. It had proven to be the perfect cover for the work they had to do. Above ground level, the villa appeared run down and neglected, paint flaking, cracked windows, and guttering stuffed with leaves.

At first, the locals considered the grey-haired, bearded man who came and went as an eccentric; someone whiling away time in isolation in a remote villa. Over time he had made a point of connecting with his neighbours, working his way into the community, sometimes meeting them for pizzas at the Pink Devil restaurant, the hub of all gossip and chatter. While he would never be one of them, for a foreigner, his knowledge of Italian language, culture, and of course, food and wine, impressed anyone who spent time in his company.

Fooling others was easy. Throughout a childhood of frustration and deprivation, he had always been angry. Angry at his parents. Angry at the schools. Angry at friends. Angry at politicians. Angry at church leaders and worshippers. He had overflowed with anger. Anything he wanted always seemed out of reach, unachievable. Not because of him, because others made it impossible. They created processes, rules, laws, structures that got in the way. Life was not supposed to be like that: always trying to achieve, get better, be compliant.

Below the villa, the two-tiered basement was another world. Tantalus was pleased with the equipment and technology accumulated and developed painstakingly over the years, truly world class. This game-changing machinery was now ready to put power back in the hands of the right people. With a little help, of course.

Bending down to lean on the hardware, he smiled and spoke in a quiet voice, aware of Mask and Arnalda on the floor above. "Ah, my sweet beauty. You are going to change the world. No more will I be frustrated by what I cannot have. You will be the catalyst for a new beginning for everyone, my sweet, to do the things we have prayed for over these many years."

As with any plan, there were some flies in the ointment, a phrase he enjoyed using with his English colleagues. His eloquence was another way to show how intelligent he was, whatever the nuances of the language. Mask's daughter was a fly. Wilson was a fly. They were just in the wrong place at the wrong time. Just like insects, at the right moment, they would have to be squatted.

He knew he had to be careful. Arnalda's father was critical to his plans. He needed to keep him close, part of the team. Mask's capabilities with technology and software were second to none. Combined with his network of maniacal friends across the world, Tantalus had all the support he now needed. The prison break had been perfectly executed. He had fun planning that operation. Shame for Martim, sometimes collateral damage is unavoidable.

He wished he could say the same about baggage. Tantalus had not realised how much baggage would come with Mask. A daughter who served no useful purpose to achieve their outcomes; she could not even cook a plate of pasta. Mask's desire to hurt Arnalda's new family and his hatred for Kiltman and Wilson were unnecessary distractions Tantalus would have to manage.

The Kiltman box had been ticked. Wilson would be next.

They were nearly ready for the Papal elections, a few more loose ends to be addressed. He would decide how to deal with Mask and his daughter later. For the time being, Mask would be part of the plan. His insatiable thirst for evil acts was at times off-putting, but he was the perfect ally. At least for the next couple of days.

The Final

The Galatians were playing like a different team. They were stronger in all parts of the pitch. At times, it seemed as though they enjoyed playing with Chesters, rather than against them. They juggled the ball just to show they could, and their passing play was impressive. The first half included a period where they passed 34 times without the Scots touching the ball - particularly demoralising when it resulted in a goal.

Ten minutes remained on the clock before the final whistle. The Scots were 1-0 down, although morale-wise, the score felt like 10-0. In theory, while technically they could still win, scoring a goal felt impossible. They were going through the motions rather than believing in themselves. Coach Stone had not stopped shouting and cajoling, but it seemed even his energy was beginning to wane.

They had just spent the last twenty minutes in their own half, endeavouring to limit the defeat to one goal. Until an errant pass from Jo-Jo bounced off a Galatians defender, to go out of play in the opposing half.

"Roddy!" Reilly had the ball in his hands preparing to throw. "Let's do the Drumchapel play."

They had practised this in training. It had been more of a joke, than a real move. They had called it after their Drumchapel adversaries, because they had seen it performed by them.

Roddy walked towards Reilly. They exchanged a wink. Roddy turned his back to the ball and faced a Galatians defender. Their faces were as close as boxers before a championship bout. Roddy closed his eyes and grimaced. He positioned himself at a 45-degree angle five metres from Reilly, bracing himself – his back tensed, ready for impact. He waited for Reilly to launch the ball, putting all his pent-up frustration and worry into tightening his back muscles. Still, the impact of Reilly's throw nearly winded him. The ball whacked him with much more force than his teammate had used in training.

It had the desired effect. The ball bounced down the line towards Galatians' goal into space free of defenders - who had all committed themselves to marking the Chesters players. Reilly sprinted towards the free ball and pushed it forward towards goal. The keeper came out to close down the angle, which Reilly had expected. Slipping his foot underneath, he executed the perfect chip. It sailed over the goalie's head into the top of the net. 1-1.

Roddy ran towards Reilly. He waited until the goal scorer had completed two somersaults, and a knee-slide towards the corner flag, before he hugged him. Reilly punched the air and shouted, "Brilliant! What a pass!"

They both laughed before being swamped by the other players – the usual bedlam that comes with a goal. As they walked back towards their own half before the game restarted, Reilly shouted to the team, "Come on, guys. We are going to win this! Let's do it for Angie!"

From the second the whistle blew the Galatians knew they were facing a revitalised team. The onslaught was overwhelming. Whenever a Chesters player hit the ball, they shouted 'Angie'. Legs that had been sluggish and heavy had a renewed spring. Especially Jo-Jo. She was a defender in all respects; so much so her teammates joked with her about never going into the opponent's half in case she got a nosebleed. Today was different, she wanted to make Angie proud.

When the ball landed at her feet, with one minute to go, she did not think. She reacted, letting her leg do the rest. The ball pierced the top right-hand corner of the goal. Chesters players ran and jumped on Jo-Jo. The squeals and shouts drowned out her cry, "You guys are crushing me!"

It took them a few minutes to calm down and walk back to the centre of the field. The referee blew the whistle to restart the match. Before soon blowing again to end the game, and the tournament. Chesters were the champions.

The Galatians' disappointment was etched on their faces. Shoulders slumped, some kneeling, heads obscured to hide the tears.

"Come on, team!" was shouted from the middle of the pitch. It was Brit. "*Brothers and sisters, like Isaac, you are children of promise*." Her message was clear – there was more to life than a football match.

Brad shouted from the bench, "4, 28!"

As if on cue, the players reached inside their shirts and took out their medals. They lifted them in the air before kissing the shiny surface. This had the desired change in their demeanour. They walked forward to Chesters and hugged and congratulated their opponents. By this point, Coach Stone had made it to the centre of the pitch, commiserating with the Galatians and congratulating the Scots, whoever came into his line of sight.

Roddy was off to the side, looking skyward, saying a quiet prayer for Angie and his father. He was happy for the team but could not get beyond the gnawing sense of loss and growing concern for their safety. He had still not accepted the news that Mask had escaped from the so-called *high security* prison; he was convinced Mask was responsible for Angie and his father's disappearance. That morning Roddy had tried to track the telephone numbers, there had been nothing. Before the match he had called his mother; to be informed there was no news about his father.

He really wanted to be a *child of promise*, but he could not shake off the weight of despair. He just needed one piece of good news, was that too much to ask?

"Hey, Roddy. Talking to yourself now, are we?" Jo-Jo said as she placed a protective hand on his shoulder. He had not realised he had spoken aloud. She continued. "Angie and your dad will turn up. If we can win a game like that, anything can happen. We just have to believe." She waited a moment and then offered, "You know, if there's anything I can do, just ask."

Esperança

The whole village were at the riverbank to watch him depart. Kiltman held onto the steering wheel as they pushed the boat into the river. As soon as the boat touched the rushing waters, it shot off like a bullet from a gun. He nearly fell over the side, stumbling to catch his hand on the steering wheel. Fortunately, the frantic realignment of weight helped straighten the boat, saving him from toppling overboard.

By the time he had righted himself, he was a hundred metres downstream. He turned to give a hearty wave and blow a kiss to the people who had saved him, watching their smiles disappear into the distance. He could detect a hint of bemusement as they watched this demi-god scrambling to navigate a boat, whilst coming close to undoing all their healing and caring a few seconds after being left to his own devices.

That age-old African proverb was true after all: *it takes a village to raise a superhero*. Close enough, he thought.

As the vessel hurtled along the river, he could detect no other signs of life - of the human form, although plenty of wildlife – to give him hope he had made the right decision. He was well aware that he had thrown caution to the wind. Now he had to focus on staying positive, recognising that he was lucky to be alive.

Over the next twenty-four hours he had dozed on and off, trying not to succumb to a deep sleep. While there were some calm, peaceful moments, the reality was the journey was fraught with danger. The fast-flowing current tugged at the boat, sometimes spinning it in circles, threatening to overturn its flimsy structure. Yet it stayed afloat. A combination of Kiltman's whisky-imbued nautical skills and massive amounts of luck meant he was progressing along the river at a fast pace.

The heat and humidity were proving to be oppressive. It would have been unbearable were it not for his channelling of Hair o' the Dog to his nervous system, dialling down its sensitivity to heat and light. Unfortunately, he had no such remedy for the flies and gnats biting and chewing at his neck, legs and hands.

In between fighting to stay afloat and awake, he ate from the provisions the villagers had given him. They had stocked the left side of the cabin with food and water, and the right side with creams and leaves. They had gone to painstaking lengths to demonstrate how to apply the cream and when to eat the leaves. Their whistling and clicking had reached a crescendo when he performed the cream application himself and demonstrated that he knew how to eat a leaf.

He could now sense the boat slowing up as it settled into a more tranquil flow, the incline of the river easing to an even current. He took the moment to sit down and examine his wounds. There were too many scratches to count on his arms, and midriff, crisscrossing and blending in a pattern not too dissimilar to the tartan on his kilt. None of them were of concern except for the hole on his right arm where the villager had inserted his fingers.

His legs were much worse than the rest of his body, full of deep gashes like the one on his arm. The villagers had applied stitches using a thin, leafy twine, pulling the skin together. They had left just enough room between the flaps of skin to insert cream into the cracks.

He lifted the earthen container with its makeshift wooden lid, scooped a handful of goo, and rubbed it into his cuts and scrapes as they had instructed, feeling the soothing sense of healing.

He could have sworn most of his wounds had shrunk since the last application. Hair o' the Dog was an incredible potion, born in a far-flung galaxy, raised to its full potential in a house in Scotland. While it magnified his senses to extraordinary levels, he was in no doubt, it was not responsible for this healing process. As a chemistry student he had spent many months analysing and studying scientists who employed various combinations of elements to find cures for a range of diseases. Nothing like this had ever been discussed or even contemplated. The cream was nothing short of miraculous.

He was already chewing on a leaf, enjoying its succulence and bitter-sweet aftertaste. The texture did not give into the constant mashing of molars. If anything, it changed from a rubbery plant to a form of chewing gum, allowing its painkilling powers to enter his bloodstream at a pace suited to his nervous system's ability to cope.

The pot of cream rolled along to bump against the cabin wall. An innocuous movement that in another situation would have been unremarkable. Yet for Kiltman it was a warning sign. The pace of the boat's drift was beginning to pick up again. He stood, shielded the sun from his eyes and squinted into the distance. Other than the fast-flowing river, there was nothing but large trees and bushes in his line of vision.

Yet the change in the river's pull was unmistakeable. The vessel began to bob from side to side. Gripping the wheel, he had to work harder to keep her straight. Up ahead, a cluster of rapids appeared as he navigated around a sharp bend. Angry waters crashed off scores of intimidating rocks protruding dangerously above the water line. Despite her name, Esperança would struggle to handle the impact. They would reach the rapids in moments. He grabbed handfuls of leaves, stuffing them into his sporran; and tightened his grip on the earthenware jug full of cream. He steadied himself for impact.

Esperança's hull just managed to survive the first group of rocks, shuddering and crunching with each impact. As it crashed along a gauntlet of jagged boulders, he knew she had reached the end of the line. Ten metres beyond was a precipice. While he could not see how high the drop would be, he knew that the boat had run out of *esperança*.

The next crash shook every bone in his body, before flipping the vessel up into the air. He found himself hurtling above the rocks, the boat below him crumpling into driftwood. He saw a flat rock over to the side closer to the bank. Twisting his body, he worked hard to take his momentum in that direction. The impact would hurt but at least he would have something to hold onto. His effort paid off, allowing him to land square in its centre. He breathed a sigh of relief. Just before the force of his fall and the smoothness of the rock turned it into a slide firing him over the water's edge.

As he fell through the air, white waters spilling and crashing around him, he tucked himself into a ball. With the healing cream held tight in his grasp, Shakespeare's words in Measure for Measure came to mind: "The miserable have no other medicine but hope."

Change of Plans

"Mum, I've got Coach Stone here beside me. Please talk to him." Roddy passed the phone to the Coach, who was celebrating with a bottle of local Christian Moerlein beer.

"Hello?" He took a hefty slurp before stifling a belch away from the phone.

"Hi, Coach. This is Roddy's mother, Fiona. Congratulations on winning the tournament. You must be pleased."

"Eh, yes, thanks. The team did well. They are a great bunch of kids." He changed the tone of his voice. "I know you haven't heard from Angie yet. I spoke to the police this morning and they are doing everything they can. I wish we could do more here. It's heart-breaking for all of us."

"Thanks, Coach. I appreciate your support, I really do. I wanted to talk about Roddy. He has asked if he can go to Rome for the Papal elections. I said, yes. He needs something to distract him from the stress of Angie being missing. His dad's partner is there already, so she will look after him. You know his dad has not been in touch?"

"His father, too? Really? What happened?" Coach looked at Roddy, who seemed to find the cream on his donut worthy of focused attention.

"Oh, yes. His dad went on holiday earlier this week and has not contacted any of us. It has been tough for Roddy."

"Of course, it is. Yes, if you are okay with him going to Rome then I am too. It will be an amazing time to be there, the election of a new Pope. You never know, Cardinal Damascus from here in Cincinnati could be in with a shout." He winked as Roddy gave him the thumbs up.

"That's good. I reserved a seat on a flight this evening, which lands tomorrow morning. I'll go ahead and confirm now."

Coach said goodbye and handed the phone back. He put an arm around Roddy's shoulders, gave him a squeeze and said, "See you back home. You played brilliantly. Good luck."

"Thanks, Coach. I appreciate it." Roddy smiled as Coach turned his beer bottle upside down, drooping the corners of his mouth. He failed at looking sad - although pulled off a credible Robert de Niro expression. He turned around and walked in the direction of the fridge. Roddy stepped outside to the carpark. Once out of earshot, he spoke into the phone. "Are you still there?"

"Yes."

"You were amazing, thanks a million."

"No problem. Safe travels."

"Will do. I owe you one." He looked across the carpark to where Jo-Jo was sitting on a car bonnet. They gave each other a wave. She was going to do well in drama school.

Sicily

"Detective Inspector Wilson. It's my great pleasure to meet you." The officer extended his hand to greet her. She shook it, struck by how he clasped hers in both of his. It was more of a hand-embrace than a shake.

"Thank you," she said, pulling back gently. There were two officers in plain clothes. The other - not engaging in pleasantries – was holding identification badges for him and his colleague. The hand-shaker was Officer Albano and the other, Officer Monte. They looked like twins. Typical Italian. Tall, dark and handsome. It never got old.

"How was your flight?" asked Officer Monte.

"Short," she answered. It had been little more than an hour, just enough time for a coffee and pastry; although not cannoli.

"Please, let's go to the car. We can go directly to the station and plan your next steps." The officers stepped to the side to let her pass. She had checked her phone on landing. There were no messages.

The drive from Palermo airport to the police station took longer than it should. Traffic jams seemed to appear from nowhere and in an instant. Monte drove while Albano asked questions about the investigation, assessing how much progress she had made so far. Every now and then Monte would shout and gesticulate at another car. Sometimes, even when there was no other vehicle, he shouted anyway.

Once they had reached the station and established themselves in a small room, filled with files and computer screens, Albano said, "Signora Wilson, would you like a coffee?"

"Yes, please. I would kill for one," she answered.

"Sorry?" Albano said. Monte stopped arranging his papers on the desk.

"Oops," she laughed. "Just an expression. Yes, please."

Albano looked at Monte, who nodded and left the room. He returned ten minutes later with three large, double espressos. The two officers downed theirs in one gulp and placed the cups on the tray. Wilson - in an effort to regain some respect – did the same.

They sat around the table where Monte had laid out pictures of the four faces that had been attached to the whiteboard in New Scotland Yard.

"Thank you for your update in the car. I believe I am comfortable with where you have got to in your investigation. If I can summarise, please. Will you allow me?" Albano's formality and precision in enunciating every syllable made her feel a tad uncomfortable. She had picked up a pen and was twisting it around in her fingers, up and down, backwards and forwards. She noticed Monte observe her fidgeting.

"Yes, of course, Officer Albano, please go ahead." Wilson put the pen down and picked up her Styrofoam cup. She began to break it into little pieces, placing them inside the container. She wondered at what point she would run out of cup.

"Okay. Sacco is killed. Clearly not suicide. I agree with your conclusion. As you can imagine, we have a lot of fake suicides in this part of the world." She began to smile at what she believed was Albano's sardonic sense of humour. She shifted mid-smile to a half-cough and forced sneeze, realising that neither Albano nor Monte were finding this comment the least bit droll.

"Banco d'Aiuto receives regular deposits from accounts connected to these four individuals. We will not call them suspects. Not yet, at any rate. In the last year these have amounted to 10 million euros. You have evidence showing that they have been making deposits for around 15 years, adding up in total to around 70 million euros. Am I on track so far?"

"Yes, you are correct." She moved the cup to the side of the table. As she moved to pick up the pen, she knocked the cup over, spilling the tiny pieces of Styrofoam on top of the pictures. "Oh, sorry. So clumsy." When she tried to gather the pieces in her hands, she pushed them across the table onto Albano's jacket sleeve.

He said something under his breath she could not quite catch. Monte stood and ran his hand across the pieces and pushed them into a trash can. Albano picked the white bits from his sleeve and did the same. He waited until he had removed all the chunks before he started to speak again. She noticed a twitch at the corner of his mouth that had not been there earlier.

"Okay, let's keep going. Banco d'Aiuto apparently transfers over half of its deposits to Banco Discepolo. This includes payments from the accounts in question in addition to a lot more besides. You said around one billion euros in the last year alone?"

"Yes, one billion." She nodded. Her hands were safely tucked under her legs.

"Now, based on this evidence, you want to meet some or all of the account holders? Who all happen to have alleged links to organised crime?" Albano pointed at the photographs.

"Yes, that's about the extent of it." She paused and looked at Albano, then Monte. "Look, we have something here. I know it. Our forensics work can show the money flows. Until we speak to them, we will not know why they are paying money into Banco d'Aiuto then allowing it to be transferred to Banco Discepolo. If they can help us with this, then we might know why the funds are being managed in this way. Then we might understand why Sacco was killed."

"Two *mights*, Signora Wilson." Albano said, folding his arms.

"What do you mean?"

"Normally one 'might' is tenuous and will be discussed for hours, sometimes days, before action is taken. You have two 'mights' and are asking us to approach these individuals and enquire about their banking practices."

She nodded.

"How would you recommend we initiate these conversations?" He looked at Monte and smiled.

"Well, that's why I'm here. I was hoping you could help with this." Her heart had been pounding – she was beginning to feel it ease off.

"DI Wilson. With all due respect. We...." he nodded his head at Monte, "are the last people they will want to see. These men are not the type where officers just show up at their door to ask some questions. They have established processes and protocol for meeting people. They are not in a hurry to meet anyone from the justiciary or police."

He paused and looked at his colleague.

"I know, you may find this bizarre but, believe me, things have to happen a certain way in this part of the world. If we are, what is the word, em, cavalier," he snapped his fingers, "we can create a lot of problems. None of them small."

"So how can you help me then, Officers?" She could feel her temper ticking up a notch. "Are you telling me this has been a wasted journey?"

"No, not wasted. We can help you understand the men you want to meet. You will need to be prepared for them and recognise that they have, how would you say, uniquely unusual backgrounds. Once we have done that, then it's up to you." His arms were still folded resolutely. There was nothing subtle about his message that their support was limited.

"Okay, that makes sense." Arguing would be pointless. "Who would you recommend I talk to first?"

"Good question," Monte said, "Before that, would you like another coffee?"

"No, thanks," she answered, "not unless Officer Albano wants some more sticky white things on his nice new jacket."

Capos Galore

The faces were spread out on the bed with a page of scribbled notes under each. Once Albano and Monte started to talk, they could not stop. Their information download started with home addresses and phone numbers; and went on to paint a picture of the capos' childhood through to alleged, but unproven, crimes in adulthood. There had been several attempts over the years to hang a conviction on each of them. All failed. Either because of flimsy evidence, or absent witnesses, or witnesses who changed their minds at the last minute. She sensed the witness protection programme famous in US movies was much harder to implement in Italy.

She picked up Roberto 'Mucky' Marciano's picture. He was 51 years old, groomed to an appearance no older than 35. Slicked back hair, sporting a wayward curl above his forehead; eyebrows unnaturally thin; cheekbones and nose sharp and to the point. It was his eyes she focused on. Clear blue. Not the blue of a summer's day – rather, icy cold grey blue, like the sea on a winter's morning. Allegedly - an important word in Sicily - he had worked his way up the family ladder by disposing of anyone who got in the way.

Gianni 'Pirla' Sconi's round, beaming face filled most of the frame. His combover reminded her of the Glasgow comic, Rab C. Nesbitt - a half-hearted attempt to salvage a long-lost dignity. His features were soft and generously squidgy, his skin glinting under the camera flash. He enjoyed his pasta and vino, not afraid to show it. He looked as cute and cuddly as an urban fox. Albano had made a point of looking her in the eye, when he said, "Don't be fooled by his bonhomie. This guy would have you disposed of for as little as..." he waited a few moments and then said, "spreading Styrofoam specks all over his jacket." He laughed but the smile did not reach his eyes. He then put his thumb to the corner of his right eye and said, "*Occhio!*" She made a point of looking it up later.

At the opposite end of the spectrum was Mauro 'Zio' Papetti. Lean, chiselled and an air of charisma that rarely comes across in a photograph. Although it did for him. He was the youngest of the four capos, trusted by the others. Monte made a point of emphasizing the role he played across the group. He was the glue that kept them connected, non-combative and intent on peace. Zio's angle was that there was more to lose than gain in fighting. They were in it for the money and security, not the violence. Brooklyn hits and New York drive-by killings might sell movies, but they did not work for organised crime on a Mediterranean island.

Carlo 'San' Babila was the most interesting. Born and bred in Brooklyn, he had returned to Sicily twenty years earlier. On his father's death, he was duty bound to come back and run the *business*. He had been living a happy life with his wife and children in New York, working as a lawyer on Wall Street. His reputation as a legal eagle had been known far and wide. The link to Sicily was not uncovered until he resigned and returned to his Italian family. Seen by many to be the contemporary face of an age-old institution, he was respected for his wisdom and problem-solving.

It was clear from Albano that the four Mafia dons worked independently yet were connected on all aspects of security. The island had the lowest rates of crime across Italy - people were aware of the consequences of stepping out of line.

Her next steps were to figure out which capo to visit first. She had no idea how to approach them other than walk up to their front door and explain she was investigating an international crime. Were it not for the challenges she faced on searching for Angie and tracing Kiltman, she would have been able to take her time.

After Crawford's Vatican sighting of Mask, she was convinced that Angie was the girl he saw in the square. Pisacane had issued photos and descriptions to all the Rome precincts. He understood the seriousness. He made a point of holding Wilson's hand when explaining that he had a fifteen-year-old daughter. This was personal for him, and he would not give up until he found them.

Kiltman's disappearance was breaking her heart; yet she refused to accept it. Something good had to come of this. Just like when she had ignored the fuel gauge warning on last year's driving holiday. They had broken down in the middle of the Scottish Highlands, no petrol stations or shops within an hour's drive. She had blamed him for not filling up before leaving Inverness, while he argued she should have paid more attention to the gauge. After a few minutes of bickering and stone-cold silence they turned to look at each other. Before reaching out and embracing for as long as they had argued. They realised at the same time they had broken down in one of the most stunning glens in Scotland surrounded by beauty beyond compare.

Wilson was not a natural optimist. In her line of work, she found that optimists did not solve many crimes. She was determined that, despite drowning in a sea of setbacks and obstacles, she would find a clue worth believing in.

Hens On Tour

"Hi, gorgeous, can I buy you a drink?" Tommy preferred the old-fashioned approach.

"That would be nice," Gina said, pushing the tiara back to the top of her head. It was hard to keep it in place when dancing on a chair. He had been enjoying watching this pretty woman with soft brown eyes and tanned skin dance as if she were on her own.

"She's spoken for, Scotty-boy!" A blonde woman with clear blue eyes and a welcoming smile tapped him on the shoulder. "She is Gina and I am Hilda." She extended her hand to shake Tommy's.

"Oh, I see. That's what the sash saying *Happy Engagement* means!" He laughed. "I want to buy her a drink to congratulate her, not to chat her up. You on the other hand…"

"No chance," Hilda's German accent became stronger when she was having fun. "I've got a Scottish boyfriend. He's a bigger version than you."

"It's not my day," he shrugged. "Oh, hello, girls!" He turned to see another two of Gina's attractive hen party coming back from the bar with a tray of drinks, smiling at him and Hilda; or maybe it was just Hilda.

"Forget it," Hilda said. She winked at Gina. "Michelle and Carina have Scottish husbands. I think you'll need to fish in another pond."

"Do you think I'm only after one thing? If so, then you're right!" The party girls nodded at each other recognising the 'typical Scotsman' charm they had all fallen for. He put his hands in the air. "Guilty as charged! I am looking for a party. Nothing more. I didn't expect to meet a group of gorgeous Scottish WAGs in Sicily."

"Well, you've found the right group," Gina said, jumping off the chair. "Who are you here with?"

"On my own, just flown in from Estonia. I've never been on a hen do before. Cheers!" He lifted his glass to theirs. They took a moment to introduce themselves.

While they came from different countries - Gina-England, Hilda-Germany, Michelle-France and Carina-Italy - the girls proved to be the lynchpin in bringing together a group of Scottish men who met playing football for a pub team in Milan. When Tommy remarked that the Scots were probably punching above their weight, none of the girls argued.

It was a late Saturday afternoon in Palermo. He had dropped his bag at the Pensione, round the corner from the pub. He had gone for a twenty-minute walk to stretch his legs, enjoying the city's unique art nouveau architecture. Not someone who usually noticed structural genius, he was impressed at the subtlety of the Arab influence, impacting city design and culture in equal measure. He then decided to do what he had done in cities across the world. Walk into the local pub, bar, bodega, watering hole and have a party with whomever was willing and able.

"What are you drinking?" Gina asked. "I insist. Bride to be's right and honour. My fiancé would be horrified if I didn't buy a roaming Scotsman a drink."

"Oh, well, if you put it like that. I'll have a *Nasty Blue*. Or as the Italians like to call it, Nastro Azzuro. Thanks."

As he waited for the beer, his phone rang. He had called Maggie when he arrived; it had gone to voicemail. Whatever case she was working, he hoped she would be able to take a break for a refreshment.

"Hey, pal! How are you?" he asked.

"All a bit crazy just now to be honest. I listened to your message. You're here already?"

"Maggie, I live in Estonia. Not Australia. Last year we became part of Europe. Getting to exotic European locations is much easier now. Anyway, I've popped into a pub for a drink and met a group of girls on a hen party. Why don't you come along to join us? I think you'd like them."

"Tommy, I am so busy with everything on my plate, I can't think in a straight line. Text me the name, and I'll come and meet you."

How Many Lives does a Kilt Have?

The wispy, misty cloud made the hiker think someone had lit a campfire behind the bushes. It caught her attention as she walked towards the river to fill their water bottles.

"Hey, Patrick. Quick, over here." Jane pushed through the thick, sprawling bushes to the clearing on the other side. They had descended a long, winding trail from the tall, thick trees above them. Despite the precarious slope, they realised this may be their last chance to find water for a while. The figure was lying on his back looking skyward, half covered by the bush. Steam rose with the sun beating down on his sodden, crumpled clothes.

"Hello! Hello!" she shouted. Can you hear me?" Her Welsh accent sounded quite lyrical in the wilds of the Amazon.

"Hi," he said, his voice weaker than he had wanted it to be. He had been lying there for no more than twenty minutes - performing a mental inventory of his physical parts.

"My God, what happened to you?" Jane bent down and held his wrist to check his pulse: it was fast. Kiltman pushed on his elbows and levered himself into a sitting position, her arm behind his back.

"Jane, what's going..." Patrick burst through the foliage much less gracefully than his wife. He had been distracted by a flock of exotic birds, clicking his camera with an insatiable thirst to make use of last year's Christmas present. He was determined to defeat the curse of snapping the obvious when the more exciting subject was just a flash of inspiration away.

"OMG!" He pronounced each letter as if it were a word. He pulled the water bottle from his belt and held it to Kiltman's mouth. He drank several noisy mouthfuls, holding up his thumb in acknowledgement.

"You're the Kiltman guy, aren't you?" Jane asked. "What on earth are you doing here?"

He managed to smile and groan at the same time. "Now that's a great question. Although I don't have time to answer it."

He had not expected to meet anyone when he left the villagers' camp. It had been a last-ditch effort; he had run out of options.

"Fair enough," Patrick said. "It would be good to at least get the Reader's Digest version."

Kiltman took a deep breath. "Okay. Man flies in helicopter. Man falls from same helicopter. Survives fall. Is brought back to life by indigenous tribe of Amazonians. Finds a boat. Goes crashing over a waterfall." He pointed to the river, where they could see a cascade of surf 25 metres high. "Lands in water. Meets two strangers. Asks if they have a phone that gets a signal."

They both smiled before Jane said, "Sorry. No, we don't. Look, there is a Save the Planet camp not far up the trail. Have you heard of them? They're doing a lot of work to protect the Amazonian rain forest. We are here with them; they may have a phone you can use."

"Yes, my ex... I mean, a friend of a friend is at the Paris convention." Kiltman stood on shaky legs, placing his hand inside his sporran. Flask and leaves were there, intact. The jar of cream was still in his hand - his fingers hurting with the robustness of the grip. He extracted a leaf and stuffed it into his mouth, before taking a swig of Hair o' the Dog. "Ah! That's just what I needed. Sorry, I'd offer you some but it's a form of medication."

Jane and Patrick watched, exchanging glances.

"Yes, I understand, I don't fancy eating grass. But what about the whisky? It smells amazing." Patrick's hand was moving forward.

"Aw, I'd love to give you some. But that's also a special form of medication. Look, it's a long story. Can you show me the way to the camp?" He walked towards the bushes; and turned his head back towards them. "Please?"

"Sure," Jane said, giving Patrick a reassuring pat on the back. "Go straight through and turn left."

When Kiltman stepped forward, Jane nudged her husband and pointed at the back of his legs. The cuts and scratches were crimson red, glistening with the goo he had plastered over them. She looked at Patrick and mouthed an exaggerated *Ouch*.

"I know," said Patrick, pausing to snap a passing parakeet. "I've never seen such a tattered kilt."

Reunion

Wilson walked into the pub, hoping a drink with Tommy would give her the energy to think straight and move forward. She was stressed and anxious about breaking the news to him about Kenny.

When she left the hotel, she had received a text from Roddy to say he was on a flight to Rome, arriving the following morning. It had been sent just before take-off – deliberately, to make sure she could not stop him.

An unprompted flight across the Atlantic without a word of warning was something his father would do. It was in the boy's genes. She had called Fiona to let her know. As she expected, he had not told his mother. Fiona was upset, worried another child could be in danger. Wilson had calmed her with assurances that she would keep an eye on his safety.

When she closed the phone, there was a brief moment of panic; until she remembered Valentina. Wilson did not know her, other than she was sweet and had captured Crawford's heart. The call took just a few minutes. Crawford had made no progress since he had been taken into the critical care unit. Valentina wanted to help anyway she could. Picking Roddy up and keeping him with her until Maggie returned from Sicily would be a pleasure.

At least Roddy had been dealt with; for the time being. When he arrived, he would want to get involved in searching for Mask and Angie. That was tomorrow's problem. Today she was in a rut, frustrated by the absence of clues and direction. Angie and Kiltman missing, no clue as to where to find them. Then there was the Sacco investigation. She was in the right place at the right time, without the right to investigate. Albano and Monte had made it clear, their job stopped with the delivery of a few facts; information she could have picked up from a simple Google search.

"Maggie!" Tommy walked towards her swinging his hips from side to side.

"I take it you've been getting on well with the bride to be."
She smiled despite herself, pointing at the tiara and sash he was
wearing.

Tommy reached across and wrapped his arms around her
petite frame. "Good to see you. It's been a while."

"Too long, Tommy. Good to see you too. I need to tell…"

"Ah! Ah!" He put his finger on her lips. "No business talk.
First things first." He pointed towards the bar where the hen party
was in full swing. "In the middle of that gaggle of em, hens,
there's a large glass of Primitivo. Nice Italian red wine. Right up
your street."

She found herself close to tears. A bit of Dutch courage was
not a bad suggestion. "Okay, Tommy, lead the way."

"Maggie!" shouted Hilda. "Is that really you?"

Hilda's shout attracted her friends. Within seconds they were
hugging and kissing the Scottish detective. Gina, Michelle and
Carina joined Hilda in a group hug. Tommy watched the scene
with a sense of disbelief.

"So good to see you, girls. Who's getting married?" Wilson
asked once she had escaped the cluster of arms and heads
scrunched into a friendly scrum. He realised he had one job to
do. He placed a glass of wine in her outstretched hand.

"Gina is joining the Scottish - what did you call it, Tommy -
club?" Carina said, her attractive face, with strong Italian
features, beaming at Wilson.

"Em, the WAGs club!" he answered, feeling less confident
than the first time he had suggested it. Something to do with the
arrival of a Scottish Detective Inspector.

"Really? You're getting brave, aren't you?" Wilson's smile
was warmer than he expected. "Congratulations, Gina. He is a
lucky man." She embraced Gina, who settled in for another hug.

"Excuse me, did I miss something here? How do you all know
Maggie?" Tommy was standing on the periphery of the group,
where minutes earlier he had been at the centre.

The girls found it quite easy to ignore him. They had already
started to realise he did not expect people to react to his
comments.

"Ah, memories. Kiltman and I had a fun night with these girls
in Milan a few years back. Night before San Siro." Wilson

winced, remembering their run across the centre of the park in full view of tens of thousands of supporters.

"I remember that. You took out two Italian police officers with a tackle Wullie Miller would have been proud of." Tommy raised his glass.

"Yes, let's move on." Wilson laughed. "Look, girls, I need to talk to Tommy about something. I'll catch up with you in a minute." Her words were lost in their spontaneous rendition of Gloria Gaynor's *I Will Survive*.

She put her arm around his shoulders and led him to a table in the corner of the room. He sat down with his back against the wall. His youthful, impish features were usually perfect for lighting up a party or cracking a joke. Wilson's command had turned his face a patchy shade of pale - worry did not suit him.

"What's going on? Don't keep me in suspense."

How to start this conversation was her challenge. She wanted to talk about Kenny's disappearance, it was embroiled in Kiltman's absence. If she started, she would have to open up about his alter ego. She cast her mind back to a discussion with Kenny a couple of years earlier, not long after Mask was imprisoned. He had wanted to tell Tommy then, on the grounds they were best friends, and the role his friend had played in helping catch Skink and Mask. Maggie had dissuaded him - reminding him that once the genie is out of the bottle, there is no turning back. In the end, they decided to wait until they had no choice.

She realised this was the moment - once she had taken a large mouthful of wine. Placing the glass on the table beside her phone, she said, "Okay, there's no easy way to say this. It's complicated. You see..."

Bzzz. Bzzz. She looked at the phone, to see it vibrating on the polished wood. A +55 number. Brazil.

"I'm sorry, Tommy, I need to take this."

He nodded, stood and walked back towards the bar, shaking his head at how mobile phones dominated life these days. So much for the pre-conversation hype, he thought. Typical Maggie, making a mountain out of a mole hill. The queen of hyperbole. One day he would tell her that. Over the phone.

Finally

"Okay, I've got a signal. It's ringing." Nishav had worked for Save the Planet for over five years. After a childhood spent in India, he had moved to London to find a way to give something back to society. The organisation realised they had found someone with natural diplomacy underpinned by a hard work ethic. Throw in a sense of humour that lay somewhere between quirky and edgy, they knew he would be a strong ambassador in their camp somewhere west of Manaus. His family had cautioned against taking a role in a place so far from home, yet he knew it was the right thing not only for him, but for the planet he was committed to saving.

Kiltman stood beside him, holding a satellite dish aloft. They had walked to the summit of a nearby hill after arriving at the camp; a smaller set up than Kiltman had expected for such a critical project. There were a handful of scientists and ecologists working together to protect the forest. They were intent on collaborating with the local Brazilians to find sustainable ways of retaining and growing the Amazon foliage.

"Hello? Hello?" Nishav shouted. "Can you hear me?"

"Barely." Wilson had her hand over the mouthpiece to minimise the background noise. "Let me move outside." Nishav was sure he could hear a man's voice singing *I Will Survive* in the background. She stepped out onto the arid, dusty cobblestones. "Hello?"

"Hi, is that Maggie Wilson?" Nishav asked.

Kiltman yanked the phone from his hand.

"Maggie?" he shouted.

The pause felt like an age, filled with Gloria Gaynor's lyrics, more appropriate than any other they could imagine at that moment.

"Kenny?" She had sat down in a crouch, one hand on the stones keeping her balance. "Is that you?"

"Yes, it's me. Oh, God, I've missed you so much." Nishav had not seen a grown man cry since India lost against England at cricket. Just like then, he put his hand on the stranger's back and stroked him gently.

"I can't believe it. We had lost hope. Every minute has been torture. I never thought I'd hear your voice again," she said. Her tears dropped in thick droplets, dampening the dry cobbles. "Are you okay? How did you manage to stay alive?" She had so many questions, yet she was not able to think straight.

"I'm still in the Amazon, southwest of Brazil. Let's just say it has been as far from a spa as you could imagine. Listen, Mask has escaped. Angie, Fiona and Roddy are all in danger. I'm going to contact Roddy now and let him know I'm okay. Please can you make sure they are protected? I'll tell you everything when I see you."

"Kenny, we eventually figured out Mask had bolted. It took a few days; he had covered his tracks well. It looks like he already has Angie. She disappeared from the camp."

"What?" He twitched just as Nishav's back rub touched an open wound. "What do you mean disappeared?"

Maggie explained the information she had received from Roddy and the coincidental sighting in Rome. That side-tracked her for a moment, as she explained the status of her Sacco investigation. She went on to describe the attack on Crawford. Kiltman shared her pain at Crawford's battle to stay alive; and sensed her guilt. He remembered the afternoon spent in Murphy's bar in Manhattan, the crowd baiting Crawford to break the habit of a lifetime and buy a drink. Poor guy, he thought.

His attention turned to Roddy. "He doesn't know anyone in America. Where is he getting these clues from?" Kiltman's radar was up. This was not making sense.

"Someone he met on social media. At least that's what he said. Anyway, that's not the point." She was keen to bring him up to date and move the conversation along. "You haven't heard it all, though."

Kiltman had his forehead up against a palm tree. It was too late. Mask did not hang around; he had already implemented his plan. "There's more?"

"Yes, Roddy has left the US. He's on a flight to Rome, arriving tomorrow morning." This was going to be the hard bit.

"What? How did he wangle that? Are you going to meet him at the airport?"

"Well, that's the thing. I was there for just a couple of days. I'm now in Sicily following up on the Sacco killing. I just discovered he was on the flight. He hadn't told Fiona; I had to break the news to her." She could see how all this looked very messy from the point of view of someone who had just emerged from five days in the jungle.

"He can't arrive there with no-one to meet him, Maggie." No sugar, Sherlock, she thought.

"I know. So, I've made arrangements for him to be picked up at the airport." She began to feel less sure about her plan.

"Who by?"

She could have said, "A girl who works in a Pasticceria in central Rome that I only met this week".

Instead she said, "Valentina; a really lovely person Crawford and I know in Rome. She'll take him to her house until I get back there, or…"

"…I get there," he said. "Looks like all roads lead to Rome, after all. When I arrive, I'll call you. We need to find Mask and Angie. I'm sure he didn't leave prison just to take her back. He's up to something, I know it. Thanks for arranging to have him picked up by your friend."

Nishav was enjoying the role he was playing in supporting a kilted superhero. He would have invited him to dinner with the rest of the team; however, the chopper was leaving in twenty minutes. It had been scheduled to leave half an hour earlier, they had delayed it to allow Kiltman a lift. If it left any later, then several Save the Planet employees would miss their connecting flights home.

He had coughed a couple of times to get the Scotsman's attention; when that failed to have an impact, he picked a handful of purple berries from a nearby tree and launched them in the air to cascade onto his head and back. Kiltman turned to see Nishav pointing at his watch, scrunching his face into as authentic a version of frustration as he could muster, despite the absurdity of the moment.

Kiltman raised his thumb and nodded back at his smiling newfound friend who was threatening to throw another bunch of berries. "Looks like I need to go. My new pal is reminding me that there's a helicopter waiting to take me to Rio de Janeiro international airport. I'll get a flight from there. Will let you know the details."

"Oh, Kenny. There's another thing before you go. Really quick."

"What is it?" He was not sure if he could handle much more.

"Tommy flew down from Estonia and is here with me in Sicily." The line between sublime and ridiculous had never been thinner.

"What on earth is he doing there?" Kiltman asked,

"At the moment, he is doing the Rumba, wearing a tiara."

The Road to Damascus

He surveyed the peculiar, sloping square, thousands of people crammed into its confined space. The banners, posters, chants of *Damascus! Damascus*! greeted him as he stood on the balcony waving at his followers. He raised both arms in the air to quieten the crowds. His vantage point was perfectly located for an occasion as important as this. His team had linked a microphone up to speakers dotted across the square. Not the most sophisticated of communications, but enough for this evening's purpose.

Once he felt the noise had abated, he put his hands together, and scanned the crowd. "My people, my loyal Galatians. I am humbled by your support and faith in our movement. On Monday I will join my fellow Cardinals to elect our new Pope. I do not need to tell you how important this event is for the future of the Church. The fact you are all here today, wearing your medals, shows you believe in a future that speaks to Christ's true message.

"On your right, you can see the Gregorian University, where many years ago I studied philosophy and theology, under the talented tutelage of the esteemed Jesuit order. On your left is the Pontificio Istituto Biblico, the centre of advanced studies in Holy Scripture. Between these two organisations, there is a wealth of knowledge based on generations of research, investigation and scholarly analysis."

He paused and let his words sink in, silence descending across the crowd.

"At some point, we should stop and ask ourselves the fundamental question. If Jesus were to show up in physical form again, would he look at our Church and say, 'Yes, this is exactly the institution I wanted to create'? Would he want to join our Church as it is today? Or would he want to remind us of simpler times, simpler messages."

He waited several seconds, listening to a volley of responses in the crowd. He knew they were aligned to his words.

"In the coming days, when you pray, I do not ask you to hope for a particular Pope." The crowd chanted even louder: *Damascus! Damascus!* "I ask you to pray that whoever the next leader of our Church may be, that he will lead us into the future and will make our religion Jesus' first choice as the Church he would want to belong to.

"Do you want Jesus to say '*You were running a good race. Who cut in on you to keep you from obeying the truth?*': Galatians 5,7? Or should he remind us of Galatians 2,5: '*We did not give in to them for a moment, so that the truth of the gospel might remain with you.*'"

The crowd shouted in unison, "*2, 5; 2, 5; 2, 5; 2, 5;...*"

Cardinal Damascus watched as the chants grew louder and stronger. He wanted all of Rome to hear this chant, this proclamation of truth. He knew his presence at the balcony would make them increase the commitment in their hearts and the power in their shouts. Taking his medal in both hands, he raised it high in the air above his head. Hands all around him did the same thing. Unbridled enthusiasm surged through each of them as individuals and as a group, reinforcing their desire to support this man who had come from poor beginnings. The media had talked at length about his challenges. A refugee from Europe during the Second World War, he had been adopted into a midwestern American family. It was public knowledge that he had defied the odds to achieve such a position of leadership, famed for his humility and sense of purpose.

The Cardinal surveyed the square focusing on the individual members of the crowd. At the front, holding a banner with the words *Cardinal Damascus for Pope*, was a face he recognised. He had to do a double take. Yes, it was him. Coach Stone. Damascus had seen his conversion with his own eyes. Someone who understood Galatians 1:11: *I want you to know, brothers and sisters, that the gospel I preached is not of human origin.* Here he was far from Cincinnati and home. Even by the standards of adulation Damascus had grown accustomed to, this was exceptional. Coach stood, placard in hand, medal around his neck, eyes closed, swaying to the chants of *Damascus for Pope, Damascus for Pope.*

Damascus felt good to be surrounded by people who cared about his cause, knowing there were many more outside this square all across the world.

Two interested followers enjoyed watching the event on their TV in a house one hour's drive north of this gathering. Tantalus and Mask were looking forward to the role they were going to play in redefining the future of the Church.

Sunday, April 17

Wee Small Hours

The bar had been filling up as each hour passed. Soon after midnight the numbers spiked. Mainly men. Word had spread that a contingent of pretty girls had flown in for a party. The reason for the revelry was not important; the group of dancing, singing partygoers was enough to have friends calling each other, changing their Saturday evening plans. Once dinner had finished and their slow *passeggiata* with family had ended, a group of five young men left home on their Vespas to meet at the bar.

Hilda noticed them arrive, commenting on the similarity to a pack of wolves. The first to walk in was a young man around thirty - not dissimilar to the ruggedly handsome Al Pacino in Scarface - the others strutting behind, talking animatedly to one another. Their faux indifference was tangible. They looked towards the bar at the girls dancing in a circle. Tommy and a few others from the pub were singing along to The Proclaimers booming *500 Miles* from the old-fashioned jukebox.

Wilson was sitting at the bar, nursing her wine, enjoying an overwhelming sense of relief. She could breathe more easily with Kenny now alive and well. Or maybe not so well. Five days wandering the Amazon would not have been a walk in the park, she thought. Then smiled, knowing how much Kenny would have loved to own that comment. She missed him more than she could have imagined. Taking a glug of her wine, she had a momentary flash of feelgood. A wave of repressed euphoria washed over her. That last drink of wine had taken her to what she called *pivotal junction*: go home to bed or have a party. It had been happening to her since she was in university. One moment she would be putting her coat on to go home, the next on top of a table dancing with her friends.

She studied the men walking towards a table in the corner. Wilson noticed the manager approach customers who had been sitting there for over an hour. He lent his hands on the table and spoke quietly. They had been eating an array of snacks, sipping on Campari sodas. Without complaint, they picked up their drinks and plates and walked towards a corner near the jukebox. The manager wiped the table with a cloth, as a waitress gathered glasses and plates. The five men positioned chairs in a semi-circle around the table, facing towards the bar. By the time they had placed their helmets and phones in front of them, there was little room left for the drinks the barman carried over. Interesting, Wilson thought; as far as she could tell, they had not placed an order, yet the barman had brought them an array of beers and liqueurs. The leader of the pack slipped some money into the barista's hand.

One of them stood and walked towards the hen party. His strut and swagger - manicured to perfection - drew glances from others sitting around the pub. He approached Gina and whispered in her ear, before turning to saunter back to his friends.

"Hey, Gina, what did he say?" Wilson's antenna was up.

Gina laughed. "He asked us to come and join them at the table, they want to buy us a drink." Tommy had returned the tiara and sash, adding two pink balloons to her costume. "They must have missed the hidden signs that I am not available." She pointed at her party accoutrements.

"Aw, come on," Michelle said. She had been attracting attention from the other customers. Not often they had a chance to watch a glamorous French woman dance on top of a barstool, marching on the spot to the Proclaimers. "It could be fun. We came here to have a party."

"Yes, Gina, this might be the last night out for many years." Carina tried to put her wrists together in fake bondage, but forgot she was holding a glass of wine, contents splashing onto the marble floor. "Whoops!" She giggled.

"Ja," Hilda waded in. "Carina and Michelle are right; let's go."

"Okay," Gina said. "I give in."

"What's the guy's name?" Michelle asked.

"The one who spoke to me is Pietro, and the other who wants to meet us is Marco. You're right, we are here in Sicily. We might as well get to know some Italians," Gina said, filling her glass from a half empty bottle of prosecco.

Wilson saw Tommy stroll over to a table close to the five men. A couple were there already; they did not seem to mind him sitting beside them, recognising him as the man who had been happy to dance wearing a tiara a few minutes earlier. Wilson realised he was experiencing the same sense of concern she was as he positioned himself at the table with a clear view of the girls pulling up chairs and introducing themselves. She walked over and sat beside him. They did not speak a word. They leaned back against the wall, enjoying the shade of a thick wooden pillar, like a pair of foxes observing a pack of wolves.

Nothing Good Happens after 2 am

Tommy had been at the same table for a couple of hours, with Wilson settled in beside him. They had not discussed it; they both shared a sense of unease. There was something eery in the mood building in the pub: tables busy, walls lined with customers drinking, chatting, surveying. Despite a very busy bar, it seemed to him the energy in the room had dropped a few notches when the five men arrived.

Tommy turned to her. "Hey, Maggie, you know I have a friend back in Saltcoats?"

"Aw, that's a lovely wee spot on the Ayrshire coast," she answered, remembering weekends there with her family as a child.

"Well, my friend, Pat, comes from there. He's a really nice guy, passionate Celtic supporter. Anyway, he once told me that his mother had a saying." He took a gulp of his beer. It was already quite flat. He had slowed down as the evening progressed: enough time spent in pubs to know when the energy was going rogue. "She used to say that nothing good ever happens after two o'clock in the morning."

As if on cue, an old grandfather clock, oddly out of place in the bar, struck 2 am. Other than Tommy and Wilson, nobody noticed it over the din generated by the large crowd. Wilson nodded; her past experiences supported this theory.

Gina and her friends were a table away talking to the Italian men. The conversation seemed quite lively. Wilson and Tommy had shifted their chairs nearer to their table, close enough to listen in.

"One of the things that fascinates me about Sicily is the role it played in the Second World War," Gina said to the group. The men looked at each other. Until now, they had listened to the women tell stories and sing along to the jukebox. Gina had decided it was important to introduce a more serious tone to suit the mood of the brooding men. Hilda was shaking her head at the topic Gina chose to discuss.

"What do you mean exactly?" Marco asked. His posture changed from a distracted slouch to straight-backed intensity. He had said very little until that moment.

"Gina is a history teacher in Milan. In one of the international schools," Hilda said, patting her on the back. Proud of her friend.

"Oh, time for a history lesson, is it?" Pietro said with a sardonic laugh. Marco shot him a glance that would have stopped a four-year-old putting their fingers in the cookie jar.

"Go on," Marco said. More of a dare than an invite.

"Well," Gina said, distracted by the interaction between the men. It had made her uncomfortable, but she continued. "The Allies needed to find a way into Europe to counterattack the Germans. The tide was starting to turn; yet nothing would change until the Allied troops could get their forces onto mainland Europe. The problem was the Germans were too strong in Northern Europe. Even with the support of the Americans, taking the Allied troops across in boats to France would have resulted in carnage." She took a drink of her prosecco, to hide the tears dampening her eyes. It saddened her to think of all the young soldiers who lost their lives.

"The Allies had just defeated Rommel in Northern Africa and had a strong force of British and American troops there already. Thousands of soldiers who had fought long and hard and were battle ready. It was decided that they needed to cross into Europe from the South, through Southern Italy. Until then, Italy had been on the side of the Germans, although a large contingent of Italians actively opposed this alliance."

Michelle was looking intently at Gina, enthralled by the story. Tommy wondered if she might start taking notes.

"So, it was a risky move. Depending on where they chose to land could make or break the invasion. That's where Sicily comes in. In some ways, you could say that Sicily changed the shape of the war and was the catalyst for the Allied victory." Some of the men at the table, who had been quiet until now, nodded in agreement.

"This is when you have to go to the USA. Where Lucky Luciano comes into the picture. He is considered to have played a dominant role in organised crime in America. For a gangster, he had a contradictory mix of values. He was responsible for all sorts of criminal activities in New York; yet when he was imprisoned before the war, he led a petition to have a church built inside the correctional facility, one of the first churches ever built in a prison. Before imprisonment, and for a while when he was behind bars, he remained capo for the organised crime network in New York. Not a surprise, considering he was originally from Sicily. His strong links back to the families running his home island were still intact, fortified by his New York kingpin status. We all know from movies like the Godfather, the two places are well-connected."

"Great soundtrack," Carina said, clicking her fingers and humming.

"By the way, Marco," Michelle said, "you are the double of Michael Corleone in that movie." The comment earned a mouth twitch from the sullen young man.

"To cut a long story short, Lucky knew he could help the Allied troops invade Sicily. From prison, he reached out to the American government and, before you know it, convinced them that he could engineer the necessary Sicilian support via his connections; people who could *make things happen*." She made the inverted commas sign with her fingers.

"The Allied invasion took place through Sicily in 1943; a huge success due to Lucky's contacts allowing an easy entry into Europe. It was even given a name: Project Husky. They fought their way up through Italy into central Europe. Hitler stood no chance after that. Two years later, the war was over." She slapped her hands together, as if class dismissed. She chose not to say push your chairs under your desks. "Well, that's it. I think I am ready to go home." She had sensed a turn in the mood at the table.

"What happened to Lucky?" asked Michelle settling into the story.

"When the war ended, he was set free, and deported back to Italy," Gina answered, then sighed. "It's widely recognised that while Lucky Luciano was one of the reasons the Allies won the war, the downside was that it opened the door for cementing Mafia control in New York. Lots of dodgy people have become very rich because of Lucky's pact with the US. Some people say it was a high, but necessary, price to pay to stop the war."

Marco was tapping the edge of his glass with a finger. His face did not change expression during the 2 am lesson. "You think you have all the answers in your history books?" His tone fostered a wave of tension across the table.

Gina was about to answer; it was not going to be polite. She had had enough of the machismo oozing out of these men. She enjoyed a good debate. However, she had begun to sense a hostility from the young men; and was concerned the late hour was making her less aware of her audience.

The chance to address his question was quashed when the door of the bar slammed open. Two men burst through, dressed in black with dark balaclavas.

Marco and his friends reacted by throwing themselves onto the floor, pulling whoever was nearest down with them; Gina, Hilda, Michelle and Carina, all landed together in a stack of bodies. Marco pushed the table up onto its edge, shielding them from what was about to come. Glasses and plates crashed; just audible above the cacophony of screams in the bar, customers clambering for cover.

Wilson and Tommy were at the table nearest the door. They turned to see two men armed with short, stub-nosed machine guns, pointed at the upturned table. A glass - Tommy's pint of *Nasty Blue* - had left Wilson's hand before she realised what she was doing. The smaller of the two men took the full impact on his temple. His knees crumpled and the gun fired bullets into the wall.

Tommy ducked down to below waist level and punched him in the solar plexus as he fell to the ground. The gush of air was audible as he dropped his gun and collapsed in pain, struggling to catch a breath.

The other assailant fired off a volley of shots, slamming into the upended table. He did not spare a glance for his accomplice writhing on the ground. Striding towards the table, he continued to fire, breaking the table into splinters.

Wilson dived on his legs, wrapping her hands around his ankles. Before she could get a strong grip, he lashed out with his foot and connected with her head. She fell back onto the ground, dazed, unable to stand.

The man placed his hand on the table to roll it sideways, the barrel of the gun pointing downwards. His finger tightened on the trigger. One more burst of bullets and his victims would be dead. If there was collateral damage, so be it. He would grab his friend lying in a heap, escape and collect their earnings. A job like this was expected to be messy. Unlike their most recent hit in London, this one was meant to threaten. To send a message.

A man of many talents, Luca prided himself on the speed of his reactions. This time he had met his match. A woman sprang from behind the table. Her hands slashed the air, as she screamed a piercing screech. Landing on her left foot, her right leg flashed through the air at a 90-degree angle. The roundhouse kick smacked off the side of the man's head. Gina had only ever kicked punchbags in the gym and had once - for a dare - knocked the hat off Hilda's handsome boyfriend. Hitting a villain when he was a clear and present danger to others gave her an immense sense of satisfaction. He tumbled to the ground, unconscious; the gun smashing off the floor.

Tommy dived forward and grabbed the weapon. Scrambling to his feet, he pointed it at the attackers. Both lay where they fell; one unconscious, the other gasping for breath. Screams were still sounding around the bar, people running for the doors. Sirens broke through the chaos, alerting them that help was on its way, rising in volume by the second.

Wilson rubbed the side of her face; she had not felt this burning sense of pain since the Mask chase a few years ago. Nodding her respect towards Gina and Tommy, she said, "Looks like it's true: nothing good happens after 2 o'clock in the morning. Except..." She pointed at the two men, powerless on the ground.

Touching Down

A ten-hour flight was just what he needed to arrange his thoughts. He managed a fitful five-hour sleep; and a viewing of Die Hard, a definite bonus of flying alone, no parents to check the age ratings.

He was in no doubt he had crossed the line with this impromptu flight. His mother would first be shocked, then upset, followed by angry and when she calmed down, loving and - hopefully - proud of him for taking the initiative. Then most likely angry again. Classic parent emotional curve. He could handle that. His father on the other hand would be angry then angrier and then apoplectic. At that moment he would have given anything to see his dad in a rage about his socks on top of the TV; or his phone on the wall outside the house (to be fair, he had to get his keys from the bottom of the bag); or his not coming home after school for dinner; or for taking a flight across the Atlantic without permission.

It was important to stay focused. Mask showing up in St. Peter's was no coincidence. Angie would have had no choice but to go to him. Then there was his father's trip to Brazil. As the days progressed, he had more time to think about this. Maybe their spa trip was a ruse, a decoy, to cover up a visit to see Mask. Or maybe it was legit and Maggie and he were going to get their legs waxed together. He pushed that thought from his mind. It only added to his discomfort.

He was in no doubt that his father's fate and Mask's escape were inextricably linked. At that point he switched on the movie. He needed inspiration, a way to believe his father could survive whatever Mask had planned for him. If John McLean could do it, his dad could too.

His mind drifted to the Galatians and their charismatic, yet unusual, leader. It was a welcome relief to think about something other than the absence of his father and Angie. Could Damascus really become the next Pope? Roddy had to admit to himself he did not understand the machinations of the Church. Such a huge organisation with two thousand years of history. It was not difficult to see Damascus had a point in that there was a lot of pomp and ceremony layered on top of Christ's message of loving God and your neighbour. On the other hand, there were over one billion Catholics across the world. It made sense that some rules and traditions had to be introduced and followed to keep them connected and on message.

He remembered his father comparing the Catholic Church to one of Wallace Distillers' most popular whiskies: High Park 10-year-old. It had been outselling the competition globally, making more money for the company than most of the other brands put together. However, across the international markets, the local distributors were adding their own view as to how High Park 10 should be marketed. Some had billboards with views of Scotland showing peaceful sunsets, campfires and grown men fishing. The more avant-garde, usually Mediterranean, countries had William Wallace fighting the English, battle worn soldiers in ripped kilts celebrating with a High Park 10. His father had explained that while both images were valid and could be used for whisky marketing, they could not be used for the same brand. They were destined for the *'graveyard of inconsistency'*, as his father called it. The home of brands that failed to stay true to their essence – their soul.

His father had then nodded, spread his hands and said, "This is the dilemma of the Church."

It had taken Roddy a while to think it through. Now it helped clarify why Damascus was taking such a strong stand. He was not trying to create inconsistency across the Church, although a by-product of his sect was a disruption that could not be popular. He was focused on taking the Church back to its true *brand*, walking away from flashy advertising and message control. He was asking everyone to follow St. Paul in starting again, leaving the old customs and ways behind, embracing the original essence of Christ's teaching. A commendable objective, Roddy thought, although there was an edge to the Galatians that did not sit well with him. Something was not quite right with the *cult-ure* they created around them.

When he watched the news on TV in the airport, and they discussed the pending Papal Conclave, they showed pictures of people across the world wearing Galatians medals. He had seen his dad's friend, Grant MacTavish, reporting on the Galatians. Grant had coined a phrase he was clearly proud of – that Galatians are inspiring Catholics all over the world to *meddle with their medals* and seek change. Medal meddling was receiving more news coverage as the days passed.

The conclave was scheduled to start on Monday, April 18th, the day after he landed. He expected Rome to be busy with tourists and pilgrims coming to witness this rare event. Whether this made his task easier or more difficult was uncertain.

The pilot called for passengers to fasten their seat belts. Roddy tightened his, smiling ruefully at the pilot's unwittingly appropriate metaphor.

Valentina

He walked around the terminal looking for Maggie, surprised at her absence. After some minutes his phone connected to Italia telecom, followed by a few beeps of incoming messages.

The first was from Maggie to say there was good news and bad news. Bad news first, as they always agreed they would do; she was in Sicily and could not pick him up. A lovely lady called Valentina would be there with a sign. Good news, however, was that his father was alive and well. He took a moment to say a prayer of thanks for his father's return. In his heart he had always known his father was okay, while his head told him to prepare for the worst. What did this mean about Mask and Angie? Roddy was sure his father was not going to remain in Brazil. Maggie was throwing him a curve ball: an Americanism he picked up listening to Coach explain a football tactic.

He walked back to the *meet and greet* area. He could see a young woman leaning against the barrier with a board above her head. The number of arriving travellers had reduced to a slow trickle of people with trolleys overloaded with luggage. He could see her growing concern in how she nibbled at her bottom lip.

"Excuse me," he said. "I'm Roddy." He was struck with how pretty she was; olive skin, dark eyes, dark hair tied up in a precarious lump above her head, defying gravity with the aid of a pen and pencil. He smiled at the board she was holding. In flowery writing, was *Rodi*, with a rose in one corner, a sun in the other, and a heart surrounding the whole thing.

"Ah, Roddy!" She kissed him on each cheek, what his mother would have called *big slobbery loving* kisses. "Welcome to Roma! I am Valentina." She took him by the hand and led him through the crowds of people wandering around the airport, trying to find buses, taxis and loved ones.

Outside the terminal, a small van - *Pasticceria Valentina* labelled along its side - was parked across from the taxis. Two traffic wardens sat on its bonnet, eating croissants and holding cups of coffee. They waved at Valentina as she approached before wandering off to issue tickets; to those who did not offer fresh pastries and coffee.

The drive into Rome changed from exhilarating to hair-raising with every near miss and horn blare. Valentina's driving persona was inconsistent with the sweet girl at the airport. When she spoke to him in the car, she was the epitome of friendly, with lots of questions about Scotland, about what he was interested in, whether he had a girlfriend; and ultimately what football team he supported.

On arrival at the Pasticceria in central Rome, she stopped the van to get out and move two yellow cones, placed a few metres apart. Back in the vehicle, she manoeuvred it into the makeshift parking spot, bumping into cars, front and back, to squeeze into the space.

"Let's go!" she said, before stepping outside the van. There was a man leaning against the Pasticceria wall, smoking a cigarette. She threw him the key. "Grazie, Paolo!" He caught the key as he had done many times before. Opening the bakery door, he nodded to Roddy. "*Benvenuto, amico!*"

"Eh, thank you," he answered, getting the gist of the welcome.

Valentina escorted him through the bakery, full of shoppers discussing the bread and cakes on offer. She grabbed a few freshly baked pastries, a large orange juice and a bunch of napkins before leading him to a room two floors above. She arranged the food and drink on the table, making sure to place the TV remote control alongside. He looked out the window. The view out over *Piazza del Popolo* was calming. A lazy stream of Sunday morning traffic weaved around the oxymoronic, *circular square*. He had read about this part of Rome on the plane. The piazza was one of the city's highlights on any tour worth its salt. Home to another plundered millennia-old Egyptian obelisk, it served as the entrance to *Via del Corso*, the city's busiest shopping area. The square was a conduit between ancient history and bargains on the high street.

The smells wafting up from the Pasticceria tickled his taste buds. He could not imagine living in this apartment without gorging on the delights baked two floors below.

"Okay, *caro*, I need to work. I will come back in a couple of hours. Relax, have a sleep if you're tired." She pointed at a laptop on the table. "Also, I have a computer, if you want to play games."

"Thanks, Valentina. I really appreciate it." She kissed him again on each cheek, before leaving.

A minute later, he clicked his fingers and ran to the door.

She was halfway down the stairs talking into her phone.

"Hey, Valentina," he called.

She turned and looked up the stairs between the iron railings, "Hi, Roddy. I'm just talking to DI Wilson. How can I help?"

"Say *Ciao* from me! What's your password for the computer? I fancy playing some games, I'm not tired."

"Oh, I forgot to tell you; this is a bit embarrassing. I just changed it yesterday. It's, em, *Crawford.* Capital C then small letters. So that I can remember to say a prayer for him every time I log on." She shrugged. "At the end of the day, all we have left is prayer."

"I know what you mean. Thanks!" He waved before turning back into the room.

First thing he had to do was call his mother to let her know he was safe in Rome. He waited a moment to prepare for the call before dialling. The call soon turned into a freight train of emotion, his mother expressing herself as only a mother could. She followed each stage of the parental emotional journey as expected. He stopped her at the loving stage and said he had to go; he would call later.

His next call was to Maggie.

"Hi! *Buongiorno, Maggie!*" He had learned a few Italian words on the plane, intent on impressing her.

"Hey. Nice Italian accent there. Welcome to Rome! Did you have a good flight?" She sounded tired, forcing an upbeat tone.

"Thanks. Yes, all fine. Watched Die Hard, don't tell Dad." He liked being conspiratorial with her. "I was so pleased to get your text that he is okay."

"You're telling me! What a relief, I can tell you." He waited while she paused for a moment "Listen, pal. I am at the police station. I need to go; I will connect later. When we meet, we can talk more. Oh, and don't worry about Die Hard, I'll just add it to the list of things I can bribe you with." Wilson wanted to talk but not with Albano and Monte staring at her across the table.

"No worries. Speak later. *Arrivederci!*" Roddy sat down at the laptop, waiting for her to hang up first. He hoped she was still impressed with his accent.

"Oh, I forgot to ask," she said. "I assume Valentina managed to pick you up okay. I thought she would have let me know."

Interrogation

"Let me get this clear, DI Wilson," Albano said. She could see he was caught somewhere between disbelief and respect. "You and your friends just happened to be celebrating a…" he looked at his notes, "…*hen night*, whatever that is. Which includes you socialising with members of the Marciano gang, before preventing their assassination." He did a strange thing with his hands, as if he had salt pinched in his fingers pointing them towards her. She assumed this was his way of showing he found the explanation ridiculous.

"Not quite," she replied. She had told the story three times already. It was 9 am, she had not slept, her nerves were frayed and her patience non-existent. She closed her eyes and focused on being patient. "I was not there to participate in a hen party. Which, by the way, is an event to celebrate a woman getting married. I bumped into them by chance in the pub, I knew them from a trip to Milan a few years ago. I know how it might appear, yet coincidences do happen."

She put her hand in the air to head off their next comment. "My friend, Tommy MacGregor, flew down from Estonia for a holiday when he knew I was here. I know that sounds far-fetched; let's just say, he is rather, em, spontaneous." She grimaced. "Thanks to Tommy, we were able to stop them from murdering some of your local citizens. By the way, have you found out who the two thugs are?"

"Excuse me, Signora Wilson, we are questioning you. It is not your place to interrogate us. When we feel it is appropriate, we will let you know. All I can say, is that they are being interviewed in another room." Albano looked at Monte before continuing. "Now, tell us about how you knew the Marciano gang members."

"We didn't know those men belonged to Marciano's gang. If I had known, then I may have taken the opportunity to ask a few questions of my own." She omitted to mention that Marco had taken her to the side when the police arrived. He made a point of thanking her, Gina and Tommy, emphasizing the word *rispetto* -

respect, one of the most important words in Sicily. He pushed a card into her hand and asked her to call him. He wanted to thank them for saving his life and his friends too. Something told her not to discuss this with Albano.

"That's it. I'm tired; and need some coffee. So please, let's wrap this up. You know where I'm staying, if you want to reach me." She stood, picked up her phone and placed it in her bag. Albano looked at Monte. They both made a peculiar facial expression and nodded their agreement. Next time she came to Italy, she would find a dictionary that translated body part movements into English.

She left the station, head spinning from the nonstop questioning. She walked a few blocks to clear her head before entering Bar Palermo, where she had agreed to meet Tommy. He was sitting at the counter with a coffee and an array of pastries. As she walked in, he signalled the waitress with a wink and a wave, which prompted a broad smile. The waitress was around their age, attractive in a Sophia Loren no-nonsense way; strong Italian features and proud of them. She came over as Wilson sat on the stool beside him. Before she could place an order, the waitress reached across and nipped Tommy's cheek with her fingers, squeezing for a few seconds, "*Sei troppo birichino!*"

She turned her gaze to Wilson, "Is he your husband?"

"God, no. I mean, no," Wilson said. "Why?"

"That is good. I just told him that he is very, how do you say, cheeky!"

Wilson laughed. "On that, I agree one hundred per cent!"

"*Cento percento!*" The waitress smiled and gave Wilson a high five. "You for coffee?" At first Wilson thought she had just been sworn at, then replied, "Oh, yes please. A cappuccino would be great."

"My name is Luisa, and I will be your waitress this morning." Luisa threw her head back and guffawed. "I love saying things like Americans in the movies." She walked off to the coffee machine giggling to herself.

Tommy turned to Wilson and spoke before she could say anything, "I'm going to marry that girl."

"Excuse me?"

"Luisa will be my wife. I know it." he glanced towards the waitress, who was being steamed by the old-fashioned De'Longhi coffee machine. He stared at her for a few moments, sighed then said, "I think she knows it too."

"Okay, Romeo." Wilson put a hand on his arm. "I admit she's very cute, but you met her this morning for the first time. She might be married or at least have a significant other."

"Hey, I'm only here till tomorrow. No point in messing around." He took a mouthful of his cappuccino.

"Okay, if you want to make this work, you might want to lose the moustache." Wilson wanted to mother Tommy whenever she met him.

"Oh, right." He used his sleeve to wipe the milk residue from his top lip. He caught Luisa's eye as he did so; his heart gave a little half jump.

"Can we talk about what just happened a few hours ago?" she asked.

"Yes, sure," he said. "That was surreal. At one point I thought a film crew would jump out from behind the curtains and shout 'Cut!'"

She nodded. "I know. We were lucky. You were very brave."

Luisa returned and placed a coffee cup in front of Wilson. "Si, I agree Signor Tommy is very brave."

"Excuse me," Wilson said. "Do you know what happened last night?"

"Are you joking? This is Sicily. Everyone knows everything. You too, Detective. Also, very brave." She stopped and looked Wilson in the eyes. "Now you two must be very careful. When you make one man happy in Sicily, you make another man angry." She dragged her thumb along the corner of her eye.

"*Occhio!*" Wilson responded before Luisa could speak, running her thumb down her cheek. The waitress nodded. "Look after this sweet man. I do not want him to stand me up tonight."

"Sorry?" Tommy said. Then blushed when a hint of understanding crossed his eyes. "Meet you at steps of San Domenico at seven?"

"*Perfetto.*" She made a loud kissing sound with her full lips, before walking to the other end of the bar to serve a group of elderly men. As she walked towards them Wilson could see their faces light up. They did not come to Bar Palermo for the coffee.

Wilson cocked her head at him.

"This never happens to me." Tommy's face was scarlet. "Now it has. My dream is about to come true."

Wilson laughed. "You know, Tommy, I don't think I could last one day in your world. Where do you get the energy?"

"Hah! You don't do so bad yourself. Rugby tackling a guy with a machine gun."

She rubbed the side of her head, flinching at the touch. "I'm getting too old for this." She reached across and hugged him. She had not meant to, it just happened. "Tommy, I know we all joke a lot, but really, you are a great guy. You were amazing last night."

"Shh, Maggie." He put his finger to her lips. "Luisa might hear you."

Welcome to Rome

"*Benvenuto a Roma, Signor Shaunery.*" The immigration official stamped and handed the passport back. Cornelius Shaunery, a name he saved for missions like this. He kept the passport alongside his Kiltman and Kenny Morgan passports in a secret, waterproofed compartment of his sporran.

Technically he was stepping outside his boundaries. He was sure Gemmill would use this phony passport to bring him down - if he found out about it. He was never sure if the Chief Constable truly disliked him or just found it impossible to respect him. He only used it when he had no other choice. This was one of those situations. Kiltman flying into Rome would be reported in the media. Travelling as 'Kenny Morgan' was also not advisable. Either name would alert Mask that he was still alive. It was already difficult to catch this madman without sending a signal he was coming after him.

He walked through the terminal towards the taxi rank dodging hordes of pilgrims and tourists. They were dressed in clothes befitting a Papal Conclave campaign, determined to take every opportunity to convince the Cardinals of their preferred candidate - hats and t-shirts with names stitched or painted on: Bergoglio, Ratzinger, Martini and Damascus were the most common. Under their arms, they carried folded banners and posters, no doubt to be unfurled in St. Peter's Square later that day. Many of them had medals around their necks that would not have looked out of place at a Metallica concert. Some held them in their hands, rubbing with their fingers.

He had seen enough on the airport terminal's TV to know this particular Papal contest was considered a watershed moment. A juxtaposition for the Church to either stay on the same path or to step back and refresh. The question then became how much of a refresh could be delivered and would be acceptable.

He was in no doubt this was the reason for Mask showing up in Rome. He loved the big stage; he tried to kill hundreds of United Nations representatives in a single smash of his lethal gas container in New York. A Papal election was another huge platform. What exactly he intended to do was still a mystery. It was important to understand these intentions before he could find out how to catch him. He looked at the clock above the exit: 10.55 am; less than 24 hours until the cardinals were behind locked doors in the Vatican choosing who would lead them on the next chapter in the Church's history.

He stepped out onto the kerb and flagged a cab.

"Si, Signor, where we go?" It always impressed Kenny how airport cab drivers knew which language to address a customer, just by looking at them. Kenny had purchased his clothes from a second-hand stall outside Rio's airport. He asked the seller to allow him to change behind the curtain. He had packed his Kiltman garb in a backpack and changed into khaki trousers and a Guns 'n' Roses t-shirt. In the light of day, the t-shirt showed its age and lack of washing. Like those mornings when he thought his teeth looked good; until he smiled after applying shaving foam.

"Just a sec," he said. His phone - purchased at the airport – beeped to let him know it had just connected. He had already sent Maggie a message from Rio with his new number.

The driver was becoming impatient. "Signor? You go or no go?"

"Patience, my friend, is a virtue." He tapped on the phone. Maggie had sent him the address for the Pasticceria: central Rome.

"It's your lucky day, pal." He showed the driver the address.

"Ah, si, very nice." The driver rubbed his fingers together in the international sign for money, before opening the door. "I got something you like. Come."

Kenny stepped into the back of the car and fastened his seat belt. The driver started the engine, beeped his horn at nobody in particular, before screeching out into a small space between moving cars. He pushed a CD into the player on the dashboard, turned up the volume and gave a thumbs up in the mirror.

Sweet Child O' Mine blared from the car's speakers. The driver began to sing along, bopping his head from side to side. After a few seconds, he said, "Come on, singa with me!"

"Eh, sorry," Kenny touched his throat. "Sore!" Then coughed to drive the point home, regretting his choice of t-shirt.

The driver dropped him at *Piazza del Popolo,* unimpressed by his fellow Guns 'n' Roses fan's knowledge of lyrics. Kenny did not notice the driver's discontent as he focused on Pasticceria Valentina, easy to spot with its queue snaking out the door and round the block. He walked across the square to sit on the edge of one of the piazza's fountains. Roddy would not notice him in the chaotic mesh of cars and scooters buzzing around this gateway to *centro storico*.

He searched inside his bag, finding the sporran. He extracted one of the Amazonian leaves and his flask. He chewed on the leaf, realising the longer he stored them in his sporran, the more succulent they became. He pressed his thumb against the flask's side, where he had embedded a secret button; the top popped open. He could tell by its weight there was not much left. With no access to his stash back home, he would soon be out of Hair o' the Dog. Each drink had to be well-timed. Now that he was in Rome, he needed to imbibe. While he did not yet have a plan, he had to be ready for anything. He would wait in the square until he caught sight of his son, and then figure out what to do next. The whisky would have kicked in by then.

He took a careful sip, enjoying the sensation of gentle burn and warm tingling. Someone touched his hand, prompting him to look up, flask still at his lips. An old nun, bent over at an awkward angle, with a kind, lined face, placed a twenty euro note in his hand. He realised she had taken pity on this aging rocker with the tattered t-shirt and trousers, drinking alcohol and eating some sort of weed on a Sunday morning in a public square. In this charitable nun's mind, he was a poster child for destitution. She placed her hand on his head and closed her eyes, mouth moving in silent prayer.

Her touch startled him. It jolted him to his feet. He pulled her into his chest and wrapped his arms around her frail body. It was not the feeling of her hand on his head that prompted his sense of urgency. He had felt something; he had to increase the physical connection to analyse it. This had happened a couple of times in the past when he had just taken a drink of Hair o' the Dog. Normally it returned nothing other than what the other person had eaten that day. This nun was different. The contact triggered an alarm: she was in danger.

Tiber Island

Holding her close, he concentrated on where this feeling was leading him. He imagined himself inside her brain, wandering through arteries and mushy greyness. His supercharged ability to remember every synapse, vein and electrode he had studied in biology all those years before allowed him to navigate to the blood flow. In the middle of one of her arteries, he could feel the blood moving more slowly. As her heart pumped, more and more pressure pushed against the artery's sides. The structural strength of its collagen fibres was dissipating with each beat; the artery was ready to burst.

He whistled at a taxi.

"*Signora, dobbiamo andare all'ospedale.*" he said, thankful for Hair o' the Dog's linguistic empowerment. They had to get to a hospital fast. The nun looked up; eyebrows scrunched as if she wanted to ask something yet was not sure what the question should be. Her watery blue eyes framed her puppy innocence. She waited a moment, searching his face for an indication she should follow his instructions. Not one to walk away from a challenge or a miracle in the making, she saw the kindness in his eyes. No look like that could conceal evil intent.

She nodded, "*Ripongo la mia fiducia in te.*" *I place my faith in thee* - a statement of acceptance and trust common to the old and new testaments she recited every day of the week.

The cab had screeched to a halt in front of them. The driver opened the passenger door; and helped her settle into the backseat. Kenny ducked in beside her, casting a glance at the Pasticceria. At a second-floor window, he could see a slight figure chomping on a croissant.

A few days ago, he thought he might never see him again. Now, when he was within metres of a father-son hug, he was off on another escapade. There was so much he wanted to say to Roddy. One of the more sensitive matters would be the acne outbreak across his son's nose and forehead. He would have to find a delicate way to discourage the pastry consumption.

He looked at the nun, who returned his gaze, patted him on the knee and said, *"Andrà tutto bene"* – he hoped she was right, and all would be okay. She scrunched her face, concentrating on the words. *"My namo iss Robertina!"*.

"Okay, Sister, we are going to take care of you." He patted her arm feeling like he had just delivered a line from a John Wayne movie. He turned to the driver. *"Ospedale, per favore!"*

The driver nodded. This was an emergency. Italian cab drivers did not need an excuse to speed; especially when they had a valid reason - and a sick nun was as valid as this driver needed. The car sped through narrow streets, convincing pedestrians to fight the desire to jaywalk. Kenny continued to monitor her brain's activity with his hand on her arm, watching her lips move in prayer, rosary beads slipping between old, wrinkled fingers.

Within half an hour, they reached Rome's oldest working bridge, leading to the hospital on Tiber Island. At two thousand plus years, *Ponte Fabricio* had seen thousands of patients traverse its cobbled stones in search of healing on the other side. The driver refused the twenty euro note Sister Robertina had given Kenny earlier, accepting a blessing from her instead.

Kenny let her hook an arm in his to walk across to the hospital door. They soon found the reception and a congenial receptionist, who grasped the urgency of the situation. Doctor Massimo was called to meet them.

"My name is Cornelius Shaunery. I am a doctor and work at St. Thomas' Hospital in London. This nun, Sister Robertina, has an undiagnosed condition in her brain. I have seen signs in her behaviour that indicate she is in imminent danger of an aneurism."

Dr. Massimo, a tall, elderly man with a stern face, rubbed his chin. "Doctor Shaunery, this is highly unusual. We can't just accept a patient into the hospital without a letter of recommendation, or unless there is an emergency. And without causing offence, the basis of your diagnosis has not been made after careful medical procedures, but solely because of 'behaviours'. No disrespect, if praying openly in public and appearing in a spiritual trance are the *behaviours* you refer to, I would need to bring in half of Rome for an examination. She seems perfectly fine to me. This may be acceptable in London, although I doubt very much it is. In Rome we do not work this way."

Out of politeness, Dr. Massimo did not comment on this doctor's garb. He understood the British were eccentric; however, dressing in this way must breach at least one section of the Hippocratic code.

"I know, Doctor. I agree. This is not how things should be done. That makes this all the more urgent. If I, as a doctor, am begging you to do this, then you must know that it's a major emergency. My sense is she has a couple of hours before the blood vessel bursts."

They both looked at Sister Robertina. She reached across to the doctor, raised her head from its bent position and touched his arm, *"Ripongo la mia fiducia in te."*

The doctor sighed and turned to the receptionist. Within a few minutes they had arranged an MRI scan. Two young nurses came along with a wheelchair to take her to the examination. As they pushed her along the corridor, she looked back over her shoulder and waved at her saviour. He nodded and blew her a kiss that made her smile.

"Thanks, Doctor. Please, get her onto blood-thinning drugs as soon as possible. Before the MRI." In for a penny and a pound.

"Okay, now I am starting to become annoyed." Dr Massimo's face became sterner. "Trust me to know my job. Since I am already placing my faith in your diagnosis, you can rest assured I will be giving her blood-thinners immediately." He walked off after the wheelchair, shaking his head, muttering under his breath.

Kenny breathed a sigh of relief and gave the receptionist his details. "I'll call later to find out how the examination has gone."

"No problem. I can give you a card with our number. Just ask for me." She pointed at her nameplate. "Toni Desiderio."

She bent down to take a card from a box. Something dropped out from inside her shirt and dangled above the array of papers and pens on the desk. He saw the **G** glinting, the same insignia as he had seen on the medals in the airport.

"Excuse me, what is this medal I keep seeing?"

She took the medal in her fingers. "Ah, this is the future of the Church. We are Galatians. We pray that Cardinal Damascus will become the next Pope and help us all find the true message of Christ." She smiled at him; he could see hope in her eyes.

"Good luck, then," he said, not sure of what the appropriate comment is when someone is vying for a particular Pope.

"Prayer and divine intervention are what we need, not luck." Her beaming smile showed there was no spite in her words. "I was at mass with him yesterday evening. He is a walking saint. I even waited outside his apartment last night, praying with my fellow Galatians."

"Oh, where is he staying?" he asked, surprised at his own curiosity.

"*Piazza della Pilotta.*" He continued to stare at her medal. "You can touch it if you want. You are a good man, bringing us a nun you were concerned about. Even if she is in good health, it's your gesture that matters above all." She leaned forward towards him and whispered, "*Bear each other's burdens, and so fulfil the law of Christ.*" Galatians, 6, 2."

He shrugged not knowing how to react to scripture quoted at him, then reached across and took the medal between his thumb and forefinger. "Ow!" he shouted, yanking his hand back.

"Did you get a shock?" she asked.

"Yes, I did." He shook his hand in the air.

"It happens regularly in the hospital when you touch metal objects or people," she answered. "Don't take it personally." She laughed as she handed him a card with the hospital number.

The only shock he felt was the realisation that something sinister was connected to that medal.

Connecting

"I can't leave you two alone for an evening." He tried to be flippant, but his mind was racing. Maggie and Tommy had come close to being killed in a bar brawl.

Wilson laughed aloud to lift the mood settling into the call. "So, have you seen Roddy yet?" She was outside the café where Tommy was leaning against the bar talking to Luisa. Wilson was finding the sound of vespas and car horns therapeutic.

"I've not spoken to him although I saw him at the window of the Pasticceria. He seemed fine, judging by the size of the croissant he was eating."

Wilson laughed again. "Like father, like son."

"God, I hope not," he said. "I hope he does better than that."

She heard his tone. "Kenny, listen. You are the best father Roddy could ever have had. These days you've been away have given me time to think. You're a brilliant dad. Not just because you are intrinsically a good father. It's because you and Roddy are a team. You may both have gone off piste lately, but you are a brilliant double act. You just have to remember why you are so good together."

He was looking skywards. He found it easier to hold back the tears when he looked at the light. He was standing against the wall outside the hospital. She was right, he knew it. He also knew that those words applied to them as a couple too.

"Thanks. You always know how to break it down."

"You said you *saw* him at the window. Are you no longer near the Pasticceria?"

"Well, that's the thing. There was this nun. You see, she thought I was homeless. She prayed over me. Then I realised she had an aneurism about to burst. I got her to the hospital and am hoping they can do something about it."

Wilson pinched the top of her nose. All he had to do was stand outside Roddy's window and wait for a moment to see him. Now he throws in nuns and aneurisms. She had to remind herself of something he had told her one night when they were having dinner: "Bad choices make great stories." She decided to let it go since she knew she would have done the same thing in similar circumstances. Then it struck her.

"Which hospital are you at?"

He stepped back from the wall and looked at the sign. He had never seen so many letters in the name of anything since driving around Wales the previous summer. He concentrated as he enunciated each letter. "It's called *Ospedale San Giovanni Calibita Fatebenefratelli*."

It took her a moment to process what he had said, as she paced up and down outside the bar. "That's where Crawford is! On Tiber Island, right?"

"Yes, we're on the island. Small world." And then grimaced at his choice of words. "I'll go and see how things are with him. Love you, Maggie!"

She told him the ward and floor number before they hung up. He decided not to mention the discussion with Toni the Galatian. The medal-shock was beyond explicable. Something had pulsed through his fingers into his nervous system. It would have gone further if Hair o' the Dog had not magnified the role of his enzyme inhibitors, blocking any foreign stimulus from invading his body.

He walked back into the hospital and found a map on the wall explaining the layout of floors and departments. Just like hospitals back home, the map left him none the wiser. On a table beside the entrance, there was a scattering of pamphlets explaining the history of the hospital. He picked one up and leafed through the pages. It had been built nearly half a millennium earlier. Not a surprise. He had found the architecture quaintly antique, although not the place he wanted to be in an emergency medical situation. He read on.

During the Second World War, when the Germans occupied Rome, they rounded up and arrested the Jews. A local physician, Doctor Borromeo, realised he had to act quickly and with authority. He registered around one hundred Jews to a special ward under his care within the hospital. Whenever Nazis came on their searches, he had the patients coughing and spluttering, victims of this strange illness, he had christened Syndrome K. In fear of risking their own health, the Germans refused to enter the ward, saving the 'patients' from being discovered and marched off to the death camps.

He could not think of a better hospital to bring a charitable nun and a brave accountant. After a few minutes of wandering, his legs and arms drawing glances from medics in the corridors, he found the room where Crawford was lying motionless in his bed. As he approached, a Scottish voice said, "Hey, who are you?"

Good question. Was he Kiltman, Kenny or Cornelius?

"Oh, hi. I am Cornelius Shaunery, a London-based doctor. Just thought I'd check in on Crawford. Who are you?"

The man had been sitting on a seat that could only be described as uncomfortable; straight wooden back, with a layer of scuffed fabric that used to be a cushion. His character-filled face looked tired. "I am Crawford's father." He turned to a lady in the corner who rose from her seat to introduce herself as his mother.

He grabbed a chair and sat beside them. "So, how is he doing?"

"No change since he got here," the mother said. "We've not lost hope. Crawford is a fighter. We believe he will pull through."

He took her hand. "I've heard how brave your son has been. He put his work before his own safety; he did that because he believes in right above wrong. I've got no doubt those values came from both of you." He could see tears welling in their eyes.

The door swung open. A young woman entered carrying two coffees and a pack of freshly baked pastries.

"Oh, hello," she said, surprised at another person in the room.

"Hi, my name is Shaunery, Con Shaunery." He stood and extended his hand.

"Pleased to meet you. I am Valentina." She squeezed his fingers, one of those connections that falls short of a strong handshake. He could sense the nervousness in her grip. She handed the coffees and food to Crawford's parents. Their appreciation was palpable, thanking her several times.

It took a moment, until she asked, "How do you know Crawford?"

"Oh, well, I don't really know him," he answered. "I know DI Wilson. She knew I was, em, working in the hospital, so she asked me to look in on him."

Valentina's head inclined to the side. There was nothing wrong with her BS antenna, as she scanned his mottled t-shirt.

"In fact, she mentioned you to me. She said that you've been amazing in keeping an eye on Crawford."

"Thank you. He's a good man. It's my honour to help." She smiled at the parents, who were picking at the warm croissants.

"She also said that you were looking after a boy who flew over from America on his own. What was his name?" He scratched the side of his head.

"Roddy," she said. "Lovely boy. He'll stay with me until Maggie comes back from Sicily."

"That's good. You really have been so helpful to Maggie. She already has a lot to worry about." He waited a moment. "You must be busy between your Pasticceria, looking after this Roddy lad, and also visiting Crawford and his parents here at the hospital. I have an idea. If it might help you, I could take the boy out for a walk or an ice cream. I understand he's Scottish too. I'm sure we would find a lot to talk about."

She paused for a few seconds, struggling to hide her sense of discomfort. "I would need to check with Maggie."

"Of course. Please call her. I'm sure she'll agree that this is a good idea." He waited a moment, then said. "I have a child the same age. I know how to connect with teenagers." And get them home to where they are supposed to be, not running wild round Europe.

Back Soon

"I am sorry, Signor Shaunery, you cannot see Cardinal Damascus. This is highly irregular." The priest spoke through a narrow slat.

"Why not? I want to wish him well for the Papal Conclave. We are friends from many years ago. I visited with him in America, and he was very kind to my family." Con Shaunery seemed to be full of deceit and trickery beyond Kenny's simple wiles; it felt like an amateur form of method acting.

"Look, sir. Behind you are thousands of people who would also want to speak to the Cardinal. Clearly that will not happen." He was well aware of the crowds, the singing and chanting hurt his highly tuned hearing. "If this continues, I will have to call the police." The priest was no more than thirty years old. He had the collar of a cleric and the face of a teenager. He was finding this confrontation very uncomfortable.

"Look, all I want is five minutes. Is that too much to ask?"

The secretary sighed, "Well, yes, it is. You see, the Cardinal is not here." He paused before leaning into the slat. "He left this morning to go and seek some solace and quiet in Rome. He wants to be in the right frame of mind when he enters Vatican City tomorrow."

"Are you telling me you don't know where he is?" His radar had been activated.

"Cardinal Damascus is a leader in the Church. I cannot see why you feel we should keep tabs on him when he is in pursuit of alone time. He has told me he will be back soon. I will let him know you were here. Now, I have had enough of this discussion. Goodbye." The slat closed with a metallic crunch.

Kenny turned and walked to the bottom of the square, memories of his two prior visits to Rome coming back to him. The first - and fuzziest - was with Tommy on his stag weekend, when they stumbled across the house where Bonnie Prince Charlie had lived and died, after failing in the 18th century's second Jacobite rebellion. By chance, the house was at the bottom of *Piazza della Pilotta*, metres from where he was standing.

The next visit was with Wilson, defusing a bomb Cullen Skink had set to go off in the Prince's house, releasing a lethal gas that would have killed thousands of people.

He realised as he walked along the side of the square that since he had been in Rome, he had found two reasons not to go directly to Roddy: a nun and a cardinal. Pasticceria Valentina was a twenty minutes' walk away.

He had called Maggie to alert her that he had met Valentina, and that he was going to visit Roddy under the guise of a good friend taking him on a tour of the city. She asked why he would not just say he was his father, why had he created this whole fabrication. He had to think about it himself; it had started when he told the doctor he was Con Shaunery. He had stayed in role when Valentina showed up, reacting to the smallest of niggles in the back of his mind.

Maggie agreed it made sense not to promote the fact that Kenny or Kiltman were in Rome. She would call Roddy and ask him to pretend to not know his dad. Come to think of it, they decided, he was already an expert in playing that role.

Mafia Meet

Wilson had called Marco soon after leaving the police station. He was effusive in his appreciation of their bravery, recognising that Wilson, Tommy and Gina had saved his life. The least he could do was invite them to his father's home later that day for lunch. Wilson knew this was her chance to pull together some of the frustrating, loose ends dangling out of reach related to Sacco's death.

Tommy reminded her that they could not arrive empty handed. They discussed what present to bring to a Mafia don's house when you have been invited to lunch. Tommy shook his head when she suggested going safe with a bottle of wine. He challenged the safety of giving *vino* to someone who probably owned half the vineyards in the area. God forbid, they gave a bottle from another 'family's' winery.

After a few minutes of debate, Tommy thrust his hand down into the bottom of his rucksack, before producing a Scotland flag. He explained that it was his lucky mascot which he had taken to the 1998 World Cup in France. When Wilson asked him how lucky it was if Morocco beat Scotland 3-0, he moved on to remind her of the fact Brazil won because Tom Boyd scored their winning goal for them.

In the end, they settled for a bottle of High Park 10-year-old, available in a local grocery shop at an eye-watering price. Against her better judgement, Maggie agreed to let him wrap it in the Scotland flag.

A black Maserati arrived to pick them up, a plastic screen between the driver and the back seat. They had just settled into the car, when Tommy nudged Wilson and pointed at a cabinet underneath the front passenger headrest. He opened it to find a bottle of grappa, three quarters full. He poured himself a glass and made to pour one for her. She refused with a shake of her head; it was important to stay alert. She had already noticed they were being followed by another car. After it had followed them down a series of country lanes, she felt she should mention it to the driver.

"Not to worry," he said. "We have bodyguards. Hah! Like Kevin Costner and Whitney Houston!" He chortled to himself driving the last few hundred metres to the house.

The villa sat high on the summit of a prominent hillock, a few kilometres outside Corleone. It dominated the hillside with its large windows and turrets, affording views of the surrounding hills and country roads.

Marco was waiting at the entrance with his friend Pietro. They were dressed in blue suits with open neck white shirts. Wilson and Tommy looked at each other: she, in her short skirt and yellow blouse; he, in the same jeans and t-shirt from the night before. She could even see a stain on Tommy's shirt just below the neck, a remnant from the previous night's *'nasty blue'* beer. Tommy no doubt had packed one pair of jeans and one other 'going out' t-shirt.

They stepped out of the car to be greeted by Marco, holding the door open for them. "It's my pleasure to welcome you to my father's house. Please follow me." Pietro acknowledged their arrival with a wave.

On entering the house, a butler invited them to place their phones in a safety box. Marco did not make an effort to 'apologise for inconveniences'; all guests followed this safety protocol. They handed over their mobiles, before passing through an electronic gate similar to an airport. Another man in black slacks and white t-shirt was at a monitor nodding his consent for them to continue.

They walked through a large atrium and down a long corridor akin to a viewing at an art gallery. Wilson noticed the paintings of obvious significance were not individually alarmed; there was no risk of anyone being foolish enough to break in. They entered a bright dining room with a pre-set table, its patio doors open wide to the infinity pool and the hills beyond. Tommy hoped Marco had a spare pair of trunks.

They walked towards a table set for five, although it looked more like twice that number based on the amount of cutlery and crockery.

The footsteps coming down the corridor sounded at a slow pace, building volume the closer they came to the dining room. Roberto 'Mucky' Marciano was every bit the image of the photograph she had studied the previous day; smooth complexion, tucked and tweaked to within a centimetre of perfection.

"Welcome to our humble home," he said, bowing to them.

"Good one," Tommy laughed. "Really humble! What an amazing palace you've got here." Wilson was standing close enough to apply a slight nudge with her elbow.

She noticed the host look at Tommy for a second beyond comfortable. "Thank you for your kind words."

"You're welcome," Tommy said, enjoying his connection with the capo. "I bet those paintings in the hall are worth a few bob."

"Sorry?" Marciano looked at his son, who shrugged as if to say – *listen, Dad, they only saved my life, they're not my best mates.*

They introduced themselves, with Marciano kissing them on the cheeks. Tommy seemed to enjoy it more than Wilson.

"Where is the other brave young lady?" Marciano smiled, although his cold blue eyes had not yet warmed up.

"Ah, Gina had to go back to Milan," Wilson answered. "You're right, she is very brave."

Marco agreed. "Her future husband is a lucky man. He will need to be very careful not to get on her wrong side." They all nodded their agreement.

"Yes, she is a pocket rocket of joy one minute and a ninja warrior the next," Tommy said. They spent a moment digesting this comment before Marco shrugged and pointed at the table.

"Please, take a seat. I am sure you are very hungry after all the excitement of last night."

Tommy moved to sit down, waving his hand in the air. "Och, that was nothing. Just like a night out in the Gallowgate in Glasgow."

Wilson could sense a widening cultural gap. "Tommy's joking. We have never been in a situation like that before, have we?" She smiled at him, hoping he would sense the need to dial it down a notch or two.

"Speak for yourself, Maggie. Try going out for a pint on a Saturday night after an Old Firm match." He turned to face the other side of the table. "An Old Firm match is when Celtic play Rangers, both Glasgow teams. Bit like Palermo playing against Messina, although," he paused for a moment and scratched his chin, "you're all Catholics down here so it's not a great example, when I think about it."

Marciano looked at his son.

Tommy had started again. "We have a gift for you." He produced the bundle of wrapped whisky from his backpack.

"Oh, what's this?" Marciano asked. He unfurled the flag as if it was the most precious garment he had ever touched. Wilson realised in their haste to scramble this present together, she had not inspected it. He took his reading glasses from his jacket pocket and studied it intently. "What is this writing?"

Tommy leant over and looked at where he was pointing at the flag. "Ah. That's John Collins. He scored a penalty against Brazil." As if that explained it.

"Oh, well, thank you for your flag. Also, for this bottle of fine Scottish whisky. I hope during this lunch we will find a good reason to celebrate with it." Marciano gestured towards the table at an array of meats and cheeses provided by two efficient waiters finding space to place plates and containers. "Please, enjoy!"

Marco poured red wine into their glasses. Wilson could feel Tommy's beaming smile, she did not need to turn around to see it.

"That would be lovely," Wilson said. Her foot was resting on Tommy's now. She intended to apply pressure whenever she sensed he was about to put one of his own in the wrong place.

Celebrating

The conversation moved from football to culture and cuisine then back to football. Tommy encouraged them all to recognise similarities between Scotland and Sicily none of the others felt existed. When he realised he was not making progress, he played his trump card.

"Jim Kerr lives in Sicily." He was faced with blank expressions. "Front man with Simple Minds." He waited for acknowledgment.

"Of course," Mucky Marciano replied with a snap of his fingers. He stood up from the table; and sang in a thick operetta base. *"Don't you forget about me!"*

"There you go," Tommy rose from his seat, closed his eyes and began to sway, singing, *"Don't, don't, don't, don't!"*

"Don't you forget about me!" Marciano sang again, with Tommy joining in. Wilson and Marco looked at each other and attempted to smile as if there was nothing awkward about this duet.

After a couple of verses, Marciano sat down and wiped his forehead. "Ah, that was fun!" He reached for the second bottle of wine and filled their glasses. "You know, my favourite movie is Braveheart. I have watched it more than ten times."

Wilson and Tommy nodded their acknowledgment of his good taste in cinema.

"I like the movie for many reasons; particularly, I enjoyed the message of *vendetta*." He looked at them. "In Sicily, *vendetta* is an important word. Maybe Scotland and Sicily do have one thing in common after all."

"Cheers to that." Tommy reached across with his glass to clink Marciano's. Their host continued. "William Wallace wanted a peaceful life. Another country attacked his people first. He had no choice but to take the fight to England. He had to show them that he and his countrymen were strong." He turned to look at Wilson, who had become quieter as the meal progressed.

"Maggie, are you okay?"

"Yes, Signor Marciano, I am fine."

"I think our conversation has become boring for you. How about you tell us something interesting." It was more a challenge than a request.

Wilson looked at each of Marciano and his son in turn. She felt Tommy begin to speak, in an attempt to take the pressure off her. She pushed her foot down gently. Tommy picked his glass up and took a slow sip.

"You want to hear something interesting?" She wiped the corner of her mouth with the napkin before folding and placing it at the side of her plate.

"Yes, please, Signora." Marciano was curious.

She folded her arms. "What's the difference between intelligence and wisdom?"

Marciano scratched his temple. "Hmm, a very good question. Is it that intelligence is knowing what to say, while wisdom is knowing when to say it?"

She shook her head. "Good try, although I need something more memorable."

Marco spoke up. "I've got it. A Chinese philosopher said that 'knowing others is intelligence, knowing yourself is true wisdom'.'"

"Nice one," she answered. "Not what I was looking for."

"Okay, my dear, please go ahead. We are intrigued." Marciano looked at his watch.

Wilson leant back in her chair and twirled her glass. "Intelligence is knowing that a tomato is fruit. Wisdom is knowing not to put it in a fruit salad."

Marciano laughed aloud and clapped his hands. He pointed at her. "Perfect! I will remember that. Sicilians love explanations that involve food. It helps us remember."

He looked at his watch again. "Ah, it's one o'clock already. Let's watch the news." He picked up the remote control and clicked onto the RAI channel. The TV was halfway up the wall across from the dining table. Tommy and Wilson exchanged a glance.

The news channel's introductory jingle was similar to Reporting Scotland on STV. Tommy hummed along and decided that he should mention this connection. He felt Maggie's foot press down on his; and decided to keep the thought to himself.

The first image on the screen was of a female reporter outside a police station talking with a high degree of animation. Wilson leaned forward, "Hey, that's the station we were at in Palermo this morning." Marco and Marciano nodded, not moving their eyes from the screen.

"Apologies," Marco said. "Let me translate." The picture changed to a scene outside the police station earlier that day, with a time highlighted in the corner: 12.30 pm. The reporter's excited, fast-paced voice continued in the background. The picture was quite grainy, but as they focused, they could see two bodies lying on the ground, arms and legs spread motionless.

Marco coughed before relaying his translation, enunciating each word clearly. "Today, just after 12 o'clock, two men were gunned down and killed in broad daylight as they left Palermo police station. Apparently, they had been brought in for questioning related to an incident that took place in the early hours of the morning. An attempted shooting in a local bar. They have been linked to Gianni Sconi, one of the main Mafia dons here in Sicily. Gianni Sconi, also known as *Pirla*, has denied any association with the men."

Wilson gasped. Tommy spoke. "They're the same guys from the pub." Their dark clothes were unmistakeable; now a shade darker, blood-saturated patches dominating the material.

Marco continued to translate. "They were released on bail today, pending further investigation. As they left the police station, a car drove past, and shots were fired. The victims died instantly. We have no further details. We will let you know when we have more to report."

Marciano turned off the TV. "Some more wine?" He lifted the bottle above Wilson's glass.

"Eh, no. No, thanks." She placed her hand across the top of her glass; she had lost her thirst and her appetite. Her mind was racing. Why had the police released them on bail? It was clear they were the shooters in the bar. No police force in their right minds would let them go so soon after such a violent attack. She looked from Marciano to Marco. Their faces registered neither displeasure nor joy, poker inscrutability.

Marciano took a moment before he spoke. "Well, it looks like someone extracted the tomato from the fruit salad." Wilson was not sure how to interpret the comment. Their host reached across the table. "Now I think we have found the perfect opportunity."

"Perfect opportunity?" she asked.

He looked at Tommy and winked as he twisted the cap. "To open this fine High Park 10-year-old."

Missing

"Roddy!" Valentina called up the stairs. It was the third time, without a response. Kenny knew something was wrong. It was only him that his son ignored; he was polite whenever anyone else spoke to him.

"Let me go and see," he offered.

She held up her hand for him to wait at the bottom of the steps, before she ran to the room. A minute later she was back with a note, reading it aloud as she descended. *Hi Valentina, I've gone for a walk. Don't worry. I'll be back later. R xx*

She walked past him and spoke to the staff working behind the Pasticceria counter. He heard them answer, *"Non è passato di qui."* He had not gone through the shop.

Kenny walked out onto the street underneath the window he spotted Roddy eating at earlier. A drainpipe ran from the window down the wall onto the pavement. He touched it and closed his eyes, allowing himself to analyse the casing of the pipe. He could feel Roddy's DNA. Holding it for a moment longer, he knew that his son had left half an hour earlier.

"Do you think he left this way?" Valentina was at his shoulder pointing at the pipe. He could sense the concern in her voice.

"Maybe." He looked at his watch. "Well, looks like I won't be hanging out with him then this afternoon. I hope he comes back before dark."

"Seriously?" she asked. Her face was tilted at an angle bordering on unnatural.

"Look, I only wanted to do Maggie a favour and keep him busy. Looks like he has his own agenda after all. Don't worry, I'm sure he'll be fine. He sounds quite resourceful." Before she could reply, he waved his hand. "Bye then, see you soon."

He walked round the corner onto *Via del Corso* and made a point in losing himself in the crowds of shoppers and strollers. His mind was busy, trying to piece together the latest turn of events. This was out of character for Roddy. While he would happily ignore or shirk his father, he would never do something as rude and churlish as escaping from someone who had been kind and generous. Unless he had a good reason.

He typed his son's number into the burner phone, surprised that he remembered it.

"Hello?" Even with two syllables, Roddy's voice sounded like Beethoven's fifth. Safe, secure and memorable.

"Hey, pal, how are you doing?"

"Dad? Is that you?"

"Yes, it's me. It's good to hear you."

"Oh, Dad," Roddy cried, tears flowing down his cheeks. "I've really missed you. There's so much I have to talk to you about."

Kenny worked hard not to cry. It was so unusual to hear his son being emotional. He could not remember the last time. "Don't worry, son. I am in Rome. I've just been at the Pasticceria. Seems you left there in a hurry."

"Yes, I didn't feel comfortable. I'm not sure I can trust Valentina."

"Oh?"

"Probably nothing. I'll explain when I see you."

"Okay, I'll come to you. Where are you?"

"I'm walking towards the Trevi Fountain area of the city."

"That's nice; have you decided to visit the sites?"

"Not exactly, Dad. Do you remember your friend Shuggy brought a priest round to see us a year or so ago?"

Kenny felt a pang of guilt. He had not seen Shuggy since the previous summer. They had been close years earlier at university, then drifted apart when Shuggy became a priest. On leaving the priesthood to marry the love of his life, Lulu, Shuggy had asked Kenny to help him navigate life on the outside. Dinner at Uisge Beatha last year was an opportunity for Kenny to impart some words of wisdom. In hindsight, he had struggled to find one helpful suggestion. At least the evening was not a complete wash-out, as they got to meet Shuggy's seminary friend.

"Oh, yes, that's right. What was his name again?" he asked.

"Father David Montrose," Roddy responded.

"I remember now." He recalled a tall, elegant priest with a shrewd intellect and capacity for storytelling. When they were washing up later, he saw how much Roddy was taken by the man. They sat with Maggie around the table for an hour or so chatting about what made this man so charismatic. He was quietly spoken, yet authoritative. When he expressed an opinion on any topic, he seemed to own the room.

He had them all laughing at the catalyst for his decision to become a priest. He had been unemployed in Scotland living from meagre weekly social security cheques, in the doldrum Thatcher years not long after the shipyard and factory closures. One particular Christmas time, he had made many sacrifices to save just enough money to buy presents. They would be modest, but at least he could hold his head high knowing he was not empty handed. On the way to the shops, he bumped into an affable taxi driver he knew from his local area. It did not take much discussion for the driver to convince David to go for *just the one* beer. Several hours later, all his money spent, and no Christmas presents, David realised he needed to change his life. He had not looked back since.

Roddy deciding to place his trust in him made perfect sense.

"Are you going to see him?"

"Yes. I need someone I can trust. I just remember him being such a dependable person. I had his number in my phone, so called him on the off chance."

"Good thinking. Where are you meeting him?"

"He's at the university today. I'm going to meet him there."

"Is it not closed on a Sunday?" Since Brazil he had been struggling to remember which day it was, although the constant ringing of church bells left him in no doubt today was the Sabbath.

"Yes, apparently he is doing some research and using the university library." Hopefully computers were available too.

"Okay, I'll come and meet you. Where is it?"

"The Gregorian University at *Piazza della Pilotta*," he answered.

"That's weird," Kenny said. "I've just come from there."

Pizza Time

"So, have you completed it yet?" Tantalus was fiddling with the controls for one of the many keyboards distributed around the room.

"Everything's going according to plan." Mask did not like the way Tantalus spoke to him; the air of a boss addressing a subordinate. "We need to be vigilant 24/7. Anything can happen once the Vatican doors close on the conclave." He turned to his daughter, sitting in the corner of the room reading. "What are you thinking, Arnalda? You've been very quiet since we showed you our *technology suite*. Are you not impressed?"

Angie looked up, as if she had been reading intently. She had not turned a page in the last twenty minutes. Her mind was racing. Tantalus and her father were about to unleash an act of horror she could not have imagined possible.

"Oh, I'm fine, father. Yes, this technology is mind-blowing."

"Ha! Good one!" Tantalus laughed. "Your daughter has a sense of humour, unlike her old man."

She did not want to be a source of humour for either of them. "Can I go and get some fresh air, please?"

"Sure, Arnalda. I left some fruit in the back garden for you." Mask made a note of another put-down by Tantalus. This was not going to end well for him if he did not rein in his condescension.

Angie rose from her chair, and walked out through the door, trying to ignore the incessant hum of their computer. In their 'technology suite' they had video screens showing every room and staircase in the house. The windows and doors to the outside were locked and barricaded, save for the kitchen.

She climbed the stairs to the kitchen and walked out into the garden. Her father made it sound like a small piece of paradise; *fruit in the garden*. Two apples and a banana lay on a wooden table in a space no larger than a living room, surrounded on all sides by 8-foot walls; with a gate to the outside world barricaded with strips of iron welded onto its railings.

She chose an apple and took a bite. The sour taste hit the back of her throat. It was old. Like everything else in the villa, full of food and drink purchased by Tantalus two weeks earlier in preparation.

She picked up the fruit bowl - the banana more black than yellow - and walked back into the kitchen to throw the contents into the bin. On the worktop underneath the microwave, she noticed a plastic box. It contained an array of phones, various makes and models. Her father and Tantalus had purchased them the previous day. Burner phones they called them, ready to be used, fully charged with sim cards already installed. They prided themselves on being prepared for any eventuality.

Until now, the crippling fear of Roddy and Fiona's safety had prevented her from considering escape an option. However, having caught snippets of conversations between her father and Tantalus, she realised there was so much more at stake. She had seconds to decide and act.

The camera in the room was above the doorway. By turning to face the microwave, she could obscure the phone. She took a slice of cheese and a hard roll lying on the table and made a sandwich. She opened the microwave door and placed it inside. If her father was watching, it would look like she was melting the mouldy cheese, while leaning her arm on the counter watching it turn around and around.

She pressed the keys on the phone. It was the only number she remembered, or at least she hoped she remembered. She had to be quick.

Reilly. Am in Rome in Villa on Via Cassia area called Tomba di Nerone dad plotting horrible things. DON'T REPLY TO THIS PHONE. Please help me. A

She hit send.

As the microwave beeped, she deleted her sent message from the phone's memory and placed it back on the worktop.

"Hey, Arnalda, you having a sandwich?" Tantalus asked. She had not heard his footsteps on the marble floor.

"Yes." She opened the door, grabbed the hot bread and took a bite. It was even more disgusting than it looked. At least it was hot.

"I just came to get my phone," Tantalus said, looking at the phone beside her elbow. He picked it up and scrolled down through messages and calls. He looked up at her. "Do you miss not having your phone? I bet you have a boyfriend back home who is missing you, eh?"

She shrugged.

"Not very talkative, are you?" He walked around her to the sink to pour a glass of water. "You wouldn't be up to something now, would you?"

"Seriously?" she asked. "It's not exactly the most fun place in the world, cooped up with you and my dad for days on end. What can I get up to? I'd love to know."

"Ha!" he laughed. "I like your spark. Don't worry, soon this part of the adventure will all be over. Not sure what your father will do next. If you ask me…"

"Tantalus!" They turned to see Mask in the doorway. "That's enough!"

"Steady!" Tantalus placed his hands in front of him. "Just having a chat with your girl. No harm in that, eh?"

"Don't push me, you will not live to regret it, I promise you. I do not make idle threats." Mask's face had hardened. Angie knew when he was ready to blow; he was close to unleashing his temper.

"It's okay, Dad." She held up her sandwich. "I can't eat this. Can we order a pizza or something, just this evening?"

Her father's face tightened when he saw she had taken a bite from a lump of hardened dough oozing yellow and blue gunk onto her fingers.

"Yes, you're right. Tonight, we'll have pizza. Tantalus, what's the name of the place you sometimes go to? Do they do deliveries?"

"The Pink Devil." Tantalus finished his water. Unlike her father, she could not tell what mood he was in. His features changed little whatever the conversation or emotion in the room. "Yes, I can call them." He sighed slowly. "They do all the usual pizza flavours and toppings." He paused. looked at each of them and smiled. "Please don't ask for pineapple. It will be a dead giveaway we have Brits hiding in the house."

No Time to Live

"Mister Marciano." Wilson tried not to show the growing sense of discomfort rising within her. "Did you know that those guys were going to be executed?"

"Signora Wilson," Marciano smiled. "I think you have to open your mind to how things work in Sicily."

"Okay, I'm listening." They had been sitting around the table for three hours already. The bonhomie in the room had evaporated when the news finished. She was back in full Detective Inspector role.

"First thing I want you to understand is that I was not responsible for those deaths. The order did not come from me." He poured water into his empty wine glass, before swirling it gracefully to collect red splodges from its sides. He took a slow drink before continuing. "Those two men attempted to kill my son." He nodded at Marco, who was content to sit and listen to his father educate the non-Sicilians. "If I were to seek revenge, I would attract attention to my family; and put us all in danger."

"That doesn't stop you getting someone else to do it." Tommy was enjoying the conversation more than Wilson felt he should. "You seemed quite happy to listen to the news. As if you expected it to happen."

"Ah, Mr. MacGregor, I wish it was as simple as that." Marciano rose from the table and stood behind his son's chair. He placed his hands on Marco's shoulders. "My son is very dear to me. Of this, you should have no doubt." He patted his son's shoulder slowly. "Their attempt on his life was not meant to be taken personally by me, or him. Their aim was to send me a message."

"A message?" she asked.

"Yes. You see, word on the streets was that I have been part of a conspiracy to rob their boss."

"Their boss?" she asked.

"Yes, Gianni Sconi, also known as *Pirla*. We all have nicknames. I am known perversely as *Mucky* because I make an

246

effort to look my best. Sconi is known as *Pirla* because, well, he is a *Pirla*." Marco and his father burst into a guffaw of laughter. She could see it was a laugh they had shared many times before, knowing when to rise and fall in their combined chortling. Wilson was not interested in Mafia don nicknames; she was beginning to feel irritated.

"Go on." She looked at Tommy, who was trying to spear an olive with a cocktail stick.

"Look. Our families need to get on with each other. There is too much to lose. However, every so often something comes along to create a build-up in pressure." He clicked his fingers, energised by a thought. "Think about planet earth and its tectonic plates. They may stay relatively stable for centuries then suddenly." He clapped his hands loudly. Tommy mis-cued the olive, sending it off to bounce along the marble floor.

"The plates move, and an earthquake happens. We know it will happen at some point, although we don't know where and to what magnitude. Well, due to recent events here in Sicily, some personal in nature," - he nipped Marco's cheek with finger and thumb - "and some business related, there has been a shift in our local tectonic plates. Make no mistake, the pressure has been building for a long time."

She nodded. "So why did this pressure grow to such a point an earthquake had to happen at all?"

"Now that's the right question to ask. I should add that this question may help you with your other investigation. The reason you are here in Sicily in the first place." She had not told him why she was there. Albano and Monte were no doubt as porous as a block of Pecorino. He waited for this point to settle. Then continued. "I am going to tell you a story. It will help you in your enquiry."

"Thank you for your offer to enlighten me. Why would you want to do that?" She pushed her chair back to create a distance. Her feeling of discomfort was growing with each word he spoke.

"Let's just say; that if you believe me, then you and the police may move on and leave us poor Sicilians alone." His smile bordered on a sneer.

"Okay, let's get started. Let's imagine a group of families who inhabit an isolated island in the middle of a large sea. They live together in a beautiful part of the world. However, every so often they clash and fight. Each of the families knows that the more they attack each other, the more people die, and the less harmony surrounds them. Fighting is not a solution to their problems, just an expression of rage."

He took a sip of his water, before dabbing a napkin at the corners of his mouth.

"One day, they decide to collaborate. They divide their different business operations among themselves. One family gets the rights to control fishing; another the takings from trade; another manages the pubs and restaurants; and so on." It was the *'and so on'* Wilson was interested in but chose not to ask.

"This was working well for many years, until one of the families suggested they take it one stage further. Rather than just focus on the businesses that made them money. Why not choose a charity and donate money as a group to a worthwhile cause?"

"Excuse me," Tommy interrupted. "Are you saying that the families put the *don* in donating?"

Marciano looked at him with a tilted head. "Hmm, I see what you did there. It is what you English call a pun, am I right?"

Tommy coughed and pointed at the bottle of whisky.

"Sorry, Scottish." Marciano nodded apologetically. "May I continue?"

"Yes, of course." Tommy turned his attention to a breadstick. He had moved on to trying to master the art of breaking it into three pieces, using both thumbs. He had watched Marco do it with ease earlier but was struggling to emulate his wizardry.

"So, yes, they decided to donate. Their chosen charity was the homeless in Italy. Of course, you can imagine some of the complexities involved in a venture like this."

Wilson looked at Tommy to assess whether he was believing this story. Only to see him break a breadstick into multiple pieces, crumbs scattering across the white tablecloth.

"You see, the families enjoyed their notoriety for being tough guys. The last thing they wanted to do was create an image of being kind people. So, they created a bank to help them channel their funding to the appropriate charities focused on helping the less well off."

Wilson slapped the table. "Banco d'Aiuto!"

Marciano's face did not change expression. "Of course, my story is purely fictitious. If you want to call it Banco d'Aiuto, I am not going to argue." He smiled at Marco, who shrugged towards Wilson. She assumed it was an acknowledgement of her guess.

"Anyway, they used this bank for many years. Everything was going very well. Until their accountants noticed that the charities were receiving less money than they should have been. This became a problem for the families. Someone was stealing their funds. Monies they had agreed collectively to donate. It was not only theft; it was the worst kind of theft. Stealing from the good families who ran the island and helped the poor."

She had folded her arms. If she was in the police station, she would have been taking notes on her pad. Or recording the conversation on her phone, which was being kept under lock and key by their host's guards.

"So," Tommy added, "the manager of this fictitious bank had to answer some questions before he was *fed to the fishes*?" Tommy did the inverted comma thing with his fingers.

"Or before," Maggie said, "he was left dangling *above the fishes*."

Marciano smiled the slightest of smiles, before brushing a fleck of dust from his shoulder. She did not need a translation for that gesture.

Not so Trivial

"Dad, it's so good to see you." Roddy's face was buried in his father's chest. His shoulders shuddered with unrestrained sobs.

"It's all good now, son. We're going to figure this out. Don't worry." Kenny saw his own tears glisten on top of Roddy's soft, auburn hair. "Listen, before we go and meet Fr. David, let's have a chat." Roddy nodded and wrapped his arm around his father's waist. They stayed like that as they walked away from *Piazza della Pilotta* down a cobbled street, pleased to be with each other at last. The crowds in the square had become oppressive, unconstrained screaming and shouting, waving medals in the air. Cardinal Damascus had not appeared again, but that did not stop them from calling his name in a cultish chant.

They turned a corner expecting another narrow, cobbled street; to be confronted with a wide, open area, dominated by an astounding piece of 18th century Baroque architecture. The Trevi Fountain had been the centrepiece for movies, marriage proposals, late-night revelry and now the perfect setting for a long overdue father-son tete-a-tete. They walked to a space on the wall surrounding the water, both taking a moment to absorb the majesty of the fountain and its sculptures, nestled in the middle of three roads.

In its centre, Oceanus dominated the scene employing his Tritons to quell waters that were so calm they sparkled with the thousands of coins shining in the evening light. Roddy had heard that there was in the region of €3,000 a day thrown into the fountain. He gave his father a one-euro coin. They sat together, closed their eyes and tossed their coins over the left shoulder with the right hand for full effect. They turned just in time to see them clink against each other before splashing into the water. The significance was not lost on either of them.

Roddy had learned in his research the meaning of Trevi – derived from the word TriVia, meaning *three ways*. The junction of a three-road combination was a place where Romans would share gossip and news – giving birth to the word 'trivia'.

Ironically Roddy's pending revelation would prove to be far from trivial.

Kenny turned to his son. "We have a lot to talk about. Where do you want to start?"

Roddy was unsure where this was going yet felt they were in the right place for the subject he needed to broach. On the edge of the world's most famous fountain with hundreds of people coming and going, laughing and talking, his father would have to restrain any outbursts.

"Okay. I'm not sure how much you know about Angie's disappearance. Let me fill you in." Roddy explained as best he could, starting with Angie's concerning texts, and finishing up with the attack on Crawford in St. Peter's Square.

His father nodded as he talked. The story matched Maggie's version. When it was clear Roddy had reached the end, he said. "Amazing. That was a breakthrough when you were able to reach out and contact Maggie about the meeting in the square." His father tilted his head to the side and scratched his cheek. "The thing I don't get is how on earth you obtained that kind of information? Maggie said something about you having a - what do you call it - *social media* friend in the US who helped you. Really?"

Roddy shook his head. "That's not entirely true."

"I didn't think so. Look, don't hold back. I'll be fine with whatever you tell me. Honestly, I will." He rubbed Roddy's arm. After everything they had both been through, he would never underestimate the power of this bond with his son.

"Okay, Dad." Roddy shifted in his seat as a busker to the right of the fountain squeezed out the first few bars on his accordion: the classic Italian Cornetto ice-cream song, *O Sole Mio*. He remembered Elvis's version of the same hit - *It's Now or Never*. He smiled at how fitting this was as a backdrop for what he was about to divulge. His father smiled back at him and nodded his encouragement to go on.

"Well, Dad, you're right. I don't have a social media friend in the US. That was a white lie. You see, I didn't want to admit to the real source of the information."

"The suspense is killing me! Go on." His father waved his hands in the air encouraging his son to open up.

"Well, I know you're going to find this hard to believe. It was me who was able to trace the numbers and decode their messages." He waited for his father to process this.

"How could you do that?" Kenny was not sure he should be impressed until he heard the whole story.

"Well, truthfully, I figured out the code they were using by myself. Although it would have been impossible were it not for the periodic table cup you gave me."

"Nice one, pal. I knew it would come in handy somehow. Although that doesn't explain how you knew about the texts and phone numbers?"

"Okay. For those, I did have some help; but not from someone else."

"Really? Then what?"

Roddy opened the zip on his backpack and reached down to bring out the Irn-Bru bottle. Half the contents remained.

"Irn-Bru?" His dad looked quizzically. "How can Irn-Bru help to solve these kinds of problems?"

Roddy twisted the top off the bottle and lifted it to his father's nose. Kenny leant forward and sniffed. Then jerked his head back in surprise.

"Hey, you can't drink whisky! You're far too young. Give that to me." He reached across to take it from his hand. Roddy sat back on the wall, replaced the cap and extended his arm out of reach over the water. "Dad, it's non-alcoholic whisky. It's okay."

"What are you talking about? Non-alcoholic whisky? That's ridic…" Roddy saw the light go on in his father's eyes.

Kenny felt his breathing quicken. He rubbed his head with the flat of his hand. "How did you get that?"

Roddy began to speak. The words were on the tip of his tongue, ready to free him from the burden of silence. Before he could utter them, his father jumped from the wall and threw himself onto his son. They both tumbled over into the water, splashing the tourists on either side. Roddy felt his back smack off the marble floor of the fountain, just below the surface. While he had expected his father to be shocked by the revelation, this reaction was exaggerated even by his dad's standards.

His father was motionless, flattened on top of him, pinning him to the marble floor. Roddy was desperate to breathe, his consciousness ebbing. There was no energy left to push his father off. As the blackness enveloped him, he could hear the muffled screams of tourists around the fountain.

The last thing he saw before his eyes closed was the Trevi's crystal-clear water take on a misty-red hue.

Nonna

"Ah, Nonna!" Marco said as he and Marciano pushed their chairs back and rose from the table. Wilson and Tommy did the same, watching the elderly lady shuffle across the room towards them. Small and frail, the lady's back had already succumbed to a curved spine and narrow shoulders. She placed the stick purposefully in front of her as she took measured steps towards the table.

She stood in front of Wilson a moment before speaking, allowing the detective a moment to study her. The clear blue eyes sat like small jewels in the middle of a face hosting wrinkles that became deeper lines as they stretched from her eyes towards her mouth.

"Is this the young lady and man who saved Marco?"

"Yes, they are Maggie and Tommy," Marco replied. "There was another woman too, Gina. Very brave lady. She has gone home to prepare for her wedding."

"Make sure you send her a gift," Nonna answered without taking her eyes from Wilson.

"Of course, Mama. It has already been arranged." Marciano pulled a chair back for her to sit.

The lady placed her hand on Wilson's face and stroked her cheek gently. "You are a beautiful woman. However…" She tilted her head to the side to look more closely. "I see that you are worried. Something is concerning you." Nonna turned to look at Tommy. "You, young man, don't seem to have a care in the world." She smiled, and the room seemed to light up around them. "How did the two of you get together?"

"Oh, no," Wilson answered. "We are not together, just friends." Tommy tried to hide the disappointment at how quickly Maggie felt she had to correct this impression. "You see, Tommy's best friends with my partner."

"Partner?" Nonna laughed as she settled into the chair. "Sounds more like you are in business together rather than lovers." Wilson wondered if the elderly lady had sensed just how close to the truth she was.

Marco placed a plate of cheese and crackers in front of his grandmother while Marciano filled her glass from a bottle of limoncello. Tommy had noticed it in the middle of the table, nestled in a bucket of ice, wondering when they were going to open it. Marco smiled across at him as if he had known all along how tempting it had been for the Scotsman to reach out and help himself. He filled Tommy's wine glass and winked at him. Wilson covered her glass with a hand and smiled an apologetic refusal.

"*Salute!*" Nonna said, raising her glass towards them. "I thank you both, and your friend, for saving my grandson's life." She took a healthy slug of the limoncello, before placing it on the table and nodding at Marco. He refilled her glass.

Wilson could see her cheeks pinken with the warmth of the liqueur. She coughed before continuing. "These are interesting days, you know. Young men are walking into bars with machine guns. People are assassinated. Popes are being elected." She shrugged her shoulders. "What I have learned is that coincidences only exist when you stop trying to find the connection."

"I could not agree more," Wilson answered.

"I know you are a detective, so I will be careful about what I say." Nonna looked at her son and grandson. "Don't worry. I might be old, but I am not stupid, *ragazzi!*"

Their awkward smiles showed that while they knew she was not 'stupid', they were not sure where the conversation was going.

"There are many topics I cannot talk about, even though you would find them interesting, Maggie. That said, I do feel I should help you to understand some things. My gift to you for saving Marco and his friends."

She took a bite of cracker and cheese and washed it down with another sip of her drink. "You see, I come from a tradition where one good deed deserves another. What I will say now, I hope, will help you in solving the crime you are investigating."

"Any help we can get will be appreciated," Tommy answered on Wilson's behalf.

"I am sure you know what our family does. Or at least you believe you know all of what we do. Yes, we make a living from doing things that you would not condone. However, believe me, when I say, we do not treat people badly." She sipped her limoncello. "Unless they deserve it." Wilson saw a flash of menace in Nonna's piercing eyes.

"Those men who attacked you were nothing more than rented killers. Hitmen. Luca and Luigi. One of the families here in Sicily used them to dispose of people who should be eliminated. Sometimes they got it right. Like in London. Sometimes, not so right." She nodded towards Marco.

"Excuse me." Wilson sat up in her chair. "London?"

Nonna continued. "Yes, London. *Sacco* Capello."

"Luca and Luigi killed him?" If this was true, Wilson had never known such an important tipoff to be given in such a throwaway fashion.

The old lady nodded. "I'm sure with all your forensic equipment these days, you will find a match to the bricks in Sacco's pocket and the rope." She paused, letting Wilson digest the information she had come to Italy to find.

"As I said, they got this one right. Don't misunderstand me. Sacco was not a bad man. The problem was that when we decided to do something good and give back, we chose the wrong person to protect our funds. His crime was to manage a bank that did not properly control our families' monies. He failed us; and paid a price."

"Are you saying he stole from you and the other families?" Wilson asked.

"No, I am not saying that." Nonna shifted in her seat. "He did not look after what we had entrusted him with. One of the families decided to take matters into their own hands. However…" she raised her hand in the air, "…do not ask me who that family was. I will not be accused of breaking Omertà."

Wilson and Tommy recognised this as the Sicilian Mafia's code of silence. Breaking Omertà was punishable by death. Wilson knew when to stop asking questions. She had enough to take back to Rome and London; to move them onto the next stage of the investigation. Marciano and Marco had begun to fold their napkins. Lunch had come to an end.

"Hey, Nonna!" Wilson should have realised Tommy was not going to let them leave easily. "Who do you think the new Pope is going to be?" Where Tommy saw a valid conversational linkage, everyone else saw a non-sequitur.

"Hah! Such a good question. The best one to end our lunch." The lady moved to rise from her chair. Marciano and Marco were already standing at her back. "My vote, if I had one, would be for Cardinal Damascus. He has turned out to be a very good man. Despite the challenging childhood he had."

"You say that as if you know him," said Tommy.

"Well, if delivering him as a baby into the world can be considered as knowing him, then yes, you are right."

Damascus' Nativity

Nonna pointed at her glass - it had been empty for a few minutes. She had sat back down in her chair with a renewed energy. Marco topped up her limoncello – with a barely-concealed reluctance.

"It was towards the end of the war. I was in my home village just outside Naples. The bombs had been landing for days at that point. We knew the American and British soldiers were gaining ground, but we were not sure if we could survive for long enough. In the middle of the night a bomb landed on our building. It was falling down around us." She took a decent slug from the glass and wiped a tear from her eye.

"I could hear our next-door neighbour, Signora Di Maria. She was screaming. I ran into her apartment and found her lying on the floor." Nonna looked at Wilson. "I was eighteen years old. With no experience of babies. The mother was already in labour. What could I do?"

She did not wait for an answer. "I did the best I could. Although the blood would not stop." Tears were now streaming down her cheeks. "Just as I took her child in my arms, an American soldier came into the room. He was evacuating the building. I thrust the baby into his arms, and he took him away."

"What a terrible situation to have been in. You are so brave." Wilson reached across and held her frail hand. "I take it the mother died."

The old lady nodded, dabbing a napkin to her eyes.

"How do you know that Cardinal Damascus is the baby?" Tommy asked the question Wilson had been considering.

"When Cardinal Damascus was much older, he reached out. Before his father passed away, he gave his adopted son the name of the village where we lived. By the time he contacted the village council, I was living in Sicily. I decided not to contact him after the day he was born. I was sure he would consider this connection to our family in Sicily as damaging to the role he played in the Church."

She sighed and took a moment to blow her nose. "I heard about his visits to his birthplace over the years. Apparently, he enjoyed spending time there. You know what they say, once Italian, always Italian. That is good enough for me."

"What an incredible story." Wilson said. "Would you not want to meet him now?"

"Ah, my *G'mlu*," Nonna sighed and looked at Wilson. "Things are never as simple as you would like them to be."

"*G'mlu*?" Wilson asked.

Marciano spoke. "Yes, *G'mlu* is the name she uses for him. A sort of pet name since she did not know his real name until many years later. Now, I think we should call it a day. She needs some rest."

His mother flashed him a sharp look. "I can decide for myself when I go to sleep, thank you."

Marciano put his arms in the air in supplication. Wilson could see he enjoyed his mother's feisty nature. Nonna put a hand in her pocket and pulled out a shiny object. She placed it on the table in front of Wilson. The letter **G** sparkled in the light.

"Hey, I saw those medals in St. Peter's Square a couple of days ago. What does the **G** represent?"

"Galatians," Nonna answered. "*G'mlu* believes that the Church needs to return to its basic message; and move away from traditions and distractions. The letter to the Galatians was St. Paul's way of doing the same thing two thousand year ago." She shrugged her shoulders. "While we may not be perfect here in our family, we believe in honesty of action and sincerity of heart."

"Okay, Mama. That's enough. Time to call it a day. Maggie and Tommy will be tired after all their escapades last night." Marciano was firmer this time. His mother stood up slowly. Wearier now than when she arrived. Bed was beckoning. She turned to Wilson.

"You know. There is more to this story of *G'mlu*. However, I will leave it there. If you are as good as I think you are, then you will figure out the rest."

"One last question." Wilson put her hand under her elbow, helping her manoeuvre into an upright position. "Where did you learn to speak English so well?"

"Ah, Maggie. Thank you, although I am a little rusty. I worked in London for many years before my son was born."

"Oh, who did you work for?" Wilson asked.

Nonna smiled. *"G'mlu's…"*

"Mama! Basta! Non di piu!" Marciano shouted. *Enough, no more.* His mother said a quiet prayer before lifting the medal and placing it against her lips. She held it there for a second before tucking it into her cardigan pocket. She patted Wilson on the arm and turned to hobble across the floor. Marciano held out his arm and she linked her own. *"Mi dispiace, figliolo. Così dimentico che non dovremmo parlare di lui."*

Wilson knew enough rudimentary Italian to translate her words – *Sorry, son. Sometimes I forget we should not speak of him.*

Back at the Trevi

Roddy sat on the steps beside the fountain dripping water onto the ancient stones. His father lay on the ground semi-conscious, blood seeping from a wound at the side of his forehead. A young woman in shorts and t-shirt was bent over him, dabbing a white cloth against the cut.

"Is he okay?" Roddy asked. He held his father's hand, squeezing each finger one by one.

"He must have bashed his head on the wall as he fell in," she answered in an American accent. "Good news is the wound is more a graze than a cut. You were both in the fountain for no more than a few seconds. He can't have swallowed much water." She pointed at his arms and legs. "He seems to have been in a fight with a bear quite recently." He had not noticed the cuts and bruises; he had been so pleased to see his father.

Kenny spluttered into life with a throaty cough expelling a half pint of water onto the woman's t-shirt. Roddy enjoyed the sense of relief, his hand supporting the back of his father's head.

"Oh, I'm sorry," Kenny said between coughs. "I've ruined your shirt."

She looked at Roddy and smiled. "Don't worry. I'm just pleased you are conscious. You had us all worried."

Kenny looked up to see a crowd of people looking at him, standing on each layer of the Trevi's steps, as if in an ancient amphitheatre watching a slapstick performance.

"Oh, we've created quite the scene here," he said rising shakily to his feet. "Thank you so much for your help."

"You okay?" Roddy had not yet digested his father's exaggerated reaction.

Kenny turned to his son and wrapped his arms around him. "I'm fine. You okay, pal?"

"Fine. Good to see you are okay. You must have cracked your head on the wall when you jumped on me."

His father whispered in his ear. "I didn't hit my head and I didn't jump on you. I saved you." He lowered himself and Roddy onto their haunches and pointed at the wall, where it looked like a hole had been hollowed into the marble. They could see the end of a circular metal object embedded in the stone. Kenny touched his head where the blood was already congealing. He had come within a centimetre of death. He made a point of obscuring the bullet hole from the crowd. He knew it would not be long before they realised what had happened.

"Hey, Kenny! Roddy!" A tall, handsome priest ran down the steps towards them. "What in God's name has happened?"

"Hi Father David," Roddy said. "It's good to see you. We were on our way to meet you, before we ended up with two Scots in a fountain!"

"Are you okay?" Fr. David reached across to dab a handkerchief against the cut.

Kenny scrunched his nose and flinched at the touch. His reaction surprised Roddy: much like a child being offered brussels sprouts at Christmas dinner. "It's okay, Father. It's just a scratch. How did you know we were here?"

"Well, I had been hanging around the library for a while waiting for Roddy. Eventually I took to looking out a window to see if he was coming. I saw you both walking away towards the fountain. By the time I had locked up and got here, you had fallen into the water. What happened?"

Roddy could sense the crowd disperse. The American woman remained, standing beside Fr. David. "Hi, Father. I saw it all."

He turned to her. "Oh, hi." He saw speckles of blood on her hand. "I assume you were the first aid giver here."

She shrugged her embarrassment off. "It was strange; this man just jumped onto his son and pushed him into the water." Her eyes were focused on Kenny, her tone of admonishment not lost on any of them.

He coughed. "I know. It was a moment of madness. I thought I saw a mosquito on his head. He has a severe allergic reaction to mozzy bites. I just panicked." He bent down to look at Roddy's head. "Did it bite you, pal?"

"Eh, no. You got there just in time. Thanks." Roddy had never been good at lying yet seemed to be getting better by the day. He was still coming to terms with the bullet in the wall.

"Okay, let's get you both into dry clothes. We have some lost property at the university. I am sure we can kit you out." Fr. David began to walk up the steps onto the street. Kenny and Roddy thanked their nurse, who introduced herself as Florence.

"No better name. Thank you, Florence." Kenny said. Roddy hugged her before they picked up their backpacks to follow Fr. David.

Kenny heard his phone buzzing. As luck would have it, the phone had remained on the wall when he dived into the water.

"Hey, Maggie!"

"Hi, can you talk?"

"Bit difficult at the moment. What's up?"

"I think I'm making progress. Looks like I'll need to come back to Rome."

He smiled. "Aw, that would be great. We could make it three Scots in a fountain next time."

"What?"

"I'll explain when you get here."

Pink Devil Pizza

"How is your pizza?" Tantalus dabbed a napkin at the corner of his mouth. His table manners were so impeccable, they made her feel uncomfortable.

Angie did not need to lie. The pizzas and sodas had been delivered half an hour earlier by a young man on a scooter with flowing lettering on its side: *Pink Devil Pizzeria.* The thin base, liberal spread of tomato puree and delicious cheese rendered her Margherita the best thing since sliced bread. She decided not to explain it that way. "It's really tasty, sir."

"Now, now. Please call me by my name."

"Is Tantalus your real name?" she asked before taking a sip of San Pellegrino, enjoying the subtle bitter orange flavour.

"Arnalda!" her father interrupted. "I told you not to ask questions like this. The less you know, the better for all of us."

Tantalus put his hand in the air. "Mask, it's okay. We have to encourage children to express their curiosity. I am sure you did. I certainly was not shy at asking questions."

He placed his napkin on the table and looked at her. There was the hint of soporific intensity in how he levelled his gaze. "Tantalus is not my original name. I am afraid that is information I keep to myself. However, I chose the name Tantalus for a very good reason. You see, my life was not easy. I tried to achieve many things. I was very skilled at my chosen profession: information systems and computers. I was always told I had a genius IQ, unsurpassed by anyone my teachers and bosses had witnessed before me."

She noticed a fleeting glimpse of irritation in his eyes.

"Did they intervene to promote my talents on a broader scale? Oh, no. I was too much of a threat to them. They did not want to see my successes surpass their own. They tried to quash my spirit. It became clear that through no fault of my own, the goals I dreamed of achieving would always be too far away." He took a drink of sparkling water. Some bubbles nested on the rim of his grey moustache.

"Before you ask, yes, I did fall in love at one time, in my younger years. My love-life proved to be no better than my career. I once had a beautiful girlfriend; I adored the ground she walked on. I truly believed she fell from heaven. Until her great betrayal, she left me for another man. She said I was too intense. Too intense! What do you think of that?"

He spread his hands wide and expanded his chest.

"Her loss, I'd say," Angie answered in a quiet voice.

"Hah!" Tantalus laughed. He looked at Mask and pointed with his thumb at Angie. "You have a real diplomat there!" He turned his head back to her.

"Anyway. I realised after these disappointments and many others just like them that I was always destined for my dreams to be frustratingly just out of reach. So, I chose the name, Tantalus."

Angie nodded. "I know the story. It's from Greek mythology. Tantalus displeased the gods, so he was doomed to spend his life trapped between a pond he could not reach to quench his thirst; and a tree with succulent fruit that was just too far out of his grasp."

She waited a moment as Tantalus clapped his hands and said, "Bravo!"

She continued. "That's why we have the word *tantalise* in our language today."

"Okay, I think that's enough." Mask did not like to see his daughter connecting with a man he knew was capable of terrible things. It was enough she had him as a father; he did not need competition in the villainous mastermind department.

"Yes, Mask, you are right. We have just had our Last Supper before we enter the final phase of our plan. In fact, we should look on tomorrow as the beginning of the end, before the start of the new beginning." Tantalus rose from the table.

Mask nodded, "I look forward to us not using these strange beginning and ending statements anymore." He picked up his cardboard box and threw it onto a pile of rubbish in the corner of the kitchen. His phone beeped.

He looked at Tantalus before picking it up. He read the message before he kicked his chair across the room.

"I take it he missed?" Tantalus said.

"That fool had one thing to do. A single measly task." Mask looked at his partner. "We need to end our relationship with that incompetent, once and for all."

Tantalus nodded. "All in good time. Let's not underestimate what our colleague can do. There is still time."

Angie busied herself collecting the dinner waste from the table. She pretended not to notice their exchange, scraping pizza remains into the bin.

Tantalus stood, exhaled a slow sigh and left to go downstairs to the basement. She heard him talking as he walked along the corridor. "Ah, soon all of this will come to a head and make the long journey worthwhile."

Oblique Views of the Square

"We don't have much time." Kenny watched Fr. David leave the library to find some towels and dry clothes. They were sitting at a small desk in front of a laptop.

"Dad, this is tripping me out. Did somebody really try and shoot us?" Roddy was talking over his shoulder as he logged on.

"Yes. The reason I jumped on you was because I heard a click coming from a first-floor window. It came from the other end of the fountain behind us. The sound of a bullet being loaded into the chamber of a gun is unmistakeable." He paused for a moment. "Now that you're aware of Hair o' the Dog's powers, I expect you've put two and two together."

Roddy took the Irn-Bru bottle from his bag and placed it on the table. "Sorry. I should've told you before. It was not long after you came back from America, after you and Maggie had captured Mask. I didn't know how to bring it up. Then I stopped after a while, because…"

"Oh, no, pal. Please don't tell me it had an adverse reaction?"

"Eh, no. Well, yes." Roddy coughed. "My acne flares up whenever I drink it. My street cred was getting ruined. So, I stopped not long after I discovered it."

He was not sure, he thought he detected a twitch at the edge of his father's mouth. "Oh, really?" his father said.

"Are you laughing?"

"No. Something's stuck in my teeth. Anyway, let's get back to the discussion." He loved every spot on his wee boy's face.

"Well, I knew then that you were Kiltman. It all made sense. Dad…"

"Go on, you can say it. Quick, Fr. David will be back soon."

"Dad, I'm so proud of you. All those people you've saved."

"Aw, thanks, Son." They hugged for a few seconds, enjoying the frankness of their discussion. "Listen, you can't tell this to anyone."

"I know. Don't worry." Roddy was enjoying the sense of relief and wave of empowerment; until he saw his father's face adopt a disconcerting solemnity.

He leant forward and whispered in his son's ear. "Now, listen to me carefully. Fr. David fired the gun. When he gets…"

"Dad, what are you talking about? That's ridiculous." Roddy rose from the table and walked to the library window. "How could you say such a thing?"

"Several reasons." He counted along his fingers. "First, he knew you were going to be in this neighbourhood. You had let him know you were coming. Second, when he was at the Trevi, I could smell cordite on his fingers. It must have come from the gun. Lastly, look out the window."

Roddy looked out the window. "What am I looking for?"

"Point to where we walked along the square earlier today."

Roddy looked left and right through the glass. "I can't. It was in the corner down there. I can't see it from here."

"So how could Fr. David have seen us walking towards the Trevi?"

Roddy's face flickered enough for his father to know his point had registered. The door opened with Fr. David stumbling in carrying a box full of clothes and a couple of towels draped over his arm.

"Sorry, gents. I had to go downstairs for these." He threw the towels towards them. "Dry yourselves off. You can get changed here. There's no-one else around. I'll come back in a few minutes and help you log on. We can do what you had originally intended to do here. Believe me, I am intrigued." He had not noticed Roddy was already on the internet.

He placed the box on the desk and turned to leave. Roddy was starting to feel a chill in the damp clothes. He reached over to take one of the towels, looking forward to drying off and putting on whatever Fr. David had managed to muster. His father's assumption that this likeable priest had tried to shoot them did not make sense. When Fr. David left the room, he intended to challenge his father on his notion that a God-fearing priest would go around shooting at people in a public place.

Out of the corner of his eye he saw his father leap from the chair. His father covered the few metres to the door at a speed that surprised Roddy. He threw himself onto Fr. David's back, knocking the priest to the ground. The force of his chest hitting a desk forced a grunt from Fr. David on his way down to the floor.

Kenny turned him onto his back and knelt on his arms in the same way the bigger children had trapped him in primary school. He decided not to tap Fr. David on the chest as had been done to him all those years ago.

"Okay, Fr. David. I've got a good mind to knock you into next week. You need to start explaining yourself. Why did you try and shoot my son today?"

"Dad, why do you think he was aiming at me?" Roddy was unsure whether to be more surprised at the priest firing a gun or shooting at him.

"I'll explain later. All to do with the trajectory of the bullet." He pushed his knees hard onto the priest's outstretched arms.

"Hey! Have you gone mad?" Fr. David squirmed under his weight. "Get off me! What's all this nonsense about me shooting at you?"

"You need to answer a few questions!" Kenny shouted.

"Okay! Okay! Just ask. For God's sake! This is crazy!"

"First question," Kenny started. "You said you saw us walking from the square to the Trevi. That's not possible. The library windows don't show the area where we were walking."

"Is that it? You jumped on me because of that? I said I saw you from a window. I didn't say it was a library window. Yes, I waited in the library, then I went to a reading room and looked out from there because it gives a full view of the square. Now, can I get up, please?"

"Quick thinking, Father. Although that doesn't explain the cordite on your hands." Kenny grabbed a handful of the priest's black shirt. The thought of losing Roddy to a bullet had inspired a rage he struggled to control.

"Cordite?" The priest furrowed his brow letting a few seconds pass. "Of course. This morning, I was working with the nuns at our local parish of San Silvestro to arrange fireworks for when the new Pope is announced. The conclave starts tomorrow. An announcement could be made very soon. We need to be prepared to celebrate."

With each word Fr. David uttered, Kenny eased back on his knees. By the time he had finished he was still straddling him but kneeling on the ground. He could tell by the vocal intonation and heart rate racing through his elongated arms that the priest was telling the truth.

Kenny coughed. He stood up and extended his hand to help Fr. David to his feet. The priest ignored him and used a chair to pull himself up to his full height, looking down at Kenny and Roddy.

"Eh, I'm sorry, Father. Not sure what got into me." Holes in the ground just never appear when they should.

"I don't have words to express how shocked I am at your behaviour. Not only how you could've believed I am capable – apparently – of shooting a teenage boy. The fact that based on the flimsiest of evidence you manhandle me to the ground. I have a good mind to call the police." Fr. David brushed the dust off his clothes with the back of his hand.

"Father," Roddy put his hand on Kenny's shoulder. "My dad has been through a hard time lately. He just got back from Brazil where he was lost in the jungle for a few days. He's not been himself."

Fr. David looked at Kenny, whose face was doing its best to look like a confused man who had spent days walking around a rainforest. "I can see you are not the same person I met back in Scotland." The hurt and disappointment were evident on his handsome features. "One thing I've learned as a priest is that forgiveness applies to every situation. Yes, even this one. I can't say I'm not upset. However, I have to forgive you. Goes with the territory." He touched his white collar to make his point. He realised it was dangling across the top of his shirt. He fixed it back into place before extending his hand in front of him.

Kenny reached across for the handshake. The priest withdrew his hand. It would have been comical in another scenario.

"I was not offering to shake hands with you. I am about to give you and Roddy a blessing. Whatever you two are working on, I sense you need God on your side."

Kilt - Man and Boy

Kiltman held out his flask while Roddy poured a top up from his Irn-Bru bottle. He wanted to recognise this as one of the benefits of having a son who shared the powers of Hair o' the Dog. He decided not to; the whole scenario was just too fresh. And more than a little weird. He had not had time to digest the implications of his son being part of the power-imbuing, non-alcoholic whisky world. After the Fr. David mauling, he just felt lucky his son was still talking to him.

When Roddy went to the bathroom to dry off and dress, Kenny took a moment to text Maggie of his confession to Roddy that he was Kiltman. He chose not to mention his son's own superpowers from Hair o' the Dog. Some things were better not texted; just like attacking a priest. They would deal with these issues when she was in Rome.

They were sitting at the desk facing the computer. He had changed out of his wet Guns 'n' Roses shirt and shorts into his Kiltman costume. Kenny would have to take a back seat; and Cornelius Shaunery would go into hibernation until the next time total anonymity was required.

Something was going down in Rome, he was convinced. At the same time, flummoxed - there were still too many loose ends for him to formalise a proper plan. Roddy sitting there smiling at his father in his Kiltman costume eased the tension. The shredded cape and kilt begged a question, but Roddy chose not to ask. They had enough danger in Rome without replaying his father's Brazilian adventure. Roddy was wearing an Italia '90 football top and a pair of grey jogging trousers that had seen better days, perfect for the mood he was in.

Fr. David had gone to a dinner appointment with friends, leaving them alone to perform their research. He could not exit the library quick enough. His blessing was delivered in a shaky hand with a liberal sprinkling of holy water - then he scarpered.

They clicked their containers together. "*Sláinte!*" they said at the same time; enjoying a generous helping of non-alcoholic -

but tasty - whisky before they turned to the computer. While he was expert in many areas, Kiltman struggled to keep up with Roddy's mesmerising keyboard tapping.

"Stop!" His son seemed oblivious to him, entranced by the screen. Every few seconds he looked somehow into the middle distance and then back at the computer. "I said, stop!"

"Oh, sorry. What is it?" Roddy held his fingers above the keyboard.

"You've been tapping away like a crazed person. Can you tell me what's going on?"

He turned to his father. "Okay. This must seem a bit odd, I'm not going to lie." He picked up the Irn-Bru bottle. "When I drink your whisky, I end up with strange powers. Just not the ones you're famous for."

"Go on."

"The powers centre around technology. There are two levels. The first is that I can see messages and files in the air around me. I see the airwaves, I guess. It's as if they become visible and move in slow motion allowing me to read them. I can also see where they are coming from and going to. Once I access a phone or a system, I can visualise the messages. It's a weird feeling."

"Crikey, that is unusual." Kiltman enjoyed the fact Hair o' the Dog had given Roddy a uniquely special power. Although he fought back a tinge of envy, imagining what he could do with it.

"That's not all. There is a second level of power." He felt strange telling his father; yet the satisfaction outweighed the awkwardness of the revelation. "When I am online, I can access systems with ease. I can break down firewalls, decipher passwords and reach into confidential files stored in encrypted locations."

Kiltman decided not to say 'crikey' again. He needed to maintain some credibility as the more senior of the two. His mind raced. There was no end to the possibilities of such a power. He trusted Roddy but it made him more convinced of the importance of keeping the whisky under lock and key. It made him pause and consider how safe his stash was back home. If a teenager was able to avail himself of Hair o' the Dog at will, his security at Uisge Beatha was seriously lacking.

Kiltman nodded. "That's great. Let's put your powers to good use now. Can you still access the numbers you first noticed, the ones that helped you advise Maggie about the St. Peter's Square meeting?"

"Dad!" Roddy pointed at the screen. "What do you think I've been doing for the last five minutes?" Data began to trickle onto the screen from the bottom, moving in a staccato march to the top. "That +39 number is the one that was communicating with Mask's Brazilian phone."

+39 – 1892, 7566?
+44 – 8 9, 271816
+39 – 66841481, 537, 13342581.
+44 – 1619
+39 – 907, 11059
+44 – 1619

"The other number is a +44, which, as you know, is the UK. Are they using the same code?" Kiltman asked.

Roddy nodded and reached into his bag to produce the periodic table cup. It gleamed under the table lamp in the library. "Who would've thought, eh?"

Kiltman high-fived Roddy's outstretched hand. "Okay, let's test your knowledge of the chemical elements."

Roddy took a sheet of paper and pencil from a nearby desk and wrote the numbers down onto the sheet. Alongside, he scribbled the associated letters coming from the cup.

+39 – 18, 92, 7566? *AR, U, REDY?*
+44 – 8 9, 271816 *O F, CO AR S*
+39 – 66841481, 537, 13342581. *DYPOSITI, IN, BSEMNTI*
+44 – 1619 *OK*
+39 – 907, 11059 *THN, DSPR*
+44 – 1619 *OK*

Roddy began to write down a more recognisable combination of the letters, but Kiltman beat him to it, vocalising the patchy lettering.

Are you ready?
Of course
Deposit in basement
Okay

Then disappear
Okay

"You got it, Dad! What could it mean?"

"Something is being kept in, or being put into, a basement. When were the messages sent?"

Roddy flicked back through the screen. "This afternoon." He waited a moment and scrolled some more. "Look!"

Kiltman studied where Roddy was pointing. The +39 number had made a phone call earlier that evening. To another +39 number. Roddy made a quick google search and found the number that had been called. It showed up on screen under a photograph of a family dressed in white chef's clothes holding a pizza. Behind the smiling group of four, emblazoned in pink lettering, *Pink Devil Pizzeria* shone brightly.

Kiltman dialled the number and put his phone on speaker.

"*Pronto!*" a woman answered in a chirpy voice.

"Hi, do you speak English?" he asked.

"Yes, of course. How can I help you?"

"My friend ordered some pizzas earlier. However, he forgot to keep the receipt. Can you tell me how much it cost?"

"Okay, sir, however we deliver lots of pizzas. What number did he dial from?"

Kiltman read aloud the numbers on the screen.

"Ah, yes. *Via Cassia.* They ordered two Margaritas, a Pepperoni and a Diavolo. It was 48 euros. Do you want me to bring round a receipt?"

"No, thanks. I expect we will be out for a walk soon and can pick it up then. In the meantime, could you text a copy of the receipt to my number? *Grazie!*"

He hung up. A minute later his phone beeped with the text. He showed it to Roddy, the specific location on *Via Cassia* noted at the top of the receipt.

"Cool. Will we go there now? It might be Angie in that basement." Roddy had seen enough movies to know that whenever a basement was mentioned it did not bode well.

"Not just yet. Can you dig up any more information from that number? The more we know, the better armed we will be."

"I can search for an IP address linked to the location. That would give me a chance to access their computer records."

"Go for it. Don't let me hold you back." Kiltman could not deny he was enjoying this.

Roddy spent a few more minutes clicking, tapping and mousing. "Okay, I'm now connected. To be honest, it has several layers of security not normally associated with a home computer."

"Can you get into it?" his father asked.

"Probably, although it'll take time." Roddy fought back his growing frustration. "This is strange," he said.

"What is?" Kiltman was watching his son walk around the library pointing at thin air.

"That home computer is constantly generating tons of data. They must have a massive server there to process all this activity." He looked more carefully. "There are thousands of signals being emitted every second. I can't understand what this is."

"Anything else?" Kiltman asked.

Roddy walked around the room looking towards the ceiling. He began to see a multitude of rows of numbers, accompanied by dollar and euro symbols. "Yes, loads of numbers. They look like different currencies. There are headers above the columns, with the words, *Debits* and *Credits*, just like you'd see on a bank statement. The word *Cayman* keeps popping up."

"Sounds like there are transactions being processed with a bank in the Cayman Islands." Kiltman suggested. "Can you tell which bank is being used to send the money?" He had stood up and was walking around behind Roddy looking at where his son was studying the air above his head, in the hope he would see something. All he could see were thousands of old philosophy and theology books sitting on a myriad of wooden shelves.

"Yes, it's Banco d'Aiuto. Have you heard of it?"

"No, can't say I have. It does sound odd for someone's home computer to be making so many transactions between banks." Kiltman leaned against a bookcase and massaged the top of his nose.

Roddy's phone beeped back to life. A welcome distraction from the thousands of numbers floating around his head. He walked over and picked it up.

"Dad! You've got to look at this!" he called across the width of the library.

His father called back, "Hold it up. I can see from here." It would take a while to adjust to his father's superpowers. He held the phone in the air and scrolled down slowly.

Roddy, it's Reilly here. I received this message from Angie. I am on my way to Rome from the US. My dad is meeting me there. Will get in touch when I arrive.

"Reilly. Am in Rome in Villa on Via Cassia area called Tomba di Nerone dad plotting horrible things. DON'T REPLY TO THIS PHONE. Please help me. A x"

Monday, April 18

All Flights Lead to Rome

"Is that Mr. MacDonald, Reilly's father?"

"Yes, it is. With whom am I speaking?"

"Hi, it's Kenny Morgan, Roddy's dad. My son has been trying to reach Reilly, his phone seems to be turned off."

Kiltman heard him take a deep breath. "I will be quite honest with you, Mr. Morgan…"

"Just call me Kenny."

"Mr. Morgan, listen. I am not happy that Reilly has decided to fly to Rome rather than go home." Kiltman held the phone a few centimetres from his ear, surprised at the aggressive intonation.

"Hold on, Mr. MacDonald. You can't blame me for your son's choices." He looked at Roddy, who was standing beside him trying to hear the discussion.

Mr. MacDonald continued as if Kiltman had not spoken. "Please understand that I empathise with your challenges and search for Angie. However, the police are well-equipped to investigate the text she sent to Reilly."

"Where are you just now?" Kiltman was not in the mood for a stranger off-loading his worries onto him, even if he was more responsible than Mr. MacDonald was aware.

"I'm standing at the airport waiting for Reilly to come off his flight."

"Oh, you're in Rome already? That was quick."

"Yes, I am. Did you know that Coach Stone has also come to Rome?"

"That's strange. I assume Coach needed a break." Kiltman felt his blood pressure rising. Considering this was the first time he had spoken to Reilly's father; he was not in the mood to be lectured on the poor travel choices of Reilly and Coach.

"He is irresponsible, if you ask me. He has set a bad example. He should have stayed in the US and flown directly home to Scotland, rather than put this foolish notion in Reilly's mind. I intend to get my son on the first flight back to Scotland. If he contacts you, can you please support this?"

"Yes, of course. Don't worry."

"I need to go."

"Okay, tha…" The line went dead. Reilly was still on the plane. They would need to try and contact him directly when he landed rather than through the father.

It was Monday morning: they had slept little the night before. Pensione da Antonio was minimal but clean and comfortable. Near the train station, the trundling of trams and beeping horns had startled them into alertness every few minutes. Sitting at their window one floor up, they had a view of the station across the road. Their pile of takeaway plates and cups bore testimony to a carb-loaded breakfast washed down with coffee and juice. Roddy had found a McDonalds near the station. His father asked if he understood the culinary blasphemy of eating burgers in Rome. Roddy reminded him of the midnight feast of fish and chips his dad had purchased on his way home from a posh Glasgow restaurant. He was finding it easier to bat off his father's quips.

Wilson had just landed and would come to meet them at the Pensione. For some reason Tommy had decided to stay in Sicily. Kiltman tuned out when Wilson began to explain about Tommy wanting to spend time getting to know his *future* wife. At times, he could be an incredible asset. Until his love of a good-looking girl became a distraction worth dropping everything for.

"How you getting on?" he asked Roddy, watching him type with vim on a laptop they had borrowed from the hotel. Kiltman had lifted the bottom of his mask for the conversation with Mr. MacDonald, deactivating the voice-changer. He had now moved it back into position and even though he could see Roddy struggling with the mechanical, Kiltman voice, he was pleased his son did not ask him to deactivate it.

"Okay. Do you know what's really interesting about these financial transactions?"

"What?"

"Well, they all start in euros and end in dollars. However, that's not the best part. For every transaction, a tiny fraction of each goes into this separate Cayman Islands bank account. Over a year, these tiny fractions add up to millions of dollars. I'll keep going to see why this is happening."

"What about the other thing?"

"The signals?"

"Yes."

"Hmm, not much I can say about that. Just that there seems to be a complicated algorithm generating pulses of energy into the atmosphere. I'll need to keep looking at that."

If it were not for Roddy, he would have felt helpless. He walked across to his son and placed a hand on his head and ruffled his hair.

"You're doing well, pal."

"Thanks." Roddy kept his eyes on the screen. He sensed today was going to end very differently to how it had started. They had agreed that Kiltman would go to Tomba di Nerone to check out the villa where Angie was being held.

Kiltman continued. "If we can figure out what's going on with these bank transfers, it could help us negotiate Angie's release."

Or get you killed, Roddy thought.

Or get me killed, Kiltman thought.

Welcome, Wilson

She walked out into the terminal in search of a taxi rank. It was a relief to be on solid ground again. The flight had been busy. Monday morning *red eye* from Palermo to Rome, full of business folks, briefcases and laptops.

Her phone beeped with a message from Sergeant McNeil back in Glasgow: *Morning, boss. Just checking in to see if you need any help with anything. I heard what happened to your colleague at the Vatican. I'm so sorry. McN.*

She fired off a quick response: *Thanks, Sarge. I'll let you know. I appreciate your note. X*

It was not normal practice to include a kiss in a message to a subordinate in the Scottish police, but McNeil just seemed to bring out her caring side.

Until she saw Chief Commissioner Pisacane standing at the welcome area with two officers chaperoning him. "Oh, good morning, sir. This is a pleasant surprise?" It was not meant to sound like a question, but she could not hide a hint of sardonic challenge.

"Detective Inspector Wilson, we have a lot to talk about. Please come with us." Pisacane had already turned to walk towards the exit. He looked over his shoulder to see that she was not following him. "Did you not hear me?"

"Yes, sir. I did. However, I am going to get a taxi, thanks." She did not like the edge in his tone.

"I would rather we don't have this conversation here in the airport. Let's go to the police station."

"Why? I would rather go back to my hotel, shower and then come see you later. How about that?" She had folded her arms.

"Let's compromise." He sighed. "We give you a lift to your hotel and debrief in the car."

She could not argue, so nodded and followed him and his officers. Their Polizia Alfa Romeo was parked at the terminal entrance. Within minutes they had left the airport grounds and were heading for the motorway. Pisacane was in the back seat beside Wilson. He opened a cabinet behind the driver's seat and gestured to the contents. It contained a variety of juices and waters. Tommy would have been disappointed.

She opted for a litre bottle of San Pellegrino. She collected two glasses and placed them on the table jutting out from the back of the front passenger seat.

She tried to twist the cap off but could not get a sufficiently tight grip; her palm felt clammy after the confrontation at the airport. Pisacane offered his hand which she accepted. He twisted the top off with barely a flick of his wrist. The escaping bubbles broke the silence in the impromptu carpool. He filled their glasses.

"Please talk me through what happened in Sicily." Pisacane had switched on a mini recorder and placed it between them on the seat.

"I debriefed Albano and Monte. Did they not give you my report?"

"Yes, they did." Pisacane acknowledged. "More importantly, I want to know what was talked about when you met Marciano senior. Or should I say, at your three-hour lunch with him?"

"Oh, you know about that?" she asked. "I'm starting to realise Italy is a small country."

"Signora Wilson, it's my job to know what goes on. Just like it's your job to investigate Sacco's murder and the related financial implications. It seems in your hurry to ingratiate yourself with the Cosa Nostra, you have lost sight of your reasons for being in Italy."

"Okay, listen." She screwed the cap back on the bottle, channelling her ire into a tighter twist than necessary. "I'm getting fed up with your insinuations and opinions about my policing skills and modus operandi. Don't second guess me, sir. That's one way to guarantee minimal communication on my part. Is that clear?"

"Okay," he said, with a shallow nod of the head. "I am sorry if I come across as direct and, in some ways, obstinate. You should understand that this is a high-profile case. We need to find answers."

"Yes, I do understand. I appreciate your apology. Let's start again." She turned in her seat to face him.

"How do you want to do that then?" he asked.

"Let's start by you asking me how my flight went." She smiled.

"How was your flight, Signora Wilson?" He was even more handsome when he grinned.

"Great, thanks, sir. Too many suits for my liking. Thank goodness it was over before I knew it."

"That's good to hear." He seemed to be enjoying this.

"Can I update you on my meeting with Marciano?"

"Oh, that would be very useful. Thank you."

Wilson talked through their lunch conversation, focusing on the comments about Luigi and Luca and their involvement in Sacco's killing. Pisacane knew the importance of this titbit. Something they would not have found on their own. She could see he was surprised by the charitable funding initiative that had prompted someone to eliminate Sacco. All of this would require further investigation by his team, but he could not deny her lunch had moved the case forward.

They dropped her at Roma Termini, the city's central train station, close enough to her hotel for a walk and some fresh air, she insisted. She chose not to mention Kenny and Roddy waiting in a Pensione nearby. For some reason, not yet obvious to her, she felt it was better not to talk about the conversation with Nonna about Cardinal Damascus. She was not sure if it was relevant to anything, yet it piqued her detective antenna. Until she ran this by Kiltman, she was unwilling to share with the Rome constabulary. She thanked Pisacane for the lift and stepped out of the car.

Pisacane nodded his appreciation through the window and waved as she disappeared into the throng of Rome pedestrians. He may have underestimated the Scottish Detective Inspector. Just when he thought he had her sussed, she turned out to be more capable than he had expected.

Realising his glass was empty, he wrapped his fingers around the bottle cap to prise it open. After a few seconds of unsuccessful effort, he smiled. Yes, Wilson really was a force to be reckoned with.

Collaboration

"You had one job to do, and you could not even manage that."

"I'm sorry. I didn't expect him to climb out a window."

"Who is this guy Shaunery? What's he doing in Rome?"

"I don't know. He just showed up at the hospital and then the Pasticceria."

He cursed under his breath. She could hear him controlling his temper. "What happened at the fountain?"

"It was all a bit chaotic. There were lots of people around as usual. I had a clear view of them sitting on the fountain wall. Everything was under control, until this Shaunery man jumped onto Roddy. It happened in an instant, they both ended up in the water."

"In the Trevi?"

"Yes."

"And?"

"It all got crazy after that. I decided to leave the scene for a while in case I was spotted. When I returned, they had both gone."

"I am disappointed."

"I know. So am I!"

"Let me be clear. Self-disappointment is a luxury you can revel in when this is all over. For the moment, I am the only one who can be disappointed. Anyway, what condition is the patient in now?"

"There is no change. He is still in a coma."

"Why do they not just pull the plug?"

She did not answer. She expected it was rhetorical - with him she was never sure.

"What are you planning to do now?"

"I am going to find them. I have Roddy's number. I am trying to triangulate and find out where he is. He keeps turning his phone off; it's hard to lock in a signal."

He decided to end the call, he hated excuses. "Wilson is back in Rome. She is at Roma Termini, walking towards her hotel.

Find her and you will find the boy. He is up to something, I know it. They seem to be one step ahead of us."

"I understand the urgency." He was now going over old ground, the same issues he had spoken about a day earlier.

"I hope you do. Keep me informed, Valentina."

Reunion

"Excuse me!" Roddy had waited long enough.

"Oh, sorry, pal. Come here and give me a big teenage, bear hug!" she said from underneath Kiltman's armpit. It was heart-warming to see just how pleased they were to embrace each other again. After a couple of minutes, Roddy felt left out. He let Maggie and his father pull him into a group hug. After another minute or so, it began to feel uncomfortable. It reminded him of his history lesson on Stalin, how everyone clapped for long periods in fear of being first to stop. Eventually, he broke away, prompting her to say, "I guess we have a lot to talk about."

She turned back to Kiltman and began to stroke his chest slowly with her fingers. After a few moments of awkwardness, she switched her gaze to Roddy. "Please don't tell your father that I'm having an affair with Kiltman. I find Superheroes irresistible. I don't think your dad will be very pleased."

Roddy shrugged. "Don't worry. I always thought you were too good-looking for Dad. He has been punching above his weight, if you ask me." He was relieved to know his father had informed her that he was now in on the family secret. Otherwise, the scene unfolding would have been beyond weird.

"Hey, that's enough!" Kiltman said, feeling ill at ease in his mask. One of the quirks of his costume was that he never wore just part of the get up. If he put it on, then he went full Monty, on all aspects of kilt and mask wearing. "Okay, enough of the witty banter, you two. We've got a job to do. Once we get home, we can debrief on who knew what and when about my alter-ego."

Wilson dug into her backpack and produced a paper bag full of warm, sweet-smelling cannoli; to go with the coffees and juices she had placed on the table, beside the residue of their first breakfast. "Looks like you need a fuel top up, guys. It will help as we cover what's been going on over the last few days. A lot has happened. Why don't you tell me what you've been up to? I'll go last."

She sat down on the bed, Kiltman and Roddy at the table. Before long they were in full stride, covering the events of the last week. Kiltman kicked it off with a concise version of his trip to Brazil. He managed to make falling out of a helicopter and over a waterfall sound like mundane events. She would have reacted differently if Roddy had not been there; she could tell Kiltman was holding back. She would get the full version later. He showed them his life-saving leaves and cream when he spoke about the Amazonian tribe. Wilson asked if she could have a leaf, her eyes glistening at this point in the story. He passed her a spongy, square piece of Amazonian foliage, which she kissed before placing it in a dark corner of her backpack.

Roddy picked up from there. "I landed in Cincinnati a week ago. Hard to believe."

"Oh, my!" Kiltman said. "I forgot to ask the most important question."

"Yes?"

"How did the tournament go?"

Roddy reached into his shirt and produced his winner's medal. Gold, shiny and so heavy, it had created a groove on his neck where the chain rested.

"Yes!" Kiltman shouted and punched the air. "Finally, some good news this week. When we get back, we're going to celebrate. Come here, young fella!"

After another group hug, Kiltman said, "You know, it's strange to see a medal that doesn't have a large **G** on it. They seem to be everywhere."

"Dad, you know that's the symbol for Cardinal Damascus who's one of the favourites for Pope? The Conclave starts today."

Both Wilson and Kiltman nodded remembering their own encounters with the medal. Roddy went on. "I met Cardinal Damascus in Cincinnati. That's where he's based. Kind of an eccentric guy, if you ask me. I can't deny though, his followers love him. He has a massive fan club, people all over the world."

"You know what *fan* stands for?" Kiltman asked.

"Fanatics," Wilson answered.

"Angie is definitely in Rome." Roddy wanted to get back to the main topic. He had spent enough time that week in the presence of Galatians.

"Where is she?" Wilson did not sound surprised.

"In a villa on the *Via Cassia*, to the north of the city."

"How did you manage to find that out?" She was impressed.

"She sent a message to our friend, Reilly." Roddy looked at his father, who nodded. "Also, we were able to track their messages and calls, so we know exactly the address they are at."

"Seriously, how did you track them? Your social media contact…again?" She knew something did not add up. Kiltman stepped in; his son was struggling with the words.

"Roddy has, em, how can I say it, become Kiltboy."

"Guys, this isn't funny. Explain, before I lose it!"

Roddy put his hand up for his father to step back. He stood and walked towards Wilson. "I found Dad's stash and had a wee drink." He saw her face change expression. "It's okay. Don't forget, it's non-alcoholic."

She looked at Kiltman who shrugged. "Boys will be boys, I guess."

"Go, on," she said, unsure of whether his glibness was sincere or a coping mechanism.

Roddy went on to explain the powers he developed when under the influence of Hair o' the Dog. The ups of being able to capture and read messages on the airwaves to the downs of lumpy, bumpy acne. It proved hard to read Maggie's expression until she put her hands in the air and said, "Do you guys realise how weird this is becoming?"

They both nodded.

"Let's be careful about the whole *Kiltboy* thing here. Roddy has a life ahead of him. This could be a curse just as much as a benefit."

They both nodded again. After a few seconds silence, Kiltman spoke first. "We'll have to deal with this when we get home. Right now, we need to rescue Angie and stop whatever madness Mask is planning."

"I agree," she acknowledged.

"There's something else." Roddy said before she could say what was on her mind.

"Someone shot at us. Or apparently at me, yesterday."

She switched her gaze to Kiltman. "What?"

Kiltman coughed a dry, time-saving cough. "It was at the Trevi Fountain. Someone fired at Roddy. I know he was the intended target because of the trajectory of the bullet. Don't ask me how I know that. However, I do know for sure it was aimed at him. It ended up in the fountain wall after grazing me here, under the mask." He pointed at his forehead.

She moved over to Roddy and kissed him on the cheek. "Are you okay?"

"Eh, yes, thanks, Maggie. Although it was Dad who got hit by the bullet." She turned to see Kiltman with his arms spread wide. How many lives did this cat have, she wondered, before kissing him in the centre of the mask, in the general vicinity of where she thought his mouth was.

"At first, we thought it was a priest we knew. Until we figured out it wasn't him." Instinct told Roddy not to mention his father accosting Fr. David. That, and his father drawing a thumb across his throat behind Wilson's back. "We still don't know who fired the gun. Or why."

Her mind drifted to Crawford who was still in limbo between life and death. She had called the hospital when she landed. There was no change in his condition. This case was taking too much of a toll on good people. She snapped her mind back to the conversation. "Thank God, you're both okay. That was far too close."

Roddy refocused them. "I want to talk about Mask and the weird computer thing he has going on. It seems like he's up to something on quite a grand scale. I tracked the IP location and was able to see a couple of strange things going on with their computer. They've got a lot of signals being pumped out to a multitude of locations. High frequency. I can't attach any words or messages to them. At least not yet. I'm still working on it."

"Hmm, that's bizarre." She rubbed her chin. "What's the other issue? You said there were a couple of things."

"Yes. This one's a bit clearer, although not sure why it's happening. His computer is sending money between financial institutions. It seems he's able to send messages to banks to prompt them to transfer funds. The bizarre thing is that each transaction triggers another transaction, this time for a much smaller amount, which goes to another bank.”

She sat forward in her chair. “Who are the banks?”

“The money is going mainly to a bank called Banco Discepolo, and the smaller amounts are going to a bank in the Caymans.”

She rose from her chair and began to pace the room. “Which bank is sending the money in the first place?”

“Banco d’Aiuto,” Roddy answered.

“Say again?” She had stopped to lean her back against the wall. She looked at the ceiling, the hint of a smile tickling the corner of her mouth.

“Banco d’Aiuto.” He was concerned his Italian pronunciation had not been clear enough.

“Do you realise you have just given me the perfect segue into what I have been working on over the last few days?”

Pre-Conclave

"Three, Two, One. You're now live!"

Grant felt anxious. He prided himself on controlling his nerves. However, today was different. He knew the Papal Conclave was important to his boss, both on a professional and deeply personal level.

"Here we are at St. Peter's Square in Vatican City; on a truly momentous day in the history of the church." Grant stood atop a makeshift podium two metres by one metre, far enough from the ground to allow him a head and shoulders above the crowds pouring into the square. "Over here to my right, you can see St. Peter's Basilica. Behind its doors the Cardinals are celebrating mass to kick off the process for electing the Church's 265th Pope."

"*Kick off the process*! What the heck was that? Follow the script!" Dominic shouted through the earpiece.

Grant continued. "The mass is known as *Pro Eligendo Romano Pontifice*, which translates as 'For the Election of the Roman Pontiff'. After mass, Cardinals under the age of 80 when Pope John Paul II died will enter the famous Sistine Chapel to the call of *EXTRA OMNES!* - which means *Everybody Out*! Not very polite if you ask me, maybe Latin didn't have a word for *please*."

He heard Dominic's hefty sigh into his microphone.

"The longest Conclave in history took place back in the 13th century. It lasted 34 months! In comparison, the most recent Conclave for Pope John Paul II's election took two days. So, who knows how long the Cardinals will remain under lock and key in Vatican City. In fact, the word Conclave comes from the Latin *Cum Clave* – meaning *with key*. Yes, you heard it here first: on BBC, translating for the non-Latin speakers."

"MACTAVISH!" bellowed through his earpiece, prompting the reporter to cough into his elbow.

"This evening, they will have the first ballot. If it doesn't result in a new Pontiff, then tomorrow morning there will be another one. And if no new Pope at that point, then there will be another vote in the afternoon. This will continue until a winner is decided upon."

"Jesus, Mary, Joseph and the wee donkey!" Dominic muttered resignedly.

"Of course, this will be a winner in all respects. There is no greater responsibility on the planet than leading the more than one billion Catholics looking for direction and guidance.

"And in terms of the numbers needed to arrive at a decision; the new Pope will require a two thirds majority of Cardinals. There you have it; Maths and Latin in one broadcast! That's why you pay your licence fee." Grant's signature, cheeky grin filled the camera just before it panned away from him to the thousands of people in the square, singing and shouting the names of preferred Cardinals.

It gave Dominic a chance to provide feedback. "MacTavish! You have to recognise the solemnity of this occasion. Don't trivialise it, ya muppet!"

The camera came back to focus on Grant.

"There is a carnival atmosphere here right now in the square; however, let that not distract from the solemnity of this auspicious day in the Catholic Church. Rest assured we will give you updates as they arise. The only communication to come from behind the Vatican walls will be the smoke that billows up from that chimney."

A second camera on the other side of the Vatican focused in on a long, thin chimney. It stretched to just above the rooves of surrounding buildings, above the world's most famous artistic achievement, Michelangelo's fresco in the Sistine Chapel.

"If the smoke comes out black, it will signify they have not yet reached a clear decision. When it's white, you can bet all hell breaks loose. Eh, sorry, everyone will get very excited, because that means there will be a new Pope.

"This has been Grant MacTavish, live at St. Peter's in Rome." … and not looking forward to his producer's debrief.

Their Pensione television was not great quality, but they were able to catch the BBC report on the laptop. Roddy commented on the large number in the crowd sporting Galatians' medals. Kiltman and Wilson agreed, surprised that so much support was focused on an American Cardinal. There was a general sense that American leaders in the church risked upsetting the conservative, traditional approach of the institution. Roddy reminded them that this was exactly the platform Damascus chose to lead from.

Wilson clicked her fingers.

"Hey, I forgot to mention that I met the woman who delivered Cardinal Damascus when he was born. Towards the end of the war in Naples. She is Marciano's mother." She had updated them on the bar brawl and their role in protecting Marco Marciano and his henchmen. Despite the drama of the story, they had laughed at Tommy's antics and the hen party coincidence. Kiltman was still rubbing his arm from when Wilson had punched him. In retrospect saying that Gina's fiancé was 'one lucky man', was not the wisest comment.

"You know," Kiltman said, "it will be a remarkable story if Cardinal Damascus is elected. To come from such a humble beginning to leader of the Church seems quite apt."

Wilson nodded. "I know what you mean. Jesus was born in a stable."

"Yes, and he went on to transform the world more than any one person has ever done before or since." Kiltman thought about what he had just said. "You know, change is not always a good thing."

"I don't know. Depends on what the starting point is for change; and what things will be like after it." Roddy offered.

"I think you've been spending too much time in the Gregorian University library, wee man. You're becoming a bit of a philosopher." Kiltman was smiling. Although nobody noticed.

They were biding their time till dark. Roddy was working with Wilson on her laptop, digging into the *Via Cassia* IP location. So far, they had found nothing new. No messages or calls. While there was the same transmission of high frequency signals, the bank transfers seemed to be slowing down.

Wilson had been able to compare the account numbers for each of the Mafia families against the Banco d'Aiuto transactions. They were the same. The offshoot transfers to the Cayman Islands bank were tiny per transaction, but added up to millions of dollars over the years. The ownership of the Cayman bank account was anonymous, no details available on the system.

She knew a few people in Sicily who would want to have this information. Also, a Chief Commissioner in Rome. She decided to sit on it for the time being. They had to focus on rescuing Angie. Something else was niggling her too. Her gut. Not from too much cannoli - contrary to Kiltman's suggestion - just the good old Detective Inspector instinct that perceives a problem before it happens.

Kiltman was going to Tomba di Nerone alone. Wilson had argued but gave in when he asked her to keep an eye on Roddy. Resisting was not an option. She recognised it had the added advantage of allowing her to work with Roddy in investigating the multi-layered, complex systems he was navigating around. Where he was able to point to reams of data, she was better placed to pick out the anomalies and clues to analyse what was going on.

After a few minutes of silence and scrolling through pages of figures, shoulder to shoulder with Roddy, a low hum sounded across the room; similar to a throttle on an outboard motor. They turned to see Kiltman lying on the bed, snoring through his mask. She decided to leave him like that; he had a long evening ahead of him.

She looked at Roddy. He jerked his head towards his father with a faux disgusted look on his face. Wilson sighed and rose from her seat. She grabbed a blanket from the cupboard and threw it across Kiltman's motionless body. Not for warmth. Just sometimes, a true Scotsman could be in the wrong place at the wrong time, in the wrong position.

Papal Conclave

The Cardinals walked solemnly towards the Sistine Chapel. Mass had been reflective, a moment to consider the late pontiff, his legacy and the platform he created for the future. Over the days since Pope John-Paul II died, there had been time for the Cardinals to share views of where the Church should focus.

There was agreement the Church was at a turning point. It had a choice to make. Either embrace a new era; or continue straight ahead and miss the opportunity to evolve.

"So, Cardinal Damascus, it seems you have drummed up quite a lot of support. Are you feeling confident?"

Challenging a fellow Cardinal on his ambition for becoming the new Pope was unusual. He turned to face the young Cardinal. He recognised him although could not recall which African country he represented. "This is a strange question, my friend. I am not sure what you mean by 'drumming up' however, let me assure you, I pray for the best outcome for the Church, not for selfish interests or pride."

He dropped his tone of voice a notch and whispered, "*Am I now trying to win human approval, or God's approval? Or am I trying to please people? If I were still trying to please people, I would not be a servant of Christ.*" He waited, searching the African Cardinal's eyes.

"Galatians 1:10." The African Cardinal conceded. "You are right, of course. God's approval should be our guiding light. We need to move the Church forward and remind ourselves of the true message."

They bowed to each other and continued their walk towards the Sistine Chapel. Before the first ballot that evening, there would be more time to reflect and listen. More time for him to quote Galatians and remind the other Cardinals that change was needed. The more he talked of change, the greater the association would be that he was the one to deliver it.

Salvatore

"She is in a Pensione behind Roma Termini. Not the most luxurious place, to be frank. Maybe she's trying to be incognito." Salvatore sat in the driver's seat, enjoying an espresso; his third that day and it had just gone mid-afternoon. This was not the first time he had sat in a car patiently awaiting instructions.

"Is she alone?" Pirla Sconi was seated in a leather armchair in his villa overlooking a calm, blue sea, watching soft waves pulsate onto the coastline around Cefalù; one of Sicily's go to coastal towns, where Sconi had settled several years earlier. A fourth century BC settlement, Cefalù had been built by the invading Greeks to take advantage of its Northern headland jutting out into the Mediterranean, complementing the dominant large rock high above sea level. No better place to see your enemy coming. Good enough for the Greeks, good enough for the Sconis.

He sipped on his hefty grappa, enjoying the view.

"I don't know yet. I expect the boy is there too. I haven't poked my nose around just yet."

"Wise. Hold back for now. Patience is our advantage." Sconi enjoyed revenge; but loved waiting for it even more.

"No problem. Do you want a clean sweep?"

"Of course. Leave no stone unturned. She made a mistake coming here and interfering in our affairs. If she has pulled other people into her circle, then more fool them."

Sconi sighed. He had not wanted to kill Luca and Luigi; he had no choice. They would have understood their time was up when they were arrested. Loose lips sink ships. He knew it and they knew it. He would make sure their families would not suffer; at least financially they would be secure.

Wilson on the other hand was just an interloper. Coming all the way from Scotland to interfere in their affairs was an insult. The fact she did not realise how much she was being used by the Italian police eradicated any respect due her for previous achievements. Yes, she had captured an insane, evil genius with her kilted partner. However, that was a long time ago. Now she was a pawn in a game she did not know she was even playing.

"Anything else for the time being?" Salvatore asked.

"Have you had lunch?"

"Yes, I had a panini."

"Okay, once you've done the job, make sure you go to a wonderful restaurant, a few blocks from the station. It's called *Foglio di Scrisio*. I have enjoyed many a dinner there. Make sure to have the *saltimbocca alla romana*; it's incredible. It will be my treat." Sconi drained his glass. He would live vicariously through Salvatore over the next few hours.

"Thank you. I'll do that. I expect I'll be hungry by then," Salvatore said as he twisted the silencer onto the gun. He always enjoyed talking to his father before he made a hit.

Scientia Potentia Est

"We need to show you something here." Wilson said to Kiltman as she watched him yawn and stretch. "Least I could do after what you showed us."

"Sure," he said, throwing his legs over the side of the bed. Roddy and Wilson looked away. Roddy was the first to laugh, Wilson followed soon after. "What's so funny?"

"It's a long story," she said.

"Not so long, to be honest." Roddy looked at Wilson.

"I think you've just taken this one stage too far, young Mr. Morgan." She put her finger to her lips. He probably had, he thought, but it was worth it.

Kiltman shuffled in beside them in front of the laptop. "Okay, what is it?"

"Your wee boy's going to give us a Maths lesson." She pointed at a piece of paper on the desk.

Kiltman knew not to question the flow when Maggie was focused on a lead. "Go on."

Roddy sat upright in his chair. "Okay. Let's say you're Banco di Kenny and she is Banco di Maggie and I am Banco di Roddy. Banco di Kenny wants to send 100 Euros to Banco di Maggie. However, Banco di Maggie only wants Dollars. So, they need to use an exchange rate where 100 Euro translates into 128.714 Dollars. So, Banco di Kenny sends the 100 Euros. Banco di Maggie receives 128.71 Dollars. They are both happy because the transaction has gone through. Until... and this is the important bit." Roddy was scribbling the numbers on a sheet of paper. He writes the 128.714 and underneath deducts the 128.71. "Look, there is a difference of 0.004. Banco di Maggie has received \$0.004 less than she should have. Guess where that amount of Dollars goes?"

"I assume Banco di Roddy."

"Exactly!" Roddy said. "We've discovered that for all these Euro to Dollar transfers, the exchange rate is cut off one decimal point early. Then the difference is sent to this Cayman Islands

Bank. We looked at the transactions over the last ten years and it accounts for millions of dollars effectively stolen from these transactions." He waited for his father to digest the information.

"So, let's go back to the real world where Banco d'Aiuto is sending Euros and Banco Discepolo is receiving Dollars. The dollars received are always slightly smaller than they should be."

"This is insane." Kiltman was pacing the room. "There must be controls in the banking system to stop this happening?"

"Yes, there are. However, someone switched them off. Or rather, reduced them by one decimal place. At the same time, they created an offshore account to collect the difference."

Kiltman looked at Wilson. She nodded. "Sacco over-rode the systems and set this all up. There is no way he could not have known about this. That's why the Mafia are so incensed. At some point after all these years, they have added up the numbers and realised that this money has gone missing. Because of the infinitesimal amounts in each transaction, it would not have been noticed until there was a critical mass of fund transfers."

"Incredible," Kiltman said. "So simple yet…"

"Wait, there's more," she interrupted. "We've dug into the Cayman accounts. We can't see who the account holders are. However, they've been spending this money just as quickly as it's received."

"Who is it going to?" Kiltman sat down, beginning to think he should go to sleep more often.

"Major IT, software and hardware companies in locations in America, UK and Italy. But wait for it." Roddy stood up as his father sat down.

"There's even more?" Kiltman had snuggled up on the chair beside Wilson.

"A payment for €48 was made from the Cayman's account to…" Roddy paused to let his father catch up.

"The Pink Devil!" Kiltman slapped his hand against Wilson's.

"Ouch!" she shouted. "What was that?"

"Sorry, I thought you were doing a high five."

"I was about to lean across and point to the screen, at the receipt." She shook her head. "Sometimes I wonder about you."

Roddy smiled. It was good to see things getting back to normal.

Kiltman leaned forward to peer at the laptop. It had been a while since he had been to Specsavers. He needed another slug of Hair o' the Dog.

The receipt for four pizzas from Pink Devil Pizzeria sat square in the middle of the page; the delivery address noted at the bottom, same location on the *Via Cassia*.

"So basically, if I get this right," he said. "Mask is in control of the funds that have been stolen from the Mafia."

Wilson nodded.

"Do you think the families know this?"

"I doubt it," she said. "Not unless they have a non-alcoholic whisky power-imbued equivalent of Roddy nearby." She stood up, stretched her arms and back and sat on the edge of the table. She looked at Kiltman and said, *"Scientia potentia est."*

"Don't tell me you've joined Grant's Latin class?" he asked.

She shook her head. "I do remember a few phrases from my *Ecce Romani* books at high school. This is one of them: *knowledge is power*. Believe me, this kind of knowledge is the most powerful."

Marco Marciano

He had not been to Rome for several years. It was not his kind of city. Jostling for position and space among throngs of tourists and pilgrims was not his idea of fun. While he respected what the city had to offer its visitors, he had seen it all many years before on school trips. This visit was quite different. He had enjoyed the short trip on his father's jet, landing half an hour before Wilson's plane. He was in the terminal when she walked through. Her standing up to Pisacane had made him smile. The Chief Commissioner was a thorn in the side of the Sicilian families. The media saw him as a white knight come to rescue Italy from the Cosa Nostra. Marco knew enough about him to know his main objective was *Cosa Pisacane:* made up of his ego and career.

Marco was enjoying his cigarette at a rickety table outside Bar Simpatia, at the opposite corner from Pensione da Antonio. If she caught sight of him, she would not notice; the beard and glasses gave him a scholarly air. He liked the look. It suited a bar in Rome on a bustling Monday afternoon.

She had made quite an impact on the Marcianos. To gain his father's approval was not easy. He had presented many girlfriends over the years; to see his father's subtle shake of the head, before apologising and leaving the table. Marco had not given up; the family line had to continue. He and his father were aligned on this objective. Until now they had not seen eye to eye on the future Signora Marciano.

Yesterday's lunch had been the perfect way to round off the exploits of the evening before. Laying the base for a potential future relationship. Then Nonna arrived. He loved his grandmother but she had the habit of saying too much. It was impossible to enforce Omertà when she had downed a couple of limoncellos. He had discussed it with his father, and they agreed that she had gone too far. She had opened up a channel of information that Maggie should not have been aware of. Whether or not she had fully digested the information, vigilance was now necessary.

And this was one vigilante role he intended to enjoy.

Pontificating

The Cardinals were spread out across the Sistine Chapel. Some walked with an air of contemplation, looking towards Michelangelo's Last Judgement fresco for guidance and inspiration. A few gathered in corners whispering, continuing to exchange views on the Church and its challenges. Nearer to the door a larger group were huddled together. The average age of this gathering of Cardinals was a good ten years younger than the others. Their discussion was animated, opinions and perspectives expressed with a degree of passion and fervour atypical in the Sistine Chapel.

"My dear Cardinal Damascus, my brothers and I understand the importance of the Church stepping back and reassessing itself. That said, you must understand, there is a fear among the Cardinals that you are asking for too much too soon." The Cardinal had lived in Peru during the evolution of liberation theology in the sixties. Like then, when he could not fault the socio-economic drive, he feared for the political position it required of the Church's leaders. It led to a degree of disruption that threatened the fabric of the institution. Over recent years, Pope John Paul II had focused on quelling the storm. Although it was never far away.

"Ah, my dear friend. I know what you have been through and the hard times you and your people have endured in Latin America. You, above all, should not be afraid of change." He took out his medal from below his cassock. "We don't wear this because we want to look flashy or hip. It's a reminder of St. Paul's letter to the Galatians. We all know what his message was, and why it was so important to Paul to send it. I think we can all agree that the epistle was not just a moment for him to comment on what the Galatians were or were not doing. It was much more than that. It was also his way of telling future generations to be careful."

He paused to look at the other Cardinals, taking time to make eye contact with each of them individually.

"We are that future generation." He pointed at his trimmed, grey hair jutting out from under his zucchetto. "Sometimes I don't feel like a future generation, but I am."

The other Cardinals laughed. Some pointed at their own grey hair, or lack of it.

"It's not that I want to create a revolution in the Church. God forbid. However, we have a duty to heed St. Paul's words. '*Know that a person is not justified by observing the law, but by faith in Jesus Christ. So we, too, have put our faith in Christ Jesus that we may be justified by faith in Christ and not by observing the law, because by observing the law no one will be justified.*'"

"Galatians 2:16," the South American Cardinal whispered.

"Exactly. 2:16. This is the essence of St. Paul's message. Faith above law will justify our existence as a Church, and our role as Cardinals. Never has our role been more critical than it is now as we choose our new Pontiff."

He rose from his chair. "Now, in a few minutes I believe we will be asked to submit our votes. Let's take a few moments before then to ask for divine inspiration. May God be with you all."

"Amen!" the Cardinals said in unison. The group rose and walked to their assigned places. The first ballot was starting.

Pizzas Again

They walked along the edge of the *Via Cassia*, stepping onto the grassy verge whenever a vehicle sped past. At any point, a pedestrian could be on the brink of making the wrong move and being hit by a car. Before long Mask and Angie turned down a side street and strolled between rows of affluent apartment buildings. To any onlooker, they would have seemed like the perfect father and daughter, on their way to dine at the Pink Devil Pizzeria. It would be their second visit there: Tantalus had treated them to pizzas and gelato when they arrived in Rome.

The eatery, nestled in the corner of a small shopping plaza, offered quiet anonymity from the busy world of Rome and the Vatican; allowing them to get on with the task at hand.

"*Buona sera!*" the owner said through a mouthful of his own pizza.

"*Buona sera, Signore.*" Mask answered, looking sideways at his daughter; she would not have known he spoke Italian. Today he did not want to engage in small talk. The less contact they made, the easier it would be to disappear without notice. They were ushered to a table by the window, welcomed by the aroma of pizzas baking in the large oven towards the back of the pizzeria. Mask liked to see the kitchen when he was dining. It was harder for chefs to cheat on the food when they were in full view of the customers.

A waiter, identified by a nametag as Matteo, produced a bottle of sparkling water and filled their glasses. Mask picked up the menu and pointed at *Pizza Margarita*. "*Due, grazie.*"

The waiter shuffled off towards the kitchen.

Mask reached across to take Angie's hands in his. "Arnalda, I know you have been struggling this last week with everything that has been going on. However, this will all be over soon. Then we can move onto the next stage of our adventure. I promise you; it will be much more rewarding. I know Tantalus can be hard work; he is a difficult person to read. Trust me when I say he is the only one that could help make our plans come to life."

He sensed his daughter's resistance to his affection. Leaning back in his chair, he took a slow sip from his glass. "You know, it's nice that we can take this moment to be together and have a proper father to daughter talk."

"Father, for God's sake! My name is Angie! Stop this madness." She had never been so brave with him. She had started to believe she had nothing to lose. "I don't have a clue what your plan is. Why do you act as if I am part of your gang? You kidnapped me and brought me here. Why? Just to wait for you to do something evil?"

His face flinched. Barely perceptible but enough for her to notice. "Arnalda, my dear, I don't expect you to understand what we are doing. Just have faith that we are about to do something incredible." He paused for a moment and chewed on the end of a breadstick, studying the tablecloth. When he looked up, she saw the demon in his eyes that she had witnessed so often in the past. "Listen carefully, my daughter. I detest nothing more than a whinging child. If you can't be supportive then let's not talk at all. I am happy to eat in silence."

They sat and looked at each other. His eyes gave nothing away; his blank stare usually sucked her energy dry. Not today. She could feel an anger grow inside.

"Okay, Father. I am happy to stay quiet too." She looked away towards the chef. On another day, she would have found the roundness of his belly worthy of comment. He resembled the conventional pizza maker more than he realised himself. The circular lump of floppy dough rose into the air to drop onto his balled fist, before he placed it with unabashed ease onto his long-handled spatula. Akin to a Masai warrior's command of his spear, the chef inserted the dough into the large oven. He then extracted the two he had started earlier, dropping them onto plates as if it was the most important task he would do all day, every day. Matteo was there to cut the two cheesy Margaritas into six slices apiece. He carried them to their table, noticing that the atmosphere had changed between the customers.

"*Buon appetito!*" Matteo said with an exaggerated show of energy. He guessed the girl at the table was around his age, maybe a little younger. He was drawn to her. Yes, she was attractive, and in a different scenario he would invite her to meet for a gelato. He could sense her fragility; he did not like the way the man dominated. This was the father's moment to ask questions about friends, school, hobbies and interests; explore his daughter's world. Instead, he glowered at her as if she were the devil incarnate.

"Excuse me," Matteo said as they bit down on their first slice. "Will your friend be coming to join you? We can put another pizza in the oven for him."

"Our friend?" Mask asked.

"Yes, the man you came with the other day. He likes our pizzas. In fact, I think he ordered a home delivery yesterday."

"Ah, yes. You know, we have so many friends." Mask had stopped looking at the waiter, hoping he would go back to serving other customers.

"Oh! There's something I need to give you." Matteo left the table to step behind the cash register.

"What's he doing?" Mask asked. Angie could see Matteo over her father's shoulder rummaging around in a drawer.

"No idea. He's looking for something."

Matteo walked back to the table. "Here you go. Please give this to your friend." He placed a numbered invoice on the table.

"What's this?" Mask could not hide the impatience now. He picked it up and studied the document. It described the Sunday night takeaway, for €48.

"I don't want this." Mask thrust it at Matteo.

"No, but your friend may want it." Matteo was determined to interrupt their lunch even more. He was beginning to enjoy it.

"Why would he want it?" Mask's irritation made Angie flinch.

"Well, he called earlier today to find out how much it cost. I assume he wants to manage his financial records."

"No, I am sorry. I am quite sure he did not call." Mask looked at Angie. She shrugged. This was the best fun she had had all week.

"Yes, sir, he did. I don't care if you don't believe me. If you don't want the invoice, I'll take it back." Matteo tried to snatch the receipt from Mask's hand. He whisked it away before the waiter came close. Mask studied the slip of paper to see the delivery address annotated across the bottom.

"Did he ask for the address?"

"Why would he do that, Signore? He knows where he lives." Matteo smirked at Angie.

"I see. That's fine then." Mask turned back to eat his pizza, flapping the invoice dismissively at Matteo.

He extracted it from Mask's fingers and turned to walk back towards the kitchen. As he left the table, he said, "Tell your friend that if he wants a copy, it is available online in the account he set up with us."

Mask looked at Angie. His mind was racing. He had spent most of his life avoiding being captured; his natural instinct was to smell a rat. Tantalus would not have called the pizzeria. He did not even need to ask him, he was oddly eccentric but not stupid, wilier than anyone he had worked with before.

"Arnalda, bring those slices with you. We need to go. You are going to see Rome's splendid *Piazza di Spagna* up close. You will be impressed."

They each grabbed handfuls of pizza and walked out the door. Mask returned a few seconds later and gave Matteo a 100 Euro note. "You have been very helpful, young man. Much more than you could possibly imagine."

Matteo batted Mask's hand away. "This one is on the house, Signore. I suggest you spend the €100 on learning *comportamento corretto*."

"Okay, Matteo!" The owner interrupted. "Please go and help the chef." He agreed with Matteo that the customer needed to learn good manners. At that moment, he just wanted the man gone. He moved to close the door but found Mask's foot placed against it.

"Dad, come!" Angie called. She could see her father reach down towards his sock for his double-bladed knife. She felt a cold chill remembering how he had used it to stab the man in the square. "Remember our plans!" she shouted.

The seconds ticked by as Mask remained bent with his fingers wrapped around the handle. The owner looked down at him crouching on the pavement; he did not need to see the knife to feel the menacing air.

"Please, move your foot. I am closing the door."

Mask felt Angie's warm, soft hand squeeze his. He concentrated on bringing his temper under control, releasing his grip.

"I will not forget our encounter, Signore Pink Devil. Not you, and certainly not that waiter with the attitude."

"*Arrivederci!*" the owner said, before closing the door in Mask's face.

The wave of anger was just what Mask needed to revive him. He found a renewed sense of infuriation to fuel his next steps. He was not worried; their emergency contingency plan was more than adequate to manage this latest upset. Whoever had called the restaurant would think they had the upper hand. That put Mask in the best position imaginable, where the hunter becomes the prey.

Life was becoming good again.

Next Steps

"Hi, Roddy," Reilly whispered into the phone.

"Hey, Reilly. Good to hear from you. I hear you're in Rome."

"I am. Any news about Angie?" Reilly's concern sat heavy in his voice.

"Eh, no. Nothing tangible. You remember Maggie Wilson, the Detective Inspector involved in catching Mask a few years ago? Well, she's here helping find Angie. I gave her the text she sent you. She's following up on that now." He heard Reilly take a deep breath. Roddy continued. "Maybe we should meet up?"

"I'd like that, my father's really angry. He was at the airport when I arrived. I'd hoped I would get the chance to meet you before he got here. However, he beat me to it. I've never seen him so worked up." Roddy sensed Reilly was working hard to control his emotions. "Look, I can't talk for long. He's trying to get me a flight home. It looks like it won't happen today, flights are all full. I better go but will contact you when I know what's happening."

"Okay, pal."

"Please keep me updated, mate. I'm so worried about our Angie."

Our Angie. Roddy liked that. "Me too, but I am confident we will find her."

"You're the best brother she could ever have wished for." Reilly dropped his voice to a tiny whisper. "Need to go, Dad's coming."

The phone went dead. He felt Reilly's pain. Somehow it diluted his own - if even just a smidgeon.

"Okay." Kiltman tapped Roddy on the shoulder. "I'm going now." He had been waiting for him to finish the call. He ruffled Roddy's hair and turned to Wilson. She broke the rules by lifting his mask and kissing him on the lips. She had that instinctive sense an officer had when they walked into a crime scene. Whatever the outcome, things would never be the same afterwards. They all sensed the danger in this next stage of their quest. Darkness had started to fall. By the time he reached Tomba di Nerone, it would be completely dark.

He walked down two flights of stairs, before exiting onto the street; a glance left then right before beginning his walk towards the main road. There were no shortages of taxis. He raised his hand and a yellow cab pulled up to the pavement. Leaving Wilson and Roddy in the Pensione had been hard. Now standing on the streets of Rome, about to walk into a life-threatening situation, he felt a sense of isolation.

Unaware of the two sets of eyes observing him as he stepped into the taxi.

First Ballot

"The tension is palpable," Grant spoke into the camera. Behind him, the square's lighting created a dull yellow hue. Shadows began to settle on the façade of St. Peter's, the sun settling into its downward drift for the night. "The world awaits the results of the first ballot. Although it has to be said, nobody really expects a Pope to be elected in just a few hours."

Behind Grant's left shoulder and to the side of the basilica, a small chimney was the object of attention. While it was barely noticeable above the mishmash of rooves and windows, nobody underestimated the significance of the role it played in determining the Church's future.

"Look!" someone shouted from the crowd, pointing. Whispers of smoke oozed out into the night air. It was difficult to tell if it was black or white.

"MacTavish, what's going on? Keep talking!" Dominic shouted. "What's happening there?"

The camera zoomed in on the chimney. "As you can see, the first ballot has taken place, smoke is rising from the Sistine Chapel chimney. From here, it's hard to tell if it's white or black." The camera turned back to Grant who was squinting towards the smoke. On realising he was back on camera, his face switched back into its usual demure composure, against a backdrop of noisy expectation from the crowd. Until a call went out. "It's black!"

A deflated en masse sigh rose across the square. The pilgrims settled back down onto their mats and makeshift beds. It was going to be a long night.

"It's black," Grant said. "No surprise, really. That will be it until tomorrow at noon, when we will see the results of the next ballot. People near and far will need to wait patiently for the next Pope to be elected. Signing off from BBC World News, this is Grant MacTavish on his way to a plate of pasta and glass of well-deserved wine." He tugged the earpiece out before Dominic had the chance to react.

He had been watching the TV, attempting to gauge the public mood; at least as much as can be garnered from soundbites. He switched off the portable television smuggled into his room in the Vatican accommodation. He preferred BBC World News. MacTavish could be annoying, but he trusted the BBC to get it right.

A loud rap at the door startled him. "Cardinal Damascus?"

"Yes?" he answered.

"We are proceeding to dinner now if you are ready." The Swiss Guard outside his door was efficient if nothing else. Adorned with colours and a costume bordering on buffoonery, he wondered why the Vatican did not move to a less comical security staff.

"Yes, coming." He packed the TV under his bed and brushed down his cassock. He looked at his phone. He did not expect any messages. He was surprised to see a light flashing at him.

"*15577, 5, 151674*"

Sometimes he got confused with these numbers, whether to read single or double digit. Over time he had become more expert at decoding the messages. It read '*PLAN B NOW*'. This was concerning. Something had interrupted their strategy. Not good news, but not something he would let worry him. This is why contingencies were created, their planning had been impeccable.

Across the city, in a small Pensione, Roddy called Wilson over to the desk. "Maggie, quick! Quick! Come here and see this."

He pointed at the numbers on the screen. "This message has just been sent. I've translated it already. It says: '*plan B now*'."

"Interesting. Something must have spooked them. Any replies?" She placed her hand on his shoulder; in an attempt to quell his rising concern.

He shook his head and looked at Wilson. "Do you think Dad will be okay?" She sensed the same threat he did.

"Your father has got himself out of as many scrapes as he's got himself into." Words her mother used to say to her when she was a child; they seemed appropriate in downplaying Roddy's concerns. Concerns she felt rising in every sinew of her being.

Post First Ballot

He had not expected a decision on the first ballot. It was more a chance to gauge the competition. Ratzinger was at the top of the list, which was not a surprise. Times magazine had named the German Cardinal as one of the 100 most influential people in the world. For twenty plus years he had been Prefect of the Sacred Congregation for the Doctrine of the Faith, appointed by Pope John Paul II himself. His credentials were perfect for the role; if the Church was intent on a traditional leader, *Old School*. Word on the street was that he did not want the job. He had peaked in his current role, maybe the extra stretch would be too much for him.

Cardinal Damascus came towards the bottom of the top ten. At this stage, as he knelt on the kneeler in the Sistine Chapel, he could not have hoped for better. He knew his discussions with fellow Cardinals had pushed him up the ranks. He now needed to capitalise on this position; there was not much time. Cardinal Ratzinger was ahead by a strong margin, nearly five times the second placed Cardinal; the Argentinian, Bergoglio. Ratzinger was already halfway to the number of votes needed to secure victory. Each ballot was independent of previous ballots. However, once a Cardinal voted for one of the front runners, they would stick with him unless a strong reason came along to change their mind. There was no time to lose. At best, there were just a few ballots left before a Pope would be decided.

He stood up, blessed himself and walked beneath Michelangelo's Last Judgement, pausing every few steps to marvel at the artist's genius. An elderly Cardinal touched his elbow. He was not sure if it was a Scottish or Irish accent; the tone was the familiar Celtic overture of friendliness and compassion. "On the day of judgement, Cardinal Damascus, we will meet our maker. Just like the fresco tells us. Our decisions in these days will live with us forever."

He looked at the ruddy complexion and lined face of his counterpart. "Of course, do you not think I realise this?"

"Oh, I am sure you do. However, we should not forget that pride does come before the fall." The Celtic Cardinal had a beguiling mix of seriousness overlaid with a hint of humour.

He extracted his medal and presented it to the Celtic Cardinal. "All we can do here is pray that the decision we make is the right one. We also have a duty to the Church to keep it on track. Never forget St. Paul's words, written to the Galatians at 1:10: '*Am I now trying to win human approval, or God's approval? Or am I trying to please people? If I were still trying to please people, I would not be a servant of Christ.*' I am not here my friend to repeat the mistakes of the past. I genuinely believe we have a responsibility to face into change and welcome it. I suggest you bear this in mind when you make your vote."

They looked at each other for a moment longer than necessary. It was clear a gap existed in their outlook. He reached across and touched the Celtic Cardinal's arm. "You must vote with confidence and faith. Please vote in the knowledge of how the Church is connecting with Catholics in your dioceses. You have less churchgoers and many fewer vocations to the priesthood in these days. We can make excuses that there are too many distractions in the modern world; however, we must turn this on its head. We need to show that the Church should be the distraction, the inspirational craze that stops people in their tracks and interrupts their focus on the material world. Just like it was two thousand years ago." He searched the Celtic Cardinal's face for acknowledgement. He smiled when a subtle nod was returned.

"We are being asked to choose between the status quo or renewal. With the latter, the sky's the limit on what we can achieve. Or should I say, heaven's the limit."

The crinkly-eyed Celtic Cardinal sighed before turning to walk back to his colleagues. There were around thirty of them huddled together, waiting to be convinced one way or the other. Stick with Ratzinger's stay-the-course model or embrace Damascus' uncharted future: a chance to walk in St. Paul's shoes and execute the two millennia old letter sent to the Galatians. The Celtic Cardinal touched his own medal under his cassock as he walked back to his colleagues. He knew many of them wore the same item of jewellery, hidden under their robes. In their hearts they wanted to be brave enough to vote for Damascus, but did they have the courage to do so?

It was time to return to the rooms for quiet and peace; tomorrow's ballot was twelve hours away. Prayer and meditation in the comfort of his small room was so much more satisfying while holding his medal.

In Vino Veritas

"Let's go for some dinner." Wilson pulled her jacket from the back of the chair. "There's only so much screen-gazing I can do."

"Okay." Roddy stood slowly. He had spent hours searching the internet and airwaves trying to find a way to explain the pulsating beat of signals emanating from Mask's computer. Maybe a plate of pasta would inspire him.

The door crashed open with a crack of wood splintering down its frame. A tall man, wearing a cream fedora, open necked shirt and white Chinos stood in the doorway. He could have been posing for a photo-shoot were it not for the gun, and its sleek silencer, pointed at Wilson.

The man was the perfect Hogmanay first foot; tall, dark and handsome. If handsome included a darkness behind the eyes, nurtured by years of pain inflicted on others. Wilson snatched an iron lampshade from the table and launched it at him.

He caught it in his hand with ease. "Now, now, Signora Wilson. That's no way to respect other people's property." He waved the pistol at the chair. "Sit down."

Wilson sat and beckoned Roddy to do the same. He dropped back onto the seat he had just vacated. The man walked to the table and placed the lamp down gently.

"Who the hell are you?" Wilson felt a surge of anger and fear. Anger at this thug for breaking into their room; fear for Roddy, he was not supposed to be so close to this type of danger.

"Ah, *cara*. You are not the one to be asking questions. Let's just say that your interference has become problematic for some people. Your time is up." He pointed the weapon at her forehead. "When I am finished with you, I will do the same to this nosy boy."

"Huh!" Roddy said. "Missed me yesterday, so you have to get up close to make sure you don't miss this time. I'm not afraid of you."

"Listen, young man. I never miss. I will prove that to you now." He turned the gun towards Roddy and put pressure on the trigger. This was the bit he enjoyed the most. The split second between squeeze and thud made him feel at his most powerful.

A brick weighs just over a kilo. Thrown at a distance of a couple of metres renders it as a lethal weapon. This time, while it did not kill the victim, it rendered him unconscious. Salvatore slumped to the ground in a lifeless heap, the gun spilling from his hand onto the carpet. Wilson rushed to grab the pistol, but a foot landed on it instead. She looked up to see a hand extended towards her.

"Come on, Maggie. You can relax now."

She looked at the leg for a moment before turning her gaze to his face. She had already recognised the voice.

"Marco? What are you doing here?" Wilson rose to her feet her heartbeat beginning to slow.

"Maybe *thank you* would be a better first thing to do say." He smiled as he helped her up.

"Eh, yes, thank you. That was a close call."

"You're welcome. I would say you can do the same for me one day, but you already have."

There was something about him she could not place. Then she realised. He had become charming since she saw him a day earlier.

"Who is this handsome young man?" He smiled at Roddy.

"I'm Roddy, Maggie's friend." Wilson was nodding at him reassuringly; to accept Marco as an ally.

"Pleased to meet you." Marco gave a small wave of his hand. He sunk onto his knees and felt for a pulse in the assassin's neck. There was a beat. Although not for much longer, judging by the blood seeping from his cracked skull.

"He needs a hospital," Wilson said. "Who is he?"

"His name is Salvatore." Marco looked up. "One of Pirla Sconi's gang; his son in fact. Luca and Luigi were also his men. Salvatore came here to deliver *vendetta*. The price he wanted you to pay for saving me the other evening."

Wilson saw Roddy's quizzical expression. "I'll explain later."

"What are you both doing here anyway? It's not exactly the plushest place in Rome." He scanned the room's basic furniture; a bed, small desk, two chairs and a TV.

"Working a case," Wilson answered.

"A case?" Marco placed Salvatore's gun in his pocket. "What about the kilted man who left here a few minutes ago? Is he going to be back soon?"

"Kiltman will be back later. He had to run an errand."

"Ah, Kiltman, yes the Scottish superhero." Marco laughed in a manner bordering on derisory. Roddy knew not to react, although felt a rising anger. Nobody disrespected his father. Well, except his son, he thought guiltily.

Marco dialled a number on his phone and said, "*Avanti!*" A minute later two men entered. Marco pointed at the body. "*Ospedale, sbrigati!*" They lifted Salvatore and carried him out the door, not caring if he bumped into the doorframe on the way out. Which he did.

Marco looked at Wilson. "They are taking him to hospital. Pirla Sconi will know that I exercised mercy and did not kill his eldest child. It should be the end of the vendetta against you and me."

She nodded. "Thank you, I guess."

"Where were you going?" He pointed at their jackets.

"Dinner." she answered, sensing what was coming next.

"*Perfetto!*" Marco broke into a broad smile. "I know a lovely place I used to go to years ago." It was less invite, more instruction.

Wilson decided not to argue. She had experienced enough confrontation with Sicilian Mafia members in the last few days. Plus, it could be a way to glean some more information; *in vino veritas*.

Tomba di Nerone

The villa sat back from the main road, surrounded by a high brick wall. He could see its roof over the top of the gate. An alley down the south wall allowed him to creep through the overgrown bushes to the back. The surrounding wall's cracks and fissures indicated it was close to collapsing. On the plus side, it meant there were enough spaces for Kiltman to place his feet in the gaps. After a slow climb, he crouched on top, listening for signs of activity below. There was barely a noise save for a light breeze in the trees and the scurrying of roaming rodents.

He dropped down the other side and inched towards the back door. The lights were off throughout the house, no sign of life. He placed his hand against the wall. He could feel warmth. A couple of hours earlier the building had been heated from the inside.

On the ground floor, a window was open wide enough for a hand to reach in. Underneath, an upturned crate rested against the wall. The perfect height to allow him to climb in. He moved towards it and stopped, studying the box. He folded his arms and rubbed his chin, running through the facts in his head.

A few hours ago, people had been inside. All the lights were now turned off. A window had been accidentally left open. Oh, and a crate of just the right height happened to be placed underneath.

The words of his high school Maths teacher came back to him. It was during a gruelling double lesson, when he could not solve a quadratic equation. "You may be Scottish, Kenny, but you are not stupid." While he never quite understood it at the time, he knew it was a put down. The teacher may have used the same words now.

He bent down to inspect the crate. He could see a stream of coloured wires nestled underneath, extending along under the foliage. He followed them to a flowerpot a metre down the path. The wires reached up from the earth into the bottom of the pot. Kiltman scraped away some of the dirt with the edge of his hand.

To find a home-made explosive device. Simple in its construction, it was enough to bring down the side of the house on top of whoever stood on the crate.

He stepped away towards the back door. He picked up a lumpy chunk of rock. With all the subtlety of a clumsy burglar, he threw it at the door, shattering the glass. The noise echoed in the night air as thousands of pieces of coloured glass landed on the concrete steps.

His nerves were on heightened alert as he reached in and unlocked the door. It opened into the kitchen, full of smells he recognised - cheesy pizza, pasta and coffee. He placed his hand on the kettle. It had been used two and a half hours earlier, give or take a couple of minutes.

The corridor ran from the kitchen to a staircase dropping down into the basement. He stepped softly down into a large room underneath the kitchen. There were no markings on the wall, a dank smell hovering in the air. His interest was piqued. Not by what was in the room; but by what was not in the room. He walked to the centre underneath a dangling light bulb that reminded him of Callan when he used to watch black and white TV as a child. The warmth underfoot was unmistakeable. Bending down, he placed his hand on the floor. Something had been on that spot earlier generating heat and energy. Considering how much heat was escaping the floor as he stood there, he deduced it had been a large, heavy, metallic object. The source of the signals Roddy had been struggling to identify. A mainframe. He looked along the floor to the door to the stairs. He could see wheel marks of a trolley used to carry it to a ramp attached to the steps.

He wandered through the room sniffing akin to the haphazard urgency of a dog on a morning walk. He followed his nose to a door at the far end of the room. It opened to another set of steps. In Italian a one floor down basement is known as *menouno* (one less). He was now descending to *menodue*.

The scent hit him hard at the top of his nostrils, enough to make him retch. He stood for a moment trying to break down the smells that had been trapped in there. Body odour, sweat and salty tears. Whoever had been in the cramped room had been upset. The strongest smells were faeces and urine. Someone had been living here. Been kept here. He dropped down onto one knee, praying it had not been Angie, gorgeous wee Angie. He inhaled deeply, focusing on the smells. No, they were much too intense for a young girl. They belonged to a man; middle-aged, maybe older.

There was nothing in the room to indicate where Mask and Angie had gone. The emptiness and sensation of despair was powerful. He walked back up to the ground floor. He shifted his nostril's olfactory cilia to overload remembering Angie's scent, searching for her aroma around the house. There was no doubt she had been there. He found a bedroom on the floor above. Three cot beds lay alongside the walls with a table in the middle. Either the three people who slept there were very close; or there was a distinct lack of trust.

He caught Mask's scent from the bed nearest the door. It was hard to believe it was just a week earlier when he had tried to shoot him in the helicopter. The furthest bed held a smell he did not recognise; he knew he had never met this person before. Definitely male, maybe a bit older than Mask. The middle bed had been Angie's. Kiltman touched the pillow. He had not spent as much time with her as Fiona and Roddy; but had got to know her well enough to appreciate her resourcefulness. What would a girl like Angie do in a situation like this?

He pulled back the sheets and lifted the pillows. Nothing. He dropped down onto his back and levered himself under the bed. The springs were just above the floor, just enough room to squeeze under. If it had been before the Brazil adventure, he would have struggled with this search. A few days of not eating and sweating had given him a waistline he would have been proud of in any other scenario.

There it was; a sheet of paper between the frame and the mattress. He pulled it away and edged out from under the bed. He sat down on the mattress and read.

Dear whoever finds this,

I have been here with my father, known as Mask and his crazy partner, Tantalus.

They are planning something horrible. I don't know what it is. But it is connected to the Papal Conclave.

Please stop them and come and find me. I think we are going to Piazza di Spagna... wherever that is.

Help!!!!!!

Angie

Kiltman knew *Piazza di Spagna* and its famous Spanish Steps. Rome's most romantic staircase, the source of love, desire and hope, was now the go to place for a crazed megalomaniac.

Foglio di Scrisio

"This is a lovely restaurant." Wilson looked around her. She had never dined in quite so traditional an Italian restaurant. Rough, stony walls were painted in a yellowy-orange hue, partially covered with colourful paintings. The architect had worked hard to convey the image of a restaurant inside a cave. Anywhere else it would have seemed old-fashioned. In a city more than two thousand years old, with history etched into every corner and building, it was the perfect place to dine.

Roddy was less sure but had learned to be polite. "It really is, em, quite unique."

Marco laughed as he dropped a napkin onto his lap. "Typical Scots. You guys never want to be judgemental. You are famous for finding the good in everything and everyone."

"Marco, that's such a nice thing to say about the Scots. Have you met many of us?"

"Enough. I can honestly say I've never met a Scottish person I didn't like. Even your weird friend, Tommy, is a good guy."

"You met Tommy?" Roddy asked. He loved Tommy. He could not have asked for a better 'uncle'. Whether he was looking after his pub in Glasgow or managing the bars in Estonia, he always remembered Roddy's birthday. They had run out of space on the fridge door. His father had commented on checking the hinge to make sure the magnets were not too heavy. At the end of the day, it was the thought that counted.

Marco turned to look at Roddy. "Yes, he, Maggie and their friend, Gina, saved my life. This evening, I want to take a moment to celebrate. Have whatever you want. Dinner is on me." Marco waved at the waiter. "Good evening. May I see the wine list?"

The waiter, dressed in traditional white jacket and shirt, bow tie and black trousers, said. "Sir, are you by any chance from Sicily?"

"Yes, I am. Why?" Marco raised an eyebrow in Wilson's direction.

"Ah, well, you don't need to order wine. Your father called us already and purchased a bottle of wine for you. It's a classic Chianti, one of our best."

"That's very nice of him," Marco said slowly. He swivelled his head to survey the other customers. His father did not know which restaurant he was going to. "What did he say exactly?"

"He said that his son was working on an important job in Rome; and would be at the restaurant in the evening. He left his credit card details for us to charge the dinner. I hope that is okay." The waiter had started to fiddle with his tie, this was becoming awkward.

"Did he give a name?" Marco asked.

"Yes, he said to look after his son, Salvatore."

Marco concentrated on not smirking. "Yes, please bring the Chianti."

The waiter shuffled back to the kitchen. Monday evenings were supposed to be the quiet shift.

Wilson leaned forward. "Surely not the same Salvatore?"

Marco nodded. "This restaurant was where my father and Pirla Sconi used to meet whenever they came to Rome on, eh, how can I say, business. Sadly, over recent years, there has been animosity, however they did have some good times together in the past." He sighed. "Maybe one day it will be good again. I'm tired of all this fighting."

"So, what did you do to the Sconis for them to send a couple of hitmen after you?" Wilson did not want to show her disgust at enjoying generosity from the man who had sent his son to kill her; albeit rediverted generosity. She had to keep Marco talking; there was more information there waiting to be divulged.

"Ah, their vendetta goes back many years. Recently it has become worse. The latest wave is partially my fault. Or at least the fault of this." He pointed at his chest.

"Sorry?" She bent her head to the side.

"My heart," he explained. "I fell in love with Marina Sconi, Salvatore's younger sister." He shrugged and smiled. "Sicily is a small island."

"The Sconis tried to kill you because you dated a family member?" Roddy was finding Marco intriguing.

"No. It was how I stopped dating her that upset them. Let's just say that I met another woman who truly stole my heart."

"What? You cheated on her?" Wilson's expression hardened.

"Hey," he smiled coyly. "What can I say? I'm a warm-blooded Italian!"

She turned to Roddy. "Don't you ever do that; do you hear me?"

He caught the twinkle in her eye. "Don't worry, I don't want the Mafia chasing me."

"Shhh!" Marco held his finger to his lips. "We don't say that word."

"What, 'chasing'?" Roddy answered.

"No, the other…" Marco clicked his fingers and grinned. "Funny! You nearly got me there."

The waiter arrived with the wine and poured generous portions for Wilson and Marco. Roddy was pleased to have another cold San Pellegrino Bitter Orange. After they clinked glasses and thanked one another for saving each other's lives, they got down to ordering an array of courses and side dishes. It was going to be a long evening. Sconi was paying after all.

Open Exchange

Wilson had waited until they were on their second bottle of wine. She had hoped one bottle, with her sipping slowly, would have loosened Marco's tongue. She had not considered Marco had grown up in a family of oenophiles; she therefore encouraged him to order another. He chose an even more expensive Chianti, which the waiter had just brought to the table.

"What if I was to tell you we know what happened to the Banco d'Aiuto funds?" Wilson said after Marco had swirled the red wine around his glass and started to drink.

"Oh, really?" he asked before stifling a cough, a flash of annoyance crossing his features. "You wait until now to tell me?"

"I wasn't sure. Now, having spent some more time in your company, I think I can trust you."

Marco leaned forward, his demeanour softening. "You can do more than trust me, Maggie."

Roddy spoke up for the first time in a while. He had been enjoying the banter. "Excuse me, guys, I hate to interrupt but are we going to order dessert?"

"Don't worry, soon." Marco placed the back of his hand at his mouth and whispered. "I'm still wooing her. She will crack eventually."

Roddy wondered if Marco knew that she was his father's paramour. Then realised that was an irrelevance. Marco appeared to be the person who got what he wanted.

"Relax, pal. I have this," Wilson said, her eyes fixed on Marco. "Okay. Let's get back to my point. We found that Banco d'Aiuto was indeed transferring your funds to Banco Discepolo for the charitable causes your families wanted. This definitely happened. However, they were deducting a small amount from each transfer and sending it to a Cayman bank. They were fiddling with the exchange rates to make it happen. That's why it took a long time for you to notice."

Marco nodded. This information would make him popular at home. "What about Sacco?"

"We think he knew it was going on. Although I don't believe he was the brains behind it."

"So, who was it then?" Marco asked.

"That, I'm afraid, I can't divulge. At least, not for now."

"The day we know who stole from us, that will be their last day." Marco's eyes glinted with too much wine and the thought of *vendetta*.

Wilson took a robust drink from her glass. She had abstained for long enough. She would kick herself if she did not at least enjoy this smooth, rich Chianti.

"Okay, I'll make a deal with you. As soon as I have clearance, you will be the first person I tell."

"A deal means you must want something from me." He blew her a kiss with his hand.

"Well, yes. I do want something." Wilson would have laughed in another scenario. "At lunch the other day, your Nonna made some interesting comments, but I think she had more to say."

"Ah, my grandmother! She is a lovely lady but a couple of limoncellos and she becomes quite chatty." Marco fiddled with his glass. "Look, I can tell you what I think she was going to say. It's not that interesting, just not something we normally tell people outside the family."

Wilson shrugged. "I'm curious, that's all."

Marco dabbed at his mouth with the napkin before placing it carefully back on his lap. "As she said, Nonna delivered Cardinal Damascus into the world at the end of the war. However, this was not the whole story. Something else happened that night in the house outside Naples."

"Oh, really? What?"

"Well, just after she gave Damascus to the American soldier, the…"

Wilson's phone pinged. She looked at the number. Kiltman was calling. "I'm sorry, I need to take this."

She did not wait for a response. She stood and walked towards the restaurant door. "Kiltman, are you okay?"

He smiled at how she always defaulted to his superhero cover when they were on a case. "Hi, Detective Inspector Wilson!"

"Very funny. What's going on?"

"They've gone. Angie left a note of where they went to. Can you meet me there?"

"Yes, where?"

"*Piazza di Spagna.* It's about twenty minutes from the Pensione."

"Okay, but we're not at the Pensione." She looked through the window to see Marco teaching Roddy how to break a breadstick into three pieces.

"Oh?" He did not need to remind her that the plan was for them to stay put.

"I'll tell you when I see you. It's a long story." Involving Mafia hits, Mafia dinners and Mafia storytelling. "We'll meet you at the *Piazza di Spagna* in half an hour. I just need to do something quickly." Marco saw her at the window and waved.

"I hope it's not going to take long."

"No, but it might make me slightly unpopular."

Rom-ing Scots

Kiltman walked out onto the *Via Cassia*. He looked right and left, hoping to see a cab emerge out of the darkness. Every so often a car would speed past, but no taxis. On similar occasions in the past, he had been known to step out into the path of oncoming vehicles. In cities when they were driving at a reasonable speed, this was dangerous but manageable. On a speedy thoroughfare like this, that strategy would be lethal.

The rattle of the coach driving north along the Cassia caught his attention first. Soon this was drowned out by a strange sound emanating from inside the vehicle. It was approaching at pace, the noise getting louder. He could hear a song. Or at least a raucous version of a song. Bob Marley's *Buffalo Soldier* wafted through the night air. The single decker bus passed him, gears changing as it slowed, indicating left. Through the windows he could see a group of young men dressed in purple cassocks wearing priest collars. They were oblivious to him waving at the side of the road, as they belted out: *I'm just a Buffalo Soldier, in the heart of America.*

The bus decelerated fifty metres down the road, indicating to turn through an open gate. This was his chance. He ran along the street and managed to enter behind the coach, just before the iron gate closed. Then he realised.

Several years earlier he had been here as Kiltman when Cullen Skink led him and Maggie on a merry dance around Europe - The Scots College, where young Scottish men came to 'test their vocation' for the priesthood. He should have realised when he saw the address for the villa next door.

The bus doors opened, and the seminarians spilled out onto the small square in front of the college building. One of the students, small in stature with a cheeky grin, pointed at him. "Hey, is that Kiltman?" The others stopped and turned to look at where he was pointing. Whatever they had intended to do that evening, whether vespers or the college bar for a nightcap, would take second place now.

He walked towards them, his hands in the air. "Hi guys! Small world!" In the middle of Rome, he could have got away with this comment; standing in the middle of private property on the outskirts of the city rendered it awkward.

The seminarian who had noticed him stepped forward. "Hey, I'm Melvil. You can call me *Wee Man*. We crossed paths briefly when you were here a few years ago meeting Fr. Shuggy Quinn, or should I say ex-Father Shuggy."

Shuggy Quinn, his university friend, had played an influential role in the seminary, someone they all respected and wanted to spend time with. His choice to follow his heart and marry Lulu increased the esteem with which he was held rather than diminished it. When he returned to Scotland, Kiltman knew he should prioritise Shuggy and help him settle down in the secular world.

The other students remained intrigued waiting to hear why Scotland's superhero was standing on college grounds.

He shook hands with Melvil. "Hi, wee man. To be honest, just like the last time, I need your help. I was hoping someone could give me a lift into Rome."

Melvil, who could not have been much more than twenty years old, explained he had only ever driven tractors at the family farm in Ireland. Prompting comments from the other seminarians as to whether his feet could have reached the pedals. Melvil's humility was more than enough to absorb the quips, somehow enjoying the interaction. Kiltman smiled realising that even in a seminary, Celtic banter prevailed.

One of the others stepped forward. Kiltman liked him immediately. Sporting a gracious, welcoming smile, he exuded a kind demeanour that made Kiltman trust him. "Hey, Kiltman, it's a pleasure to meet you. I'm Peter. I can drive you into the city if you want. I'm one of the lucky ones with a licence."

"That would be great, I'd really appreciate it," Kiltman responded. Before he could extend his hand for a handshake, Peter leaned forward and wrapped his arms around him. It was as if he sensed this superhero needed a hug. As they held each other, Kiltman felt the warmth and humanity of the man seep into his skin, down to his soul. While he had met many people over

the years, he had never met someone with the natural charisma
this man exuded.

"Okay, then," Peter said as he stepped back from the embrace.

"Cool!" Melvil added. "I'll go with you. You might need
some muscle when you get to whatever venture you are on."
Kiltman was pleased the mask disguised his smile.

"Okay, guys. Let's go." Peter called across from the entrance
waving a set of keys at them. He opened the car door and
whispered, "There's one condition."

"Oh?" Kiltman knew a punchline was coming. He saw Melvil
and Peter look at each other and nod.

Bob Marley Remembered

Kiltman should have realised the condition underpinning the lift into Rome was that he had to sing as many verses of Bob Marley songs as he could remember.

He could sense that Peter regretted stipulating the requirement once he had heard Kiltman's tuneless rendition. While Kiltman found it therapeutic, his fellow travellers struggled with the harsh off-key notes belted out in a confined space.

"That was great," Peter said as he navigated the Fiat across *Piazza del Popolo*. Kiltman had a few lines left of the song but got the message that enough was enough. "So, what have you been doing since you arrived in Rome?"

"Not much…" Kiltman said. "Took a nun to hospital with a suspected aneurism, ate lots of pastries, stopped a wee boy from being shot, and fell into the Trevi Fountain." He nearly added '*attacked a priest*' but fought the urge to confess this incident to a couple of seminarians.

Melvil, in the back seat, said. "Hey, Peter! We can say we've done the same thing as Kiltman."

Peter laughed remembering when a Martedi Grasso/Shrove Tuesday celebration resulted in a few of them taking a dip in the Trevi and Spanish Steps fountains.

Between Peter's infectious giggle and Melvil's cheeky, sometimes funny, comments, Kiltman wished he could have hung out with these guys for longer than a car ride. He reached across with his fist into the middle of the car. All four of them fist-bumped at the same time. "Respect!" Kiltman said.

"This has been a weird weekend in Rome," Melvil laughed. "One of our friends was jumped the other day in the Greg."

"Seriously, wee man?" Peter asked. "Who was it?"

"David Montrose. Apparently, some Scottish guy just threw himself on top of him and pinned him to the ground. Happened in the Greg library." Melvil could not stop himself from laughing. "So much for all the martial arts belts he has accumulated over the years."

Kiltman felt himself slip down the passenger seat, trying not to groan aloud.

"That's odd," Peter said. "David is always looking for a chance to show his moves. I've seen him in action, he knows how to defend himself. There must have been a reason why he chose not to put the guy in his place."

"I know, that's what I thought," Melvil acknowledged.

Before Kiltman could formulate a question, the car screeched to a halt at the end of a dark, cobbled street. "Here we are. Top of the Spanish Steps, just over there." He pointed into the darkness of the evening towards an imposing obelisk.

"Thanks, guys, I really appreciate it." Kiltman exited the car and leaned inside through the passenger seat window. He saw Peter's hand in the air. "Kiltman, you have to do something before we let you go. I think you can guess."

The surreal car journey had prepared him for what was required to trigger his release. He stepped back from the car, coughed and inhaled a deep breath, reaching down into his diaphragm to find as much air as possible.

"Don't worry, about a thing,

'Cause every little thing, gonna be all right."

As he sang Marley's famous lyrics, he watched Peter and Melvil disappear into the distance, realising he had just spent precious moments with some of the finest people he would ever meet.

Piazza di Spagna

Kiltman bowed to a group of teenage kids sitting on a wall at the top of the steps; he was a tad embarrassed although pleased he had held the tune this time. They clapped and cheered, less a recognition of the quality of singing more because they had never seen a kilted vocalist.

He turned to look over the top of the steps towards the square stretching out below. *Piazza di Spagna* sat in relief against a horizon of rooftops, domes and churches stretching as far as the eye could see. The dome of St. Peter's Basilica glowed in the distance, reminding everyone that Michelangelo had left his imprint on the city like no-one before or since.

He closed his eyes and focused. He had taken position at the top of *Piazza di Spagna*'s famous Spanish Steps. Built just over a century after the Vatican Basilica dome, the 135 steps had witnessed millions of tourists, movie scenes, the cementing of lifelong love affairs and, as he had just learned from his fellow Scots, Martedi Grasso buffoonery. This was a Monday evening, same as the start of the week the world over, most folks at home recharging for the week ahead. He enjoyed the quiet murmur of conversations rising from a sprinkling of couples sitting around the steps, whiling away the evening.

It was proving hard to focus on the task at hand. It had been a long week. There were now so many things to consider; a number of loose ends that did not make sense. No matter how much Hair o' the Dog he imbibed, his logic and problem-solving struggled to keep up with the pace of the case.

He closed his eyes. He had to focus, searching for anything unusual or extraordinary. Before long he felt it. A low buzz; imperceptible to normal hearing. Even dogs would struggle to pick it up. It was there, somewhere close.

"Hey, Dad!" He turned to find Roddy and Wilson walking up the steps towards him.

"Hi, pal! Good to see you; and the gorgeous Maggie." He hugged Roddy and latex-kissed Wilson. She rubbed her cheek;

she was beginning to get a rash. "So, what happened after I left you? Did you decide to go out on the town?"

She looked at Roddy; they had agreed to downplay the incident. She leant on the wall facing out towards centro storico and St. Peter's Basilica in the distance, working hard to appear nonchalant. "You know the Sacco case I'm working?" He nodded slowly. "Well, a representative, let's call him that, from one of the families, decided to visit the Pensione. He was about to send us a message…"

"Message?" Kiltman could smell a cover up.

"Eh, well, let's just say he had a gun."

"A gun?"

"Yes, that's right. Nothing wrong with your super-hearing today."

He put his hand on her shoulder and turned her around to face him. "Maggie, you might not be able to notice because of the mask, but I am starting to get annoyed."

"Yes, he tried to do something nasty. Although you'll never guess what happened next." She paused until Kiltman shook his head in exasperation. Then continued. "A member of another Sicilian family saved the day. Surreal, eh?"

Roddy looked at Wilson, wondering why he had let her take the lead.

"Dad, second guy was great. Just knocked out the first guy with a brick and it was all over. Best part, though; he took us out for dinner. I think he fancies Maggie."

"Really?" Kiltman looked at her. She flicked her hair. She decided not to mention the long, lingering hug Marco gave her when he realised they were leaving dinner earlier than expected. It had started to become uncomfortable until Roddy coughed the word, *Ahem*, which sounded much more like the word than an actual cough.

"I've still got it, you know."

"Yes, obviously." Kiltman did not know where to start on his response. "Did this *'first guy'* try and shoot Roddy yesterday at the Trevi?"

"Well, that's the thing. I don't think so. He said he never misses." Roddy shrugged.

"Anyway, how did you get here so quickly?" she asked.

"I met some guys from the Scots College. Remember our visit a few years ago? Well, they gave me a lift."

Wilson smiled, recalling their brief visit there to gain some insights on clues Cullen Skink had left regarding Rome. It had felt quite surreal to see all these young men together in an isolated seminary, dedicating their lives to God.

Kiltman looked at her. "You know, I had to sing Bob Marley songs to get a lift." He did not miss Roddy and Wilson scrunching their faces up in fake anguish but chose to ignore them. "Okay, we can talk this all through whenever we get to the end of the case. Listen, standing here just now, I can feel something. Not sure yet what it is or where it's coming from, but there's an unusual vibe in the air."

"Roddy?" They all turned at the shout to see Reilly running towards them.

"Reilly! Great to see you." The boys fell into an impromptu embrace; with all the clumsiness expected of two teenagers who were learning how to man-hug. "What are you doing here?" Before Reilly could answer, they saw Coach Stone and Reilly's father a few metres behind, exiting the Trinità dei Monti church, at the top of the steps.

"Hello, Coach Stone and Mr. MacDonald." Roddy said.

Kiltman looked at Wilson. One thing they did not need at that moment was a Scottish reunion. A few moments were spent exchanging pleasantries before a degree of discomfiture settled around them. Reilly's father spoke first. "So, what's Kiltman doing in Rome? And the famous DI Wilson?"

"Looking for Angie," Roddy answered for them. "We haven't come up with anything yet, still looking."

"I thought your dad was here." Mr MacDonald looked around the clearing at the top of the steps.

Roddy kept a straight face. "Eh, no. He had to go back. Maggie's on teen-sitting duty. Better than Dad, to be honest. She's not as strict." He smiled at Wilson.

"Yes, I heard your dad can be a bit grumpy," Coach Stone added. "When we get back, I'll give you details of a course he can go on. It's called *Take a Chill Pill*."

Wilson coughed into her handkerchief. "Allergies," she explained, a tear escaping the corner of her eye.

"Okay, so what are you doing here?" Kiltman had to move this on.

"Well, my son decided to fly solo to Rome from the USA to help find Angie." He scowled at Reilly. His son did not react, just another admonishment.

"What about you?" Kiltman looked at Coach Stone.

"I've had a revelation." Coach blessed himself. "I met Cardinal Damascus in the USA. I felt it. I felt his power. I'm here to pray and support him becoming the next Pope. It was Roddy who gave me the idea when he decided to come here." He opened his shirt button and produced a medal. "The **G** stands for…"

"Thanks, Coach. Yes, we know about the medal and Cardinal Damascus. He has followers everywhere. Who knows; maybe he will become Pope." Roddy sensed his father's patience was fraying.

"Good for you, Coach." Wilson said. "Follow your heart. Not the worst thing to do. Look, I need to go. I was going to discuss some things with Kiltman. Can we all catch up tomorrow at some point?"

"Sure," Coach answered. His disappointment at not being able to talk more about Damascus and the Galatians seemed to furrow his brow. "Come on, guys."

Reilly and Roddy had walked off towards the edge of the steps, pointing and chatting.

"Reilly, let's go." MacDonald called.

The boys fist bumped. Reilly jogged back to the group before he and his father followed Coach Stone zigzagging down the steep steps.

"Grumpy?" Kiltman looked at Roddy. "I'll show you grumpy."

"That was before this adventure." He tried to smile his way out of his father's mask stare. "Things are different now."

Wilson hooked her arm in Kiltman's. "It's all part of your charm, honey." She winked at Roddy.

"Okay, this is another discussion for when we're back home." He unfolded his arms, shook his hands and cracked his neck. "I've figured out what we're looking for. Or to be more exact, where we should be looking."

"Where?" Wilson and Roddy asked simultaneously.

He pointed at his feet. "Right underneath us."

Spanish Steps

"It can't be!"

"Unless someone else is using his costume. He was with DI Wilson and the Morgan boy. Thing is, he looks like Frankenstein's monster. His kilt and cape are ripped and torn, and his legs and arms are covered in cuts. He looks like he…"

"Fell out of a helicopter."

"Sorry?"

"Doesn't matter." Mask hung up. He paused to study the dirt underneath his fingernails, struggling to control his temper. Kiltman's appearance in Rome was an impossibility. Whatever powers he possessed had surpassed Mask's expectations and meticulous planning.

Not only had he survived the Amazon, he had been able to identify their location in Tomba di Nerone. Somehow, he had been able to follow the pizza paper trail. But knowing about the Spanish Steps did not make sense?

He turned to Angie. "Got something you want to tell me?"

"Not really." She continued to read her book, an ironic purchase her father had made in the airport on the way out to Rome – Dostoevsky's Crime and Punishment. He slapped the book out of her hand. It flew across the room to hit the wall above *Damascocles*.

"Don't you dare try insolence with me!" She looked up to see the face she dreaded. When anger morphed into psychopathic rage.

"I don't know what you mean?" She turned for him to see she was giving him her full attention.

"Did you manage to leave any clues anywhere as to where we were going?"

"No, of course not." It was hard work maintaining eye contact.

"Give me your notebook."

"What?"

"Your notebook. The one you scribble all your teenage thoughts into when you think nobody cares." He extended his hand. "Or I will empty your bag on the floor and take it."

She took the hardbacked book from her bag and handed it to him. He flicked through the pages with his thumb, stopping halfway through. He rubbed his finger against the rough edges of the remains of a page. "What happened to this page?"

"I can't remember. I think I drew a picture I didn't like so I threw it in the bin at Tomba."

"No, you didn't. I checked the bins to make sure we didn't leave anything that could identify us." He studied the next page for a moment. It was blank. He picked up a pencil using its edge to shade the page in a light grey charcoal colour. The imprint of the writing was difficult to read but not impossible. He read aloud.

"Dear whoever finds this, I have been here with my father, known as Mask and his crazy partner, Tantalus. They are planning something horrible. I don't know what it is. But it is connected to the Papal Conclave. Please stop them and come and find me. I think we are going to Piazza di Spagna. Wherever that is. Help. Angie"

She began to mouth a response, although unsure what to say. He tossed the notebook to join Crime and Punishment on the floor.

"Father, look, I'm…"

He raised his hand in the air. "Don't apologise. Nothing you can say will make up for this." He paced the room for a few moments, before he clapped his hands together and pointed at her. "However, actions can speak louder than words."

He lifted his satchel from the table and placed his hand inside. He extracted a burner phone and threw it across the room. She caught it with one hand.

"Sometimes opportunities arise out of the strangest places. You are going to send a text. I will dictate."

Closing In

"What are they doing?"

"They seem to be discussing something. The kilted man is pointing at his feet. Wilson and Roddy are with him. No sign of the father."

"Okay, don't do anything for the time being. We need to see what's going on. The kilted man is Kiltman, a quirky Scottish crime-solver. He works with Wilson - it's not surprising he's there. If you see anything unusual, let me know."

More unusual than a man in a shredded skirt, she wondered?

"Okay, will do."

"Anything else?"

"They were talking to a group of people at the top of the steps a few minutes ago. Seem to be some sort of acquaintances. They've gone now."

"Don't worry. I already have eyes on them."

"Excuse me?"

"You are not the only one. I do have other resources in play here. Just you do what I am asking of you."

She felt as though she had been scolded, despite not having done anything wrong. The silence continued – she had learned never to hang up first.

"What about Crawford? What's the latest?"

"No change. I think they will decide to turn the machine off soon, if he doesn't show signs of recovery."

"Did your voice just tremble there?"

"No," she said in a weaker voice than she had started the conversation.

"I hope you're not invested personally here. That would not be a smart thing to do."

"Don't worry about me. I'm fine."

"Okay. Bye."

Valentina's jacket sleeve was becoming white with the wiping of salty tears.

Trinità dei Monti

Kiltman walked down the steps, flanked on either side by Roddy and Wilson. They knew not to interrupt. He was following a high-pitched frequency signal emanating from somewhere below the steps. Halfway down he could see *Piazza di Spagna* spread out in front. At the bottom of the steps, the Fontana della Barcaccia - *Old Boat Fountain* - hosted a handful of tourists, sitting on its walls, running their hands through the calm water. He smiled, thinking of his new Scottish friends running a lap of the boat.

On his left as he looked at the calming fountain, he could see the prestigious *Keats-Shelley House,* where famous English poets had lived close to two hundred years earlier, John Keats and Percy Shelley among them. The four-storey building, nestled against the side of the Steps, rich with its literary history, added another layer of appeal to an already enchanting Roman district.

He recalled reading Shelley's *Masque of Anarchy* as a youth, recognising why, years after its writing, Ghandi had used its powerful message of passive resistance to campaign for a free India. The poem was again quoted by the Tiananmen Square students in 1989 when they faced the tanks of oppression and control. The irony of Shelley's house being in the vicinity of another *Mask of Anarchy* was not lost on Kiltman.

"Dad!"

Kiltman swivelled to see Roddy holding his phone up. "Look!" He showed a message. Wilson came over and took it from him. She read aloud. *"We are in the Trinità dei Monti church. Come quickly! Angie"*

"That's the one…" Roddy turned to point towards the top of the steps. Kiltman had already begun a fast jog in the direction he was pointing, with Wilson running alongside. It took a couple of minutes - and a few supportive smiles from tourists - for them to be standing in a cluster outside the front of the church, panting with the exertion. Kiltman had his hands on his knees trying to regain his breath. He looked up to find Wilson and Roddy pushing against the church door.

It was locked. They walked around the side to find another entrance. Wilson placed her hand against the handle; it moved with a creak born of centuries of use. The door slid open.

They walked through together, careful to avoid adding more clamour to announce their entrance. The church was bathed in candlelight, spilling shadows across the pillars and paintings on walls and ceilings. While it was too dark to see the architecture in detail, there was sufficient light for them to recognise the outstanding splendour of the building. Roddy wondered why Mask chose such exquisitely beautiful places to deliver his evil plans.

Kiltman could detect a scratching from behind the altar. He placed his finger against his mouth and gestured for them to follow him. Wilson indicated she would edge around the other side of the altar while Roddy and Kiltman took the direct route. Roddy's eyes were adjusting to the darkness, allowing him to detect shapes in the shadows. Kiltman was able to see every minute piece of detail in front of them. Yet it was Roddy that saw her first. Behind a bench, tied up with rope and tape over her mouth, Angie was struggling to break free.

He nudged his father and pointed. Kiltman nodded for his son to go to her, while he surveyed the rest of the altar area. He did not see anything untoward. Wilson was still out of sight. Strange, he thought. He walked towards where he thought she should appear. He barely had time to feel the whoosh of air, before the microphone stem connected with his forehead in a crunching smack. As he fell to the ground, unconsciousness taking over, he saw a dark shape – a man silhouetted by an Easter candle - holding a rag over Roddy's mouth.

Tuesday, April 19

Mountain Trinity Trap

Wilson was first to come to. It took her a moment to register what had happened. The last thing she remembered was the rag placed on her mouth. She could still taste the chloroform. It was impossible to know how long she had been unconscious. Her eyes were adjusting to the dark; she could see other bodies lying on the floor some metres away. Her attempt to shout came out as a muffle. Her lips were shut tight with industrial tape wrapped around her mouth, encircling the back of her head; stuck fast to her hair.

One of the other bodies moved. It was Kiltman; his cape fluttered in the draught coming from under a door. Beside him, a much smaller body lay still: Roddy. She pulled with all her strength at the plastic binds tight around her wrists, behind her back. They cut into her skin with each effort she made to break them. She felt blood trickle along her fingers onto the ground.

Kiltman started to make grunting noise. His eyes and mouth were covered in tape. It was the first time she had seen him with his mask off while wearing his costume in public. Mask would now know his identity. Although at that moment, she was not going to waste time on superhero egoistic identity nonsense.

Her hands were tied to another plastic bind around her ankles. There was no chance of climbing up onto her feet. She threw herself into a tumble. At first, she managed a half roll, but then with increasing backwards and forwards jerks she turned 360 degrees. It took a couple of minutes until she landed alongside Kiltman. His muffled sounds acknowledged he knew she was there. Her mind was racing, trying to assess how to snap the binds.

She need not have bothered. The light went on, splashing a white brightness that made her recoil.

"Aw, this is so cute!" She recognised Mask's voice. He had been sitting in the dark on a broken church bench. "You waken up and the first thing you do is roll over to Kiltman. Or should I say Kenny Morgan." He laughed, a real belly laugh, that seemed to last forever. "Why I never guessed this, I don't know. It was staring me in the face. Wilson's paramour is also Kiltman. Unbelievable!" He kicked a plastic bottle of water across the floor. It smacked off her forehead. "What makes it even more disturbing is that Cullen Skink must have known this, and he never told me. It makes me even more satisfised that I disposed with him as I did."

Mask walked across the room and sat on the ground a metre away from Kiltman, his legs crossed. "I must say, I was incredulous when you showed up in Rome. How you survived the fall from the helicopter is no doubt an entertaining story. Sadly, we don't have time to engage in chit-chat. I have other more pressing matters to attend to."

He stood up and turned to hover over Roddy's motionless body. "I am surprised he has not woken up yet. Maybe my colleague applied a little too much chloroform. Pity he did not hang around, he would have been excited to know who Kiltman really is. I look forward to revealing this news to him later. The good news is that all of you had a good night's sleep. It's already nearly lunch time on Tuesday."

Wilson looked at Kiltman. He was struggling to sit upright, blood caked around his forehead, accentuating the lump and bruising that had developed overnight.

Mask stretched down to yank the tape from Kiltman's mouth and eyes. He ripped off Wilson's gag, tearing a chunk of hair from the back of her head. She did not satisfy him with a scream.

"The question is, how am I going to dispose of you three nosy parkers? I would have killed you already but it's easier to manage live bodies than dead ones."

He pinched his nose and made an exaggerated grunt of disgust. Kiltman realised their captor was trying to be humorous. Mask pushed him onto his side and walked over to a portable TV in the corner of the room.

Second Day Morning Ballots

"What a glorious day to be here in St. Peter's Square surrounded by tens of thousands of pilgrims. Reminds me of an Old Firm football match in Glasgow, except here everyone is supposed to be supporting the same team. But are they? From where I'm standing, I can see banners and posters for many of the Cardinals from continents near and far. The name that seems to be standing out - at least in terms of popular support - is Cardinal Damascus." MacTavish held his medal up in the air.

"This medal has become the most visible object around Rome. As you can see from the bold, shiny **G**, it represents St. Paul's letter to the Galatians. It has become the symbol of renewal championed by Damascus. People all over the world are *meddling with their medals* – and, yes, you heard that very catchy phrase here first."

MacTavish expected Dominic to give him an earful. However, his producer in Glasgow was sitting in his studio twiddling his own Galatians medal. On this occasion, he would allow MacTavish some poetic licence.

"Look!" MacTavish pointed at the tiny chimney in the distance. Smoke was drifting up into the sky. "You can feel the tension here in the square; a quarter of a million people holding their breath at the same time. We are all trying to see what colour the smoke is: has the most recent ballot produced a Pope?"

A few moments passed before a collective sigh rose up from the square. MacTavish turned back to the camera. "Well, here we go again. We are going to have to wait till this evening for the results of the next ballot."

Mask switched off the television and turned to face his captive audience. "Fascinating, isn't it? The world awaits a new Pope, someone who can influence millions of people; in fact, more than a billion. What wonders he could work, eh?" Mask's sardonic, guttural laugh echoed through the room.

"Mask, listen. Whatever you're planning, it's getting out of control. You can't expect to get away with it. Too many people are looking for you. They'll know we are missing and will be out searching for us." Kiltman spoke through a parched mouth, his head throbbing.

"Kiltman, or should I say, Kenny. You really don't understand, do you? Soon no-one will care about you and your precious loved ones."

Roddy emitted a slow groan, pulling his knees up to his chest. He tried to kneel upright until he fell over. The tape across his eyes and mouth hindered his orientation.

"Oh, hi, young man. Long time no see. Welcome to the party, unfortunately we have no time to have a proper catch up." Mask laughed as he yanked the tape with a flick of his wrist.

"Ow!" Roddy shouted. A small scratch appeared above Roddy's upper lip.

"Oh, come now. It's just a flesh wound. There's much worse to come, believe me." Mask produced a knife from beneath his trouser leg.

Wilson managed to huddle up against the wall, her back supported by a chair. "Come on, Mask. At least let Roddy and Angie go. They are only kids."

"Only kids?" Mask dropped down onto his knee and placed the knife against her cheek, just strong enough to pierce the skin and generate a spot of blood. "We were all kids at one point, Maggie. It's a temporary state of anticipation, before we become the people we are meant to be. I am sure if you met me as a child, and you knew what I would become, you would not have hesitated to do the world a favour. Would you?"

"You're a sick…" Wilson pulled her head away from the knife and launched herself forward to headbutt him. He leant back just far enough to avoid the blow. She fell forward onto her face, her cheek smacking the marble floor.

"Aw, were you going to give me a *Glasgow kiss*, Maggie? I didn't think you cared about me in that way." Mask pushed her over onto her side with the sole of his foot. "I am going to take a lot of pleasure, when I have time, to make you pay for that indiscretion."

A sound echoed in the room. The Mission Impossible theme tune. Mask took his phone from his pocket. "Yes?"

He listened. "Uh-huh. Uh-huh. Okay, we need to move up the schedule now. I'll be there in five minutes. Get the equipment ready."

He put the phone back in this pocket and looked at Kiltman. "Do you like the ringtone? If you were going to live beyond today, we could give you a phone with *'Donald, Where's Your Troosers'*!"

He let out another throaty rasp of a laugh. As he was about to leave, he turned back and knelt down beside Wilson. Before she could think of a comment, he leant in and kissed her on her mouth. She pursed her lips into a hard line, just in time. "Ah, Maggie. You've gone all shy on me."

He stood, blew a kiss at Wilson and left the room, closing the door behind him.

Time Marches On

The vacuum of silence was welcome when Mask had gone. Half an hour earlier they had been unconscious, unaware of the true madness of this madman. Now they had to lie there knowing full well how helpless they were.

"Roddy, are you okay?" Kiltman asked. He saw his son nod. "Maggie?"

"Yes, I'm fine. Just got a sore cheek. I would love to brush my teeth. She spat onto the marble. "Sorry." She could still taste Mask's toothpaste on her upper lip. Euthymol. The weirdest-tasting toothpaste invented.

"Any ideas, guys?" Kiltman was pulling at his plastic ties. The harder he pulled, the tighter they became.

Nobody answered. They were each working through the options available to them, their minds as empty as the room.

"Listen," Kiltman said. "I could hear the discussion on the phone. It was not entirely clear, very muffled, but I caught the gist. Mask is involved somehow in the Papal election. The guy on the other end seemed to say something about the next Papal ballot probably being the last one. They needed to move up the schedule."

"Could you recognise the voice?" Wilson asked.

"I'm not sure. It was strange. Seemed vaguely familiar. I couldn't even catch the accent. British, I think. I need another Hair o' the Dog top up. Mask didn't think to empty my sporran. It's still there. Just can't get to it." He let out a frustrated groan, pulling at the binds again.

The noise was loud. The crash reverberated across the room as the door swivelled on its hinges and crashed against the wall. A man fell through the space onto the floor, his black clothing covered in dust and wood splinters.

"Marco?" Wilson said.

"Hey, Maggie. What's going on here then? You left dinner to come and hang out in a Church's crypt with a man in a skirt?"

Kiltman was beginning to tire of people thinking Scotland's national dress was actually a dress.

"How did you find us?" She tried to sit up but fell over onto her side. Marco bent down to help her. "Ah, now I know why you didn't run to hug me." He pulled out a short, stubby knife and cut the ties. She took it from him and did the same for Roddy and Kiltman. They stood up while dusting themselves down, trying to ignore the pains in their joints and muscles from a cold night on a stone floor.

"Thanks, Marco." Roddy ran to thank their rescuer, obscuring his line of sight.

"Hey, *caro*. It's a pleasure." Marco hugged him tightly. "Glad to help."

Kiltman found the mask on the floor beside him and pulled it over his head, before walking over to Marco.

"Ah, you're that Kiltman guy. Wow, you are very popular in Sicily."

Who would have known, Kiltman thought?

Kiltman reached out and hugged Marco. "Man, so good to see you, whoever you are."

"This is Marco," Wilson said. "The brave man that saved us yesterday. It's now twice in a row." She turned to him. "How did you know we were here?"

Marco reached across and placed his hand on her back. He tugged at her jacket for a moment before opening the palm of his hand. A small piece of metal shone in the dull light of the room.

"You put a tracker on me?" Wilson had last seen one of these a few years earlier on a case in Edinburgh.

"Maggie, I do like you, that I can't deny. Although when we hugged at the end of dinner, I had an ulterior motive. It took a while to attach this old-fashioned bug. Sorry, it probably appeared a little inappropriate at the time. You are very precious to me and my family." In another scenario she would have felt uncomfortable at how he was looking into her eyes.

"You can bug me any time," Kiltman said, patting him on the back. A little tension relief was needed. Marco was quite intense, in a macho, handsome Italian way. Kiltman rarely spent time thinking about how he looked; however, when he considered Marco, he felt like a different species.

"I guess, I should say, thanks." Wilson was smiling. She made a mental note that if she got back to Scotland in one piece, she would invest in a few of those monitors.

"Guys, Mask could be back soon." Roddy had walked to the door and was looking out towards a staircase with a steep incline. "Can we go?"

They nodded and followed him, parking their underlying issues and desires until they were in a safer place. Roddy's bag and Wilson's backpack were on a table in a narrow corridor leading to the staircase. They grabbed the bags and snuck up the stairs. Kiltman reached the top first and pushed against a heavy, wooden door. It creaked open letting light into the dark corridor. They were still inside Trinità dei Monti, looking at the inside of the church. Kiltman had never spent so long in a place of worship; he would not be in a hurry to do so again.

Marco was moving down the aisle looking along the benches as he passed, waving his pistol in case he may need to fire off a round in haste. Wilson crept along the side wall, searching for clues; she hated the absence of a plan. She turned to see Kiltman and Roddy taking a slug from the flask. Would she ever get used to that sight, she wondered?

They neared the main door, clustering at the notice board, near the entrance. The door opened slowly. Everyone froze. Mask stood silhouetted by daylight, the sounds of vespas and traffic drifting in the open door. The knife was visible in his hand. Wilson saw Marco point his gun at Mask, whose other arm had been out of sight behind the door. He yanked hard and pulled Angie in front of him, dropping onto one knee. Marco's finger had already gone too far. Too much momentum in the pull for him to reverse the action. Too much experience of street warfare. Wilson threw herself into the air, flailing her arms in front of the gun. The impact of the bullet sounded dull and innocuous. It was the scream that was chilling.

A Final Bow

Mask ran from the church, cursing as he sprinted across the short clearing towards the top of the Spanish Steps. He managed to avoid hitting the *Obelisco Sallustiano*, a homemade Roman version of an Egyptian obelisk, before bumping into an elderly man taking a picture of the large, stone needle.

He had no time to think. The wall in front of him was around a metre high, but on the other side it was the equivalent of two stories above the steps. He had no choice. There would be another bullet in the chamber coming in his direction.

He threw himself over the wall in desperate hope of a soft landing. And there it was, a couple fawning over a baby in a pram. He stretched his arms and legs wide to create some degree of air resistance, before landing square on top of the pram. The mother had barely noticed the unusual shadow in the sky above them. With the instinct and reaction that comes with motherhood, she whisked the baby from the pram into her bosom. Mask landed on the carriage, its frame somehow resisting his weight. His momentum pushed it over the first step, before bumping down towards the bottom. Mask held onto the sides working hard to steer as gravity and force pulled it forward and down.

Couples and groups, who had been enjoying a quiet snack on the steps, were scrambling for the sides, shouting to others to clear space for this pram hurtling towards them.

Mask tightened his grip. He had to get to the bottom and make an escape, retrench and then execute their plan. The pram bumped and wobbled with each step, accelerating down the steep decline. It took a few moments to reach the square. It hit the bottom at a fast pace bumping along the cobbles until it smacked against the perimeter wall of Fontana della Barcaccia. Its metal frame shattered on impact as Mask was launched into the air. He prepared to land in a judo forward roll as he had been trained in an Argentinian underground military unit years before.

That training had been delivered by some of the toughest ex-military elite in the world. However it had not included a roll that would allow him to land safely on a marble boat with solid, prominent edges.

They could see it from their vantage point at the top of the Steps. Kiltman had his arm around Wilson's waist, her arm bleeding from where the bullet had grazed her before drilling into the door just above Angie's head. Roddy, Angie and Marco watched in silence. Mask flew through the air, his knees tucked into his chest, halfway around a full three-sixty. His graceful flight ended when he landed on the boat's bulging bow. The sickening crunch of broken bones hit their ears a second later. Followed by the sight of the fountain's crystal-clear waters turning pink, then red, with the final spill of a dead man's lifeblood.

Last Ballot

Restraint should come easily to a Cardinal. He knew if he showed a hint of the frustration he felt, it would expose him. He could not afford for that to happen. Not now, when they were so close.

The two ballots that morning had shown a growing support for Ratzinger. Bergogolio was the closest, nibbling at the German's heels. The support for Damascus had already improved, at a faster pace than the others, to achieve a top 5 position. The problem was Ratzinger's margin. One more ballot could deliver him a victory. While a Damascus win needed at least another day to leverage the growing swing away from the less relevant candidates. He had spent a lot of time with the other Cardinals. He knew he was winning them over. While in private some scorned his distribution of medals, they could not openly accuse him of campaigning. He had been too subtle for that.

He needed to stop the clock; he had to find a distraction.

It had just gone twelve o'clock. There were a few hours until the next ballot that evening. Enough time to disrupt the Conclave. He looked up at the Last Judgement, remembering the words from St. Paul's letter, not to the Galatians this time, but to the Corinthians: *He will bring to light what is hidden in darkness and will expose the motives of the heart.* He smiled as he surveyed the other Cardinals scattered around the Sistine Chapel. He looked forward to exposing to them the true motives of his heart. At that stage, it would be too late for any of them to do anything to stop him.

The Good, the Bad and the Fiery

They ran down the steps to a cacophony of screams. Kiltman had torn a strip of dangling cloth from his frayed kilt and tied a makeshift tourniquet around Wilson's arm. The bleeding had stopped; but they both knew she had narrowly avoided death.

Roddy and Angie were just up ahead of them approaching the fountain, his arm around her shoulders. Angie could not bring herself to hate her father. Yet, she was surprised at how little emotion she felt at seeing him draped over the edge of the marble boat. Roddy squeezed her gently to let her know he sensed her numb confusion.

Kiltman's mind was racing. Mask was already old news as far as he was concerned. Whatever he had been working on, their nemesis would have made sure his evil plan would continue beyond his own expiry date. Kiltman had to find a way to explore underneath the steps. The hum he had felt had now increased in intensity. His senses had tuned into the vibrations. He knew where they were coming from, which was the easy part. His challenge was determining how to get there.

Marco had found himself caught up in the moment running behind the others to the fountain. Gun in hand, he looked left and right for any signs of trouble, ready to shoot any of this maniac's accomplices; then stopped halfway down. He had become embroiled in a bizarre scenario, somehow out of his depth. This was not his war; he had enough to cope with back in Sicily. His desire to follow his heart was about to get him into trouble once again.

He shook his head and turned to walk back up the steps, wondering if he would have time for a plate of pasta and glass of Chianti in the *Foglio* before his flight back to Sicily.

He barely had time to register the blow.

The body that hit him came from a few steps higher, putting him at a disadvantage. The smack knocked the wind from his lungs, sending him flailing backwards. He could tell from the perfume that it was a woman, probably young. As he fell, she held onto his shoulders, rolling with him down ten or so steps before hitting the square. She landed on top. He tried to feel for his gun on the cobbles, it was nowhere to be found. Until he felt its smooth, cold muzzle at his throat.

Wilson had just taken out her phone to call the local Polizia, when she heard the thump. Marco and his assailant had landed a metre from where they had all stopped to gaze at Mask's death mask, waiting for Kiltman to crack an inappropriate one-liner. Marco had saved her twice to her once; it was her chance to even the score. She launched herself onto the woman's back and grabbed the gun. A bullet escaped the chamber breaking a window in the Keats-Shelley house. More screams rose from the petrified tourists huddled around the corners of the steps.

She sat on the woman, forcing her arm up her back. A shoulder blade at forty-five degrees told her she need not exert any more pressure. She wanted to immobilise the woman, not maim her for life. Marco crawled back onto his feet, his confusion second to his embarrassment. The woman screamed and shouted, jerking and twisting to escape the pressure of Wilson's knees. Each time she jerked, she screamed with the pain in her shoulder.

"Stop moving!" Wilson shouted. "It's just going to hurt you even more."

"*Basta! Basta!*" the woman screamed.

"If you stop swearing, I'll let you go," Wilson answered, pressing harder onto her back.

"I'm not swearing, Maggie! I've had *enough*! Stop!"

Wilson bent down and put her head on the ground, next to the woman's face.

"Valentina?"

Valentina's Day

"Valentina, you need to explain this. What the hell is going on?" Wilson had taken the knee from her back, helping the younger girl to her feet with caution. She held the gun in her hand and made sure Valentina saw it.

"Maggie! He was chasing you guys with a gun." She pointed at Marco with her thumb. "He's Marco Marciano, a well-known Mafia don's son."

Wilson put her hands in the air. "Whoa! Take it easy." She patted her on the arm. "On this occasion, Marco's one of the good guys." They heard sirens in the distance, they did not have much time before the Polizia closed the show down. "Let's talk about you for a moment. What are you doing here and how did you know Marco was a gangster?"

"Hey!" Marco stood with his arms spread wide, like a schoolboy accused of something he had not yet done.

"Sorry, *alleged* gangster." Wilson added, creating inverted commas with her index fingers.

Valentina looked at her feet for a moment, before lifting her head. "I've not been honest with you guys." She turned to look towards Roddy. "*Caro*, I am so sorry." He had his arms folded, trying his best to look stern.

"What are you talking ab…?" The screech of tyres interrupted Wilson's question. She did not know rubber could make such a high-pitched sound. Everyone turned to look. Except her. She watched Kiltman, Roddy and Angie slink away from the Steps towards the local Spagna underground station, a minute's walk from the fountain. Two vehicles missed each other by a fraction. All car doors opened at the same time as if perfected in a training ground. Chief Commissioner Pisacane was the first to arrive at the fountain.

"What on earth is going on here?" He pointed towards Mask's drooping body. His face was as close to Wilson's as he could get while staying out of range of a headbutt. He had heard about Scottish cops.

She thought about her options. While she could summarise all of it in a few sentences, she had to buy time. Kiltman had just turned the corner with Roddy and Angie.

"Where do you want me to start, sir?"

"How about where you stopped updating me about how your investigation is going?"

"Sure, I'll do that. First of all, why don't you update me on Valentina here? Your very own fake-bakery owner."

"Okay, okay." Pisacane knew when he was busted.

"Valentina is a junior police officer, working under cover. She joined a few months back. Her bakery shop was the perfect cover for her and some officers to infiltrate local gangs." He coughed. "Em, she also happens to be my brother's daughter, my niece. We thought we would give her a job shadowing you and your colleague."

"Crawford?" Wilson looked at Valentina, a hint of repulsion twitching at her top lip.

"Maggie, no, you've got it wrong." Valentina's cheeks were stained with tears. "Yes, it's true. The Chief Commissioner is my uncle, and yes, he put me on this case. Honestly, my feelings towards Crawford are genuine. How could I not like a man as handsome and courageous as him?"

Wilson sighed. A week earlier, she would have made a quick-witted riposte of 'there really is no accounting for taste'. She would not have meant it; just what Scots do when they witness an outpouring of love and affection. She looked at Valentina for a moment and nodded. She could see Crawford and this pretty woman together. Life was cruel sometimes.

"Look, this conversation is going nowhere," Pisacane said. She could see a snaky vein throbbing on his temple. "Let's take this down to the station." Several other Polizia vehicles had arrived, including an ambulance. Mask's body was being lifted onto a stretcher to be taken to the morgue. A large crowd had gathered. Pisacane clapped his hands and shouted at them all to disperse. Very few listened.

He linked his arm into Wilson's. "You are not going anywhere. You have got a lot to explain." He began to walk towards his car before turning to Valentina. "Where is Marciano?"

They all turned and scanned up and down the Steps. He was nowhere to be seen.

From behind a car across the square, watching the animated discussion, a man - with the same dark, handsome features as Al Pacino in Scarface - looked at his watch. He smiled when he realised he had time before his flight to grab that plate of pasta and Chianti after all.

Booty Lane

"Stay close, guys. We're heading towards the underground." Kiltman said. He pointed at a street sign above his head, *Vicolo del Bottino*. "Interesting name for a street, especially one leading to a criminal's lair. It means Booty Lane."

"Kiltman, I know another way in. It's through a shop near the Steps." Angie was unsure why he was adding a layer of unnecessary complexity.

"I know, Angie, but the police are swarming all over the Square now. Plus, I don't trust your father. He may have left a booby trap for us at the entrance."

She nodded. His death had not yet registered. Or maybe she had written him off years ago when he was imprisoned. She should be feeling free now but could not shake the sense of shame – it was so much easier to pick friends than DNA. It made her feel sick. She needed a subject change.

"Hey, Roddy, any news from Reilly?"

"Yes, he's in Rome at the moment too. He came to look for you."

"Oh!" Her cheeks blushed, despite the years of training by her father on how to hide emotions. "Is he on his own?"

"No, he's with his dad." Roddy's eyebrows furrowed. "We bumped into them yesterday at the Steps. He took me aside to have a quiet word. He's worried about his father."

"What do you mean?" Kiltman asked.

"The reason his father was here was apparently to meet Reilly when he flew in from America. However, he let slip when talking to Coach Stone that he had been here for a couple of days already."

"Coach Stone?" Angie asked.

"Yes, I know, it's weird. He's here too. He came to support Cardinal Damascus in his aspiration to be Pope. You didn't see it, but it seems the Cardinal cured his leg. He's limp-free now. He spent a lot of time with the Galatians when he was in the US."

"Wow, I missed a lot over there. It does seem like Rome's the place to be." She laughed. First time in a long time. Roddy smiled back, acknowledging the moment.

"Guys, we need to focus here. Angie, can you tell me what you remember from when you got to this part of town?" Kiltman dropped down onto his haunches and held her hand. "Anything at all."

"When we arrived, he stuck me in a small room. He took *Damascocles* into another…"

"Damas…what?" he asked.

"Damascocles. It's the name of the massive computer he and Tantalus were using…"

"Tantalus?" Roddy asked.

"Okay, let me explain." She paused for a moment to focus her thoughts. "There has been this guy working with him. Long grey hair, thick beard, very intimidating, in a quietly menacing way. Strong, posh English accent. He calls himself Tantalus. Apparently, he created a program this *Damascocles* computer uses. I honestly don't know what they were doing with it."

"So where is Tantalus now?" Kiltman had started to walk along the *Vicolo del Bottino*, holding hands with Angie and Roddy. It seemed Tuesdays were quiet affairs in Rome, few commuters to interrupt them.

"That's the thing, I don't know. Since we came to *Piazza di Spagna,* Father kept me stuck in a space the size of a cupboard staring at the walls."

Kiltman shook his head. It was difficult to accept that Angie had been in such danger.

"Kiltman?" Roddy was struggling not to call him *Dad*.

"What is it?" Kiltman had stopped to place the palms of his hand against the wall. He knew a tunnel led to below the Steps. He had sensed it earlier and could now feel it through his fingertips.

"You need to look." Roddy held his phone up towards him. The message was short and to the point.

'Roddy, been trying to get your dad and Maggie. They're not replying. I'm coming to Rome. Let me know where to find you guys. Love, Tommy x'

"Will I text back?"

Kiltman was unsure how to feel about Tommy joining the party. He thought for a moment and resigned himself to the inevitability of his friend's haphazard social urges.

"Pity Dad's not here." Roddy winked at Kiltman from behind Angie.

Kiltman gave a subtle nod of his head. "I know, you should advise him of that. Ask him to contact Wilson anyway. We need all the help we can get."

As Roddy texted, Kiltman continued to press his hands against the wall of the narrow street as they walked towards the underground station, feeling for a change in density. It took a few moments, but it was unmistakeable. A layer of brick separated them from the space on the other side. He stepped back from the wall and scanned the area. There were no doors or windows allowing access.

Roddy tapped him on the arm. He pointed at their feet. They were standing on a drain, a metre square. Kiltman knelt down and ran his fingers around the edge. It looked like it had not been opened in years, grime and caked mud crammed into the seam by millions of feet rushing for trains.

He looked around for something to insert in the rim to lever it up.

"*Scusa, che stai facendo?*" An elderly man had stopped beside them. Kiltman knew by the look on his face he would not leave without an answer to his question as to what they were doing.

"Good question," Kiltman rose to look the man in the eyes.

"Of course, you speak English. Or should I say Scottish." The man's face crinkled into a broad grin.

"Yes, both. I'm bilingual."

The man laughed aloud. He tapped his metal walking stick on the ground in appreciation of the joke. "I know you from the TV. You're quite the hero. What are you doing in Rome?"

"Searching for bad guys, to be honest. Look, can you do me a favour?"

"Of course. What would you like?"

Kiltman pulled Roddy towards the man. "Can I temporarily swap this young man for your cane?"

Roddy took the man's hand and placed it on his shoulder. The man sighed and handed his cane to Kiltman. "Nothing exciting ever happens in my life. Yes, take it."

"Don't worry, it won't be for long." Kiltman took the pointy end of the stick and inserted it into a space he had scratched along the manhole rim. It took a few moments of pushing and shunting until it started to move. After a couple of minutes, he had levered the cover high enough to insert his hand. The creak of rusted iron awakened from its slumber gave the same spine-tingling sensation as nails on a blackboard. He pushed it to the side allowing them to look down into the darkness. A ladder disappeared into the depths.

He handed the cane back to the man. "*Grazie tanto!*"

"Oh, no, the pleasure is all mine." The man bowed and continued his walk along the lane to catch the train home. For the first time in years, he had a new story to tell the grandchildren.

Debrief

"Maggie?"

It was good to hear Tommy's Highland brogue; she had just sat down at Pisacane's desk. "Hi, pal. What's up?"

"Just wanted to let you know I'm going to be in Rome in just over an hour. Flight's leaving soon." The noise of Palermo's tannoy boomed in the background. "Where can I meet you?"

"It's not so easy for me just now. I'm at the police station; will be here for a while." Pisacane was rolling his fingers for her to end the call.

"That's okay, I can wait. Just let me know where." She heard the Rome flight being called in the background.

"Let's meet…" She looked at Pisacane. "…where you and Kenny saved the American tourist from losing his wallet."

"On his stag weekend? Did he tell you that story?"

"Oh, yes, many times." Pisacane was turning a shade of pink. "See you there later." She closed the call down and placed the phone on the desk.

"Okay, where were we before you decided to organise your social life?" She sighed realising the truth of what her mother had taught her as a child: patience is the most valuable thing lost by people full of their own self-importance.

"Let me take you through it again." She began to count along her fingers with each point. "Let's deal first with Sacco's murder. He was killed by a couple of hitmen, Luca and Luigi, on behalf of Sicilian Mafia families. They had been sending money via Banco' d'Aiuto to Banco Discepolo with the purposes of funding Vatican-led homeless programs across Italy."

Pisacane raised his eyebrows.

"I know, go figure. Sacco used a foreign exchange rounding mechanism to syphon money to an account in the Cayman Islands. Anyway, they didn't take kindly to Sacco stealing their cash." She smiled at her own understatement. "So, he paid the price."

"Who owns the Cayman Islands bank? Sacco?"

"No. This is where Mask comes in. He has been using that account to make payments to IT suppliers; hardware, software, networks etcetera."

"Etcetera?"

She coughed. "Oh, I don't know. IT stuff." She knew her information systems knowledge was lacking; and would rather Pisacane did not realise it. "The point is there's probably still a lot left to fund crazy schemes for years to come. At some point he must have threatened Sacco to do this. Maybe he had some information that allowed him to blackmail Sacco. We might never know since both are now dead."

"Okay, so what about the '*IT stuff*'. What's he going to use it for?"

"He's got a large computer capable of extraordinary things, from what we can tell. It's sending out signals all over the world. We couldn't understand where they were going or what they were doing."

"Now where is this computer?"

"We thought it was somewhere around the Spanish Steps. However, he lured us into a trap last night, using Angie as bait. Then today, it all went a bit mad. As you know."

"When are you going to talk about Marco Marciano?"

"Oh, yes, I forgot that bit. Last night he saved us from being shot by an assassin called Salvatore."

"Yes, we found him in hospital. Marciano is lucky. Salvatore Sconi is going to survive. Should mean a respite in a growing family feud down there in Sicily." Pisacane whistled slowly. "You know, if he had died, all hell would've broken loose. It was at boiling point already. Once they know that Marciano's men took the time to deposit Salvatore at the hospital it should make amends for Marco's treatment of Sconi's daughter."

Wilson noticed that Pisacane did not stop to consider how close she and Roddy had come to being killed. It was good to know who your true allies were.

"You know about Marco and the Sconi woman?"

"Oh, yes, we know everything."

"Well, can I go now?"

"Not yet. We need to understand where chaos will rein next in Rome. What are your plans?" He leaned forward, trying to look benign. "How can we help you?"

"I need to get back to the Pensione and sleep. I am shattered, need to recharge and then find Kiltman. He may have figured out where Mask's lair was. Once I know, I'll let you know."

"Okay, I will send a couple of officers with you."

"Thank you, but that's not necessary. No disrespect, I just need a bit of time away from uniforms." She tried to make it sound genuine, before changing the subject. "How is Valentina?"

"Ah, my niece has been relieved of her duties. If we had known how this case would escalate, we would not have assigned her to track you."

"Sir, you threw her in at the deep end. Take it easy on her. She'll make a good officer one day."

"Noted." He stood to escort her from the room.

"Where is she now?"

"She's at the hospital. That Crawford fellow made quite the impact."

Funny Thing on Way to the Colosseum

Tommy stood in front of the Vittorio Emanuele II monument. Its garish white splendour and majesty dominated this junction in Rome's city centre, at the opposite end of the *Via del Corso* - 1.5 kilometres - from Valentina's Pasticceria at *Piazza del Popolo*. Also known as the *Wedding Cake* to those less inclined to marvel at its magnificence, the structure was visible in most photos of the city. The taxi driver suggested he drop Tommy there to enjoy the experience of walking alongside the Forum towards the Colosseum. Tommy sensed the driver did not want to navigate the chaos of Colosseum traffic but acquiesced all the same.

When they were in Rome over a decade earlier on Kenny's stag weekend, he had been less interested in the powerful history of the city. Too many bars and an overload of twenties testosterone guided his actions back then. Now, he was enjoying the true essence of Rome, the history and intrigue knitted into every ruin in the Forum – the exquisite appetiser on the way to the Colosseum rising in the distance.

Despite the noise of vespas and car horns, when he heard the honk, he knew it was for him. Maybe it was the incessance of its rhythm. He turned to see Wilson's head protruding from the taxi window. "Tommy!"

He walked over to the cab, parked perilously at the side of the road, cars and vans swerving to avoid it. "Hey, Maggie. Are you the funny thing that happened on the way to the Forum?"

"Get in, quick." She opened the door for him to duck into the back seat. "Spanish Steps, driver! *Presto!*"

"So, we're not going to the Colosseum then?"

She hugged him, planting a wet kiss on his cheek. "Good to see you, pal. No, we're not. I had to be a bit clandestine about my instructions. I had company at the time."

"I thought I lived an exciting life. You beat me hands down." He ruffled her hair affectionately. She hated when he did that, but it was a Tommy thing to do. She knew she would regret it if she asked him to stop making her feel like a puppy.

"Listen, Roddy and Angie are at the Spanish Steps."

"On their own? Roddy texted me to say he was here while his dad had gone home. How could he do that when there's so much going on?"

"It's okay. He knows that Kiltman is with them. The case became too complex for me to handle alone, so he came to help. Kenny's got his own stuff to sort out back at home."

"Okay, at least it will be good to see Kiltman again. I haven't seen him since New York. Is he still, you know…" He rubbed his tummy.

"I think he's lost some weight." A few days without food in the Amazon can have that effect, she mused. "By the way, what happened with Luisa?"

"Ah, Luisa." Tommy sat back in the seat, placing his head against the headrest. "Lovely girl. Beautiful, fun personality, kind and nearly perfect in every way."

"*Nearly* perfect?"

"There was one issue."

"Oh?"

He gestured to a finger on his left hand.

"No?"

"Yip. Well, not married. Engaged. Apparently, she's been with a guy for five years."

"Ouch! I bet that hurt when she told you."

"It did, but not as much as a punch on the mouth." He leant forward and pulled his bottom lip down to show a cut on the inside. It looked no more than a standard mouth ulcer, but for Tommy it was a war wound. "We were sitting having dinner, when a man walked up to our table and started shouting at me." Wilson's eyes could not widen any further. "I know! I was shocked too."

"What happened next?"

"Well, the more he spoke, the angrier he became. I wanted to explain. Then I realised that my explanation would only confirm his worst fears. That I wanted to date his fiancée. I had just started to explain when he lashed out and knocked me off my chair.

"I ended up fleeing the restaurant and hiding in the backroom of a pizzeria until morning. A very kind man felt sorry for me skulking around Palermo's side streets and let me sleep there. He probably saved my life."

"So, you came to Rome to be safe?"

He nodded. "I still want to enjoy the rest of my holiday, so Rome it is. They even named a movie about holidaying here. In fact," he bent his head at an angle, "you do look a bit like Audrey Hepburn."

"Very funny." She nudged him with her elbow. "I'm sorry Luisa didn't work out. Listen, I'm warning you, you might not get the peaceful holiday you were looking for. Our case is reaching a crunch point. Something seriously bad is going down." She waited a moment for him to digest her words. "Do you want to help?"

He looked at her for a moment before sharing a slow wink and tapping his nose with an index finger. "Is the Pope a Catholic?"

Road to Damascus

Angie and Roddy stayed close to him in the dark tunnel, holding the edge of his cape. Kiltman ran his hands along the dank walls, feeling his way for any signs of an exit. Underfoot they felt something scarper past them, and then again, a few seconds later. It felt like they were walking through a mini zoo providing mid-afternoon entertainment for the animals. Roddy was pleased Angie could not see the expression on his face. He abhorred rodents. While she loved them. Three guinea pigs in a sprawling cage in their mum's kitchen seemed quite a normal use of precious household space to Angie.

Kiltman counted in his head the distance from the *Vicolo* to where he had sensed the vibrating hum strongest under the Steps. It took a few minutes to cover the distance underground.

"That's it," Angie said. The sound was now audible to their hearing too.

He nodded and looked up at a drain cover above his head. It was half a metre out of reach. "Roddy, can you climb on my back?"

"Sure."

"Place your foot here," Kiltman said, bending down and cupping his hands. Roddy stepped up onto his father's hands and climbed onto his shoulders.

"Can you push the metal cover?" Kiltman groaned tottering under his son's weight.

"Yes, that's what I'm doing." Roddy shook his head as he pushed hard. It would not budge.

"Harder! Come on!" He tried not to let fatherly exasperation impact the tone of his voice; he hoped the voice-changer in the mask diluted any sound of annoyance. He pushed with his legs to add to Roddy's strength, but the cover would not move.

"Kiltman?"

"Yes, Angie?"

"Could I also help?"

Kiltman held out an arm for her to climb up. Roddy made room by moving onto a single shoulder. Even though Angie was petite, Kiltman could feel his knees weaken with the added weight.

"Ok, after three. One, two, three."

The two teens felt their arms strain with the effort of pushing against the immoveable drain. Kiltman's thighs and calves shook with the exertion. He let out a loud, frustrated grunt as he pressed with his last ounce of energy. The drain cover burst open, followed by the clang of metal landing on the other side.

It took a few minutes, but after a range of gymnastic manoeuvres Billy Smart's trapeze act would have been proud of, all three of them had climbed up through the hole.

The room was small, just wide enough to accommodate the large mainframe flush against the wall. The doorway had been widened to allow access; the residue of splintered doorframes and fragmented plastering littered the floor.

"Oh, my!" Roddy said. His hands were on the sides of the computer, just above the letters, *Damascocles*.

"What is it?" Kiltman asked.

"I've never seen anything so powerful." He looked up towards the ceiling at the signals emanating from the hardware, pulsating through the walls to the outside.

"It's amazing! The power in this machine is off the charts."

"Roddy, what are you talking about?" Angie touched his arm. "Are you okay?"

Roddy realised how strange this would seem to Angie. She had not seen him sink a couple of mouthfuls of Hair o' the Dog on the Steps.

"Eh, sorry. I just love mainframes. They are so ruggedly sleek." He stroked the side with the palm of his hand. "So smooth."

"This is getting very weird." Angie looked at Kiltman.

"Hormones," Kiltman said. "They affect all teenagers differently." He tapped Roddy with the toe of his shoe.

"Angie, why don't you show us around your old apartment?" Roddy's attempt to break the ice made her shake her head, a puzzled frown settling across her face.

"Okay, come on." She led them out into the corridor. The apartment had seen better days. Probably a century old, it had not been maintained with a view to keeping up with the Spanish Steps above. Threadbare carpets and paper on the walls dangling down to the floor revealed layers of decoration dating back over the decades. Kiltman began to feel at home, realising the décor reminded him of his flat back on Corunna Street in Glasgow when he was a student. Whenever he and his flatmate had considered spending money on the apartment, they would convince each other a visit to the local pubs, *Ben Nevis* or *Grove*, for a beer would be a better use of time and money.

She pointed at a door. "That's the room I was in."

Kiltman opened it slowly. Angie's bag and notebook were on the floor beside a cot bed. Monastically spartan was a compliment to the bleakness of the room.

Angie indicated a door further down the corridor. "That's where my father spent a lot of time when we came here. He locked me in whenever he was working on something. He forbade me from entering the other room."

"Well, then. Let's check it out." Kiltman turned the handle. The door was locked. He stood back a metre or so, and turned southpaw, readying himself to ram it open.

"Kiltman!" He turned to see Roddy pointing. "Look."

Above the doorframe, jutting out by a centimetre was the edge of a silver key. "Oh, right, thanks, pal."

He reached up and took it, knowing that if they ever got through this adventure, that would be the one thing Roddy would take greatest pleasure in reminding him of. He inserted the key and turned it twice in the double lock. He opened the door with care, sensing something inside. Body heat, sweat and the acrid whiff of the unwashed. "Stay back, guys. Someone's in there." He raised his hand to stop them moving forward.

He stepped back on his heels and rushed at the door, jumping through into the space ready to fend off an attack. He scanned the room quickly. It was barren save for a mattress and a blanket. In the corner, a man lay on his side, his reddish-purple clothing creased and crumpled around him.

It took a few moments before Kiltman registered who he was looking at. It was only when he spoke that he believed it himself. "Cardinal Damascus?"

Clostridium Botulinum

He had paced back and forth, stopping to talk to any Cardinal who crossed his path. It impressed him how so many could meditate and walk in a straight line at the same time. They strolled in criss-crossing lines from one end of the Chapel to the other, never once bumping into each other. A remarkable feat of navigation, he thought.

He tried to hide the feeling of gloom that had settled on him. It had become clear that no matter how many ballots took place, there were not enough Cardinals still in deliberation to swing the vote towards him. The German and Argentinian were too far ahead. He looked at the Sistine Chapel ceiling focusing on the centrepiece, known as The Creation of Adam; God and Adam's fingers separated by a couple of centimetres, representing man's inability to achieve divine perfection. He felt the anger build inside, as if Michelangelo was reminding him of his destiny to be forever tormented by what he could not achieve.

Not this time.

He had not wanted it to get to this stage; he had believed in *Damascocles'* power to influence the populus and ultimately the Cardinals. However their voices were not yet strong enough and too many Cardinals were afraid of change.

He put a hand in his cassock pocket to touch the glass vial. In two hours, there would be a coffee break, to give everyone a chance to prepare for the evening ballot. The Cardinals liked their late afternoon cuppa. The poison would work quickly; an evening in pain with stomach cramps, before facing their own Last Judgement by morning. He turned his gaze from the ceiling to look at the mural above the altar. He pictured the cardinals sitting on the clouds begging Jesus to remember all the good things they had done.

Clostridium botulinum bacteria thrive on food products lying around in the sun for too long. Also known as Botulism, it normally carries a 5% probability of death. However, if someone is unfortunate to ingest an extra concentrated dosage then it would be a miracle if they survived. Even in the Vatican. The vial he kept in his inside pocket would kill an elephant. Some of the Cardinals would not take a cup of tea or coffee, they would survive. Mercy to a few, whose cups would be untouched, brimming over. A fitting metaphor.

The others would not rise from their beds. He wondered if the Vatican would perform an autopsy to identify the mystery bug that put them to sleep for ever. It was accepted knowledge that the Church did not perform autopsies on Popes; Pope John Paul I died after 33 days, and that was not enough to convince them to do an autopsy. He wondered how they would approach scores of dead Cardinals.

He did not care - he would be long gone by then. Back in the English countryside, enjoying walks across the hills, biding his time till his next appearance.

Ode to Damascus

Roddy held the bottle to his mouth. Cardinal Damascus sipped slowly, leaning his head back against the wall. He had little energy to swallow - letting gravity do the work. Angie gave him squares of a Dairy Milk bar she had found in her backpack.

After a few minutes of sipping and nibbling, colour returned to his cheeks. "Thank you. God bless you all." To show he meant it, he blessed them with a shaky hand. He looked at Roddy and Angie. "I know you, don't I?"

"Yes," Roddy answered. "We were at the football tournament last week in Cincinnati."

"Ah, the winners from Scotland. Lovely bunch of people." He groaned, the effort to speak taking its toll.

He turned to Kiltman. "Mr. Kiltman, I don't know how you three have come to be my rescuers, I expect there is a long story. Listen, there's no time to lose. Something very dark and dangerous is afoot. We must stop it."

Kiltman nodded. "Yes, we've reached that conclusion too. We just don't know what's going on. I was hoping you could tell us?"

Cardinal Damascus held out his hand for Kiltman to support him as he pushed himself onto his weak legs. Kiltman kept his arm around his waist allowing a few moments for the Cardinal to find his balance.

"Thank you. I think I can manage now." The Cardinal grunted with a sharp pain in his leg, which had taken the brunt of his fall when he was thrown into the room. "There's a computer here somewhere. We need to find it."

"Yes, *Damascocles*, it's just along the corridor." Kiltman allowed the Cardinal to link arms with him. They walked out of the airless room. Roddy led the way. He had begun to focus on the never-ending stream of signals and electronic pulses transmitted from the mainframe. As he approached the room, he felt the overwhelming sensation of nausea. It hit his lower abdomen, forcing him to lean against the wall, taking deep breaths.

"You okay, pal?" Kiltman asked.

Roddy nodded. "Just need a minute. This machine is so powerful, it's getting under my skin like nothing before."

"What are you talking about?" Angie asked.

He put his hand up. "Sometimes I get a bit technophobic. It'll pass, don't worry."

After a few moments, they walked into the room. Roddy studied the air around them, filled with incomprehensible signals and data flows.

"Over there, the monitor." The Cardinal indicated a large screen in the corner of the room with a thick cable attached to *Damascocles*.

Roddy sat down and hit the enter button. The display asked for a password. Closing his eyes, he let his mind drift into the messages around the room, invisible to the others. He traced the data flow back into the computer to the source of the energy. From there he traced a few connection points until he was pointed to the Credentials Manager, the home of the password.

"Tantalus with a capital T and S... five... question mark," he said as he typed the letters.

The screen came to life. Rows of data moved from left to right across the page, similar to what he had been studying in the air above them.

"Can you find a database in there somewhere?" The Cardinal leant against Kiltman as he looked at the screen. Roddy typed a few letters and numbers and was pointed to a directory of files, with row after row of folders. He read the names aloud. "US West Coast; US East Coast; US Central, Northern Europe, Southern Europe, China, India..." He stopped. "I think nearly every significant country or region has a folder."

"Cardinal Damascus bent forward and pointed at a folder towards the bottom of the screen, identified as *Cardinals*. "What about that one? Please open it."

Roddy clicked and a list of Cardinals' names appeared. He reckoned there were about twenty-five in total. Damascus was near the top of the list. Roddy tapped on his name. The screen changed to another page with a range of diagnostics specific to the Cardinal.

Wearing: Yes

Activated: Yes

Contact: No

Below the details, there was a line described as: *Input Command.*

Cardinal Damascus placed his hand inside his crumpled cassock and extracted his medal. He held it between his thumb and index finger.

The *Contact* icon changed from *No* to *Yes*. Another box opened on screen, named *Choose Mood*. Various options appeared below: *Loving; Hopeful; Desperate; Angry; Violent; Murderous; Damascofile*. Alongside these options, there were other choices to be clicked: *Very Strong, Strong, Medium, Weak*.

The Cardinal tapped Roddy on the shoulder. "Under my name, click on *Damascofile* and *Very Strong*."

Roddy tapped the mouse. Cardinal Damascus closed his eyes for a moment, holding his medal tight between his fingers. His eyes blinked open. "I knew it!"

"What happened?" Kiltman asked.

"Let's just say I enjoyed a surge of overwhelming love for myself and all that I stand for."

Kiltman snapped his fingers. "With the power in this machine and its software linked to the medals across the world, Tantalus will be sending the *Damascofile* signal now. At some point, his intention will be to move to *Violent* and *Murderous*. With millions of people holding these medals, there would be carnage."

"Come now. I do believe that's rather far-fetched." Cardinal Damascus shook his head.

"Switch it to *Angry, Very Strong* for the Cardinal here."

The Cardinal still held the medal, watching Roddy click on the options. It took a second, before Damascus' face contorted, his lips drawn back in a sneer that startled them. "Get out! Get out! You three are nothing but upstarts, trying to pretend you are heroes. Get out, I say!" Damascus snatched Angie's bag from her and smacked Kiltman on the head. Despite his weakened state, he still packed a punch. "Ouch!" Kiltman shouted. "Stop it!"

Roddy deactivated the *Angry Mood*.

Damascus fell to his knees, looking at the floor. "Oh, God, forgive me! Please, Kiltman, I am so sorry!"

"It's okay," Kiltman said as he rubbed the side of his head. "It was my idea after all. I'm just pleased we didn't switch you onto *Murderous*."

"How can this be possible?" Damascus' face was creased with anguish. An inner Mr. Hyde he never knew existed lurked very close to the surface.

"We don't know enough about it yet," Kiltman said. Roddy had pulled out his notebook and was scribbling on a page. "Hopefully Roddy can help us."

"This is frightening!" The Cardinal would have scorned this situation a few days earlier. Now after what he had been through, he could believe anything.

Kiltman shrugged. "I know, when it comes to evil, there's no limit to how manipulative it can be."

Cardinal Damascus nodded; he had spent his life fighting against the Devil and his wicked ways.

Marco... again

"I need to take this, Tommy."

"Sure," he answered. While the holiday had not been what he had expected, he had grown not to expect much from any situation. He lived for the moment. The fact he had opened pubs in Estonia and Glasgow was testament to his sheer willpower and determination to fight against his innate desire for distraction and stimulation. This holiday was providing more than enough of both.

Wilson turned her head and put her hand over the phone to drown out the sound of the taxi engine and incessant horn-blaring. "Hi, Marco! I wondered where you'd gone to at the Steps. The Roman Polizia want to talk to you."

Tommy tapped Wilson on the arm and mouthed, "Marco Marciano?" She nodded. He wagged his finger and shook his head. She nodded again and blew him a reassuring kiss. He pinched the top of his nose. He would have to find a moment to remind her that just because Kenny was out of sight, he should not be out of mind.

"Maggie, my dear. They know where to find me; that is, if they ever want to come to Sicily." He took a sip of his red wine. "Listen, we didn't finish our conversation last night at dinner. I am sitting at the same table now, and it reminded me. I owe you an answer to your question."

She cast her mind back to before their incarceration in Trinità dei Monti. They had been interrupted by Kiltman's call when Marco had begun to talk about Cardinal Damascus' birth.

"Go on," she prompted.

"Do you know what the star sign Gemini represents?"

"Seriously, Marco? Trust me, we are not compatible."

"Ah, if only." He laughed a short, resigned chortle. He had accepted that she was not interested. There was too much chemistry between her and the strange man in the kilt. "Tell me, what does Gemini mean?"

"Twins. Everyone knows that. Listen, you need to get a move on. We are close to our stop." The Damascus story had piqued her curiosity, now it was becoming a distraction.

"Okay, but not just any old twins. Gemini is a Northern constellation of stars, where the two brightest were named Castor and Pollux. Twins in both Greek and Roman mythology, they had a difficult start in life. You could say they had more than their fair share of challenges especially in the earlier years. Well, the word 'twin' translates into Italian as *Gemello*." Wilson wanted to interrupt but something told her to wait.

"You know, we Sicilians like to do things, em, how can I say, differently. This also applies to language. We have our own version of Italian. In fact, people say we don't speak Italian at all. Our language has gone off on its own direction with many words originating from the same Latin origin as Italian. However, the words then took their own etymological path depending on who was invading us at the time. Probably why we are so defensive and quick to fight because we have been attacked so often over the centuries. It's now in our blood."

"Please, Marco, continue." She was impressed at him inserting a six-syllable word into a conversation in a foreign language; but she would have preferred the discussion on a different day. The Spanish Steps were a minute away; she was relying on the police cars and ambulances to be gone.

"Well, the Sicilian word for twin is slightly different. It's *Gemellu.* If you use it colloquially, it sounds like..."

"*G'mlu!*" Wilson answered, remembering Nonna's last words before Marciano senior closed her down. "Your grandmother called Cardinal Damascus by that name."

"Yes, I thought you might find that interesting, Maggie. Damascus is *G'mlu.*" Marco paused for a moment, took another swig of wine and said, "I need to tell you a story."

1943

An English Soldier Abroad

She said a quiet prayer, thanking God for sending the American soldier. The child would live a full life somewhere free of war's horror. The mother's brow was feeling cold to the touch, the sweat drying on her forehead. It could only be minutes now before she passed.

The sound startled her. The scream was like a last-ditch wail for salvation. It came from deep inside the woman. For a child she was destined never to see. The mother had started to take painful breaths, rasping with the ache she felt rising inside her. Somehow she found the energy to move herself into a position to allow her to push. The neighbour leaned back to get a better look. At first, she was unsure, but after another shriek it became clear. The tip of a head announced the coming of another baby.

"*Spingere! Spingere!*" The neighbour shouted for the mother to push.

The mother let out one last, desperate scream, pushing with all her might, as if she knew it was the baby's last chance. It took just a moment, the mother had breathed her last as the boy fell into the neighbour's arms, crying and screaming, little arms and legs clawing the air. She cut the umbilical cord and lifted the baby to place him on the mother's breast. However, she was gone. Her dying act was to give life.

She placed a towel over the mother's face and said a prayer for her soul. A superfluous act, only because it was customary and appropriate - this woman was already in heaven, the neighbour was sure.

She managed to give the baby some warmed milk that she had left over after giving a bottle to the American soldier, for the first child. She wrapped the new-born in a large thick blanket, covering his head and limbs and walked out into the noise of war.

A soldier walked towards her, a battered rifle dangling lazily in his hand, his helmet pushed back. He seemed oblivious to the clamour and chaos of the war raging around him. Bodies lying in the street, buildings on fire, bombs landing indiscriminately.

"What's going on here then?" He spoke in an English accent, the hint of a smile on his face.

"Please, kind man. Take the baby. Save his life." She fell to her knees and held the baby towards him.

He stopped and looked at them both. A flight was scheduled to take him back to London in the morning. He was on the front line in Italy because he knew the language and understood the terrain from many years of childhood holidays. He was being relieved, more than ready to return. For a few packets of cigarettes and a bottle of Italian red wine, he knew he could convince the pilot to turn a blind eye. He had made a life out of finding opportunity where others saw problems. He reached out his hands to take the baby.

"Come on. We are all going together."

(Back to……)
Tuesday, April 19
2005

Damascocles

Cardinal Damascus sat in the corner of the room, his head in his hands. "What have I done? Oh, God, forgive me for being so bold and selfish."

Kiltman and Roddy studied the monitor, playing around with options and settings. If they could understand its range of powers, they would be better placed to see its potential. The mini test on Cardinal Damascus demonstrated the linkage between *Damascocles* and the Galatians medals. Somehow it was able to generate a physiological emotion from a physical charge on the medal-wearer's thumb.

"I think I know what's going on," Roddy said. "I just can't explain how."

"Go ahead." Kiltman leant his shoulder against the wall. Angie was sitting beside the Cardinal rubbing his back, holding the remaining squares of Dairy Milk for when he was ready.

"I studied this in Physics last year. It kind of goes like this." Roddy sat back in his chair, placing his notepad on the desk. He presented his thumb to the others. "It's all about the evolution of the thumb's nerve endings, their ability to carry out intricate neural tasks. When we touch something, the brain is traditionally where we assess the geometric dimensions of whatever it is we want to handle. Over millions of years, the brain has got busier and busier coping with all our growing needs as we evolve. It has started to delegate tasks to other parts of the body, to free up space in the brain."

He spread his fingers wide, turning his hands back and forth.

"Take our hands. There are thousands of nerve endings in our fingers already doing some of the tasks the brain used to do in our evolutionary past. They are now interpreting the dimensions of objects and transmitting the details via the spinal cord, allowing the brain to focus on the task of reacting to the item being touched. Scientists are saying that if mobile telephony continues at the pace it's going, thumbs will become one of the body's most important appendages."

"Okay, so far so good." Kiltman had always loved the sciences, much of what Roddy said resonated with his own understanding. On this occasion, he was not going to interrupt. He enjoyed watching his son in action.

"Let's see then." Kiltman walked towards the Cardinal. He had already taken his medal off, holding it out for him. Kiltman turned it over in his hand. There was no seam. It had been moulded in one piece from an alloy mix of steel and chromium. They could spend all day trying to open it, but short of a press brake machine, they would not be successful.

He closed his eyes and concentrated on its contents, his fingers rubbing the sides slowly. Roddy had turned the Very Strong signal to Off. Kiltman was not ready for any aggressive mood swings.

After a couple of minutes, he could envisage inside the metal, a cylindrical object, no bigger than a hearing aid battery. He forced his sense of touch to reach down to its centre. There it was. A myriad of tiny electrodes linked to a chip with its own processing unit, packed with programs tailored to deliver the signals received from *Damascocles*. Like an infantry soldier on a battlefront, waiting for orders.

"You're right. This little thing has all the circuitry and programming needed to redirect *Damascocles'* bidding into the owner's thumb. If you think about it, it's a group hypnosis machine. One day its owners are being instructed to love Cardinal Damascus, the next to wreak havoc and murder."

"Why?" Angie asked. "Cardinal Damascus, why would you create medals like this to control your followers?"

The Cardinal spoke quietly. "Good Lord! I would never create something like this. It's horrible, something the devil would do. I want people to believe in my message, St. Paul's message. Yes, I created the idea of the medal as a physical symbol to remind people of his letter to the Galatians. It would never have crossed my mind to manipulate anyone, least of all using some sort of futuristic technology. It's absurd."

Kiltman stood in front of him, his arms folded. "Well, someone meddled with your medal. We know Mask. But who is this other man, Tantalus?"

"I don't know!" The Cardinal looked perplexed. "Tantalus is a strange person. Physically commanding with his long hair and beard, yet something familiar about his eyes. He would come to see me in the basement and taunt me. He would tell me he was the brother I never had. None of it made sense. Then he disappeared. I've not seen him since Sunday."

"Okay, let's back up. When were you kidnapped?" There were so many gaps to fill in, Kiltman was struggling to piece it all together.

"It was Sunday morning. I had been invited to say mass at a small church in La Storta on the outskirts of the city, a few kilometres further north of Tomba di Nerone. A three-hundred-year-old church, it's built on the site where St. Ignatius of Loyola received a vision to dedicate his life to God. It's special to me because I too made my decision to give my life to the priesthood there when I was a seminarian in Rome." He sighed, realising just how long ago that was, at a time when life was much simpler.

"I never got the chance to say mass. When I exited the taxi, I was attacked. Someone knocked me out with a sort of chloroform. I didn't see who it was. Before I passed out, I heard voices. One was Mask. The other British."

"Tantalus?" Roddy asked.

"No, not him. He has a posh, English accent. It was a Scottish accent, I think."

"Who knew you were going to La Storta that morning?" Kiltman asked.

"I told no-one. The only person who was aware was the parish priest; we had texted each other the day before. I am good friends with him. He is completely trustworthy."

Kiltman looked at Roddy. You did not need Hair o' the Dog to track someone's phone messages these days.

"Are you sure the accent was Scottish?" Roddy asked.

"No, not one hundred percent. I just remember it being hard to follow what he was saying."

Roddy smiled. The Cardinal still had a sense of humour.

"This isn't the biggest mystery." The Cardinal used the wall to walk the length of the small room. "Why did no-one miss me at my residence on *Piazza della Pilotta*? Or even now at the Conclave?"

Kiltman's phone buzzed.

"Hello, Maggie? Everything okay?"

"Kiltman, we're just pulling up now at the Steps. Polizia have gone."

"We?"

"Tommy's with me."

"Okay, we'll come and get you. Listen, we've found their hideaway. They had kidnapped Cardinal Damascus."

Wilson reacted with a sharp intake of breath. In her mind, she could feel a cascade of pennies dropping.

Coffee Prep

He had studied the process of coffee distribution among the Cardinals. The water was boiled in the kitchen in a large vat, before being dispensed into flasks and mixed with coffee. Once the flasks were full, the waiter wheeled them into the Chapel on a small trolley.

It was one hour until coffee would be served – the vat would be filled within the next half hour. It would not take long for the bacteria to attack their intestines. The result would not be pretty, but that was irrelevant.

Earlier that day he had noticed a waiter lean forward to pour a coffee. His nametag identified him as Pepe. The innocuous act of filling a cup was enough for him to see the waiter as his opportunity. Pepe's Galatians' medal dropped out from his shirt. He pushed it back inside; afraid he would be accused of partisan feelings towards a particular Cardinal. It seemed to go unnoticed by the other Cardinals, or at least was not considered worthy of comment.

Pepe was now busy clearing up cups and saucers dotted throughout the Chapel. Soon he would be wheeling a trolley back into the kitchen to fill the dishwasher. That would be the moment for him to accompany Pepe, in the spirit of recognising the waiter's Galatians loyalty.

Puzzle Solving

Roddy walked out onto the *Piazza di Spagna* into dazzling sunlight. It felt as though they had been underground for most of the afternoon, yet it had been less than an hour. Long enough to turn the machine off and deactivate its signalling. It now lay redundant under the Steps, although just how much damage it had caused was still uncertain.

He waved at Maggie and Tommy standing near the fountain. She would have suggested they sit on the wall, but memories of Mask's body were too fresh.

"Wee man, long time no see!" Tommy hugged Roddy, rubbing his thick red hair. "Been too long! What are you and Kiltman up to?"

Roddy looked at Wilson. "We can explain it when we get inside." Roddy held the door open to a clothing retail shop, with a large red sign on the window: closed for *'ristrutturazione'*.

"Do you think we can find a cloak and dagger in here?" Tommy whispered as he followed Wilson in. She made a mental note to check the whereabouts of the owners. Mask would have eliminated any loose ends, just like Martim in Brazil.

Kiltman had already checked for booby traps and trip wires. There were none. Roddy locked the door and pointed towards a gate at the back of the shop. It opened onto a wide staircase leading down into the basement. Wilson noted the fresh scratch marks along the wall and ramp on the steps.

Kiltman was waiting at the bottom of the stairs with Angie and Cardinal Damascus.

"Hi, Angie!" Tommy said with a wink and a thumbs up. Before bowing towards Cardinal Damascus as if just noticing him. "Oh, hello, your honour."

Kiltman laughed. "I think you've spent too much time in court over the years, pal. After embracing Tommy like someone who is pretending-not-to-be-a-friend-but-is-still-pleased-to-see-him-because-of-prior-adventures, Kiltman turned to the Cardinal. "Actually, what should we call you?"

"Grateful! Hugely grateful." The Cardinal smiled. "Although now I am very worried about what they have planned to do next."

Wilson stepped forward. "It's a pleasure to meet you, despite the circumstances, Your Eminence. I am Maggie Wilson, from the Glasgow police force." She shook the Cardinal's hand.

"Your reputation precedes you, my dear. No need to introduce yourself." The Cardinal nodded encouragement for her to continue.

"I'll get straight to it then. I think I have the missing piece of the puzzle." She looked at the Cardinal. "Did you know that you have a brother?"

"No, Maggie, I'm sorry, that's incorrect." The Cardinal shook his head. "My parents adopted me after my adoptive father took me to America as a baby. I checked the local parish records years later; my mother had no children when I was born. She died in childbirth with me." He blessed himself slowly.

"Well, that's what your dad probably thought." She waited a moment for the Cardinal to focus on what she was saying. "You're actually a twin."

The Cardinal sighed. "Please, let's not make this situation any more bizarre. I cannot…"

"No, you are. After you were taken away by your adoptive father, your mother delivered a twin brother, just before she died. An English soldier took pity on the baby and the midwife and smuggled them back to England. She became the nanny who helped rear the infant. She's the mother of Mucky Marciano who leads the Sicilian mafia family. Her grandson explained it all to me."

"That's impossible!" The Cardinal rubbed his grey hair. "Why would I not have met this brother? We were painstaking in following up with local records in Italy, nobody mentioned it."

"That's because they left immediately after he was born."

The Cardinal let the knowledge sink in for a moment. "Okay, even if that's true, what's it got to do with what's happening here in Rome?"

"It's Tantalus!" Angie spoke up. She had been silent since Tommy and Wilson arrived.

"Sorry?" Cardinal Damascus asked.

She put her hand on the Cardinal's arm. "He didn't look like you because his hair and beard covered most of his face. It's the eyes. There's no mistaking those clear blue eyes; just like you."

The Cardinal sat down on the bottom step and looked at the ceiling. Maggie bent over him and stroked his back.

"That's it!" Kiltman clicked his fingers. "You're right. That's the missing piece. The reason why nobody has reported the Cardinal missing. Tantalus has shaved his hair off and gone to the Conclave. He's trying to influence the results of the ballot. With all the mind-bending medals around, this has been the plan all along. Tantalus is aiming to become Pope Damascus."

The Cardinal did not look up, he had already reached that conclusion. "We need to stop him." He spoke through shaky hands as he rubbed his face.

Kiltman nodded. "Yes, of course we do, but we can't go to the police, it would create mayhem. If Tantalus thinks he's cornered, he will react."

He looked at Maggie. "We need to get into the Vatican."

Affable Swagger

"I know how we can get in." Cardinal Damascus had a renewed sense of energy. Roddy could see a light in his eyes that had been missing in the darkness of the basement. "But it's not going to be easy."

Kiltman folded his arms and scratched his chin. "You can say that again, Cardinal. The security in the Vatican is going to be impossible to breach. It's impregnable at the best of times, but during a Conclave, it will be like Fort Knox." He paused for a moment and rubbed his chin before adding. "The American version; not the Presbyterian Scottish variety."

The Cardinal closed his eyes and grimaced in the same way Wilson had learned over the years; he rested his hand on Kiltman's shoulder. "Just get me to Castel Sant'Angelo and I will take it from there. Trust me."

"Who's going?" Wilson asked. "It's not safe for the Cardinal."

"My dear Maggie. It needs to be me. The world thinks I am at the Conclave already. My fellow Cardinals are making a decision we will all have to live with. Or die with. It's imperative I get in; we are losing time talking about it." He stopped and took her hand in his. "I finally have hope for the first time in days. You have given this to me. Thank you."

"Okay, let's split up. I'll go with the Cardinal." Kiltman put his hand in the air to stop Wilson before she articulated a protest. "You guys need to be ready to tell the Polizia and the media if it all goes Tantalus' way."

"Excuse me, guys." Tommy coughed a dry hack. "What the hell are you talking about?"

"If I may be so bold." The Cardinal approached him. "May I say that you have the affable swagger we need to make our plan successful."

Tommy's chest rose visibly. He had been called many things in his life, some good, some not so. If the Cardinal thought he was capable of *affable swagger*, then he would do whatever he could to prove him right.

Limoncello

Tommy, Kiltman and Cardinal Damascus sat in the cab outside Castel Sant' Angelo. It had taken half an hour to cut across Rome's *centro storico* on a lazy Tuesday afternoon. The Cardinal had shed his cassock and had squeezed into a pair of Tommy's jogging pants and *Terviseks* t-shirt. A baseball cap stretched across his short-cropped, grey hair was pulled down to just above his eyes.

They had discussed their plan on the way, huddled together in the back seat. Either they would be successful and gain entry to the castle; or get arrested. The outcomes were limited, confirming Kiltman's view that the best plans are always based on binary actions.

"Okay, let's go!" Kiltman said, reaching for the door handle.

"Just one moment." Cardinal Damascus placed a hand on each of them, touching their foreheads, and closed his eyes. "Dear Lord, please help us on our mission today. We approach this task placing our faith and trust in thee."

He looked at them.

"Oh, Amen!" said Tommy.

"Yes, me too," Kiltman added.

"Guys, when we are through with this mission, it might be worth us chatting about your faith."

They both nodded. With everything else going on, Kiltman was surprised at how uncomfortable he was beginning to feel. "Can we go now?"

The Cardinal sighed. One day, he thought, people would understand his sense of humour.

They exited the car and waved farewell to the driver. A citizen of Genoa, he had wanted to engage Kiltman in a conversation about Scottish footballers in Italy, whether Graeme Souness was a better player than Torino's Dennis Law. Kiltman was pleased to be able to sidestep the question, he did not want to disappoint the Sampdoria supporter.

Tommy walked a few steps ahead of them towards the entrance of the castle. He had taken a camera from his bag, snapping photos of anything from daisies to buildings, pointing and gesticulating. By the time he arrived at the entrance, four security guards approached him.

"Hello, guys!" He extended his hand to shake theirs. No-one responded, their faces inscrutable. "Aw, I just wanted to say hello. No harm in that, eh?"

Kiltman and the Cardinal strolled behind at a thirty-metre distance.

"Sir, you are not allowed in if you have been drinking alcohol." Tommy had picked up a bottle of limoncello at the airport. Half-finished, it was sticking out of his jacket pocket. It had pained him to pour half of this local Sicilian product down a street drain. He pulled it from his pocket and tugged the cork off. With a wipe of his sleeve, he offered it to the guards.

"Please, sir. You must leave. We have authority to arrest you if you create a disturbance." The tallest guard was taking the position of leader, the other three ready to pounce.

Tommy reached across and touched one of the guard's jackets. "Is that Gucci?"

The guard snatched his arm away. "I am warning you."

Kiltman looked at the Cardinal. They were thinking the same thing. Tommy's swagger was more laughable than affable.

"Aw, come on, big man. Can you not take a joke?" He stood closer to the guards and took a swig of limoncello. As he moved to put the cork back on the bottle, he tipped it to the side to spill a decent measure on the guard's jacket sleeve.

"*Merda!*" The guard shook his arm, splodges of yellow landing on the other guards' shoes. He reached across to grab Tommy, although the Scot was quicker than he expected. He stepped back nimbly, placing his weight on his back heel ready to move. The others moved to surround him. He noticed they all had gun holsters. Why had he not noticed that before?

Tommy threw the bottle high into the air above the guards' heads. This was Kiltman and the Cardinal's cue to approach the gate. They were still a few metres away behind a group of tourists who had stopped to enjoy the entertainment.

The bottle fell back towards the paved path. The guards had no time to step away. Tommy had not reattached the cork off before hoisting it, yellow globules of sticky limoncello dropping onto them as it spun towards the ground. The taller guard stepped forward and reached for the bottle, leaving space for the Scot to dodge through the gap.

Tommy had run for Scotland in national cross-country championships. Shin splints had forced him to give up at an early age, yet he still had a spurt of speed when he needed it. The guards chased him across the park towards the river, trying to gain on him as he sprinted past the holidaymakers and pilgrims on their way to the Vatican.

Kiltman and the Cardinal waited until the guards ran to head him off at the river before he made it across the bridge. As hoped, the gate was left unguarded.

"Okay, now follow me." Cardinal Damascus found a spring in his step. Kiltman followed him as he slipped through the entrance.

Unholy Water

"So, Pepe, how long have you worked here at the Vatican?" Tantalus had linked arms with the waiter as he pushed his trolley into the kitchen.

"Not long, Your Eminence. Just since last year." Pepe was starstruck. He had attended many events at the Vatican, catering for the Pope, Cardinals and foreign dignitaries. The last couple of days had bordered on overwhelming with over one hundred Cardinals to be taken care of. He felt humbled in their presence, unable to make eye contact. From a young age, his parents had instilled in him the importance of respecting the collar. Now he was walking arm in arm with the Cardinal he admired above all others.

"Just last year? Yet, you are so meticulous and careful in how you meet the needs of all of us. *Complimenti!*"

"*Grazie*, Cardinal Damascus!"

"Pepe. I would like to help you make the coffees for this afternoon. Would that be okay?"

"Oh, no, Your Eminence. You should not feel..."

"Nonsense, my son. You would be doing me a favour. Giving me an opportunity to fulfil scripture: ... *as we have opportunity, let us do good to all people, especially to those who belong to the family of believers.*"

"Galatians chapter six, verse ten," Pepe said without thinking.

"Yes, my son. This is my opportunity to help you, a true brother in our *family of believers.*"

Pepe bowed. "My honour, Your Eminence. Come this way."

He led Tantalus into the kitchen. There were several trolleys laden with cups and saucers, ready to be pushed out into the Chapel. Snug against the wall, a large steel vat bubbled with gallons of steaming water. Tantalus pointed at the vat and at the jugs containing coffee granules. "Why don't you take out the crockery and I will fill the pots?"

"Yes, Your Eminence. Be careful, the vat is very hot." Pepe moved to take the first trolley out to the Cardinals. Today was a day he would never forget. To spend time with such a humble and caring man, who would change the face of the Church. He pushed the trolley out smiling back at the Cardinal, who had taken the lid from the vat and was peering inside. Strange, Pepe thought, maybe he was not used to making coffee.

When Pepe exited the kitchen into the corridor Tantalus poured the contents of the vial into the boiling water, smiling as he did so. Normally the heat would kill the bacteria; however, he had this poison developed in a Russian laboratory years earlier for use in any situation. He studied the container to make sure a couple of drops remained. For emergencies.

"A little yeast works through the whole batch of dough," he said aloud. "Galatians chapter five, verse nine." He laughed, thinking that St. Paul's letter really did have a quote for every occasion.

Waiting

Wilson leant against one of the many large Doric columns flanking St. Peter's Square. She had chosen to wait between the colonnades, underneath the window where the Pope appeared every week to give an address to the pilgrims in the square. It afforded a good view of the entrance to the basilica, with *Via Porta Angelica* to her back. Angie and Roddy were a couple of columns to her right, waiting for Reilly to arrive. Angie had texted him that she was safe and well. He insisted they meet. Wilson did not think it a good idea, but Angie had pleaded with her. Considering everything she had been through, it had been impossible to decline. Underneath the Pope's window seemed a fitting place to gather while allowing her to be close to Kiltman and the Cardinal on the other side of the Vatican walls. *Porta Angelica* had an entrance leading to the Sistine Chapel, that might come in handy.

Phone in hand, she was ready for his call. She knew their plan was as solid as a *shoogily* nail on a splintered, wooden door, but it was all they had. Time was not their friend.

"Hey, Angie!" Reilly was running through the colonnades towards them. She opened her arms, tears dripping down her cheeks. He pulled her into a snuggly hug. "It's so good to see you, Angie!" he sighed as he rested his head on her shoulder.

"You too, Reilly. I can't believe I'm free." She gently levered herself away from the hug. She had been enjoying it until she became aware of Roddy standing beside her.

"Wee man!" Reilly high-fived his outstretched hand. "How on earth did you manage to find Angie?"

"It's a long story, trust me. We can explain it all later." Roddy pointed. "Look, there's Coach Stone and Mr. MacDonald."

"Hi, Angie. Good to see you." Coach Stone hugged her awkwardly; he rarely hugged the players. "You had us all really concerned."

Reilly's father squeezed her shoulder. "Reilly has been super worried about you, you know."

"I know. I missed Reilly too." Her cheeks flushed.

"Hi, everyone." Wilson had watched the reunion. Were it not for Tantalus running free inside the Vatican, she would have taken pleasure in the moment. Mr. MacDonald gestured hello with a raised hand. Coach Stone had his medal in hand, holding it aloft.

He bent his head and closed his eyes. "Thank you, Lord, for returning Angie, safe and well." He kissed the medal and turned to the others. "We should say a group prayer."

"Eh, no, that's okay, thanks." Angie snatched a look at Roddy. This new evangelised version of the Coach was going to take some getting used to. "We can all say our own prayers, if that's okay."

"Ah, you're right, Angie. *Those who have faith are children of Abraham.*" He looked at each of them, before announcing. "Chapter three, verse seven."

Angie studied her shoes. This was quite bizarre.

"Thanks, Coach. What should we do now then?" Reilly asked.

Wilson spoke. "I want to stay here and see how the next ballot goes. It'll be announced soon, I think. If you guys want to go for a bite to eat somewhere, I can come meet you later." Such a large group hampered whatever surprises she needed to manage.

She looked at Roddy. He knew her well enough to take the cue. "Good idea. There's a restaurant near here on *Via Giovanni Vitelleschi*. My dad told me about it; called *Tirolese*. Apparently does an amazing plate of *fettuccine ai quattro formaggi*."

Il Passetto di Borgo

Il Passetto di Borgo, a kilometre long passage leading from Castel Sant'Angelo into the Vatican, was a Middle Ages legacy, a means of escape for Popes who found themselves under attack. Over the years at least two of them fled capture by running through the long corridor embedded high up a thick wall that seemed to camouflage itself against the strong, square buildings surrounding the Borgo area of Rome, running along the Vatican perimeter.

With Tommy's escapades proving successful outside the Castle, Cardinal Damascus navigated towards the *Passetto* entrance, normally guarded by one of the men chasing the Scot towards the Tiber. He punched a code into the small box on the wall. The door opened wide enough for them to push through.

The Cardinal noticed Kiltman's head at an angle. "I should explain, I guess. I have been on so many tours of Rome over the years, I have memorised all the various codes and entry processes. I am fortunate to have a photographic memory. Whether I want to, or not, I just notice things." He shrugged his shoulders and smiled. "Maybe I have a superpower like you."

Kiltman nodded. "Looks like it's coming in handy today. Let's go."

Damascus led the way, jogging along the corridor, which was in better condition than it should have been. With the Papal Conclave happening, tours of the Castle had been cancelled. There was an eery quietness to this part of Rome contrasting with the shouts and songs drifting through the windows from thousands of people crammed into St. Peter's Square on the other side of the colonnades.

Kiltman knew that Wilson was close, waiting in the colonnades below the *Passetto*. If he had time to concentrate, he would be able to pick up her scent. He smiled. She had told him once not to refer to her natural odour as a 'scent'; it made her feel like a border collie.

After a five-minute jog along the corridor, they reached a large door with a similar coding system. Kiltman was impressed at how well the Cardinal ran despite his age and recent kidnapping. The Cardinal typed in the numbers. Nothing happened. He tried again. No result.

"They've changed the code." The Cardinal closed his eyes and prayed.

Kiltman placed his hand on the electronic box and let his touch connect through to the other side where wires led to the locking mechanism. He moved his palm across the digits, his fingers stroking the sides. It took a few moments, the Cardinal's eyes still closed, until they heard a click. Kiltman pushed the door open to the sound of a squeaky hinge. It had not been opened in a long time.

"Ah, the power of prayer," the Cardinal said, oblivious to Kiltman's intervention.

"I'll go first." Kiltman slid through the space trying to minimise the door's creaks. A table with a warm cup of coffee and a half-eaten panini indicated the guard on duty would be back soon. Even the Swiss need to go to the bathroom, he mused. This was a bonus. Kiltman's belt had various tools of the trade, one of which was a stun gas. With a flick of his wrist, he had intended to spray the guard. It would have knocked him out for a couple of hours. Kiltman kept it in hand, as they crept along the corridor. Their guess that most of the guards would be centred around the Sistine chapel or around the external gates had proven true.

"This way," Damascus said.

After a few minutes of ducking below windows and weaving along corridors, they entered the sacristy. Late afternoon, with Mass celebrated in the morning already, the sacristans had done their work for the day. The following morning's robes hung from the hooks along the wall, similar to a football changing room, absent the numbers on the back.

"Okay, let's see what we can find inside."

The Cardinal gave Kiltman a self-conscious fist bump before stepping into the sacristy's spacious wardrobe, in search of spare cassocks and collars.

Tirolese

They had ordered five plates of the Tirolese's signature dish, *fettuccine ai quattro formaggi* – long thin pasta saturated with four creamy cheeses. Coach and Mr. MacDonald were enjoying litre glasses of Spatenbräu, with the teenagers sipping on a variety of San Pellegrino flavoured juices.

"Cheers, everyone. It's a relief to have us all back together again." Coach raised his glass and clinked the others' proffered cans and glasses. Angie and Roddy exchanged glances. They were far from feeling relieved.

"So, what happened, Angie? It would be good to hear why Reilly had to dash across the world to Rome and have us all changing our plans." Reilly's father looked at Angie, without hint of emotion.

"Easy, Dad. It's not Angie's fault." Reilly was not used to speaking up to his father.

"Maybe not, but I still want to know. So, tell us, Angie, why did we all have to turn our lives upside down this week?"

"Dad, you're not being fair." Reilly was going for broke. "Yes, I had to change my plans; you didn't. You are acting as if this has been a massive inconvenience for you. When you were in Rome already."

His father looked at him.

"I saw your tickets. You left them on the dresser in the hotel. You have been here since Friday. The only inconvenience was in coming to the airport and having to spend time with your son. That makes a change."

"Okay, Reilly, let's ease up a bit." Coach said. "This has been a stressful few days for all of us." He threw a lump of bread into his mouth before taking a gulp of beer. "I don't think it's appropriate for me to listen to this conversation. You guys have a lot to discuss. I'm going to head up to the square and see if the next ballot comes in with white smoke."

Plates laden with pasta arrived just as Coach stood up.

"Sorry," he said to the waiter. "Can you put mine in a takeaway box? And if you have a plastic knife and fork, that would be great."

The waiter's face worked hard to stay neutral despite the sacrilegious request. Coach did not notice, as he drained the Spatenbräu.

"Yes, sir." The waiter dropped the plates on the table and turned back to the kitchen with Coach's meal.

"Hmm, bit grumpy, if you ask me." Coach whispered before following him. As if an afterthought, he called back over his shoulder, "See you guys later."

"Reilly, I had my reasons for being here. I don't need to share them with the whole table. Now, I'm waiting for an answer to my question. Angie?"

Angie looked at Roddy, who shrugged. "If you must know, Mr. MacDonald, I was kidnapped by my father. He escaped from prison and brought me here."

"Why here?" Something about Mr. MacDonald's questions irked Roddy.

She looked at him. Roddy shook his head just enough for her to notice.

"I don't know, to be fair. Not long after we got here, he disappeared."

Reilly's father leant forward and placed his elbows on the table. "Young lady, there's something you're not telling me." He sat upright and studied the nails on his hand as if considering a manicure. "I too will not be having lunch with you three. Once you have decided to tell me the truth, I will happily hang out with you. Until then, why don't you discuss how to become more honest with the people who care."

He threw his napkin onto the table, before standing up and pushing his chair back. The screech on the floor attracted attention from the other diners. He seemed oblivious, grabbing his bag and walking out onto the busy street.

Roddy looked at his friend. "Reilly, please don't take this the wrong way. How well do you know your dad?"

Breaking into the Vatican

Cardinal Damascus smiled at Kiltman and winked. "You certainly look the part."

Kiltman glanced at himself in the mirror. There was still enough of a paunch, despite his Brazil forced diet, to fill out the midriff of the cassock. The Cardinal placed a scarlet zucchetto on Kiltman's head, taking pains to place it at the right angle.

It had been Damascus' idea for Kiltman to change into cardinal cassock and collar. Wandering around the Vatican in a cape, kilt and mask was never going to work. They had been lucky to get as far as they did. Before Kiltman took off his mask, he considered the implications of the Cardinal seeing his face. After a moment's consideration, he realised if he could not trust a Cardinal, then who could he trust?

Damascus did not comment when Kiltman removed his mask, he had other concerns. Like how to navigate through crowds of his fellow leaders in the Church. He knew that while the Cardinals were a small group, remaining discrete was not impossible. Pope John Paul II had created more Cardinals than previous Popes; many of them meeting for the first time at the Conclave. There were now over one hundred, some he knew, but the majority he had never met.

He placed his hand on Kiltman's arm. "From now on I will call you Cardinal Andrew, named after the patron saint of Scotland, a brave and noble country. In recognition of Tommy's bravery, your diocese, if anyone asks - and God forgive me in advance - is the country of Estonia. Most of the Cardinals will assume this is one of the new Cardinal positions. Just do as I do, until we have sight of Tantalus, then we follow the plan."

Damascus raised his hand in the air and nodded. Kiltman bowed his head when he saw the gesture, he was learning. When the blessing was complete, he asked, "Does that make me a Cardinal now?"

"Very funny, Kiltman. If one day they are handing out honorary Cardinal-ships, I'll put your name forward." They shook hands and turned to walk along the corridor into the Sistine Chapel.

They entered the centuries old chapel to see groups of Cardinals standing around in groups, heads nodding, arms gesticulating. There was a high degree of energy. It was 3.30 pm; the next ballot was about to take place. They knew they were very close to a decision.

Kiltman knew what he was looking for, a carbon copy of Damascus. They had to spot Tantalus, before he spotted his brother. He walked several metres behind Damascus, trying not to be distracted by the beauty and magnificence of the walls and ceiling. He remembered going to Rome on his stag with Tommy. When they had tried to enter the Sistine, the queue was several hours long; they opted to go for a cold beer instead.

Some of the other Cardinals nodded at Damascus as he passed. He was doing a decent job of appearing reflective and prayerful, his eyes scanning the room from left to right as he strolled through the group. He could hear the conversations, many wondering whether Ratzinger would achieve two thirds this time.

"Your Eminence!" A waiter stopped and bowed at Damascus. The Cardinal returned the gesture. "Thank you for helping with the coffee preparation. It is truly humbling, but I thought you were still in the kitchen."

"Oh?" Damascus looked over his shoulder at Kiltman. "Can you please show me where it is again?"

"Cardinal Damascus, are you okay? It was a few minutes ago. I expect you must be very tired." Pepe was feeling uncomfortable.

"Yes, I am quite tired." Damascus rubbed his eyes with the balls of his hands. "Please show me, if you don't mind."

Pepe nodded and turned to walk back to the kitchen, pushing an empty trolley. Damascus and Kiltman followed, trying to avoid eye contact with the other Cardinals.

As Pepe approached the kitchen, Damascus raised his hand and placed it on the waiter's shoulder. "That's fine. I know where I am now. Momentary confusion. What kind of Pope would I make? Ha! Can you please just give me some time in the kitchen alone?"

"Your Eminence, I need to distribute the coffees." Pepe knew how cranky some of them could become if they did not get their refreshment on time.

"I assure you; I won't be long." Damascus did not want this innocent waiter falling foul of Tantalus' madness.

"Okay. I'll wait out here." Pepe answered nervously.

Damascus walked into the spacious, open-planned kitchen, Kiltman at his back. At the far end they saw a Cardinal filling up coffee pots from a vat of boiling water. Kiltman closed the door behind them, pushing a chair underneath the handle.

Tantalus looked up when he heard the door close, holding a pot in hand. Damascus stopped and cried, "My Dear God in Heaven, this cannot be true." Even from a distance of ten metres, he could see the resemblance. Tantalus had shaved off his beard and trimmed his hair exposing his true features; they were identical twins.

"Well, well, this is a surprise." Tantalus placed the container on the counter. Kiltman could smell the poison; the clostridium botulinum bacteria were so strong, they made his nose smart. He had to close down his olfactory cilia to cope with the onslaught on his senses. He did not need them to smell the evil in the kitchen.

Twins

"Well, well! Of all the kitchen in all the towns in all the world, my twin brother walks into mine." Tantalus looked to be enjoying the moment, his face lit up into a broad grin. In only a few words, Kiltman saw the same magnetic charm Cardinal Damascus possessed. It was evident how Tantalus had pulled off this charade, to hoodwink the leaders of the Church.

Damascus struggled to hold back the tears. He could not believe the man he was looking at was the same person who had kept him imprisoned in squalor in a basement. The beard and hair were gone, but the eyes were unmistakeable.

"Look, can we please talk? This has gone far enough. It's not too late. We can leave here together and work this through. We have so much to share."

Throughout his life, he had missed having a sibling. It had been more than an only child loneliness. He always felt there should have been someone alongside him growing up, someone who could help balance the load of childhood, adolescence, vocational soul-searching and decision-making. When those moments came along, he would turn to seek out the person he thought should have existed. It had been a yearning beyond explicable. When Maggie Wilson had explained the missing jigsaw piece, it fell into place, purging him of his lifelong frustration that someone important in his life was missing.

"Aw, you're such a softy, Saul. That moment has slipped away, a long time ago, in the history of time and distance. Although that doesn't mean we can't embrace as long-lost brothers should." He stretched his arms wide, walking towards his twin. He spotted Kiltman leaning against the door. "Who is this gentleman taking up the rear? He seems a bit too young to be a Cardinal, and maybe even a tad more weather-beaten than one would expect."

"This is my friend. He has helped me to be here with you now." Damascus held his arms out. Kiltman did not like the look of this reunion.

"Ah, Saul. I can only imagine he is someone who wants to make a name for himself by getting involved in our family."

Kiltman decided not to respond, wrapping his fingers around the top of the chair.

Tantalus edged forward. "Come on, brother. Why don't you quote me one of your Galatians' lines? What about Galatians six, one: *Brothers and sisters, if someone is caught in a sin, you who live by the Spirit should restore that person gently.*"

Tantalus stepped forward close enough to touch his brother.

"Don't you see, it really is too late. I have set myself on a path that cannot be changed. Life is like that. Things happen and create irreversible destinies." Tantalus stopped and looked at Damascus then sighed. "If I had been born before you, I would have grown up in America. I would have been wearing this cassock as a Cardinal, not as a pretender to the position you have taken. My destiny was to grow up in a cold, heartless house in London.

"The midwife who delivered us was the only relief in the madness. Even she could not stay, leaving me to fend for myself. So, yes, I am resentful. Can you blame me? Watching you from afar becoming the new face of the Church, when I was confined to a life of frustration." He stood in front of Damascus, a look of sadness flitting across his features. "Please know that none of this is personal, aimed at you. I have my own plans based on my life and destiny."

Tantalus hesitated to close the gap. Saul stretched his arms wider. "Come, brother. Let's make this the day that changes our lives for ever."

What happened next seemed to flow in freeze-frame snapshots. Tantalus moved with the speed of a snake, but for Kiltman it played out as if in slow motion. He snatched at his twin's arm, pulling him towards him. The Cardinal seemed frozen with the shock of the savage attack. Tantalus extracted a long-bladed kitchen knife from under his cassock and thrust it at Damascus' chest. With more instinct than planning, Kiltman wheeled the chair round and launched it towards the twins.

Tantalus, focused on driving the knife into his brother's chest, did not see the chair in flight. It crashed against his forehead, bloodied splinters flying into the air. The leg of the chair hit

Damascus on the back of the head. Both twins fell to the ground, the knife bouncing off the marble floor beside them.

Kiltman walked towards their motionless bodies, wrapped in each other's arms like twins in a womb.

Turning Off

"Hello? Hello?"

"Hey, Valentina, what's up?" Wilson had cupped her hand around the mouthpiece to drown out the commotion and noise of the square. Still, she could hear the anxiety in Valentina's high-pitched syllables.

"It's Crawford."

"What's happened?" Wilson's voice hit a higher note than she intended.

"They've made a decision. This evening at seven o'clock they are going to turn his life support machine off. It has already been several days and there has been no change in his vitals. The decision is irreversible."

Wilson looked at her watch; 3.45 pm. The ventilator had been the only thing keeping Crawford alive. She had hoped he would find a way through. "That's terrible news. Can they at least delay it until later in the week, or tomorrow at least?"

Valentina began to cry, sputtering out a stream of unconscious thoughts. "I know I met him just a few times; but I really connected with him. Crawford has a huge soul, a genuine caring side. I know things were complicated because of what my uncle asked me to do. It never stopped me loving him. You need to understand that. I can't explain it; we are destined for each other." Her words disappeared into a litany of wails and sobs.

"Valentina, you must stop this. You did nothing wrong. Your loyalty to Crawford has been unflinching. Now you have to be strong. Are you sure they cannot postpone this?"

Valentina stifled a helpless sigh. "Yes, I'm sure. Can you come to the hospital and be here before they turn the machine off? I realise we don't know each other but it would mean a lot to his mum and dad. They are at his bedside, praying and holding his hands."

Wilson paused, pinching the top of her nose. Her own tears were streaming down her cheeks. "It's complicated."

"Mask is dead, Angie is free. What more do you have to do? You can't let him down. He was loyal to you." Valentina let the words hang in the air.

"I know. God, don't I know. I will do my best. It's just that I can't guarantee I'll make it. You have to trust me."

Valentina waited a few moments. "Maggie, something else is going on. The Mask issue is not over, is it?"

"Don't push me. Please don't." Wilson could not take any more of this. "I need to go. I'll try to call you when I have a better idea of what's happening." She rubbed her forehead with the back of her hand. "Give Crawford a hug from me."

She hung up and leaned her head against the Doric column. Standing less than twenty metres from where Crawford had been stabbed, she could not bring herself to look in that direction. Where a young man's life and dreams were brought to a halt by a maniac whose plans were still alive even when he was dead.

Mr. MacDonald

Reilly turned the can of *limonata* in his hand. "It's hard to explain." The restaurant had filled up since they arrived. There was a buzz of conversation, the next Pontiff the main topic. The waiters were rushing between tables picking up and setting down, as if energised by the busy ambiance of the restaurant.

"It's okay. You can speak to us." Angie reached out and touched his hand. Roddy nodded, encouraging him to speak..

"You ask 'how well do I know my dad'. The truth is, I don't." Reilly took a drink then wiped his mouth with the edge of his sleeve. "Dad has been absent for years. Ever since mum died, he has become more and more distant. Fact is, I'm used to him being away more than at home."

"How do you cope?" Roddy asked, realising the issues with his own father were irrelevant in comparison.

"Aw, you know. You get used to things. It's pretending everything is okay, that's the hardest part. Dad hates it if I hint at him being distant and not involved. Before I came on the football trip, it had got really bad. I threatened not to come home and run away in America. It worried him because he kept trying to talk me down. Of course, I would never have done it, really." He looked at Angie. "Having said that, I guess I ran away to Rome."

She smiled and rubbed the back of his hand.

"That's the thing. Dad was already here. I told you about the tickets. He had been here since Friday; before he knew I had redirected my flight to Rome. Why? Something is going on. It doesn't make sense."

Roddy looked at Angie. She shook her head slightly. The less said the better.

"Dads are funny," Roddy said. "Look at mine. He went back to Scotland already, leaving me here with his girlfriend and a man in a kilt to look after me."

"Not exactly the same, bud." Reilly smiled. "Although I see what you're trying to do."

"Reilly, what does your dad do? I mean, for income?" Angie asked.

"That's the thing. He always said he was a Computer Consultant and had to travel to different places to meet clients. He rarely told me where he was going or what he had been doing. It's like…" Reilly looked around the restaurant for inspiration, resting his eyes on a painting of the Austrian Alps. "…he is a blank canvas. There is a frame and a place ready to apply paint, while the colour is missing."

"What happened to your mum? You've never spoken about her." Roddy decided to go for broke.

"Mum died when I was five. I have vague memories of her, all of them beautiful." Reilly took another drink before holding the can clasped in both hands. "She went away for the weekend with Dad, apparently a business trip. There was a car crash. He survived although she died."

"I am so sorry, Reilly." Angie was now leaning her head on his shoulder, arms wrapped around his thick chest.

"Yeah, me too, pal. You've had it rough." Roddy considered resting his head on the other shoulder. Although stopped himself when he realised how weird the scene would look. "Does your father ever talk about it?"

"Whenever I bring it up, he gets angry. It's as if he blames himself. He won't talk about it."

Cardinal's In

"Damascus! Damascus!" Kiltman had to admit, slapping a Cardinal on the cheek was as close to a guilty pleasure as he could imagine. Not sure why, it appealed to his inner sense of rebellion. It seemed to do the trick, along with the ice he had placed on his wrists and neck.

"Oh, dear God. What happened?" Damascus woke with a splutter and cough, pushing himself up onto his elbows. He rubbed the back of his head. While there was no blood, his zucchetto struggled to cover the egg-shaped bump.

"I had to act quickly. Tantalus was going to kill you." Kiltman helped him up onto his feet and pointed at the knife.

"Yes, I remember now. Where is he?" The Cardinal looked around the kitchen. Kiltman walked over to a long breakfast trolley and lifted the edge of a tablecloth. Tantalus lay unconscious on top, hidden underneath several table coverings and tea towels, his hands and legs bound tight with wires Kiltman had cut from a kettle and toaster. While waiting for Damascus to regain consciousness, he had emptied the vat of tainted water and smashed its valves and temperature control, rendering it useless. The contents of the coffee pots had been poured down the sink, before he put them in the dishwasher, at maximum temperature. Wilson would have been both impressed and surprised at his adeptness in the Vatican kitchen.

He placed the towel back on top of Tantalus. "He's going to waken soon. I need to get him out of here. You should get out there and vote, they have called the ballot. If you're found missing, security will be triggered, and they'll close the place down completely. I've sorted the kitchen out as best I can to eliminate the poison." He clicked his fingers. "Oops, not forgetting this!" He bent down to pick up the knife and placed it in a drawer.

Damascus was nodding, still rubbing his head. "What are you going to do with him?"

"No idea, other than get him out of the Vatican. If we let security know about this, all hell will break loose here. We need to contain this as much as possible. Get him into Rome Polizia custody."

"How?"

"The way we came, I guess. I'll figure it out as I go."

They heard a knock at the door. Cardinal Damascus turned and ran towards it, to see Kiltman had replaced the chair with a broom handle, jammed under the handle. He could hear Kiltman push the trolley out of sight through the back door into the corridor. The Cardinal waited a moment before removing the broom.

The waiter edged his head around the entrance. "Hey, Pepe!" Damascus said, looking at the nametag. "How are you?"

"Okay, Your Eminence. Why did you block the door from the inside? Is there something wrong?"

"Oh, I just wanted to take a moment before the ballot." He heard the other kitchen door close, leading out to another corridor.

"What was that?" Pepe looked over Damascus' shoulder.

"I expect it's the dishwasher, the coffee pots are being cleaned."

Pepe walked towards the dishwasher. "But we haven't poured the coffees. Why are you washing them?" He turned back to the Cardinal. "Your Eminence, are you sure you're okay?"

"Never better, my good friend. I need to go out and vote now. Here's to the next Pope." Damascus hurried through the door leading to the Sistine Chapel.

Pepe heard one of the Cardinals shouting in the distance, "Ah, here he is now. Quick, Cardinal Damascus, you are the last to vote. You must hurry."

Pepe looked around the room; he prided himself on keeping it shipshape. The Cardinal had set him back half an hour. Even more concerning was the state of his kitchen. Why was his big trolley missing? And why was the leg of his break-time chair broken? He walked to the vat to fill it up again. Valves and temperature gauges lay smashed on the floor. He shook his head and said a silent prayer, wondering if he had been wise in placing his allegiance in a Cardinal who had such little respect for Vatican property.

Sister Maria

Kiltman pushed the rickety trolley along the corridor, clunking across the smooth marble floor. The Vatican was a warren of corridors, chapels and halls, peppered with rooms of varying sizes. His sense of direction was waning, he needed a top-up. With more luck than strong navigational prowess, he found himself outside the sacristy.

He settled the trolley against the wall and ran in to grab his costume from the wardrobe. Within a minute he had opened the sporran and taken a mouthful of Hair o' the Dog. Even after Roddy's contribution, it was nearly empty. Just enough for one more swig.

For the moment, he enjoyed the exhilaration from the gulp of amber, meteor-inspired whisky, feeling his senses fill like the fuel gauge in a car, bringing with it a warm sense of security. At the bottom of the wardrobe there was an *Esselunga* shopping bag. He stuffed his costume and sporran into it and pulled it over his shoulder.

Tantalus was still under the towels when he came back into the corridor, although one of them had fallen onto the ground. An elderly priest was walking towards them, rosary beads in hand. He stopped to pick up the towel and place it on the trolley.

"Your Eminence, you should be in the Chapel. All the Cardinals have voted, Cardinal Damascus was a bit later than expected. We are waiting for the results to be counted."

Kiltman put his finger to his lips and winked at him. "Yes, Father. I will be there. I just have a surprise in here for later."

"Ah, this is unusual. God Bless!" The priest shrugged, bowed and walked away. He had not made it to the end of the corridor when Tantalus let out a grunt and kicked the wall. The priest turned to look back. "Are you okay, Your Eminence?"

Kiltman rubbed his cassock around the tummy area. "Oh, yes! Just too much carbonara at lunch time." He turned and pushed the trolley away, not looking back at the priest. The cleric continued his walk and rosary, deciding to say an extra decade for the leadership of the church.

After another long corridor, he could see the entrance to the *Passetto di Borgo*. There were three Swiss Guards leaning against the wall, talking. They seemed energised, enjoying the pending decision to elect a new Pope, a new boss. They did not notice a *weather-beaten* Cardinal peeking around the wall, assessing his chances.

Kiltman considered how to explain why a Cardinal wanted to exit the Vatican through a forbidden passageway, pushing a trolley laden with a twitching object. No rational explanation sprang to mind. There was only one other option. He dug into the *Esselunga* bag and extracted his phone from the sporran. He spoke quietly. "Maggie?"

"Kiltman! What's going on?" Wilson walked between the columns, avoiding the incoming crowds hurrying to see what they hoped would be white smoke.

"Can you meet me on *Via Porta Angelica*, at the gate? In a couple of minutes?"

"Yes, I'm a minute away."

"Listen, bring a car."

"A car?"

"Yes, I have Tantalus with me, unconscious on a trolley, covered in tea towels. He could wake up any minute."

She wanted to say, "Where can I find a car in two minutes?" However, she knew Kiltman would have less of a clue than she had. He already had to navigate his way out of the Vatican, smuggling a carbon copy of Cardinal Damascus past the guards, with hordes of Galatians supporters on every corner. Finding a car did not seem like such a difficult task.

"Okay, see you there. Good luck!" She hung up and looked along *Via Porta Angelica* towards the gate. There was one car, an Alfa Romeo that had seen better days, parked near the colonnades with its hazards blinking. She ran across the road.

A young, fresh-faced nun looked up from the comic she was reading. "Oh!" she said as Wilson yanked the door open.

"Sister! I need your help." Wilson placed her hand on the nun's arm.

"What's wrong?" the nun asked in an American accent, pushing the comic under her seat.

"One of the Cardinals is ill, and we need to get him to hospital. He's coming out of the *Porta Angelica* gate in a second. Can you let me have your car to take him to the hospital?" Wilson was surprised at how easily she lied to a nun.

"Well, I don't know. I'm waiting for my Mother Superior to come back from the shops. She'll not be happy if I don't have a car." The nun had spent so many years being obedient, she struggled to deny Wilson her bold request.

She pulled out her Scottish police ID. "Sister, she will be even more unhappy if a Cardinal dies because she wanted a car to take her home."

The nun unclicked her seatbelt and stepped out. "I've just recognised you! Maggie Wilson! I was in New York when you stopped the UN disaster. Go with God! The convent address is in the glove compartment when you're finished. I am Sister Maria, if anyone asks."

Wilson did not enjoy the fame that came with preventing Mask from killing the UN representatives. However, if it gave her credibility in the sisterhood, then that was already a bonus. She thanked the nun again and jumped into the car, wheeling it round in a U-turn to arrive on the other side of the road across from the gate.

She kept the engine running, enjoying a momentary silence before the looming chaos erupted onto the streets.

Her phone buzzed. Roddy.

"Hey, pal, what's up?

"Maggie, we just spoke to Reilly. There's something going on with his father."

"What do you mean?" She watched the gate as she spoke. Swiss Guards walked backwards and forwards in their purple and orange striped costumes, and long sloping black berets, as if this was normal attire for a Tuesday. Their weapons added some degree of protection, although a long pointy spear at home in mediaeval museums did little to add authority to their appearance.

"His dad has been here since Friday." He let the words settle. "Plus, he's admitted to having been worried about his dad's coming and goings for years."

"What's that got to do with anything?" Wilson said, thinking that could apply to many of the fathers she knew.

"You weren't there when we found Cardinal Damascus. He said that he had been kidnapped by someone with a Scottish accent. He didn't see the face, but he was sure the accent was from Northern UK somewhere." Roddy's voice drifted into a quieter tone the longer he spoke. He began to realise how far-fetched it sounded when he relayed it aloud.

"Look, thanks for letting me know. I don't think we should get distracted just now. Where is Mr. MacDonald?"

"That's the thing, he left the restaurant. Coach Stone did too. The conversation went in the wrong direction."

"Stay in the restaurant and wait for them to come back. It'll be fine. I need to go."

She closed the phone. There was a clamour of activity on the other side of the gate. The Swiss Guards were shouting at each other, giving commands. They had lost their trademark cool, detached manner; rushing to open the gate while shouting at priests, nuns and pilgrims to stand aside.

Her phone beeped again. A text from Tommy, asking where to meet; he had shaken off the guards. She messaged back with the address for the Tirolese, to meet the teens there and await her call.

She inched the car forward towards the gate. Game on, at last.

Breaking out of the Vatican

Kiltman had reached the elevator on the first floor, sensing the energy in the Vatican build with the frenetic activity of clerics scurrying along corridors in all directions. Word had got out that a decision had been made. White smoke was about to billow out of the Sistine chimney. He could not have prayed for a more effective distraction. A Cardinal pushing a lumpy trolley along the corridor did not warrant attention.

The elevator doors opened, and he pushed the trolley inside. Tantalus had fallen back into unconsciousness; Kiltman was concerned it would be short-lived.

"Your Eminence!" A Swiss Guard standing at the back of the elevator bowed towards him. He studied the Cardinal pushing a long trolley,

"My good guard, how are you?"

"Fine, thank you. Why are you not in the Sistine Chapel? We have just heard white smoke is about to be released. God Bless our new *Papa*."

"Yes, God is Great." Kiltman uttered the words before realising he had mixed up his religions.

The guard looked at him with furrowed brow, before plucking up the courage to ask, "What are you doing with a trolley, Your Eminence?"

"Thank God, I met you. I need your help." Kiltman whispered. He pulled back the edge of the tablecloth.

"Oh! Cardinal Damascus! What happened to him?" The gash across his forehead had stopped bleeding, a pink scab starting to form.

"What's your name?" Kiltman spoke with the assertiveness that comes with a Cardinal's cassock.

"Petrus, Your Eminence." The guard looked shaken.

"Okay, listen carefully, Petrus. You are the rock the Church relies on at this time."

The biblical connotation was not lost on the guard.

"What do you want me to do?"

"Cardinal Damascus fell and cut his head badly. As you can see, he has lost consciousness, we need to get him to hospital."

"I understand. I will contact the emergency services immediately." Petrus reached for his phone inside his orange-blue striped uniform.

Kiltman placed his hand on Petrus' arm. "No!"

"Why not? He needs help."

"Petrus, if an ambulance comes to the Vatican gates for a Cardinal at the moment when white smoke appears, it will create all sorts of chaos and rumours, detracting from this glorious moment for the Church." He paused and focused on the Swiss Guard's eyes. "Cardinal Damascus would never want that to happen. Do you understand?"

"Yes, I do. How…"

"We have a car meeting us at *Porta Angelica* gate. As soon as the doors open, we have to get the Cardinal into the car."

On cue, the doors slid open. Petrus ran out first shouting at his fellow guards. It was clear he had the right degree of authority to stimulate the others into unquestioning action. A younger soldier ran to the gate and opened it. Kiltman pushed the trolley out into the fresh air and along the cobbled paving hoping Tantalus would not fall off. He saw Wilson in the car waving at him. People were running towards the square, singing and shouting, a growing sense of euphoria gripping the Borgo streets.

Petrus exited with Kiltman and opened the car door. Between them they managed to haul Tantalus onto the back seat. "Do you want me to come with you to the hospital?"

"No, thank you, Petrus. You have done enough. God bless you!"

Without thinking, Kiltman blessed the guard in the same way Damascus had blessed them earlier that day. Petrus dropped down onto one knee and crossed himself. Wilson placed her head against the steering wheel and realised that she had seen it all now.

Barrel of a Gun

Wilson steered the car around the corner onto *Via Giovanni Vitelleschi*, searching for a quiet spot to park up and talk next steps. They passed the Tirolese on the right, before pulling up in a quiet alley. She could hear Kiltman rustling in the back, replacing the cassock with his costume.

"Ah, that feels better. You know, Maggie, I might be the only person to go *true Scotsman* in a Cardinal cassock." She chose not to respond. He checked Tantalus' pulse; slow but not concerning.

There was a loud rap at the front passenger's window. Mr. MacDonald was leaning against the car. Wilson leant across to roll the window down, the old Alfa Romeo still manual in nearly every respect. "Hey, Mr. MacDonald, everything okay?"

"What's going on here?" He leaned forward bringing his head into the car, studying the situation. Tantalus was splayed across the back seat, Kiltman - as Kiltman - holding his wrist. She followed Mr. MacDonald's gaze to the backseat. When she turned back, she was confronted with the barrel of a pistol, pointed at her forehead. "Don't try anything silly. I am not in the mood for your nonsense." He opened the door and slid into the front seat.

"What on earth are you…?" Kiltman began.

"Don't ask any questions! I am in control here. Understand?"

Wilson nodded. Kiltman's mind was racing. There was nothing he could do with a gun pointed at Wilson.

Mr. MacDonald turned to look at the unconscious body in a crumpled, blood-stained cassock. "You two really have bitten off more than you can chew. It's now time to…"

The passenger door flew open and two thick, hairy arms reached in, grabbing Mr. MacDonald's jacket. He was yanked out onto the street, crashing onto the paving stones with a loud thump, the gun clattering along the pavement. Wilson and Kiltman clambered out of the car, to see Coach Stone pummelling Mr. MacDonald. He was unleashing a cascade of punches, concentrated on the head and stomach. Kiltman grabbed Coach, pinning his arms behind his back. "Easy, easy!"

"That reprobate was going to shoot you! Why? What the hell has got into him?" Coach took deep breaths, trying to calm down - although as Kiltman eased his grip, Coach took an opportunity to kick the comatose figure on the ground in the midriff, once more for good measure.

"Thanks, Coach. You may have just saved our lives," Wilson said.

Kiltman checked Mr. MacDonald; he was out cold, blood seeping from cuts on his cheek bones and nose.

Coach bent down and looked inside the car. "Cardinal Damascus! Oh my God! What happened?"

When he tried to enter the back door, Kiltman held him back. "Listen, Coach. That's not Cardinal Damascus. It's an impostor. It's a long story we can tell you at a later date. Right now, we need to figure out what to do with him."

"He is his double!" Coach had extracted his Galatians medal, holding it between thumb and forefinger. "Are you sure?"

As if on cue, Tantalus coughed, groaning as he stretched his arms and legs. They bent down to look inside the car to see his eyes open with effort. It took him a moment to focus until he saw the three of them peering in at him.

"Well, well, Tantalus! Looks like your little charade of taking over the Church and then the world has come to an abrupt stop." Kiltman enjoyed the moment when he nailed the criminal. Wilson had admonished him on a couple of occasions saying he made too much drama out of an already dramatic closing scene. It did not stop him adding a Colombo moment.

Tantalus looked back at them. His face broke into a broad smile. Far too congenial for the situation he was in. "Really, do you think so?" He pointed past Kiltman's head. Wilson and Kiltman turned to see Coach pointing the gun at them.

"Get in the car! Now!" Coach said. "Don't give me a reason to use this."

White Smoke

Tommy felt exhilarated. The security guards had chased him along the Tiber and across to the other side of the river into *centro storico*. There were moments when he thought they would catch him; their pace faster than he would have expected for a group of guards looking after a castle. He was surprised at how diligent they had been in their pursuit. Clearly, pouring limoncello onto a guard's uniform was an insult bad enough to warrant a madcap chase through central Rome.

It took a few hundred metres before his muscle memory kicked in and allowed him to ignore the pains in his shins. With a renewed burst of energy, he had lost the guards in a warren of narrow streets speckled with groups of tourists.

Now back on the Vatican side of the river, he walked through St. Peter's Square. He knew he was witnessing a moment in history, white smoke belching out of the chimney. He could not stop a growing sense of unease as to whether Kiltman and Cardinal Damascus were okay. He had been given the easy job. How they were going to escape the Vatican with Tantalus was beyond him.

"Hey, Tommy!" He looked up to see Grant on a shaky, improvised platform, surrounded by screaming, chanting crowds.

"Hi, Grant! Looks like you've got some news to tell now!" Tommy reached up and shook hands with Kenny's ex-university colleague.

"What are you doing here?" Grant's antenna was up. Even Tommy noticed the hint of journalistic hunger in the question.

"On holiday. Looks like I picked the right time to be in Rome." He was edging away from Grant, making it difficult for their conversation to progress with the growing background noise.

"Too right. They're going to announce who the new Pope is in an hour. Don't miss my bulletin." Grant switched back to looking into the camera lens, angling his profile to catch the sunlight bathing the square.

"Can't wait!" Tommy smiled and waved back. He turned his attention to a small map of the area he had pulled from his pocket. *Via Giovanni Vitelleschi* was less than a five-minute walk away, if he avoided the crowds by nipping down a couple of side streets. He could feel the hunger pangs growing in his stomach. He was ready to murder a plate of pasta.

After a few minutes of half-trotting, he stepped onto *Vitelleschi*, traffic bustling backwards and forwards, horns beeping, drivers shouting. Anywhere else it would have felt like bedlam, but in Rome, it was unremarkable. He began to walk towards the Tirolese, stepping past a bundle of clothing on the ground.

When it moved and grunted, he gave it a second look. After the second glance, he was in no doubt. A man, covered in torn clothing with blood dripping from his face, was lying in a foetal position holding his stomach.

"Hey, are you okay?" Tommy shouted, bending down to help him sit up. He pulled his water bottle from his backpack and handed it to the man, who took several gulps before pouring the remains of the bottle over his head.

"Thank you!" he said in a shaky voice. He rubbed the water into his hair and face, and shuffled up into a sitting position.

"Are you Scottish?" Tommy asked.

"Yes."

"What happened?"

"I was accosted by someone who has just kidnapped some people. They are in grave danger."

Tommy did not need to ask. His face drained of colour. "Kiltman and Wilson?" he said in a flat tone.

"Yes, do you know them?"

Tommy nodded. "You can say that. Who are you?"

The man leaned on Tommy's outstretched arm and pulled himself up into a standing position. "I am Donald MacDonald." He pulled a scuffed wallet from his pocket and opened it to show his ID card. "I am an agent with Interpol."

MacDonald's Whopper

"Dad!" Reilly sprang from the table and rushed to the restaurant door. Tommy was beginning to weaken under Mr. MacDonald's weight. It had only been a couple of hundred metres, but he had struggled to hold him upright, his legs giving way every few steps. Angie and Roddy joined Reilly and Tommy in helping him into a chair at their table. Angie dipped a napkin into a glass of water and dabbed at the cuts on his face. First look showed they were not deep, although still painful. He jerked back each time she touched him, then leant forward for more.

"Thanks, guys." He reached out to the water jug and took a hefty swig, most of it dribbling down his shirt.

Reilly's face was pale. He placed a hand on his father's arm. "What happened, Dad?"

"I found him at the side of the road." Tommy poured himself a glass of red and drank half its contents, before letting out a satisfied belch. "Somebody had given him a good going over."

"Hey, Tommy. Good to see you." Roddy looked at Reilly. "This is my dad's friend, Tommy MacGregor."

"The famous Tommy your dad talks about all the time?" Reilly asked.

"Yes, one and the same." Roddy smiled. Tommy winked at Reilly. One more member of his fan club was always welcome.

"Look, we don't have time," Mr. MacDonald interrupted. He turned to Reilly. "I'm sorry, son. I've not been honest with you." He exhaled slowly and pointed at a glass. Tommy did the honours, pouring a liberal portion of red wine.

"I am an Interpol agent." He put his hand up to stop Reilly's reaction. "It's true. I used to be undercover, until, well, until now." He took a sip from his glass. "I'm in Rome because our tech guys had seen some unusual data activity coming from around here. They are constantly monitoring the airwaves and found strange data signals - sometimes more like massive waves pummelling transmitters across the world, emanating from Rome.

"So, I was sent to have a look because I'm an expert in computer science and radio transmissions. They traced the recipients of the signals to these bizarre medals being worn by Cardinal Damascus' supporters. I asked Coach Stone about his medal, and he got quite upset with me. I sensed something was up, so followed him when he left at lunchtime. I always had an inkling about him not being quite what he seemed." He took a sip of his wine and placed the glass on the table in a shaky hand.

"Then, I stumbled upon DI Wilson and Kiltman in a car with a beaten-up Cardinal Damascus. I was sure they were up to no good. I was about to arrest them, when Coach Stone arrived."

He pointed at his face. "He did this to me. When I woke up, they had gone."

"Seriously, Mr. MacDonald, why would Coach hit you?" Roddy could not believe what he was hearing.

"I'm as surprised as you are, trust me." Mr MacDonald grimaced when Angie rubbed the cloth across a cut under his eye.

Roddy's mind was racing. He was struggling to accept the situation coming together in his mind. "Did you honestly think Maggie and Kiltman were criminals?" His father and Wilson were now in serious trouble because Reilly's father had jumped to conclusions.

He put his hands up. "I know, I know. It was just when I saw Cardinal Damascus beaten up in the back seat. I was stupid and impetuous. Not the first time." He looked at Reilly with a care in his eyes his son had not seen in years. "When we get back, I'll explain everything. I'll make it up to you, Reilly. I promise."

Mr. MacDonald turned to look at Roddy. "I know one thing for sure. You lot know more than you are letting on. Spill the beans. If we have any chance of rescuing Maggie and Kiltman, we all need to pull together." Roddy looked at Tommy, who nodded.

"Okay." Roddy cleared his throat. "I'll make this quick. Cardinal Damascus has a twin brother, called Tantalus, he didn't know about. As luck - bad luck - would have it, Tantalus went rogue and decided to kidnap his brother and replace him in the Conclave. He had already hijacked the Galatians medals, inserting chips into them that manipulated the behaviour of the holders."

MacDonald's eyebrows raised.

"I know, it sounds far-fetched. However, it makes sense if you think about it. We are using thumbs more and more; their connections with the brain are developing rapidly. Tantalus has developed a technology that leverages this and amplifies its impact. Effectively, he created a way of brain-washing the medal holders."

He looked around the table as he relayed his hypothesis; the more he explained it, the less believable it sounded.

"The end game was to get as many believers as possible pushing for Damascus to be Pope, which would influence the other Cardinals to vote for him. But the reality was that Tantalus was masquerading as his brother, Damascus. Pope John Paul II's death may have come too early, not allowing Tantalus enough time to execute his plan. He got Mask out of prison in Brazil to help, but it was probably too little too late." He looked at Angie, who had taken to studying her glass.

Mr. MacDonald rubbed his head. If he had not been briefed by Interpol tech department on the weird airwaves oscillating from Rome, he would have challenged Roddy's account. "Okay. We need to find them. This Tantalus guy is not going to wait around now. Wilson and Kiltman are hostages. They will be disposed of as soon as they are no longer useful to Tantalus' escape plan."

"I've got an idea." Roddy was not sure if this would work; he could think of no other option. "Tommy, can you dial Maggie? Mr. MacDonald, can you dial Coach? And I will call Kiltman."

"Why?" Mr. MacDonald asked. "I can't see this nutter allowing them to answer their phones."

"Just trust me. Does anyone have a map of Rome?"

Tommy reached into his pocket and pulled out his scruffy map of central Rome. He handed it to Roddy, deciding not to question his motives.

"Ok let's start dialling." Roddy hit his father's speed dial button, hiding the screen under the palm of his hand, lest anyone saw the name he was calling. He did not need them distracted by why Roddy called Kiltman *Daddy-ghoul*.

The map lay flat on the table, glasses and saltshakers placed on its edges to keep it in place. He placed his finger on their location in the Tirolese. MacDonald and Tommy had also dialled and pressed the phones against their ears, watching him. Roddy waited for the phone signals to be activated, nodding as he saw the air above their heads colour an orange hue with the electronic pulses. He let his mind track each of their signals watching them exit through the door.

He stood up and grabbed the map, knocking the glasses and condiments onto the floor. He followed the signals onto the street. The others walked behind him, unsure why they were doing so, but realised they should stay quiet and watch. Roddy walked along *Vitelleschi* looking up into the sky tracking the signals to a radio mast overlooking Vatican City. Sweat meandered down his forehead as his brain pushed itself to the limit. He could feel his consciousness reach outside his body to follow the signals. His mind was stretched to bursting point, like chewing gum attached to the underside of a shoe. He sat down on the bonnet of a parked car and looked back at the map. As the signals bounced off the mast, he could follow their trajectory above and beyond St. Peter's Basilica to a street on the other side of St. Peter's Square; less than a kilometre from the Tirolese.

Roddy was hunched over on the car bonnet staring at the ground, his legs felt like jelly. He was not sure if he could stand up without falling over. From the recesses of his recent memories, he recalled the American player, Brandon Scobie telling him: *"Don't be afraid to fail, be afraid not to try."*

He took a deep breath and looked up to see Reilly's hand extended towards him. "Come on, Roddy, you can do it!"

Angie, Tommy and Mr. MacDonald were looking at him as though he had two heads – on reflection, he realised, he had a version of that condition. He smiled at Reilly and accepted his hand to help him up. Holding the map out to them he said, "*Viale delle Mura Aurelie*, we need to run."

Last Call

"Is that not the cutest thing to happen today?" The inside of the car sounded like an ice cream van at the beach, an orchestra of clanky tunes and jingles reverberating around their heads. "Open the window!" Tantalus barked at Coach. "Turn them all off! The time for talking to loved ones is over."

Coach smiled at his phone; MacDonald no doubt wanting to give him an earful. It felt good that he was able to show his true colours. Acting as a loveable football coach for so long had started to turn him into a nice person. God forbid, he chuckled as he switched his phone off.

Kiltman and Wilson exchanged glances, taking their time.

"I said, turn them off!" Tantalus shouted from the back seat, his knife pressed against Kiltman's throat.

Not to be outdone in the art of intimidation, Coach pressed the pistol against Wilson's head. "I may have missed Roddy at the Trevi the other day, but at this distance, you are unmissable. Now do what Tantalus says."

"So, it was you! How could you do something like that, least of all to one of your players?" Wilson spat the words at Coach, her anger dominating her sense of safety.

"It was easy. The team and the competition were all part of our plan. Winning the cup was of no consequence to me. I'd heard from the Cincinnati police that Roddy had been able to identify information on the internet related to Mask's escape. Of course, we couldn't let a cocky computer geek like that foil our plans." He paused and tapped the gun against her head. "Turn the phone off."

"How can I? You told me to keep my hands on the steering wheel." Her eyes glared back at Coach.

He lifted his hand as if ready to whack her on the temple with the butt of the gun.

"Stop, Coach!" Tantalus said. "No point in dragging out the inevitable. The time for rough stuff is over. Check to see who is trying to call her, and then put a bullet in her head so we can move on. I want Kiltman to see this before I take pleasure in finishing him off too.”

Coach reached into Wilson’s bag and extracted her phone. “Who’s Tommy?”

She shook her head. He made to throw it at her head but chose to toss it on the floor instead. Kiltman noticed she did not flinch; he had never seen rage in her eyes like she focused on Coach. His mind was racing. He was looking at a man who had shot at his son; and now was intent on killing Maggie. If he moved to grab him, Coach would pull the trigger and Tantalus would slice Kiltman’s throat. If he did nothing, Coach would pull the trigger and Tantalus would slice Kiltman’s throat.

“Can we at least talk for a moment?” Kiltman asked.

“Nothing to talk about.” Tantalus picked a fleck of dust from his cassock and dropped it onto the floor.

“How do you guys know each other?”

“Oh that? Ha!” Tantalus laughed. “Will you tell them, or will I?” Coach shrugged.

“My dad, or should I say, adoptive dad, liked to pick up waifs and strays. Some people adopt dogs, he accumulated people. Some he kept; some he discarded. I was one of the ones he kept, Coach here was not so lucky. Or maybe he was. Depends on your threshold for pain, I guess. Dad got rid of him after a few years, handing him over to a Scottish family when he was leaving primary school in London.

“We kept in touch over the years without my father knowing. Coach’s football prowess allowed him to travel all around the country. We were able to get up to our escapades in lots of places. It’s hard to hit a moving target, they say.”

Tantalus tilted his head and looked at Coach. “Let’s be honest, you weren’t the most well-behaved of kids, were you?”

Coach exhaled a long slow sigh. “Life is what you make it. I made enough money trying to be a footballer. My coaching experience allowed us the perfect cover to find a way to connect with Damascus. The tournament in Cincinnati fell into our lap.” He laughed a dry, raspy cackle. “I even had to pretend I had a limp that was miraculously cured.”

Tantalus put his hand in the air. “Enough. We don’t need to tell them our life story. All you two need to know before you depart this earth, is that this Rome adventure is not our first outing; and certainly, will not be our last."

Tantalus' face switched from relaxed storyteller reminiscing about the past to a hardened, expressionless glare.

"Okay. Pull the trigger."

Sister Acts

Sister Maria had not always wanted to be a nun. Some would have said that growing up in an Irish-Catholic community in Boston, her vocation was inevitable. One day, she was living a carefree teenage existence, considering which college to attend after high school; the next, she was having her hair shorn and being fitted out for a nun's outfit.

In school, she was the student who spoke in class when the others had already realised their teacher was about to erupt. Her impetuosity was a growing distraction for her and anyone unfortunate enough to sit beside her. Her parents had met the teachers so often, they were on first name terms. They would meet at weekends for a coffee - sometimes something stronger - if Maria was frustrating them more than normal. She used to call them her MA group - *Maria Anonymous*; they had to accept she was part of their lives, but needed reassurance and empathy to manage the challenges that came with her.

One thing that had helped temper her behaviour was baseball. She was a great pitcher, hitter and catcher, an all-rounder. The US Eastern seaboard baseball circuit was excited about her strength, accuracy and work ethic; all the skills they needed for the women's game.

She was not the only one to be surprised when she applied for the convent; her teachers, parents and brother all asked her more than once, if she was sure about what she was doing. When she left home to join the sisterhood, she had not worried about the celibate life, or the vows of poverty and obedience. The biggest challenge of all was giving up her beloved sport of baseball.

It had been five years since she arrived in the Eternal City. There were many things to be thankful for: witnessing Pope John Paul II's last years, and then final days; enjoying the white smoke announcing a new Pope to be elected within the next hour or so; and passing her driving test in Italy, allowing her to be the convent driver. It had taken three attempts, countless rosaries, and a few euros - for the examiner's children's Christmas - for her to succeed in passing her driving test. Yes, God works in mysterious ways, she mused.

She looked at the back of her Mother Superior's head. They had barely spoken a word since she returned to where the car was supposed to be. The more Sister Maria tried to explain why she had to give the car to a Scottish police officer, the more ludicrous the novice nun appeared. Silence was the best option on their walk back to the convent at the top of Gianicolo, one of Rome's highest hills; while it did not make the magnificent seven, coming eighth was a reminder of the folly of pride. She reminded herself of this whenever she walked its length, as they were doing today.

Sister Maria had decided to walk a few steps behind Mother Superior, allowing the more senior nun to dictate the pace, while staying out of her line of vision. Her young arms were straining under the weight of three shopping bags full of Vatican bric-à-brac; umpteen sets of rosary beads, pictures of each member of the Holy Family at all stages of their lives, and the one that made her smile, a large snow globe. As she walked, and the globe jostled around in the bag, snow would fall over the Nativity scene depicted in the small, colourful characters and animals. She wondered if it ever snowed in Bethlehem.

"Sister Maria!"

"Yes, Mother Superior."

The older nun was pointing at a dark blue Alfa Romeo on the other side of the street. "Is that our car?"

Sister Maria took a moment to digest the situation. Yes, the most obvious thing was the car. However, her attention was drawn to what was going on inside, beyond the open window. Specifically the pistol pointed at DI Wilson's head.

Without thinking, and with her impetuosity - curtailed for so many years – rising to the fore, she found her hand reaching down into the bag for the snow globe, her fingers wrapping around its smooth, heavy frame in breaking ball grip.

Breaking Ball

Angie and Reilly chose to return to the Tirolese with Mr. MacDonald. He had tried to run but gave up when his legs buckled under him. He put his energy into calling the Polizia and directing them to *Viale delle Mura Aurelie*; Chief Commissioner Pisacane was on his direct dial. Reilly and Angie held Mr. MacDonald's hands; time was not their friend. They sat around the table not knowing what to talk about, an air of tension settling around them.

Tommy and Roddy were ducking and weaving between pilgrims along the edge of St. Peter's Square. The Basilica's bells were audible above the clamour and festivities breaking out around them, complementing the quieter, more subtle communication of billowing white smoke. It took a few minutes to cross the square and reach *Viale delle Mura Aurelie*. Mr. MacDonald had described the car, so they knew what they were looking for.

Roddy pointed. At first, he thought he was seeing things. After the intensity of following the phone signals, his head felt like mush. Tommy followed his outstretched, shaky hand. The young nun in white clothing, head covered, leant back in classic pitcher mode, left leg raised high, her right hand behind her head. In a flash, her arm lashed through the air, releasing a multi-coloured projectile.

Tommy and Roddy stopped in their tracks unsure as to what just happened. The colourful object streaked the ten or so metres to the car in a second, dipping just before its entry through the passenger window. The inside of the car flashed a momentary silhouette of its occupants before they heard the high-pitched crack of a pistol.

The back door of the car burst open; someone in cardinal's clothing stumbled out onto the street. Tommy looked at Roddy in panic, thinking it was Damascus.

"I think it's Tantalus," Roddy said with a reassuring pat on his back. "Let's hope Damascus is in the Vatican."

Tantalus scrambled to his feet, working hard to gain an upright position. He started to run towards the square. After a few steps, he stopped and brought his hand up to his face, blood dripping from his fingers onto the ground. The realisation that he had a hole in his chest registered on his face at the same time as he sank to his knees.

In a matter of seconds, this small corner of Rome became a hub of activity and attention. Three Polizia cars screeched to a halt on either side of the road. Kiltman and Wilson exited the car and ran to Tantalus. He had one hand on the pavement, holding himself upright, a pool of blood spreading around him underneath his cassock. Tommy and Roddy arrived to find the young nun kneeling beside Tantalus crying hysterically. Her Mother Superior had her arm around her shoulders, squeezing soothingly.

Wilson dropped down to her knees beside the nuns. "Sister Maria!"

Sister Maria was choking on her tears, her hands shaking. "Oh, no! What have I done! This is a Cardinal. Oh, God, forgive me!" She dropped her head into her hands, shoulders shuddering with grief.

"Sister!" Wilson took hold of her shoulders and shook her just enough to get her to look up, her face awash with tears. "That's not a Cardinal. He is a criminal who was pretending to be Cardinal Damascus. You have saved our lives! And God knows how many others. You did a great thing."

A few moments earlier, Wilson had been gripping her seat expecting a bullet in the brain. Only to be sprayed with water and members of the Holy Family nativity scene, as the snow globe smashed off Coach Stone's head, forcing him forward. The gun had hit her headrest, redirecting the nozzle towards Tantalus. As Coach fell unconscious, he squeezed the trigger.

Kiltman bent down to look at Tantalus. He could hear the Polizia running from their cars, shouting and screaming. It was difficult to concentrate, his ears still ringing from the gun blast, but he got the gist of their frantic calls to step away. Tantalus looked up; his face contorted into a twisted grin. Through a mouth full of blood, he managed to gargle the words, "*Habemus… mortem.*" He collapsed lifeless onto his blood glistening on the ground, as it seeped down through the cracks in the cobbles, sharing the same journey his soul was on.

One Last Thing to Do

"Can you turn the TV to BBC World News?" Kiltman asked the elderly barista as he sat down at the first seat inside the bar.

"*Si, certo!*" Gianni clicked the remote until he found the channel, turning the volume to max. He had seen many famous people over the years, foreign dignitaries and eminent leaders of the Church. This was the first time a Superhero had entered his bar. Gianni had to arrange the chairs around a Formica-covered table to allow them to sit together. His bar was just big enough for a small number of guests to sit comfortably. He was used to pouring coffees for people on the move from one tourist location to another, usually the Vatican. It was rare for people to want to huddle around a table in the confines of his small locale, Bar Speranza.

He placed coffees and soft drinks on their table watching them listen to the TV. Gianni was pleased to have been able to find BBC for them. An attractive lady, a curiously young-looking adult and a tired-looking teen had sat down at the table beside Kiltman. Normally, Papal elections carried an air of lightness and hope. This group seemed to be disenchanted, unsettled, going through the motions of watching the news.

"Well, it has finally happened." Grant's face was lit up by the late afternoon sun. "It's five minutes to five here in the Vatican, and it truly is a crackerjack moment. Cardinal Medina, the Church's Cardinal Protodeacon, has just spoken the words, *Habemus Papam*. We have a Pope. He has been announced as…"

Kiltman looked at Wilson. She had extracted her phone to see if there had been any more messages on Crawford. Nothing. She looked up at the screen.

"Grant! Are you waiting for a drum roll? Just say the name, for goodness' sake!" Dominic already knew who the new Pope was, and while he liked a degree of suspense in reporting, MacTavish was dragging out this announcement as though he were a game show host.

"...Cardinal Ratzinger, the German Cardinal. Yes, he has been the favourite since the start of the Conclave. So, it's not a surprise, to be honest. At the moment we don't know how close the others came, although it does mean that he had a two thirds majority. Cardinal Medina also informed us that he has chosen the name Benedict. That will make him the sixteenth Pope Benedict."

Grant pulled a notepad from his inside pocket and flipped it open. "Interesting to note, the original Saint Benedict from the sixth century is patron saint against poisoning. Apparently during his life several attempts were made to kill the saint with poison. Yes, you heard it here first!"

Kiltman grimaced at the irony.

"Not only that; Saint Benedict is also known for a very distinctive medal, that shows the wearer's trust in God's authority over evil."

Wilson looked at Kiltman. "Please, no!" she said, before shaking her head. "We've had enough medal mayhem to last a lifetime."

"It was Saint Benedict who had the medal hundreds of years ago, Maggie, not the new Pope. Relax!" Roddy smiled and touched her hand; he sensed the anguish she was trying hard to control.

They saw Grant touch his ear. "Nice one, MacTavish." Dominic was impressed with the correspondent's titbit of Saint trivia he had never heard before.

MacTavish looked down to his left and placed his hand over the microphone. He spoke a few words to someone off camera.

"What's going on?" Dominic shouted. "You've just lost us."

Grant turned back to face the camera, holding his hand out to help someone up. "Talking about medals, here is Cardinal Damascus to say a few words."

The Cardinal took the microphone, the camera closing in on his face. His eyes were filled with tears, yet his face relaxed and at peace.

"I wanted to take a moment to say a few words. First of all, to thank God for our new Pontiff and to wish Pope Benedict grace and wisdom in his appointment. This is a great day for the Church."

"Also, I must bow my head and ask for forgiveness. From all of you who believed in me and my words, and I ask God for his understanding too. I have led a campaign of change, using St. Paul's letter to the Galatians as my platform to encourage us to walk away from traditional constraints and embrace a new way, closer to Christ's original message and guidance.

"In my pursuit of this new path, I lost sight that we already have a strong Church based on the love and dedication of its members. I flew in the face of everything the Church has achieved over the centuries, acting as though I was some sort of modern-day St. Paul.

"I prioritised my way over the right way. I was focused on Revolution rather than Evolution. In the last few days, I have come to my senses. I have seen how my pride can create fresh soil for evil to take root and grow.

"Thanks to the help and support of some incredibly brave people, who have shown me what true caring and love for your neighbour means, I am now ready to change my ways."

Tommy looked up from his coffee and pastry, crumbs splattered across the table. "Is that us?"

Kiltman and Wilson exchanged glances before smiling at him. There was something endearing about Tommy's ability to always be ten seconds behind everyone else. They looked back at the TV.

"Over the days ahead, I will come back with a more structured and hopeful message, one that seeks to support the Church in being the organisation Christ will recognise when he comes back on the last day. For those of you who wear Galatians' medals, please dispose of them. We should not need a piece of metal around our necks to guide us." He opened his cassock to extract his medal. The force with which he broke its chain startled MacTavish. "If we have Christ's message in our hearts, we will not stray. Let's pray for a strong Church, one that grows to accept our differences and embraces the changes we desire. We need to see the Church as our home in times of refuge and our family in times of isolation. God Bless Pope Benedict!"

He turned to hand the microphone back to Grant. The reporter was distracted, his mobile phone at his ear, his finger in the other blocking the noise from the square. He nodded before turning to swap the phone for the return of the microphone. "This call is for you, Cardinal Damascus."

"What the hell are you doing, MacTavish? You took a call while on air?" Dominic Gallagher struggled to get the words out.

The Cardinal placed the phone at his ear. "Yes?" After a moment, he nodded and looked into the camera, his thumb in the air. "I will see you there."

Grant waited for Damascus to leave the podium. "Sometimes, when amazing events happen like the election of a new Pope, other phenomena occur that are inexplicable and just downright bizarre." He shrugged. "There is one thing we can say about Cardinal Damascus. He may not have been elected the Church's leader, but his ability to challenge the existing order of things means that others have to step up.

"This is Grant MacTavish signing off on the day a new Pope was elected."

The news bulletin closed, the camera panning back to take in the Basilica and thousands of people in the square. Kiltman looked at Wilson, hunched over the table, her phone held tight against her ear. She placed it back in her bag and wiped a tear away with the edge of her sleeve. "We need to go."

Families, eh?

Tommy remained in the bar with Roddy, finishing his third pastry. Their next task was to meet Angie, Reilly and Mr. MacDonald and make sure they were okay. They preferred this rather than going to the hospital to watch a man die.

Wilson and Kiltman were standing outside the bar trying to flag a taxi. It was proving difficult with burgeoning crowds growing around the Vatican, hordes of people coming to rejoice at having a new Pope. The celebrations were not limited to Cardinal Ratzinger supporters; everyone was enjoying the fact they had a new leader in the Church.

A car pulled up beside them. The driver stepped out and walked around to the back door. He opened it for them and beckoned them to step inside. Kiltman clambered in after Wilson.

"Tiber Island, please, driver. As fast as you can," he said as he buckled up.

"Kiltman!" Wilson whispered in his ear.

"What?" He was distracted with his belt which seemed to be knotted in the middle, not stretching as far as the buckle. He needed a swig of Hair o' the Dog.

"There are two people in the front!" Her whispers were getting louder.

He looked up to see a man sitting in the passenger seat. He wanted to say something then hesitated. Maybe the driver was taking his brother home or picking a friend up from a long lunch.

The man turned around to face them.

"Hello, Kiltman and Wilson."

The collective intake of breath was audible.

"Don't worry. We are not kidnapping you. I think there has been enough of that for a while."

The man extended his hand. "Let me introduce myself. I am Mauro Papetti."

Wilson tapped her knee against Kiltman's. "Well, well. I was wondering when the good-looking capo would turn up. Mauro

Papetti, more commonly known as *Zio*. Everybody's favourite uncle. Until they get on the wrong side of him."

Kiltman nodded. Darn, if he saw one more dark, hunky man, he would cry into his sporran for a week. It was just not fair.

"Hah!" Zio tapped the driver on the arm. "Very funny. Thank you for your compliments. I am not sure the driver will appreciate them as much as I."

"Really?" she asked.

"Yes. You see, our driver is Carlo Babila. Your police charts may have him nicknamed as *San*.

The fourth family capo, San, turned to look at them. He smiled as he tapped his flat cap with his forefinger. "Pleased to meet you. You've made quite the impression on Rome and Sicily this week."

Kiltman was pleased to see that he was less dark, less handsome and more downtown Glasgow in his gruff appearance.

"Look!" Wilson leant forward in her seat. "This is not the right time. We have to be at…"

"…the hospital," Zio said. "Yes, we are here to make sure you get there on time." He pointed through the windscreen. Two large, black people carriers were ten metres in front of them. As they sped along the road, they could see the vehicles bumping against other cars, edging them over to the side, creating a break in the traffic to let them through.

Kiltman and Wilson exchanged glances. After a few moments of watching their lead cars control the road, she said, "Why?"

"Finally!" San said from the driver's seat.

"Okay," Zio said. "We have watched the events unfold over the last few days. I have to say, at first, we thought you were in Sicily to challenge us. We now know that you Scots just want to do the right thing. You genuinely care and want to prevent *evils* turning *lives* inside out."

They waited as Zio took a long drag from his bottle of water. San nodded his respect at his fellow capo's clever use of English.

"In Sicily, we have been trying to do the right thing too. Don't get me wrong; we still like to do the wrong thing." He laughed. San extended his hand, and they slapped palms.

"Honestly, we are trying to get better. Hence why all four families got together to donate money to the homeless. It's our way of turning ourselves around. I know, it will take time. But we have to remember; the first steps are the most important.

"Sacco made a big mistake. He has paid the price." Zio drew his thumb along his neck. "Mask and Tantalus, people we did not know existed until today, paid the same price. Thanks to you." He bowed his head, a form of appreciation which felt awkward in the circumstances.

"There is this guy, Coach, however." He paused and looked at his nails. "In captivity, although not yet paid the price for his actions. We have time."

"Okay, thanks for the Sicilian perspective on the week's venture, but what do you want with us now?" Kiltman was sitting forward in his seat.

"Ah! You see, we need nothing from you. You have already given us so much. We are now in your debt. It does not happen often in our world. When it does, we honour our obligations. It's our duty to take you to the hospital to spend your last minutes with your brave, fallen colleague."

San screeched to a halt at the bridge outside the hospital.

Kiltman and Wilson unbuckled their belts, thanking San and Zio, who smiled in acknowledgment at their appreciation.

As they left the car, Zio shouted. "One last thing. Any friend of yours is a friend of ours. Your *amico*, Tommy, is also protected. Tell him, he will always be safe in Sicily."

The Last Rite

Kiltman followed Wilson into the hospital; she beckoned him to follow her down a corridor as she walked at a pace bordering on a jog. As he stepped in behind her, he narrowly avoided a woman in a wheelchair, being pushed by an orderly. Despite the bandage wrapped around her head, her face looked much younger than the last time he had seen her a couple of days earlier.

"Sister Robertina!"

She reached out and took his hand. "*Sank you!*"

She knew who he was, even though he was in his Kiltman costume. His hand on her arm was enough for her to feel the same compassion that had saved her life by getting her to the hospital in time for the lifesaving operation.

"Kiltman, come on!" Wilson had shouted the words before she turned to see him hugging an elderly lady. Something told her not to call again. He looked up. "Maggie, meet Sister Robertina, the nun I met outside Pasticceria Valentina."

Wilson shook the nun's hand, feeling a wave of goodness and love in the hard-worked fingers. Sister Robertina turned to the orderly and said something in Italian. The orderly, a fresh-faced young man not much older than Roddy, said, "Sister thanks you for saving her life. She also says that she senses you are both very worried. She is going to pray now for whatever is causing you concern; that God grants you the miracle you are looking for."

"*Grazie!*" Wilson and Kiltman said at the same time. Sister Robertina nodded and closed her eyes, before extracting her rosary beads. The orderly smiled and waved as she pushed the wheelchair along the corridor.

They had no time to discuss the chance meeting. Wilson started running, Kiltman in pursuit, drawing looks from patients and nurses. He hated these moments, when it looked like a man in a skirt was chasing a pretty woman. He wished he had time to stop and explain.

They arrived at Crawford's room in less than a minute. They entered to the haunting melody of Chris Martin singing Yellow:

"Look at the stars, look how they shine for you, And everything you do, Yeah, they were all yellow".

Wilson noticed a small CD player had been placed on top of a cupboard, with several CDs to the side, a mix of Coldplay and The Proclaimers. She thought of Crawford sitting in the office, with his formidable glasses and combed back hair. She had joked with him that he may have been the Proclaimers' triplet who got away.

The clock - showing 6.45 pm - on the wall above his bed ticked the seconds away until life support was to be switched off in quarter of an hour. The ventilator churned out its mechanical breaths to a backdrop of his parents resting their heads on the bed, weeping quietly.

Valentina rose from her chair when they entered the room. She hugged Wilson like a long-lost family member. They held each other for a moment before they turned to focus on Crawford. Wilson walked towards the bed working hard to control her rising sorrow; she had to be strong. With Tantalus and Mask dead, and their accomplice Coach in custody, she should have let the pain and grief break through. She could not allow herself this moment. Not now. She could not remember a journey harder than the walk to his bed. His parents stood up and stepped back towards the door allowing her through. At his bedside she whispered her thanks for his indomitable spirit and character; and begged his forgiveness for leading him into such danger.

Kiltman watched her bend down and take his head in her hands. The plastic mask with extended hose created a surreal image she did not want to remember; she took a few moments to stroke his cheek with her fingers. His parents, Valentina and Kiltman looked away at this intimate farewell.

After a few moments, Kiltman whispered to the parents. "I'm very sorry for your troubles. Do you mind if I say goodbye?"

"No, of course not," his mother spoke in voice laden with grief. "He always admired you, Kiltman. He would have been proud to know that you were here."

He walked down the other side of the bed from where Wilson had been. She sidled along to the back of the room to stand beside Valentina. They wrapped arms around each other and watched Kiltman hug the peaceful body. They watched him take hold of the edge of his cape and drape it over Crawford. It reminded Valentina of her family custom of placing a large, black cloth over the entrance of the deceased's house. After a minute, he rose and rearranged his cape around his back. This was one of those moments when a mask was not helpful, the inside awash with salty, sticky tears.

The door opened again. All eyes turned to see Cardinal Damascus in the entrance, the gloom of the room emphasizing the dark rings under his eyes. Wilson walked to him. "Thank you, Cardinal. This means a lot."

"Ah, Maggie. This poor man, caught in the middle of evil criminals and their wicked acts." He turned to Crawford's parents. "I am so sorry for what has happened to your son." He held their hands wishing he could explain to them just why he was so sorry. "May I pray with you?"

"Of course, Cardinal. It would be an honour." Crawford's mother said, beckoning him forward. She looked at her husband, overwhelmed at the arrival of a Church leader.

The Cardinal knelt at the bedside, the cue for the others to do the same, creating a horseshoe of sadness around the bed. The long hand of the clock above their heads touched 12. On cue, a doctor and nurse arrived in the room. This was not the first such scene they had witnessed. Nor would it be the last. They approached the ventilator respectful of the sadness in the room. It took just a minute to check Crawford's vitals – no change – before they turned the machine off and removed his mask. The absence of the mechanical breaths that had dominated the room created a crushing sense of emptiness.

"Dear God," Cardinal Damascus interrupted the silence, "please take pity on this man, Crawford. He is being taken from his family and friends at far too young an age. We know that you work in mysterious ways, and many times we struggle to cope with the reasons why life takes the turns it does. Today, Lord, in this moment of sadness and despair, please shine your compassion on this man."

The silence was profound, interrupted by tears and sniffles, shoulders shaking, heads bowed. The despair reminded Cardinal Damascus of Michelangelo's Last Judgement, so many people in such a small space begging for God to hear their prayers. He felt a wave of guilt at the unwitting role he had played in this man's demise.

"God, I beg you!" he shouted at the top of his voice. The others looked to see him with his arms in the air, anguish etched across his face. "Do this! Please!"

The sound they heard was no louder than a weak cough. Wilson turned to Kiltman, considering he had the best hearing in the room. He was already standing up. Damascus and the parents looked at him. Crawford's eyes were open, staring at Kiltman.

"Kiltman, is that you?" he whispered. There was no time for an answer, his parents and Valentina clambering up onto their feet to hold an arm, a leg, whatever limb they could find.

Cardinal Damascus looked at the ceiling. "Thank you, God." Kiltman saw his arm wrapped around Wilson's shoulders, her face embedded in the shoulder of his cassock, her back rocking with unshed tears she could now let flow.

Wednesday, April 20

Penultimate Epilogue

It seemed an age since they had all been in the house together, yet it had just been a week and a half. It had been a lot longer since they had sat together on the balcony enjoying Uisge Beatha's view of the Firth of Clyde. A pleasant, calm spring evening, the river stretched out in front of them as far as they could see. The evening light allowed a golden haze to settle on the misty waters.

Kenny and Wilson held hands, drinking tea, with Roddy across the table sipping on San Pellegrino. He had grown to enjoy the bitter orange flavour. Maisie hovered around their feet, sleeping one minute, then exploring the kitchen the next. The ferocity and vigour with how she had welcomed them made Kenny wonder if she had sensed how much danger they had endured.

They were settling into a relaxed evening now that everyone had left Rome. He had just read out a text from Tommy:

Hey Kenny! Bet your legs are as smooth as you now ;-0

You've missed all the action here in Rome. Sure Maggie's told you everything. Just to let you know I'm in Sicily again! Luisa broke up with her boyfriend. Apparently, she said because I know the Marcianos I am Untouchable (move over, Sean Con.!). Wish me luck! Tommy

It made them all smile. Even Maisie, with her head bent to the side, seemed to understand that Tommy could fall into the sea and come out with a salmon.

Angie had stayed for a quick snack before being picked up by Fiona. Fiona did not want to hang around, intent on getting Angie back home. She was happy to let Roddy stay the night at Uisge Beatha since he *'had not seen his dad in such a long time'*. Nobody contradicted her.

Angie had agreed with him to minimise the week's events to just the bare details. Even then, Fiona would have a fit. Angie's father dead, Coach gone to prison and Mr. MacDonald recovering from his injuries. Hardly non-events by anyone's standards, least of all Fiona.

Mr. MacDonald was home with Reilly. He had confided in Wilson that he would focus first on repairing his relationship with his son, his body later.

Reilly was looking forward to his first official date with Angie that weekend. Roddy wondered if Angie would include that in her short summary of the Rome story shared with Fiona.

Crawford was still in hospital, Valentina at his bedside. His vitals were back on track. The doctors could not explain how he regained consciousness when the ventilator was switched off. Cardinal Damascus was more convinced than ever of the power of prayer.

Kiltman did not have the heart to tell the Cardinal that he had surreptitiously poured a sliver of Hair o' the Dog on Crawford's tongue during his caped hug. On the flight back home, he took pleasure in telling Wilson that Hair o' the Dog had life-giving powers.

When she realised how pleased he was with his stealthy application of the whisky, Wilson decided not to tell him that she had torn a piece from the Amazonian leaf he had given her and placed it inside Crawford's mouth. If it could revive a broken body in the Amazon, then it was worth a try.

They would never know the truth. Maybe that was not such a bad thing, she mused.

On leaving hospital Crawford was looking forward to taking extended leave to recover from the stabbing. Wilson was quite sure he would have the chance to enjoy lots of cannoli with the love of his life. He deserved it.

Crawford's parents decided to make the most of their Rome trip and do some sight-seeing, giving their son and his Italian lass some space. They were looking forward to welcoming Valentina - and her pastries - into the family, if that was what destiny had in store for them.

The Cardinal returned to the US a more chastened, humble version of the man who had arrived a few days earlier, determined to support the Church on its journey, rather than disrupt it. The Church had avoided ruin, with only a handful of people aware of how close Tantalus and Mask had come to being victorious.

Sister Maria had exchanged numbers with Wilson, resulting in a flurry of texts since the snow-globe hurling moment. Her Mother Superior was so impressed, she was going to allow the nuns to play baseball in their recreation time, assigning Sister Maria the responsibility for creating a team to participate in The Italian Baseball League, based in Rome. Sister Maria's last message to her was:

"Dear Maggie. I joined the sisterhood fully aware of the sacrifices involved. You know the old joke 'nun of this, nun of that' ;-)'. Now, thanks to our adventure, one of those sacrifices has been redeemed to me. God is good. x"

All in all, life seemed to have a chance of settling down to some semblance of normality.

Epilogue

He had been quiet for most of the trip home that day. Wilson and Roddy were worried about him. Between the Rome adventure and the Brazilian rainforest, it looked like he had peaked out. On the plane, he had been withdrawn and fidgety. They would have passed it off as delayed tiredness, were it not for the uneaten ice cream left on his tray. Wilson managed to grab the bowl before the steward cleared up on landing. She offered it to him, but he waved it away with the back of his hand. After three years in a relationship, firsts do not come along very often. This was a first.

Now, as they enjoyed the breathtaking view of the Firth of Clyde, they were content in the evening silence, punctuated by Kenny's regular stirring of his tea. Wilson and Roddy had exchanged glances at this peculiar habit they had not seen before.

Kenny pushed his chair back and stood up. He coughed and placed his hands in his pockets. "There was something I had meant to do last week, but because of everything that happened, there just wasn't the chance to do it."

Roddy had never seen his dad look so ill at ease. He was pleased to see him talking although it felt uncomfortable.

"It did cross my mind in Rome. Then it was all too chaotic and dangerous, I guess."

"Dad, what are you on about? Just say it!"

Kenny looked at the sky, then the floor, folded his arms then unfolded them. As Maggie got up from her seat, he dropped down onto his knee. He had the ring in front of her face before she could react.

"Maggie Wilson! Make me a happy man. A happier man! The happiest man alive!"

She was still in the process of standing up when she saw the ring. She fell down onto her haunches beside him; an instant reaction, concerned that he had stumbled.

She could not speak. The silence seemed to last an age, the nighttime breeze whistling along the side of Uisge Beatha.

"Well?" It was Roddy. "Maggie, come on!"

She looked at the ring, and then back at Kenny. Breaking into a wide smile, she wrapped her arms around him. "Yes, yes, yes!" They both settled into a hug, feeling the weight of the last ten days fall from their shoulders.

Roddy sat on his seat unsure what to do. He had to make a decision. Wait and let them hug or…

He landed on top of them, all three falling flat on the ground. Joined by Maisie, licking whichever face came closest to her wet nose. After a few minutes that involved cuddling, tickling and pushing each other over, they were all back at the table, Wilson sitting on Kenny's lap.

"How long you been planning that? You're a dark horse!"

"Oh, since I met you, I guess. The second time I mean. Not the first when…"

She put a finger on his lips. "I get it, no need to explain. We have a unique story, we do." She kissed him on the mouth, happy he was not wearing his mask; then realised they may be stretching Roddy's patience too far. He was still a teenager after all.

"So, young man." She looked at him with a twinkle in her eye. "What are we going to call you?"

"What do you mean?" he answered, wiping a tear away. "You can call me son if you want."

"No, that's not what I meant. I already see you as my son."

"Roddy's fine. Never Roderick and certainly not Rod."

"Ah, yes, I know what you mean. Now that he has superpowers, what should his name be?" Kenny stroked his chin.

"Come on, guys, what's going on here?" Roddy spread his arms wide.

She stood and paced the balcony, scratching her head. "Should it be Kiltboy?"

Kenny smiled and said, "Maybe, although a bit obvious."

Roddy shook his head, his cheeks tinging red, acne flaring.

"Okay, then what about *Wee* Kiltman?" Maggie offered.

"No chance," Roddy said. "That's just weird!"

Kenny clicked his fingers. "I've got it! We can call him Kiltlad or even Kiltladdie!"

Roddy put his head in his hands. "Enough! Just call me Roddy. I'll become Kiltman when Dad hangs up his flask. How about that?"

They all laughed. A good compromise, all things considered.

A few moments passed as they sipped from their drinks and enjoyed the night air, listening to night fall across the Clyde Valley.

"Where's Maisie?" Wilson asked.

"She wandered into the kitchen," Roddy said. He sat up in his seat. "Dad, did you leave the Dairy Milk out?"

Kenny jumped up, remembering the half-eaten bar of chocolate on the edge of the kitchen table, the perfect location for a dog to poison herself.

Wilson and Roddy were in the kitchen before he got there.

"Oh, dear!" Wilson said.

"What a nightmare!" Roddy added.

"What is it? Is she okay…?" Kenny looked past them to see Maisie on the kitchen worktop. She had knocked over his opened flask of Hair o' the Dog, licking its contents thirstily as it spilled over the edge. She looked back at them, her small nose and intelligent eyes framed by white fur and floppy ears.

"Oh, dear!" Kiltman said, wondering what the future held.

Acknowledgements

There are many people to mention for bringing this book to print. I am pleased to be able to thank *my hugely talented team of editors*, even though they probably do not realise they are members of an illustrious team. They are the embodiment of the quote: 'good stories are not written, they are rewritten'.

Kiltman® 3: Once Upon a Time in Rome was rewritten several times thanks to the following clever people:

Bruce Strain Collins enjoys noticing things; his attention to detail is remarkable for a twelve-year-old. It was only natural to ask him to apply his eagle eye to Kiltman's next adventure. What an amazing job he did, reminding his old man that punctuation was not a take it or leave it option. At bedtime for several weeks, he toiled over this novel finding nits and gnats that would have defied the most committed of readers to stay the course. Despite late nights highlighting errors, he still managed to grow four centimetres in the process; which is a commendable height accomplishment in our vertically challenged family.

Max Strain, for his imagination and quirky insights in the development of the plot and creation of the characters. A natural storyteller at heart and a brilliant actor, Max is a thespian who exudes inspiration daily, generating an environment of creativity and brainstorming (how close Tommy came to his demise will remain a secret confined to our kitchen table).

Martin Delve, whose many gifts and talents are second only to his self-effacing humility. Once again, Martin has done an amazing job with his painstakingly careful review of the details and logical narrative. Despite multiple priorities, he always finds time to help Kiltman pursue that next adventure much more credible than he started out in early drafts.

Patrick Dodds, a man of great humanity and vision, provided depth of perspective and support in making Kiltman® 3 relevant and fresh. A very special thanks for his clever, artful design of the front cover - a work of art in its own right, capturing the essence of the story I set out to tell. Patrick harnessed the tricks of the *AI* trade to create a striking image that defines the essence of this Kiltman adventure, developing a skill I like to describe as *pAtrickI*.

Pat Brusnahan, a gregarious and warm man with a huge soul, spent many years working in the Amazonian jungle. Pat corrected several of my geographical errors regarding Brazil, helping me with the benefit of his time in Manaus. His insights are especially welcome considering our shared backgrounds, years on the Coca-Cola audit trail and mutual friendship with the amazing Pat Friel, an incredible man who is missed every day. Love to Evelyn, Regina and all the beautiful Friel clan.

A huge thanks to gorgeous Georgie, the heart and soul of our family; and the inspiration for fearless Gina, her *Hai Karate* moves and spontaneous history lessons. Georgie has been massively supportive, energetic and passionate in helping me communicate that there is a superhero in all of us waiting to come to life. Her insightful and numerous edits added layers of sensitivity, empathy, kindness and compassion to a plot that ran the risk of forgetting the humanity of the characters. X

Tom Brucato has inspired me over the years with his commitment to the art of writing. Although he was not directly involved in editing, Tom is a great example of what dedication, friendship and positivity can look like. A brilliant author with a gift for creativity, Tom's novels are treasure chests of unfettered imagination interwoven with the authentic and personal events we face in our daily lives. Also a visionary, Tom predicted the longevity of Abba and the Star Wars franchise; way back in 1982 when we sat around sipping Christian Moerlein beer and scoffing Skyline Chili (5-way, of course) in Cincinnati.

At our 2022 New York reunion I had the privilege to catch up with a great bunch of people who have influenced the NYC forensics team in Kiltman® 3: Hugh *'bodhrán'* Armstrong, Brian *'58840'* Loughman, Adrian *'Pelé'* Waters and Ramsay *'buy-back'* Urquhart. Over a late-night beer, Rams took the opportunity to share with me his intimate knowledge of the *Kiltman* characters; and went on to provide valuable feedback and carefully considered hints for improvement in Kiltman® 3. He particularly influenced the personality of our keen-eyed accountant, Crawford, his character hewn from a sturdy slab of Aberdonian granite. I should also take a moment to thank Rams for inviting me to sleep on his couch in the Big Apple all those years ago when I was between homes. I will be eternally grateful for having had somewhere to lay my head and enjoy such an uninterrupted night's sleep.

My final teenage years were spent in Rome, a time when I was blessed with a plethora of unique adventures and unforgettable experiences, shared with friends and fellow seminarians at the Scots College. Our unfettered embrace of culture and adventure saw us splashing in fountains, scarpering along cobbled streets, eating in wonderful restaurants, spending time in churches (every day at least one), and singing Bob Marley songs on the way to University, led by two seminary heroes: Paul 'Jake' Kierney and John 'Quinnie' Quinn.

Summer '22 marks the tragic loss of an amazingly kind, generous and loyal friend, Steve Schnall. Three decades ago in New York, we shared an apartment on the Upper East Side. Over the ensuing years, as we took different paths, we enjoyed watching each other grow through life, surrounded by good people and loving families. To this day I have not seen anyone wear a kilt with the elegance and charisma as Steve when he came to our wedding with his beautiful wife, Sherri. Steve has left a huge vacuum, and all we can do is count ourselves blessed to have had the privilege of being able to call him a friend. Thoughts and prayers are always with Sherri, Jack and Luke.

During the writing of the first draft, I received the heartbreaking news that my great *sõber* (friend), Vladimir Sapožnin, had passed away. We worked together in Estonia in the early 1990's when the country was coming to life after years behind the Iron Curtain. As we built a business against the odds, Volli became an inspiration and a rock in so many ways. Over thirty years, he has never been far away when I needed a friend, a beer, or both. Together Volli and I, along with our Estonian pals, introduced the pub crawl to Tallinn in 1994. We wandered the streets of that city over the years arm in arm, blessed in our friendship. My heart goes out to his lovely wife, Ave, and their family, Georg, Pille and grandchildren: *mu süda on teie kõigiga.*

Kiltman 3 - Once Upon a Time in Rome is dedicated to Steve and Volli. XX